Frances Gordon is the daughter of an Irish actor and after a convent education worked in newspapers and the legal profession. She now lives and writes in Staffordshire. She is the author of four acclaimed fantasy novels, written under the name of Bridget Wood, and three previous horror novels, BLOOD RITUAL, THE DEVIL'S PIPER and THE BURNING ALTAR. Her most recent novel, THORN, is the first in this series of contemporary fairy tales, and is based on the legend of 'Sleeping Beauty'. All of her novels are available from Headline Feature.

D1262269

Changeling:
An Immortal Tale

Frances Gordon

HEADLINE
FEATURE

Changeling:
An Immortal Tale

PART ONE

There was once a miller who had a very beautiful daughter of whom he was so vain and proud, that one day he boasted how she could spin gold out of straw . . .

German Popular Stories, Translated from the *Kinder und Haus-Marchen*, collected by M. M. Grimm from oral tradition, 1823

Chapter One

Tod Miller was uneasily aware that he might have got himself into a potentially embarrassing situation.

The trouble was that the dream was within reach again; the dream that had been so dazzling and that had seemed so promising twenty years ago, but that had somehow tarnished over, was within his reach again. It was hovering like a will o' the wisp on the horizon once more, and Tod was damned if he was going to let it turn to dross in his hands this time.

Rebirth. That was not too strong a word, because it was what was happening here in this over-furnished room with the myopic, balding-pated little man seated behind the enormous desk. He forced himself to pay attention to Gerald Makepiece's squeaky excitement: something about how it was going to be a new venture for Makepiece to be financing a West End musical, something else about how Makepiece was going to find it all so very interesting. How Gerald knew all about Mr Miller's earlier fame because of some local company having put on an amateur performance of the *Dwarf Spinner*. Tod at once assumed his expression of polite and interested sincerity, although amateurs were always reviving the *Dwarf Spinner* and none of them ever really managed to convey the creeping menace of the story, or the gargoyle evil of the dwarf-magician who spun the straw into gold and extorted the terrible pledge of the gift of the heroine's first-born child.

'Really a very effective story,' little rabbity Makepiece was saying. 'It's the old Grimm's fairytale, isn't it? Rumpelstiltskin. My word, I did enjoy it, Mr Miller.'

Tod smiled faintly and looked at his fingernails.

'Of course, they didn't do the final scene on stage, you understand. The one where—'

3

'The dwarf tears himself into two pieces in a tantrum,' finished Tod. 'No. Amateurs never do.'

'Well, no. Quite. But how you ever conceived of such a thing I can't imagine.'

Tod made a faint deprecatory gesture with his hands.

'Well now,' said Gerald, happily, 'to our muttons, as the French say. Time to talk about this matter of money, Mr Miller.'

'Ah yes, the sordid subject of coinage.' Tod thought it would be overdoing it to pinch the bridge of his nose between his thumb and forefinger, but he managed to convey high-minded disinterest.

Gerald assumed a businesslike manner and said, 'Exactly how much would be necessary to finance an entire show, Mr Miller?'

'Are we talking about the whole shooting match, Mr Makepiece?' Tod knew perfectly well that they were, but it was as well to get things straight at the outset. He said, 'You do mean the entire works? From first read-through to opening night? Theatre rental, sets, designers, costumes, cast, rehearsal rooms, orchestra, publicity—'

'Oh yes.' Little Makepiece was fairly wriggling in his seat with delight, as if the words that Tod had plucked more or less at random were a magical invocation. 'Yes, I do mean all those things. How much would they all cost?'

Tod told him.

It would be too much to have said that Makepiece blenched, since he was of a putty-coloured complexion to begin with. But the albino-rabbit-lashes certainly blinked several times. Tod waited. Fiscally speaking, he was prepared to haul down his flag a bit, but he was not going to make the first move.

Mr Gerald Makepiece did a few sums on a minute calculator, muttering as he did so. At last he beamed and said, 'I think that amount might be possible, Mr Miller. Yes, I think that subject to a couple of trivial conditions, it might be perfectly possible.' He tapped the end of his pen thoughtfully on the desk-top. 'You could write the music and the – what is it called? – the term you use for the story and the dialogue in a musical?'

'The book,' said Tod.

'Oh yes, the book. You could do it all?'

Tod felt a sudden lurch of panic, treacherously mingled with rising excitement, and Makepiece said happily, 'Well, that's a ridiculous question, isn't it? I'm talking to the man who wrote the *Dwarf Spinner*.'

He beamed and Tod said, 'Quite. Yes, of course I could do it.'

The pity was that he had had to come out of London, to this cold, ugly northern town, to revive his beautiful dream. The tragedy was that so many people would know it.

This was not good. Tod knew what they said about him these days: there's Tod Miller, they said. Good old Toddy. Bit of a failure, poor old chap. Bit of a back number. Wrote that brilliant pop musical in the sixties and then never wrote another thing. His wife died and he dropped into obscurity. Makes his living writing baked-bean ditties and jingles for cheese biscuits now, and segues for local radio. No one's supposed to know, but everyone does. Very sad. There's a grown-up daughter as well, rather a stunner by all accounts.

It was a pity that the biscuit and baked-bean adverts had become public knowledge, although there was nothing shameful about them. It was honest work and it was not unrewarding, and a man had to eat. A man had to provide for his only daughter, as well. It had not been easy either, what with Aine having died when Fael was barely five, what with Fael crashing her own car eighteen months ago, and her injuries taking so very long to heal. A man was entitled to feel a bit aggrieved over losing his wife to a jack-knifing oil tanker on the M1 and his daughter to a wheelchair.

The trouble was that when you had been the toast of London's theatreland for a season and when you had even had your own affectionate soubriquet – 'Hot Toddy', they had called him – you were entitled to want to keep the beans and biscuits quiet. Tod wanted to be remembered for the *Dwarf Spinner*: the dark gutsy musical of the Grimm Brothers' fairy story, rather than as the man responsible for the Beany Boppers' Beanfeast ('*Bop your way to high-fibre bean-health*'), or somebody-or-other's Spreadi-Crackers-and-Rolls: ' "*Stilton Squares and Cheddar Snaps. Edam Sticks and Gouda Baps*", sung by your own, your

5

very own, Miss Camembert Crumpet . . .' (Wearing a cheese-cloth bikini and sporting a stick of celery in each hand.)

Tod was not really ashamed of the Crumpet, who had earned him a reasonable living over the last couple of years. But it was hardly *opera bouffe*. It was hardly Gilbert & Sullivan or Gershwin or Andrew Lloyd-Webber either, and Tod was worthy of higher things. In his most cherished press-cutting, a critic had actually likened the *Dwarf Spinner*'s final scene to the scene in Marlowe's *Dr Faustus* where the devils drag Faust down to hell to tear him apart and claim his soul. 'Both present the same phenomenal problems in staging,' he had said. 'But both are such dazzling pieces of theatre that every possible effort should be made to overcome the problems. I hope that in years to come, people won't flinch from staging the *Dwarf Spinner*'s closing scene on technical grounds, as they do from *Faustus*'s. Because while one must have every sympathy with the difficulties, it would be a great pity if this remarkable piece of *Grand Guignol* theatre should be lost.'

It was an even greater pity that the *Dwarf Spinner*'s acknow-ledged creator – the man who had almost been compared to Marlowe, for goodness' sake! – was reduced to such embarrass-ing straits to earn his living! But it was all about to change. Tod could refer to the Crumpet and the Beany Boppers with a deprecatory shrug now. Mere froth and fluff. One had actually rather enjoyed working in that side of the business. And all the while the frustrations and the shabbinesses – the pitying *kindnesses* of the last twenty years would be sloughing away. Rebirth.

He beamed at little Gerald Makepiece and waited to learn what the trivial conditions attached to this financial arrangement might be.

Whatever they were, he would meet them.

Fael Miller finished playing the Chopin *Nocturne* which had suited her mood this morning. It might as easily have been Cole Porter or Brubeck or Lennon & McCartney (she did a terrific moody blues version of 'Hey Jude'), but it happened to have been Chopin. Professor Roscius, who had taught her music all those years ago, had said that to do justice to the filigree quality of Chopin's work the pianist needed extreme depth and breadth of soul. He had had a way of painting wonderful word pictures about music and composers, as well as imbuing his pupils with his own passion for music. Once Fael had got past the adolescent stage of being secretly in love with him, which was a stage most of his female pupils went through, she had learned a great deal from him, before he went back to Ireland and died there. She did not think she had any more depth and breadth of soul than anyone else, but she enjoyed playing Chopin and remembering what the professor had said about Chopin's music.

She closed the lid of the piano and wheeled the chair into the kitchen. It was unlikely that her father would get back to London in time for lunch; in fact it was unlikely that he would be back for supper. It was anybody's guess how long he would be in Yorkshire.

As Fael heated soup and buttered a roll to go with it she hoped that Tod was not doing something squirm-making or outrageous or both in Yorkshire. He could sometimes be hugely embarrassing, button-holing people in a bluff confiding manner and outlining plans to them for spectacular new shows which they did not want to hear about. He did it with visitors to the house as well, and he even did it in restaurants, interrupting people who did not want to be interrupted. Sometimes it was obvious that they were with companions they ought not to be with, and you could see them flinching. It was dreadful to feel so embarrassed by your own father, and it was appalling to want to disassociate yourself from him at those times.

But the times when he acknowledged his failure and talked about his inadequacies were worse, because that was when he drank himself into a black depression and said the world was against him and he might as well be dead, and in any case he was the victim of jealous conspiracies and envious hatred. Quite often Fael ended up shouting that Tod was childish and egocentric and plain bloody maudlin on these occasions, and then Tod stormed crossly about the house slamming doors and ringing people up to tell them how he was misunderstood by everyone, even his own daughter, and how it was sharper than a serpent's tooth to nurture a thankless child.

It was a relief to be spared all that for a couple of days,

especially since there was this afternoon's concert at the Disabled Children's Clinic, which was an important event for the clinic. Fael had got involved while undergoing the physiotherapy that was gradually helping her to walk again: it was a very long job indeed and it was exhausting at times, but at least she could get across a room with only a stick now, although anything beyond that was still impossible, and stairs were hopeless.

But a few weeks ago one of the physiotherapists had asked whether she might like to help with the disabled children, and one thing had led to another and Fael had found herself enjoying it. She liked trying to make the children take part in ordinary activities: there were some very sad cases, but there were some very intelligent children as well, and it was terrific to see them responding. She read to them a couple of times a week and played the piano for singing sessions, and encouraged them to write stories which they had to read aloud. Quite often she illustrated the stories by playing the piano – there were always bits of Prokofiev that could be used, or the pieces Debussy had written for his daughter, or Leopold Mozart's *Toy Symphony* or the *Nutcracker Suite*. There were pop songs and TV jingles as well. Two of the children were having piano lessons as a result and three more were learning the recorder.

Today they were going to act out *Peter and the Wolf* which Fael had adapted, producing a simplified version. Parents and family were coming and staff from other parts of the clinic as well, and everyone was looking forward to it. Fael was looking forward to it as well. She was going to wear a black silk jacket and tight black trousers with high black boots with a silver stripe down the side. She mostly wore boots, because people tended to admire the boots rather than wonder embarrassedly about her legs. There was nothing much wrong with the shape of her legs, as it happened. She thought there was nothing much wrong with the rest of her either.

The trivial condition that Gerald Makepiece had referred to was not trivial at all.

Tod, who simply wanted to get out of this slab-faced town and back to London with Gerald Makepiece's assurance (written

8

assurance, it had better be) folded in his wallet, thought that trivial was the last word you would use.

'Not a leading part, you understand,' little Makepiece said, tripping over his words with excitement, pouring Tod a glass of sherry from a decanter behind his desk. Sherry at eleven o'clock in the morning? Nobody drank sherry in the morning these days, for God's sake. Tod downed it anyway.

'Ah. Not a leading part?'

'Oh no. One wouldn't want to be thought guilty of nepotism.' Makepiece looked properly shocked. 'Not that she isn't perfectly capable, of course, although she'll tell you she's a little rusty. But I shouldn't take any notice of that if I were you.'

'No?'

'Oh no. She's really done some very good stuff – you might like to see some of her press cuttings . . .' Little Makepiece lost himself amid a welter of half-sentences and excitement.

Tod said, 'A – hum – a lady friend, is this?' Makepiece did not look as if he had the balls for that kind of thing, but you never knew.

'Oh no, I'm talking about my wife,' said Gerald, proudly.

'Ah. Oh, yes I see.'

'She was *professional*, you know. A singer. Light opera and musical comedy mostly – do they still call it that? And she was doing *very* well, but when we got married eighteen months ago – I should explain she's a *little* younger than I am – she gave up her career, even though I said it wasn't necessary.'

Tod thought: back row of the chorus in a touring production of the *Mikado*. Voice like a corncrake and a barmaid's disposition.

'A touring production of *Iolanthe*,' said Makepiece. 'Only a chorus role, you understand, but a voice like an angel, and a *generous* disposition.'

Near enough. Tod said, politely, 'I shall be interested to meet her.'

Gerald Makepiece was pleased that Mia had dressed with care for the lunch with Tod Miller. Of course, she had an eye for colour, and she really looked very smart in the fur coat that it had been Gerald's delight to buy for her. He had been a little surprised at the request: he had thought ladies did not care to wear fur these days because of conservation and save-the-seals and so on, but Mia had said, no, it was perfectly acceptable providing the fur was not *cheap*.

And of course she knew just what to say to Tod Miller, both of them having been in theatrical circles, although it was a pity that Miller did not seem to know any of the people Mia was mentioning. Gerald beamed all through the lunch which was at the Royal on account of wanting to properly impress their guest. A proper lunch they had, with different sauces served with the entree and the steak, and a good burgundy to drink. Mia enjoyed burgundy; she said you could tell a gentleman by the wine he drank. Tod Miller clearly enjoyed burgundy as well, because he drank quite a lot of it and they had to order a second bottle and then a third. Gerald did not grudge a drop, because this was the man who would give Mia her great breakthrough. Miller had a couple of large brandies afterwards as well. Of course, people in the theatre world did drink quite a lot.

They talked about the *Dwarf Spinner* and about the new venture. Miller was cagey about that; he was still working on it, he said, and it did not do to discuss things too early. Sometimes that was the way to abort a promising idea. Gerald did not really understand this, but he nodded slowly several times as if he did.

Mia had some very good ideas to offer. Gerald was proud to listen to her, and Tod Miller listened as well, refilling his wine glass several times, doing so absently as if he was so absorbed in the conversation that he was not really noticing what he was doing. Once or twice he said, 'Now that is a very interesting idea, Mrs Makepiece,' and Mia said at once that he must call her Mia, they were going to be friends. This was characteristic of her and one of her most endearing traits; she wanted always to be on terms of friendship with people. No one ever took advantage of it.

They parted on the steps of the Royal, Miller making a joke about how he had drunk so much he would have to be decanted onto his train, and Mia laughing with him and saying that as far as she was concerned, the afternoon had better be spent in bed. From another lady this might have sounded a bit suggestive, but Mia was as innocent as a kitten.

Tod Miller would be telephoning from London as soon as he had begun to put things in hand. There was a great deal to do. A small office in central London would have to be found, although their registered company address would be Gerald's own, of course. Miller had been glad to accept this suggestion, explaining that he knew very little about business. Every man to his own trade, he said, and then changed it quickly to profession. 'But really, Mr Makepiece, it's more usual to call in an established production company fairly early on.'

Gerald said, 'Oh, I don't think we want that, Mr Miller. I think we want to keep control of everything.'

'Ah.'

'And I believe I could very easily create a new, properly registered company within Makepiece Enterprises.'

'Ah,' said Tod again. And, 'Could you now?'

'We might even,' said little Makepiece with a nauseatingly uxorious glance at his lady, 'even call it Mia Productions, what do you say to that now?'

Tod thought that what he would like to say would not be very well received, so he murmured that it was certainly a thought. He betook himself to his train amidst a general air of approval and optimism.

Gerald Makepiece, waving their guest off, remarked happily to Mia that the day had gone remarkably well.

Apart from little Makepiece's ideas of finance, which were generous, the day had been alarming.

Tod stumbled into a carriage, and fell into the grubby railway seat. Makepiece was a gullible old fool – although he was a very rich gullible old fool – and his lady was the worst kind of greedy has-been. Tod resisted the thought that it took one to know one, because he was not a has-been and no one had ever thought it; he was going to make the most terrific comeback ever known in the West End, although he would prefer not to do it with Mia Makepiece hanging on to his coat-tails. He would postpone telling little Gerald this, however, until he saw what roles were available in the show. They might be able to palm her off with something minor.

He would begin writing the show as soon as he got back. He

would probably get an idea quite quickly once he put his mind to it. He would come up with something that would knock the *Dwarf Spinner* into obscurity. Well, he would have to, because he had told Makepiece and his lady that he would, making one of his impromptu speeches at the railway station and punctuating it with the huge expansive gestures that the public had always loved from him. Ah, the old, grandiloquent Hot Toddy was still alive! He did not think it had mattered that he had stumbled over a porter's trolley while speaking: you could not be looking out for such mundane things when you were in full and eloquent rhetorical flight. He did not think that little Makepiece or Mia had noticed that the burgundy had given him wind in the gut, either.

He closed his eyes and fell into not-quite-silent sleep which lasted most of the way to Euston, when he woke with a sour taste in his mouth and a bilious headache.

He took a taxi to Pimlico, only to find that Fael was still out at her stupid children's hospital concert, there was no supper left out for him, and there were two letters propped up on his desk. He opened them to discover that one was from the agency handling the Spreadi-Cracker account, saying they were very sorry, but it had been decided to discontinue national TV advertising for the present, due to a down-trend in sales.

The other was from Barclays Bank, reminding him with thinly-veiled impatience that the house mortgage was now five months in arrears.

Chapter Two

Peter and the Wolf was a riot. The children were serious and absorbed, their faces intent on the story and on remembering what Fael had told them. Fael, who had thought she had successfully quenched all maternal instincts since the car crash, suddenly found that she wanted to scoop them all up and hug them for doing so well.

They used the small hall which served as a lecture theatre and Christmas-disco venue. There was a good-sized stage, and two of the male nurses helped with curtains and some quite professional spot-lighting. After it was over several of the parents stayed on to meet her and thank her, and the consultant in charge of the adult paraplegic wing wanted to talk about the possibility of a more ambitious show, with the adults as well as the children taking part. This was a very intriguing suggestion, and by the time they had finished discussing it, it was half-past seven, so the consultant suggested he took her out to dinner in a nearby Greek restaurant. He was rather intriguing himself, so Fael was glad she was wearing the silk jacket and the silver and black boots.

It was as she was spinning her wheelchair down the ramp to meet the consultant, who was fetching his car from the staff car park, that she was suddenly and uneasily aware of being watched. She halted the chair at once, and looked about her. The clinic was a modern symmetrical building, with polished corridors and plate glass everywhere, but adjoining it was a large Victorian house, standing in dark, rather tanglewood gardens. The house had been annexed for offices and sleeping quarters for night staff, and the old gloomy garden with its tall old trees and a thick gloomy shrubbery was still there. To reach the staff car park it was necessary to go through this garden, and Fael usually rather liked doing so because the nodding trees and the shiny-leaved laurel cast a smeary, green twilight, which made you think about all the old tales of dark romance. But at half-past seven on a November evening there was nothing romantic about the place at all, in fact there was an unmistakable aura of menace.

Fael had just framed this thought and she was thinking it might be better to spin her chair fairly rapidly towards people and lights, when there was a soft footfall on the gravel path somewhere behind her. She spun the chair around at once, and the footfall came again. Fael's heart began to beat faster. There *was* someone here. It was almost certainly someone who had every right to be here, but—

But there was something extraordinarily furtive about the sounds. Fael received the impression of someone standing in the shadows, using the trees as a screen.

And then the shadows seemed almost to part as if a hand had thrust them arrogantly aside like a curtain, and the figure of a man wearing a long, dark coat, with a deep-brimmed hat shadowing his face, stepped out. Fael only just managed not to gasp. A soft voice said at once, 'I'm sorry – did I startle you?'

'Well it – yes, you did a bit.'

'I didn't mean to.'

He stayed where he was, and Fael, who had been about to turn her chair again and go haring off in the direction of the car park, hesitated and looked at him again, trying to penetrate the shadows. This, surely, was someone she had met. 'Do I know you?' she said, at last.

He appeared to consider this, and then after a moment, he said, 'We've never actually been introduced.'

Fael had the impression that he had chosen these words carefully. And he speaks as if he can't quite pronounce some of the letters – as if his mouth wasn't quite designed for human speech. Still, this is a medical place, after all. But I wish that doctor would hurry up with the car.

But the feeling of familiarity remained, and she said, 'Were you at the show this afternoon? Is that where I recognise you from?' Because if he was a parent or someone attached to the clinic it would be silly and even a bit rude to scuttle off without just exchanging a few words.

'You recognise me, do you?' he said.

'Not exactly, but I have the feeling that we've met,' said Fael guardedly and thought if it had not been for this sensation of recognition, she might have been quite frightened.

'I didn't come to see the show,' said the dark-clad figure. 'I came to see you, Fael.'

He knows my name, thought Fael. Oh lord, I'm not sure if I like this. I'm not sure if this mightn't be a potentially dangerous situation. If I could see his face I'd feel better. Aloud she said, 'Why? I mean, why did you come to see me?'

'I was curious,' he said, and then, as a light went on at a window somewhere above them he stepped back. He's flinching from the light, thought Fael, in horror. He's dodging it. But she could see now that he was a slenderly built, quite youngish man. But wasn't he somehow deformed? No, not exactly deformed, perhaps, but there was something wrong, there was something just very slightly out of kilter somewhere. And I still can't see his face at all, thought Fael, and with the framing of this thought, another coil of fear spiralled up. She glanced over her shoulder to see if there was any sign of the doctor.

And then the stranger said, 'I wanted to see if you were like your mother, Fael,' and Fael turned back at once, because this was instantly interesting. Her mother had died so long ago that Fael had only the dimmest of memories of her and Tod did not like her mentioned. ('Too painful,' he always said with a sigh, when Fael asked questions. 'Don't ask me to talk about her.')

But if this unknown young man (*was* he unknown?) had really met her mother, it might be good to talk to him, even though it was still not a reason for trusting him. Fael said, 'Where did you know her? How?'

'From my home in Ireland. Aine visited it once or twice when I was very small.'

He pronounced the name correctly – *Aw-ne* – which not many people did. Fael registered this, and then said, 'Yes, she was Irish.' Something prompted her to add, 'A lot of people know that.' And thought: yes, and it wouldn't be hard to find out the correct pronunciation of her name, either.

15

'Your father based the heroine of the *Dwarf Spinner* on her.'

'A lot of people know that as well.'

'You're very defensive,' he said, and there was a blurred note of amusement now. 'But truly I don't mean any harm.' He appeared to study her. His face was still in shadow, which Fael was beginning to find very disquieting indeed. If he moves forward I'll yell for help, she thought. And then – or will I? There's a darkness where his face ought to be. Oh God, I wish I hadn't thought that.

'You're very like Aine,' he said, unexpectedly.

'So I've been told.'

'You have her hair – like liquid moonlight. And you have her eyes. Like melted aquamarines.'

He was deliberately referring to the *Dwarf Spinner* again, of course. 'Melting the Moonlight' was one of the high points of the show, where the heroine was imprisoned in the drug baron's house, and the baron's hippie followers, high on marijuana, sang and danced mockingly around her, conjuring up their drug-induced rainbows and pouring them into the great melting-pot centre stage, and then spinning up the glittering living lengths of gold that she is unable to produce, until the dark, evil dwarf-magician finally appears. Anyone who had ever seen the show, or one of its amateur revivals, could have made that remark.

As if he had picked this up, he said at once, 'Tod Miller's work is well known to me, Fael. That's one of the reasons I was curious to see you.'

'Oh. Well, now you've seen me and you know what I look like, and—' It would be the height of bad manners to tell him to sod off, and he had not actually done anything to warrant it, so Fael said, 'And now I must be going – someone is collecting me.'

There was a moment when she thought he was going to step out of the twisting shadows, and she drew in a deep breath, although she had no idea whether it was to yell for help or simply to prepare for some kind of an attack. And then car headlights sliced through the darkness, and Fael turned her head and saw with thankfulness the consultant's car coming towards them. The stranger made a gesture that might have meant anything at all, and stepped back into the trees.

16

Like a thick black curtain coming down, the shadows fell silently into place again.

It was almost midnight when Fael got back to Pimlico, and it looked as if Tod had returned from wherever he had been, cooked himself a meal and gone out again. He had left the cooker switched on, which was going to send that quarter's electricity bill sky-high, and there were plates with the dried messy remains of what looked like spaghetti bolognese. Fael cursed him, and switched off the cooker but left the plates in the sink for him to wash in the morning because she was damned if she was going to be Tod's skivvy. The heat of the cooker had left a faint, burnt-food odour everywhere. Fael boiled the kettle for a mug of tea, and then wheeled through to her room which was next to the music room.

The burnt-food smell had not penetrated in here. At this time of year there were the wet-earth smells of chrysanthemums and the sweet-scented tobacco plant beneath her window. It was nice to lie in bed like this and sip a mug of tea, and think back over the evening. Her bed faced the window which looked over the garden. It was a large garden by most London standards because of the house being mid-Victorian, and Fael always left the window open and the curtains drawn back when she went to bed. She had spent hours lying here in the first weeks after the car crash that had injured her legs and part of her spine, when the fear that she might never walk again had blotted out almost everything else. But they had pretty much put her together again, the doctors had said, kindly. She was almost as good as new. The main problem was that nerves and their casings in the spine had been quite severely damaged – rather in the way that protective conduit tubes around electrical wires could be damaged – but the prognosis was good, and they were fairly confident of an almost-complete recovery. There was already a degree of sensory response and motor control in her legs.

'I'll walk again?'

Yes, certainly, said the surgeon, who had a thin, intelligent face. He added, carefully, that it would be a long haul and a lot of work. It might be as much as two or even three years, and she would probably never be able to run marathons, but if she was diligent about exercises and physiotherapy, in time she would walk again.

It had not been until after they explained all this that they told her about that other, invisible injury: the loss of the child she had not even realised had been conceived. But there was no irreparable damage done, they had said quickly. There was nothing to suggest that further children could not be conceived and born with absolute normality.

That bastard Simon, Fael had thought, hazily, lying back in the narrow hospital bed. Simon and the failure rate of the condom. Two per cent, was it? Well, Simon could sod off and take his two per cent failure with him. It looked as if he had done that anyway. She did not care. She only cared about walking again.

It had been a long time before she had dared believe she would walk again; and there had been a great many nights when she had lain here, with sleep as far away as the moon. She knew the garden by moonlight and sunlight and she knew it under leaden, rain-swollen skies, and under rose and gold dawns when the birdsong trickled through the garden like quicksilver. She knew its every mood, and it knew hers, and it had helped her through some very bad hours indeed.

She had managed to put the strange, shadowy young man to the back of her mind, and she had nearly managed to forget the oddly compelling voice as well. She was not going to think about it any more. A chance encounter with an off-beat, that was all it had been.

The Greek dinner had been enjoyable, and the young consultant had been good company. You tended to miss out a bit on men when you were tied to a wheelchair; most of them ran a mile.

Over dinner, they had talked about the consultant's plan to put on a show with the adult patients, but they had talked about other things as well. Fael rather hoped he might ask her out again. Even if he did not, it was a good feeling to know she had achieved something solid and worthwhile with the disabled children. Adults might be harder to cope with, or they might be easier. She switched off the bedside light and leaned back on the pillows, turning over suitable themes.

18

It would have to be something fairly simple, but not so simple that it would be patronising. Disabled limbs did not automatically mean a disabled mind. Look at Stephen Hawking. Look at yourself as well, Fael, only don't look too hard or too long because you might start to get bitter and self-pitying – you might start counting up how many months or years are still ahead before you can walk down a street without sticks.

Several of the consultant's group were apparently studying for Open University degrees: English Literature and History courses, which made Fael wonder if it would be possible to do a scaled-down version of Chaucer's *Canterbury Tales*. You could have a lot of fun with all the characters telling their different stories and it might be possible to use actual medieval music and soup it up. Professor Roscius had always shown mock-horror at her habit of syncopating Bach and Handel, but actually he had enjoyed it. Fael could remember terrific jam sessions when she and his other pupils had virtually taken over the ground floor of the narrow, friendly Chelsea house, and improvised to their hearts' content, switching from rock to jazz to baroque and back again. Roscius had loved it; he had encouraged them and helped them, and produced cider and lager when their creative flow finally gave out and they flopped down on cushions on the floor. Sometimes he would send out for pizzas or fish and chips, and they would all eat and talk a great deal, and then start up again. Fael missed those evenings. She still missed the professor.

What else could the adults do? There was Dickens, of course: *Nicholas Nickleby* would work well and it did not need to be a huge, grand, RSC production. Perhaps it might be a bit dark. How about Joan Littlewood's *Oh, What a Lovely War*? That was more or less a series of musical sketches centring on World War One and it could be quite simply staged. Everyone, including the audience, would enjoy joining in the songs: 'It's a Long Way to Tipperary', and 'Keep the Home Fires Burning', although it would depend on how many of the patients could sing reasonably in tune. This began to seem like a reasonable idea. One would have to find out about royalties ... And costumes, and lighting ... Two or three very strong spotlights against a dark background to depict the Blitz ... ? Had they called it Blitz then, or had that been only the Second World War . . . ? The sound effects would need to be convincing . . .

Fael was tumbling over the warm shifting boundaries of sleep; she was in the pleasant half-stage where she was not quite awake but not quite asleep either. But sleep was certainly starting to fold around her and intriguing dreams were beckoning. She could hear the river tonight, just very faintly. You could only hear it on very quiet nights, but tonight was one of those nights. There it went, splashing away to itself, like a Vivaldi concerto. It made her feel warm and secure.

She could hear the tiny night sounds of the house as well. All houses had their own sounds, and you grew so used to them that you stopped noticing the fridge switching off or the central heating switching on, or the timbers settling in the roof at night. Even though Fael's room was downstairs on account of the wheelchair, she still heard the roof timbers and sometimes the scrabbling of house martins.

It was at this point that there was a sound and then the blurred impression of movement somewhere outside of sleep. On the wrong side of sleep. On the waking side. She frowned and tried to banish it and burrow back into sleep, but it came again, insistent, tinged with some kind of warning. There's something wrong, thought Fael, opening her eyes. There's something intrusive. With the acknowledgement of this, sleep fled, and she sat up sharply in bed, pulling the sheets around her, listening intently.

Yes, there it went again: soft sounds, oddly regular, with a furtiveness about them. Footsteps? If you wanted to really frighten yourself you could say they were footsteps, creeping along the side of the house. A prowler, thought Fael, her heart thudding painfully. There's a prowler out there, an intruder. The step came again.

Fael reached to the bedside table for the cordless telephone she kept to hand, and remembered she had left it in the kitchen. Panic bubbled up, and in the same moment, the soft green light of the moonlit garden shivered, and the outline of a man, blackly silhouetted against the trees, stepped in front of the window. A gloved hand came up to tap on the glass.

Fael drew breath to scream, and a soft remembered voice said,

'Fael? Don't be frightened.' The words were low, but because the top window was open they came clearly into the room.

It was the man she had seen outside the clinic earlier that evening. Fael shrank back, her eyes on him. But he knew she was here, of course. He could see her quite plainly. Oh God, why didn't I draw the curtains? Oh God, what do I do? With a feeling of incredulity, she heard her voice say, 'Who is it? Who's there?' and was conscious of the grim humour of the words, which were the words uttered by every time-honoured, beleaguered victim to the sinister stranger at the gates. Stunning lack of originality there, Fael. But what else did you say? She called a bit louder, 'Who are you? What do you want?'

'We met earlier, Fael. We acknowledged that we had met somewhere or other, sometime or other. It might have been in another time or another world, and we might have been different people. But we recognised one another.' The words were unreal; they had a dream-like quality to them, and they were all mixed up with the moonlight silvering the old garden. He moved nearer to the window. But I still can't see his face, thought Fael, trying not to panic.

'Didn't you know I would be back, Fael?'

'No, of course I didn't! What do you want anyway?' There I go again, behaving like some crass, witless, romantic heroine. Some romance. Some heroine. 'You'd better leave now,' said Fael. 'Immediately. Or I'll scream. In fact I'll yell bloody murder.'

'Scream away,' said the stranger. 'Tod's out, isn't he? And the neighbours are too far away to hear you.'

'He—' Fael looked involuntarily at the bedside clock. It was one a.m. When Tod went out he almost always found his way to one of the small clubs frequented by actors. Most of them did not open until around ten or eleven at night when the theatres were spilling out, and most of them did not close until three or four in the morning, which meant that Tod was unlikely to return for some time. Then I'm on my own. Panic welled up again. She said, 'There's some money in the house if that's what you want. I'll tell you where it is, and you can—'

'I'm not a burglar, Fael.' The contempt was impossible to miss.

He was not a burglar. But he might be a rapist. He might be one of the weirdos who got their kicks from crippled females. And if he broke in, there would not be very much Fael could do to get away. She could get herself out of bed and she could just get from the bed to the door or the window or the phone. But it was still a long, difficult process. And if I start for the kitchen phone now, or the one in the hall, if he's really determined, he could be in here before I've got four steps. It wouldn't be all that difficult to smash the window and reach through to lift the latch. Oh God.

She dredged up her courage and said, 'You ought to know that I have a knife under my pillow. If you try to get in, I'll stab you.'

Unexpectedly he laughed. 'I'm not a rapist any more than I'm a burglar, Fael. I'm here because I want to get to know you.'

'It's a screamingly peculiar time to call.'

'It is. But then I'm a creature of the night, Fael.' And then, with a kind of silken allure in his voice that brushed Fael's senses like velvet being stroked the wrong way, he said, 'May I come in?'

You did not, unless you were completely witless, let anyone you did not know into the house if you were on your own. Especially you did not let in sinister gentlemen who stood in the shadows and spoke in persuasive, slightly sibilant tones. Fael was not about to do it.

He had said earlier that he had known her mother, and he had certainly been familiar with the *Dwarf Spinner*, but this was still not sufficient reason to invite him in. Also, it was possible that this was some kind of plot: that he thought the family was very rich because of the *Dwarf Spinner* and was planning a break-in, or even – horrid thought! – to kidnap Fael and hold her hostage for a huge cash payment, which Tod would not be able to pay.

She said, hotly, 'You've got a nerve creeping around in the dark and asking to be let in! No, of course you can't come in.' And tried to think what she could do if he really did break the window and climb through.

But he stayed where he was, and as the moment lengthened, a patch of moonlight slid across the window. The man stepped back at once. He's flinching from the light again, thought Fael. That's what he did earlier.

'Listen,' he said, and although he still spoke softly, his voice was infused with a different note that sounded far more genuine. 'Listen, Fael, I think something's about to happen – something connected with your father – that's going to affect you. But I think it'll be something I can help you with.'

'What?'

A pause. 'Tod's just returned from the north, hasn't he?' said the stranger. 'He's been trying to get a backer for a new show.'

'He's always trying to get a backer for a new show,' said Fael impatiently. 'Everyone knows that. He never succeeds.'

'But if he did succeed, Fael, have you thought what might happen? Have you thought that it might be more than he could cope with?' Another of the pauses. He does that for effect, thought Fael suddenly, and felt even better. He's a creature who has to hide from the light, and he's a creature who has to make use of planned effects.

'Have you thought,' said the soft voice, 'that it's nearly twenty years since your father created the *Dwarf Spinner*? And that he's done nothing worth mentioning since then? He's a spent force, Fael.'

'No he is not!' said Fael, so angry that she forgot about being frightened. 'But even if he does bite off more than he can chew, what's it got to do with you?'

'Listen now,' said the voice, and again there was the haunting familiarity. 'Listen, Fael, if Tod brings this deal off, you might need—'

'What deal? And what might I need? I might need a whole lot of things, but I don't see where you figure in any of them! Whoever you are,' added Fael for good measure, and thought she sounded quite reasonably angry and unafraid.

'You might need a friend,' said the voice.

'Oh sure, some friend who tries to break into the house in the middle of the night!'

'Didn't I tell you I was a creature of the night?'

'You're only saying that for effect!' said Fael, crossly, and thought: I don't believe I actually said that. I don't think this is really happening.

'Yes, but it works, doesn't it?' This time she caught the faint amusement. 'You know, you are going to need me,' he said. 'You're going to need— We'll call it a familiar,' he said. 'A dark, satanic familiar.' The expression seemed to afford him a rather bitter amusement. Fael could almost feel it ruffling the surface of his mind. 'Someone to be summoned in time of need.'

'How? Are you leaving a telephone number?' demanded Fael sarcastically. 'Or do I just summon you out of the night?'

'Something like that.'

'Well, I won't! I think you're mad. If you turn up here again you'll have the police to face!'

'Oh Fael,' he said. 'You won't turn me over to the police.'

'Don't be too sure.'

'You won't. You're too intrigued.'

'And you,' said Fael, furiously, 'are too arrogant for your own safety!'

He moved back, but this time the shaft of moonlight was too quick for him, and Fael glimpsed darkness where his face ought to be. A mask? Dear God, was he wearing a mask? Fear trickled back and she said, very sharply, 'You know, if you'd tell me who you are – or where I know you from – I might be more inclined to trust you.'

For a moment she thought he was not going to answer, and then he said, 'We have a mutual acquaintance, Fael. A mutual memory.' The measured pause once more. 'James Roscius.'

'Oh, the professor! Then you were one of his pupils!' said Fael. 'But why, for God's sake, didn't you say?'

'I can't imagine,' he said, and there was a whisper of sound and then he was gone.

The mask could only be discarded when the privacy of the tall, narrow house near Christchurch Street was reached. The young man with the soft, blurred voice peeled it off impatiently and tossed it onto a table and then sat down to think.

Fael Miller was so like her dead mother that it had set all the old memories tumbling. Aine had been a shining, slender creature with luminous skin and silver-gilt hair; to the small

24

boy who seldom left the house on Ireland's wild, west coast and who wove dreams on the dark stuff of Ireland's legends, she was a being straight out of Celtic myth. Aine, the daughter of the sinister seductive cave spirits . . . To a lonely child who peopled his world with the creatures of the old legends, she might well have become the focus upon which he would one day weave the illusions and the fledgling passions of moonish youth. Because whoever loved that loved not at first sight? thought the young man in the tall, narrow, river-side house. And I might have been faithful to you, Cynara, in my fashion, or then again, I might not. Except that he had never dared allow himself adoration or affection, or even admiration for any other living thing.

But it could have happened. He might have kept the memories and he might certainly have penned a sonnet or two, a madrigal or so, on the strength of a romantic child's dreams. That he had not done so was partly due to Tod Miller. Because fifteen years ago, Miller's famous *Dwarf Spinner* had been revived for a single charity performance in Galway.

It should have been a magical night to a boy of fourteen who lived a hermit life, seldom seeing anyone other than his clever musical father, and whose schooling had been at the hands of a series of solitary tutors who had been sworn to secrecy. Aine Miller was long since dead by then; she had died just before the *Dwarf Spinner*'s dazzling first night. The boy's romanticism had already started to tarnish. Because I knew what I was by then, he thought grimly. But traces of the romantic lingered, and he had sat bolt upright in the stage box taken by his father, with the discreet curtains partly drawn, drinking in everything on the brightly-lit stage, absorbing the flashing gold and silver, and the shimmering colours through the pores of his skin, intoxicated by the music. Yes! he had thought, clenching his fists, tightly. Yes, yes!

I might have become a writer or a composer or a playwright on that night, he thought bitterly. I was neither lunatic nor lover nor poet, and I might still have been tipped over into any one of those things.

It had been Tod Miller's grotesque finale that had jerked him out of his tumbling dream, and spun his senses into appalled horror and then into a cold, burgeoning hatred. He had gripped the padded parapet of the box, staring down at the stage, unable to look away from the final agonies of the dark, twisted creature who had served the captive heroine and spun the rainbow-dreams for her gaoler. The scene scalded into his senses and etched itself into his mind like acid, and he felt every death-pang of the lonely dwarf whose macabre face and evil witchery were only revealed in the closing minutes.

When it was ended – when the audience were cheering and Tod Miller was persuaded onto the stage to receive the acclaim, the hatred for Miller and the thing he had created had hardened and set.

Because what had been the genesis of Tod Miller's deformed, evil villain? What had been the leaven, the stimulus, that had caused him to create the macabre Rossani? The programme explained that Miller had plundered European folklore for his story, and there was a brief article by Tod himself, telling how he had wandered not only in Central Europe, but also in Russia and Icelandic sagas for his tale. To the uninitiated it might have sounded as if Miller had travelled amongst the remoter villages and hill farms and mountain colonies of far-flung places.

Rossani was the name by which the Italian story was told, and Rossani was the dwarf-magician of that version of the legend. But to have depicted the creature so precisely Tod Miller must have had a role-model.

The son of his old friend Professor Roscius? The child whose first breath had been drawn against a background of its mother screaming in revulsion? Had Tod known of that child's exist-ence? Memory stretched back over the years, to Aine Miller, a close friend of his father, one of the very few people permitted to visit the Irish house. Tod had never accompanied Aine, but supposing Aine had told him about Christian? Supposing Miller had seen it as the springboard for his plot? The thought was black, bitter gall. But why had Miller called his villain Rossani, the name so close to Roscius?

Christian Roscius, no longer a child, certainly no longer an impressionable romantic, fastened down the thrusting, hurting memories, and reaching for the concealing silk mask, went with his soft, cat-pawed tread out into the night once more.

Chapter Three

'And now,' said the dwarf, 'in return for spinning the straw into gold for you, you must promise me that when you are queen, your first-born child will be mine.'

'That may never be,' thought the Miller's daughter, and knowing no other way, promised.

German Popular Stories, Translated from the
Kinder und Haus-Marchen, collected by M. M.
Grimm from oral tradition, 1823

Tod got up from the desk and threw the screwed-up paper into the waste-paper basket in black fury.

He had made some notes for the new show in which little Makepiece was going to invest so generously; in fact he had made quite a lot, but so far he had not hit upon a single idea that would work. He had not, in fact, hit upon anything that would straggle past more than a solitary page of A4-size paper. He had explored any number of avenues: some had been allegorical and some had been historical and some had been political. Quite a few had been pantomimic and one had even been mildly pornographic. And not one of them would do.

He knew a moment of extreme self-pity. Here he was, an acclaimed composer and writer (yes he was!) and he was unable to apply his mind to his proper work. And why not? Money, that was why not! Wretched vulgar coinage!

Tod hoped he had a soul above such materialism but he defied anyone to work properly while being harried and nagged by creditors. He would just like to know what kind of stuff Lloyd-Webber and W. S. Gilbert and Offenbach would have churned out if they were constantly being plagued by pettifogging money-lenders and usurers. The richness of this last phrase pleased him so much that he instantly sat down again to draft a version of Christ in the Temple with the Money Lenders, but really all that Biblical stuff had had its day – *Jesus Christ Superstar* and *Joseph and the Amazing Technicolour Dreamcoat* and so on. He wanted something different and something original. He wanted to write another *Phantom* or *Evita* or *Les Miserables*.

He could not think of a single thing. Everything was ending in screwed-up balls in the bin. You might even go so far as to say that this was representative of his entire life, which was screwed up and ballsed-up and might as well be thrown into the bin and flushed into the Thames. He was supremely unloved and monumentally neglected and his muse had abandoned him and he was in arrears with the mortgage and there was no whisky in the house.

But now that he thought about it, was there any reason why he could not lay the entire scheme before the bank and suggest that they might care to take a financial slice of it? No reason in the world. They would accord him a bit of respect on account of it as well, instead of sending him coldly polite letters with silly phrases like 'feel sure you would like to know . . .' and 'regret to have to inform you . . .' There was nobody in the world who really wanted to know about a rapidly-accelerating debt, and so far from being regretful the bank were very likely laughing up their sleeves the entire time! Jealousy, plain and simple, that was all it was, but they would change their tune when they saw how very famous and wealthy he was about to be, by God they would! He would make an appointment to see the manager this very afternoon, and he would point out that here was a very good opportunity for a bit of sponsorship. You often saw things like 'sponsored by such-and-such a bank', or 'such-and-such company' on theatre programmes and on football stands and at golf tournaments.

Planning the actual company cheered him up. He would direct the show himself, of course (whatever it turned out to be), but he would need all manner of people to work for him. Stage managers and designers and electricians and publicity people. The image of himself seated at a large desk with several telephones presented itself pleasantly, and was followed by others, equally pleasant: rehearsals with himself at the centre of it all, his actors listening respectfully to him, carrying out his directions admiringly. He remembered that there were several quite reasonably-priced rehearsal rooms near St Martin's Lane.

Stephen Sherry would be the ideal choice for stage manager: the boy had done some good work at Bristol and Coventry and had an amiable custom of paying for the drinks whenever he and Tod met in the Greasepaint Club. It had been worth keeping up his subscription there, even though Fael said it was an extravagant frittering of money they did not have. But you met people there; you made contacts there.

Yes, Stephen would be a useful man to have, and his rich papa might be even more useful. Tod was not altogether sure what role Sir Julius Sherry played in the theatre these days, but he thought that there was some kind of managerial involvement with the Harlequin Theatre. Chairman of the governing board? Trustee? It had been the Harlequin that had seen the original West End run of the *Dwarf Spinner* and it would really be very nice if the Harlequin could be available again. Tod tried to think what was playing there at the moment and whether it was likely to close. He wondered as well if it might be possible to tell Julius Sherry that the bank were considering an investment, and then to tell the bank that Julius was considering one. He could certainly do it, but the difficulty was whether he would get away with it. It was not being deceitful or even particularly devious, of course; it was simply good business sense. He jotted the two names down.

For the designer he would very much like Flynn Deverill. He wrote the name down and looked at it doubtfully. It would be a bit of a risk to engage Deverill, who was outstandingly talented but notoriously difficult to work with. However, you did not become successful without taking a few chances and Flynn was certainly a chance worth taking. It was regrettable that a trail of rows and chaos tended to follow in his wake, and that he was said to drink and womanise to an alarming degree, but possibly a good deal of this was exaggerated. The Irish tended to

29

flamboyance, of course, and Deverill was very flamboyant indeed; Tod had not been present at the famous Inigo Jones Award ceremony (owing largely to the petty-mindedness of the organisers who had deliberately omitted his name from the guest list), but the speech that Flynn had made on being announced as the winner had become a legend. The BBC had reportedly been on the verge of signing him up to design an extravagant serialisation of Pepys's *Diaries*, but since he had denounced the entire awards system as tin cups for amateurs and the panel of judges as venal provincial sycophants, and had done so live on prime-time television, they had understandably changed their minds. Half the guests said afterwards that Flynn had been drunk, but the other half said he had never been more sober.

But he would have Flynn if possible. He remembered that the boy had been Professor Roscius's protégé during the professor's later years and that Roscius had certainly been responsible for Flynn's early involvement with the Harlequin – there you were, the Harlequin connection again. A good omen, surely! And Tod would be able to control Flynn; the boy could not be more than twenty-nine or thirty, and he would naturally treat with respect an older man and an erstwhile colleague of Roscius's. Dammit, Roscius had been musical director for the *Dwarf Spinner* all those years ago. He had come up with one or two suggestions for the musical side as well – only a tweak here and there, of course; the thing had been pretty near perfection before it went into rehearsal, but Aine had thought Roscius's suggestions good.

Of course, from one point of view, it was a pity that Aine had died in the road smash just before the first night. But looked at from another point of view, it had prevented any potentially embarrassing scenes. Also, it had meant that Tod had been able to deliver that marvellous emotional speech at curtain fall, referring to her as his inspiration – 'My splendid spur' he had called her, unashamedly wiping the tears away. It was a good thing that no one had known that the phrase was a direct pinch from the memoirs of an old Victorian actor-manager called John Martin Harvey.

And after all that, it was going to be a screaming irony if the years of writing about Beany Boppers and Camembert Crumpet had seriously impaired his skills. He drew the ruled pad towards him again.

Fael was absorbed in the new project for the clinic when Tod came plunging into her room. He appeared to have come straight from the rather seedy club he insisted on belonging to in Soho, which was more or less a gathering-place for fifth-rate actors who could not get work. Some people said it had other uses as well, and told darkly of a basement room beneath the wine cellars, which acted as a kind of secret headquarters for a particular band of Soho prostitutes. Fael, who had only been in the Greasepaint twice in her life, thought this might even be true because it felt like the kind of place where you might encounter anything from a hookers' trade union to secret IRA meetings, or even gatherings of those impassioned little societies for restoring the Stuarts to the throne of England. London was probably spattered with such things and Soho probably had a minimum of four per street.

Tod was not precisely drunk this afternoon, but he smelt of whisky and stale cigarette smoke, and Fael thought he was in the blustering stage that often tipped into embarrassing self-pity.

She put aside the notes for the hospital show and listened to what he had to say. It was depressingly familiar; Fael could almost have written the script. But it would provoke a row to say this, and there was always the possibility that one day Tod might really find someone to take him seriously.

In fact it was starting to sound as if this might actually turn out to be the day. Fael began to listen with more attention. The name of Gerald Makepiece came up a number of times – mostly preceded with adjectives ranging from 'little' to 'rabbity' – and it appeared that there had even been serious discussion about actual amounts. Whoever this Gerald Makepiece was he was either very rich or very silly, or possibly both. There was an obvious chance that he was very mad, of course.

But when Tod began to disclose the extent of the arrangement alarm bells sounded in Fael's head.

She said, 'You have done *what*?'

'I don't see why you have to glare like that, it isn't—'

Fael said, 'Let me get this clear. You have agreed with some unknown white rabbit called Gerald Makepiece to form a theatre company, write a new musical and put it on in the West End?'

'Well why not?'

'You're mad,' said Fael flatly. 'Were you sober at the time?'

'Of course I was sober!'

'Well, was he?'

'Yes, of course! He's a very respectable factory owner if you must know,' said Tod crossly. 'They make parts for – for something or other, *I* don't know what.'

'He'll need to be a very rich factory owner if he's going to finance a West End musical single-handed! I suppose you've checked him out, have you?' said Fael. 'I mean his financial position? No, I thought you hadn't.'

'I shouldn't dream of being so ungentlemanly.'

'You could ask the bank to do it for you. Or a solicitor. Banks don't mind about being ungentlemanly. Solicitors certainly don't. Supposing the rabbit's a screwball rabbit? Or a schizoid rabbit? And what if you start things rolling with your own money – not that you've got any – and he turns out to be an escaped lunatic? A *bankrupt* escaped lunatic. Have you thought about that?'

'He's not an escaped lunatic and he's not bankrupt,' said Tod, irritably. 'He seemed to me a very responsible person.'

'He seems to me a piss-artist.'

'I wish you wouldn't swear!'

'I wish you wouldn't do things to make me!'

They glared at one another. Then Tod said, 'Anyway, the thing is that I'm – hum – a trifle stuck with the actual writing. A tad bogged down – well, more than a tad, really. I've been trying all yesterday and the day before that, and all morning and—'

'And you're having difficulty,' said Fael. 'Writer's block. There's no shame in that.'

'Oh no, of course there isn't. No, absolutely not.'

'On the diet you've given your brain for the last ten years it's not surprising if it needs a bit of a kick,' said Fael. 'I should think even Mozart would find it a struggle to write something halfway decent if he'd spent years mushing his brain with washing powders and cheese-whiz biscuits and – what was that other thing you did? – Lily Laguna Lima Bean.'

It was unfair of Fael to bring up Lily the Lima Bean, which had not been one of Tod's most conspicuous successes, but surely to God a man was allowed one failure. Tod paced around the room a few times, and finally came to sit down again. 'Fael,' he said. 'It's more than writer's block. I can't do it.'

'You mean you really can't?' said Fael. 'You mean you really have got a promising backer – the real McCoy this time—'

'Of course he's the real McCoy—'

'And you're going to muff it because of Lima Beans and Crumpet Cheeses?'

'I wouldn't like to put it quite so *hurtfully*—'

'Well, how else would you like to put it?'

There was an uncomfortable silence and Fael remembered the unknown young man's words. *It's twenty years since your father created the* Dwarf Spinner, *and he's done nothing worth mentioning since then. You're going to need my help, Fael* . . . Something unexpected brushed her mind. Anticipation? Exhilaration?

Fael said, bracingly, 'Listen, now. If this rabbit really is prepared to put up the money you'll just have to keep at it. Maybe you haven't given yourself enough time.'

'It isn't that,' said Tod, and something unfamiliar showed in his eyes. The dying embers of a burnt-out man? *He's a spent force, Fael* . . .

And then the odd furtive look vanished as quickly as it had come, and Tod said, 'Fael, all those things you've done at the hospital – the shows you've written and set to music—'

'You're not suggesting I write this thing, are you?' Fael stared at him. 'Oh God, that's just what you are suggesting! Oh God, now I know you're mad! Listen, those were little concerts for *children*, for heaven's sake! They weren't original – they weren't even particularly good. They were therapy projects, to help disabled kids. Versions of other people's work – scaled-down, simplified—'

'Oh, everything in the world is a version of something else!' said Tod, instantly. 'There're only five or six basic plots, anyway, just as there are only five or six basic melodies. Anyone will tell you that.'

'But I can't write music. I've never composed anything in my life!'

'Only because you've never tried. Roscius taught you the principles of composition, didn't he? Well, I know he did because he told me before he went back to Ireland. As a matter of fact he thought rather highly of you.'

'Nice of you to pass that on after all these years,' said Fael, sarcastically.

'No, but you understand music at least as well as I do.'

'My God, there's an admission!'

Tod reached out and took her hand. This was something he hardly ever did, and Fael felt a sudden chill. *He means it. He really means it. He's going to force me to do this. Not with whips and beatings and starvation, but by appealing to my better nature. I haven't got a better nature. Yes, but I can't let him look a fool in the eyes of the world and the white rabbit. We're broke, as well. If this is all genuine, I can't let him miss such a chance.*

Tod said, 'Help me, Fael,' and this time his voice was humble and his face was pouchy with panic. 'I can't do it. But I think you can.'

Could she? The thought brought a churning blend of panic and fear, but underlying it was a burgeoning excitement.

And astonishingly, diluting the panic, was the shadowy memory of the dark young man. *You're going to need a dark, satanic familiar, Fael,* he had said.

A familiar ... An eerie, compelling twin-self with a voice like melted honey, or a black cat's fur, who would come stealing through the dusk-laden garden and help her to spin a dazzling spell-binding tale out of nothing.

Fael had no idea if she could do what Tod wanted, but there was nothing to be lost by trying. She drew the wheelchair up to the desk in the music room, and slotted a sheet of paper into the typewriter. Almost at once an unlooked-for bolt of excitement sliced through her. It was like facing an enormous blank canvas with a palette of vivid sizzling colours. It was like seating yourself in a roller coaster and waiting for the invisible machinery to rocket you helplessly onto its spinning, breathless track. *I'm about to walk into a make-believe world,* thought

Fael with fearful delight. I'm about to enter the world of illusion, and I've got to forget that the creatures who people that world aren't real: they'll have painted faces and their swords will be card and their jewels paste and pinchbeck. But I mustn't see that. I mustn't see that the castles are only plaster and timber either, or that the mist-wreathed lands are only misty because somebody's pumping out fake fog. I can't see the ending of this, thought Fael: I don't even think I can see the beginning. But here we go anyway.

A small fire was burning in the hearth, and the desk lamp cast a pool of radiance. The room was warm and safe. But night was creeping over the garden outside her window, and the shadows were becoming edged with violet. The garden was sliding into its dark, sinister shadow-self; it was turning into a place of black enchantments and spider-web witchery. The twilight thrummed with unseen forces and with strange murmurings and Fael thought it was the kind of night when anything in the world might happen. When creatures who had been sleeping at the heart of the trees might lift their three-cornered and inhuman faces and look about them . . . When horned and cloven-footed beings might dance through the gloaming, and faceless young men with blurred velvet voices prowl through the undergrowth, or dark, disguised heroes approach the doorless tower and climb up a plait of yellow hair because it was the only way in . . .

But other than that, it was not looking like a night when barnstorming award-winning musicals were created. Fael scribbled a few more notes, and acknowledged crossly that the moonwashed garden was becoming a distraction. Because I'm watching for him? Because I know he'll come, or – jarring thought! – because I know he won't?

You're going to need a dark familiar, Fael . . . You're going to need someone you can summon . . .

Well, all right, I'm summoning you, said Fael, silently. I'm conjuring you up, whoever you are, and if there's anything at all in telepathy you'll appear now! I don't know if you're a genie or a banshee or the ghost of Christmas past, and I don't even know if you're simply a figment of a disordered imagination. But I'm commanding you to appear now!

35

For a moment the shadows seemed to flinch, almost as if a strong light had suddenly shone down onto them, and Fael felt her heart begin to beat faster.

He's here. He's approaching. I can't hear him, but I can feel him. He's coming along the old river towpath, through the lych-gate that Tod always meant to have blocked up and never did . . . Through the dark trees . . . He's coming softly and slowly, because he doesn't tread quite like other people, and he's keeping to the shadows because I don't think he looks quite like other people, either . . .

She remained very still, trying not to make any sound that might break the spell, trying not to breathe, fiercely aware of her heart pounding in her chest. And then with a lurch of half-fearful, half-delighted panic, she suddenly saw that he was there, and that he had been there all along, part of the night, part of the twisting darkness, part of the interlacing branches of the old trees.

Like the old Irish legend of the Castle of Shadow and the beings that walked silently there and only appeared when it suited them – what was its name? – *Scathach*, yes that was it! He was a *Scathach*, a shadow being.

He came up to the window and stood for a moment silhouetted against the dusk. The soft voice Fael remembered so vividly said, 'Invite me in, Fael.'

A thrill of horror brushed Fael's skin. Am I really going to do this? Tod's out, and I'm on my own. In a kind of daze she heard her voice saying, 'Yes. All right. Go round to the garden door, and I'll unlock it.'

'First you must quench the lights.'

'Why?' The word came out hard and aggressive, which was at least something.

'Oh, because firelight is so much more restful. Because firelight and twilight mingle together to bring dreams. What do you think, Fael? Shall we sit by the firelight together and see what dreams we can spin? Shall we see if we can turn dross into gold or straw into silver, Fael?'

In the same half-dream, Fael wheeled the chair into the large square kitchen, and unlocked the door. She waited, but he stayed just beyond the focus of clarity, and after a moment she spun the chair back to the music room, and positioned it before the desk, watching the half-open door. The fire burned up as the little current of air fanned it slightly and then died down to a dull glow.

There was a blur of movement, the whisper of silk brushing the ground and he was there. Fael received the impression of a long black cloak and of a deep-brimmed hat with flowing locks beneath it. Covering his face . . .

'Shall we write your father's musical for him?' said Christian Roscius and crossed the room to sit in the darkest corner.

'Why?' said Fael. 'Why would you help me to do this? I don't know you. Even if we do have Professor Roscius in common, I still don't really know you – you won't even tell me your name.'

'It's midnight,' said Christian suddenly, half-turning his head to listen. 'Can you hear? Somewhere a church clock is chiming midnight.'

'All right, so it's midnight. So I'm a night-person – that's why I'm working late. You said you were a night-person as well. What about it?'

'Midnight is the time when all unholy alliances are struck,' said Christian. 'Are we going to strike a midnight bargain, Fael?'

'I'm not striking any bargain with— What kind of bargain?' said Fael, curiosity momentarily overcoming anger.

'If I help you, and if this reaches the stage, I'll want recognition and acknowledgement.'

'So that you can share in the profits?'

'No. The money doesn't interest me.'

'Then you're very unusual indeed,' said Fael. 'You're probably unique, in fact.'

'I probably am. Well?'

'No,' said Fael hotly. 'I'm damned if I'll enter into a ridiculous melodramatic bargain with somebody I don't know! Tell me your name and where you live, and then I'll think about it.'

'No,' said Christian. 'That will have to be part of the deal. But if we create between us something acceptable to your father's backer, on the opening night I'll tell you who I am. I'll be there with you in the theatre.' He stopped, and then said, half to himself, 'The Harlequin.'

'How do you know it'll be the Harlequin?' demanded Fael.

'I do know. The strands are all being gathered up. And on the opening night I will be there, Fael. When Tod acknowledges you, you'll tell them the truth. Then I'll tell you who I am.'

'My father—' This was fiercely disloyal, but it had to be said. 'I don't think you should count on him giving me acknowledgement,' said Fael. 'He's not above letting the whole thing go through as his own. Especially if it looks like being a success. You do realise that, don't you?'

'I do realise that,' said Christian.

There was an abrupt silence. Then he said, 'But I'll still do it, Fael. I'll help you – we'll work together in secrecy and I'll come here at night. For as many nights as it takes.'

'Why does it have to be in secrecy?' demanded Fael. 'And how do you know I won't yell for help and have you on a charge of trespass or breaking and entering or harassment or something? I might very well do that,' said Fael. 'I might trick you.'

'You won't.'

'Why won't I?'

'Loyalty,' he said at once, and Fael stared at him, and had a sudden unpleasant vision of Tod's wrath if he knew she had told a stranger that he could no longer write. And that he had had to ask his daughter to write a commissioned show for him. This disturbing young man was right: if the mad alliance really was struck, Tod was the last person she would dare tell. But it might be possible to do it on the crest of a wave. On opening night, with everyone delighted with one another; with Tod restored to fame. She could imagine saying, 'I had some help, of course. With the musical side. Let me introduce you –' Yes, it would be easy and natural and honour would be satisfied on all sides. But there was a long journey to be taken first, and if it had to be taken in company with this stranger—

She said, sharply, 'How do I know you aren't a maniac or a psychopath?'

'You don't. You'll have to take it on trust.'

'Well, how do I know you're even capable of helping me?' This had to be the maddest conversation anyone had ever had.

The stranger made a brief gesture that might have indicated amusement. 'You'll have to take that on trust as well,' said Christian. 'You'll have to put me on probation for a few nights. It's up to you.'

'And if I simply say, thanks, but no thanks? What then?'

'I'll vanish and never bother you again.' He leaned forward, and Fael caught her breath. But he seemed able to judge the flickering firelight, and the deep-brimmed hat with the long flowing hair under it still cast a darkness over his face. 'But between us, Fael,' he said, 'we could create something that will make everyone sit up and blink. Something memorable; something to lift people out of their workaday worlds for a space. Something that will spin an enchantment about them, so that they remember that there was once magic in the world.'

Once there was magic in the world ...

Christian said, very softly, 'We could take the cynical, materialistic, twentieth-century audiences into worlds they have forgotten. Worlds they believed in as children: worlds that live beneath a curtain of fir woods and heather ... Worlds where the moon is low and foxgloves grow on the hills ... Where the fair humanities of pagan religions still have the force and the beauty, and where ancient beckoning bewitchments still have the power to snare human souls—'

He paused, and Fael, torn between a growing fascination and an irritated suspicion that she was being manipulated, said, 'That's a jumble of quotations if ever I heard one. In a minute I suppose you'll start talking about being ill-met by moonlight and Queen Mab's chariot of an empty walnut—'

'It was a hazel-nut, actually. But the images are there, for all that, aren't they? Midnight revels and the lost languages. The vanished peoples of the earth ...'

Fael said, half to herself, *'Nicht die Kinder bloss speist man mit Märchen ab.'*

'It is not only children one feeds with fairytales,' said Christian at once. 'Precisely.' He leaned forward, and this time the firelight fell across the lower part of his face. For the first time Fael caught sight of what looked like thin black silk completely covering his face. A mask? But he moved back into the dark corner at once, and when he spoke again his voice was prosaic. 'I think you could write a story like that, Fael,' he said. 'I think you could plunder the old myths and the half-lost legends and weave them into something very memorable and beautiful.'

The spider-web idea was already solidifying into something stronger and something that was beginning to look violently exciting. Fael's mind was starting to tumble with vivid images: warrior kings and heroic quests; witches and giants and dark sinister enchantments. And beneath it all, like a bubbling under-current, a sub-text: a faint scattering of contemporary glimpses. Battles that mirrored the Bosnian war or Vietnam. Kidnapped princesses that echoed terrorist hostage situations. Parvenu dictators and greedy royalty and howling packs of paparazzi with faintly wolfish features . . . A light thread of modernity going all the way through. He's given me the germ of it, thought Fael with sudden delight. He's pointing out the way. She found herself wanting to say, Go away, go away quickly and let me get all this down on paper!

But when she spoke her voice was guarded. She said, 'Yes, I see. I think I could do that.' And thought: Oh God, yes, of course I could! 'But,' she said, very levelly, 'I couldn't compose the music.'

'No. But I could.' The silence dragged itself out again. The midnight chimes had long since died away, but Fael thought that something of them stayed on the air; a shivering awareness, a faint, far-off thrumming, like the prickle of electricity before a storm.

'Well?' said Christian, at last. 'Is it a bargain?'

To plunge fathoms down into this exciting, beckoning world . . . To make that journey, hand-in-hand with the dark compelling creature, this mysterious satanic familiar . . .

'Yes,' said Fael, softly. 'Yes, it's a bargain.'

Chapter Four

Tod seated himself at the oval mahogany table in the Greasepaint's upstairs conference room, and looked around him with gratification.

This was it, this was the start of the marvellous journey he had dreamed for so long of making. This was the journey that would take him back to the centre. He put firmly from his mind the memory of Fael seated at the desk in her room, smudgy circles of fatigue beneath her eyes. Fael would do it, she would not let him down.

He had prepared a little speech – nothing very much, really, but he dared say people would be expecting it. Once the preliminary introductions were over, and everyone was supplied with a glass of wine or sherry, he was going to deliver it. He would do it with humility and modesty and it would be very well-received, although he would have to be careful that he was not forestalled by Julius Sherry, prosy old fool, who had always been too fond of the sound of his own voice, and who already appeared to consider himself in some kind of senior position in all this. In fiscal terms Julius's contribution was minimal – he had suggested putting up a paltry fifteen thousand which was a mere flea-bite for a man of his substance! – but his position as a trustee of the Harlequin made him worth four times that sum and he would therefore have to be treated with a degree of respect. The old goat had obviously lunched well if not wisely, which was unfortunate, because he was eyeing Mia Makepiece with a bloodshot eye and a roué's mien. Tod frowned. They could not afford to upset Gerald Makepiece at this delicate stage of the proceedings. Once the cheque was signed and cleared Tod did not care whether Mia Makepiece screwed the entire company and half the audience as well.

On Julius's other side was the representative from Tod's bank, who wore an air of strong disapproval and looked as if he might disclose the embarrassing extent of Tod's liabilities to his masters at the least provocation. This was another anxiety Tod could have done without, because the bank's involvement was a very hefty one indeed, in fact there had been an extremely unpleasant interview earlier in the week, at which expressions like 'serious breach of agreement' and 'call in the first mortgage' and even 're-possession of the property' had been freely bandied about. Tod had come away feeling positively flayed.

Tod cleared his throat, waited pointedly for Julius to stop patting Mia Makepiece's hand, rose to his feet and gave of his best.

Gerald Makepiece had been enchanted to find himself scurrying along into the heart of steamy Soho, and charmed to be entering a place that was apparently Tod Miller's club. Gerald's experience of clubs was limited to seemly emporiums for the pursuit of golf or bridge, so that the Greasepaint came as a bit of a surprise.

He had been prepared for Soho, of course – one saw the place on all kinds of TV documentaries and news items – and he had expected the streets to be teeming with humanity, and to be liberally sprinkled with sinister-looking clubs and cinemas, as well as dozens upon dozens of bistros and wine bars and restaurants of every creed and colour and persuasion. But it had not previously occurred to him that people held important business meetings in shabby-fronted buildings with the facade peeling and a lingering smell of stale tobacco everywhere. He was also slightly disconcerted by the Greasepaint's doorman, who looked like an ex-pugilist.

The upstairs room to which they were conducted was a mite better, although Gerald would not have dreamed of holding any kind of meeting in a room where the windows were so grimy you could not see out of them. But he must remember that he was in a different section of society now. Raffish. Bohemian. The words pleased him.

He was entranced to find himself shaking hands with Sir

Julius Sherry, the famous theatre magnate. Tod Miller had introduced Sir Julius as one of the trustees of the Harlequin Theatre, and said there was a good possibility that they might secure the Harlequin for the show. Gerald knew about the Harlequin; he had gone to his local reference library to read up about London theatres in preparation for today, and the book he had found had devoted quite a large section to the Harlequin. It was very well thought of by the book's author, who said it was one of the oldest sites in London, and told how it dated back nearly to Charles II's day. The book also said that during its years under the musical direction of James Roscius, the Harlequin had gained its present reputation for musical shows.

Sir Julius was a far more robust person than Gerald had been expecting; he had clapped Tod Miller on the back on his arrival, and immediately launched into an anecdote about some luncheon he had just attended, which appeared to necessitate the use of several words Gerald had not thought people employed in mixed company. But he thought he managed to laugh in the right places, and he began to think he was not acquitting himself so ill. Mia, of course, was completely at home here; she was able to laugh with Sir Julius as if they were old friends, and then to talk in a serious and responsible fashion with somebody called Simkins, whom Gerald vaguely understood to be representing some kind of bank investment.

They were all given a glass of wine to toast the new venture, and Gerald opened the notebook he had brought, with its orderly headings about 'Salaries', and 'Staff', and 'Premises', and 'Profit and Loss'. Tod Miller made a little speech and Gerald listened attentively. Most interesting it was, all about how they were about to take a journey together and how they were about to become wayfarers in the motley land of chance with Tod at the helm. It was unfortunate that Sir Julius belched rather loudly at this point, but he covered it up quite well and everyone was mannerly enough to pretend not to have noticed. Of course, he was not a young man, Sir Julius, although Gerald noted wistfully that he had a good head of snowy hair. But set against that he was stout and florid-complexioned and very nearly grotesque, so that it was generous and sweet-natured of Mia to listen to his stories so tolerantly and not to mind when he patted her hand and leaned close to her.

Tod had reached the part in his speech about steering them all through turbulent waters and reaching the haven of success, when the door at the end of the room was flung open and a derisive voice said, 'Jesus God, Toddy, are you speechifying again? It's time someone broke you of that habit, for it's a terrible bore to everyone.'

Framed in the doorway was a young, or at least youngish man, with untidy black hair that needed cutting, a long, belted raincoat that looked as if it had been dragged on in the dark, and black-fringed grey eyes.

He received a rather mixed welcome.

Sir Julius, with a mischievous look on his jowly face, rose at once, and said, 'Flynn. My dear boy, come in.' And then to the table at large, 'Flynn Deverill. One of my co-trustees of the Harlequin, ladies and gentlemen. Flynn, this is Gerald Makepiece, his wife, Mia. And – ah – Mr Simkins.' The glance he sent to Tod crossed from faintly mischievous to definitely malicious. 'I asked Flynn to join us, Toddy,' he said. 'The board likes to have two trustees present when considering new ventures. And I knew you'd be glad to welcome him on board your – ah – storm-tossed ship.'

'Toddy's ship sounds more like the *Hesperus*,' said the irreverent young man. 'But so long as it doesn't turn out to be the *Marie Celeste* or – God forfend! – the *Titanic*, and us the rats scuttling away from it, it won't matter. Will I sit down now that I am here?'

'I suppose you'd better,' said Tod, ungraciously.

'Oh, do sit here,' said Mia Makepiece, who had fixed her eyes on the newcomer the minute he appeared. She leaned forward and smiled, patting the vacant chair next to her. Flynn appeared to consider this and then walked to the other side of the table and took a chair opposite Sir Julius.

'How far have you got?' The grey eyes that were far too beautiful for a man surveyed the company. 'Has Toddy milked you all of your life savings yet?' said Flynn. 'Or promised you the riches of the world if you'll bow down and worship him? I wouldn't believe a word he says if I were you. He wrote one musical twenty years ago and after that he sold his soul for a mess of pottage.'

Tod said very coldly, 'I didn't know you were on the Harlequin's board, Deverill.'

'Why should you?'

'Flynn was one of Professor Roscius's protégés,' said Sir Julius.

'Well, I know that, of course. I didn't think boards and finance were your style, Flynn.'

'Did you not?'

'Roscius was instrumental in involving Flynn in the Harlequin's board,' said Sir Julius.

'Ah yes, Professor Roscius guided your early footsteps, didn't he?' said Tod.

'He did, but it was the devil who guided them afterwards,' said Flynn. 'Is that wine you're serving us? Then I'll have some, unless it's that rubbish Toddy gets off the wood.'

'Oh, give him a drink, somebody,' said Tod, crossly. 'Flynn, the meeting started half an hour ago. If you knew about it, I do think it might have been polite of you—'

'Oh God, has somebody told you I'm polite? Don't believe him, whoever he was. The thing is, you see, that I wanted to miss your speech, Toddy, and I almost did, only – God Almighty, is this your idea of wine? *Is* it? Well, all I can say is, it's not mine.'

Mr Simkins, who privately agreed with Flynn, said reprovingly that they had a lot to get through and he had another appointment.

'Then get on with it, Toddy, before your man here sends in the bailiffs. Are you wanting me for design director of your little concert, by the way? Because if so, you'd better make sure you can afford me.' He tilted his chair back and rested the heels of his boots on the edge of the table, addressing the company generally. 'That was something Roscius taught me, you know – that people will always take you at the value you put on yourself. So I always put a very high value on myself indeed.'

Mia Makepiece said, warmly, 'I'm sure any fee *you* charged wouldn't be too high, Mr Deverill,' and Gerald said carefully that of course they would want to engage the best they could get.

'You see, Toddy? That little fowl with leggings over there wants me in the company.'

'I didn't actually say—'

'Oh, yes you do want me,' said Flynn, instantly. 'You really do, you know.'

Gerald interposed a hesitant question as to the amount that might be in question here, and turned to the page headed 'Salaries', his pen poised expectantly. Flynn grinned and named a figure, and Gerald's pen skidded across the page.

'But I'm worth it,' said Flynn. 'Because I'm very good, in fact I'm probably the best in London. And it so happens that I'm free at the moment, aren't you in luck?'

'Stop showing off,' said Sir Julius repressively, and Flynn grinned again, and raised his glass. 'And take your feet off the table.'

'I thought it would be cleaner than the floor,' said Flynn, but did as requested. 'And now, will we talk about forming this company and finding out what Toddy's going to write for us all, before I'm sick on the mat from that terrible wine? And we'll hope we don't have to repair to the wine bar downstairs, because the claret they serve's even worse than this horse-piss Toddy's giving us, and Bill lets the hookers in for half-price booze at five o'clock.'

Gerald Makepiece went back to the small, quiet Kensington hotel, his mind in a happy tumult.

The afternoon had not been like any afternoon he had ever experienced, and the meeting unlike any meeting he had ever attended. At Makepiece Enterprises they had serious and responsibly-minded conferences, where people presented reports; where figures were carefully considered and budgets balanced to the farthing. Coffee was served if it was morning, and tea if it was afternoon, and on Gerald's birthday, or if somebody was retiring or getting married, they all had a glass of Crofts dry sherry, and it was all very orderly and respectful.

There had not been a great deal of order about this afternoon's meeting, and there had not been very much respect, either! But despite it, they appeared to have formed the nucleus of a company, the articles of association for which Gerald's solicitors would draw up, and the directors of which would be Tod Miller, Julius Sherry, Gerald himself, and Miller's bank. Gerald had wanted Mia to be included, but she had very prettily declined.

'I shouldn't know the first thing about being a director,' she had said, and Sir Julius had at once made a joke about sleeping partners which made everyone laugh very heartily.

Then there had been some question as to whether Flynn Deverill would be drafted onto the board as well. Sir Julius had been inclined to favour the idea on account of the Harlequin connection, but Flynn had refused point-blank.

'I'll design Toddy's concert for him, but I'll only do it as a paid employee.'

It had not previously occurred to Gerald that anyone would refuse a seat on any board, and he had stared at Flynn in fascination.

Sir Julius Sherry said in an exasperated voice, 'For goodness' sake, Flynn, why not?'

'Oh, if you make me a director there'll be no authority for me to challenge,' said Flynn. 'I like challenging authority, in fact it's the very breath of life to me. And my best work's done when I'm quarrelling with people.'

Julius said, in a resigned fashion, 'The fighting Irish.'

'Exactly. So you can pay me that enormous salary the little fowl's got written down there, but you can leave me below the salt. I'll lead the mutinies and foment the unrest and stir up rebellion amongst the all-licensed fools and the rude mechanicals.'

'How appropriate,' said a lugubrious voice from the other side of the table, and Flynn at once raised his glass of the disputed wine to Simkins of the bank.

There had been a point in the discussions when Gerald had been afraid that Tod Miller was going to fly into a real rage with Flynn, and throw the disrespectful young Irishman out of the Greasepaint Club neck and crop. Miller had actually started up out of his chair, his face purpling in a way that made Gerald wonder uneasily about heart attacks and strokes, but the bank representative cleared his throat and began to say something about the need to get swift returns on investments, and Tod Miller had said 'Hrmph', and sat down again. In the end he had agreed to accept Flynn as the company's designer. Gerald had no very clear idea of what this entailed, but had grasped that it was a position of some importance and that they were fortunate to have Flynn.

'It's the most important thing of all,' said Flynn. 'And you're very fortunate indeed to have me. I'll design you the most startling show you ever heard of. You'll see. Toddy, when will we see the book?'

'Oh hum, well, when it's finished,' said Miller, and Gerald saw Julius Sherry look up sharply.

'There's no problem, is there, Toddy?'

'Oh no, absolutely not, my word, no problem at all. It just isn't ready for anyone to see it yet.'

'Hasn't Toddy been telling us all for years he's got a drawerful of West End successes just waiting to be staged?' said Flynn. 'Six musicals in search of an angel.' He looked at Tod through his lashes. It was ridiculous for a man to possess such extravagantly long lashes. It was a very good thing indeed that Mia had no eye for these insolent young men, as well, because Flynn Deverill possessed the kind of startling good looks that ladies sometimes became silly about. But he was shockingly rude, and Mia would not care for that.

'It's all very fine for the rest of you to make jokes,' said Tod, crossly. 'But you'll have copies in plenty of time.'

'Well, could we have a general idea?'

Tod said irritably that writing was not like working on a factory bench. 'Dammit, I'm an artist. I'm a creator. I can't be yoked and fettered.'

'I'm sure no one expects it, Mr Miller,' said Mia.

'Well, no. Thank you, Mia.'

Flynn Deverill remarked that a full-blown musical would inevitably take longer to dash off than a handful of television commercials. 'It takes a bit longer than Stilton Hooker, doesn't it?'

'Camembert Crumpet,' said Tod, infusing the words with as much dignity as was possible. He stood up, pointedly ignoring Flynn. 'Julius, are you getting a taxi back, because if so—'

But Sir Julius, it appeared, had agreed with Mia that the two of them would just nip across to the Harlequin Theatre together. 'Only a very quick nip,' he said. 'Our little lady is not familiar with the house, and we're going to review the ground. So to speak. You don't mind do you, Makepiece? No, I didn't think you would. Flynn, can we drop you anywhere?'

It was not immediately clear to Gerald how or at what point this arrangement had been arrived at, or quite why it was necessary for ground (what ground?) to be surveyed, but since Mia was going to be involved, she would want to know as much as possible about what was ahead of her. It was extremely kind of Sir Julius to go to such trouble.

Gerald stepped cautiously out into the street and waited for a taxi to drive past. There were certainly quite a lot. He placed his left foot on the kerb edge and lifted his right hand in a hailing gesture, which was what you saw people do in films. He felt very daring and nonchalant, and he managed not to appear too startled when it actually worked.

As night began to shroud the London streets, the Greasepaint's doorman went quietly down the stair that led to the wine cellars, and unlocked the subterranean room that was only ever used on Sunday nights.

The Sunday meetings at the Greasepaint were a queer old set-up; the doorman had to say they were very strange indeed. Normally you got your girls and you got your pimps, and as a rule the pimps went to the girls' flats or to the nearest pub to settle up all the monies and so on. Sometimes you got trouble between them, and the police had to be called, and quite often you got trouble of a more private kind as well: pimps poaching girls, or girls poaching territories, and private feuds and jealousies and scores to be settled. Sometimes the police got involved with those and sometimes they did not. It was mostly how it operated and although the system was a bit rough and ready, everybody knew the rules and on the whole it worked all right. If you lived or worked in Soho you knew about it almost without thinking about it, although probably it was different with the class girls who had maids and regular bookings. It would probably be a whole lot different in Mayfair and St John's

Wood; the doorman was not very familiar with those areas.

The main thing that stood out about the Sunday night meetings was that they were *organised*. In fact the doorman had only remarked the other week to Bill on the bar, that if this arrangement ever caught on they'd find themselves with a hookers' trade union, and Bill had said, well, why not? The girls worked their arses off most nights, poor cows, why shouldn't somebody take up their cause? He had not actually said 'cows', and he had not actually said 'arses' either.

The room had to be ready at midnight, to the tick. Neither of them knew where the initial instructions had come from, but they knew the arrangement had been there for two or three years and that payment for the room was made scrupulously but anonymously each Sunday, the cash left in a sealed envelope on the table after everyone had gone. The arrangements were fairly easy, really; there had to be the table at the far end, with the velvet cloth thrown over it, and there had to be the thick crimson curtains drawn behind the table, so that they hid the small door that opened onto the passage leading to the area steps. The area was sometimes used as a delivery yard and not many people knew it was there, but the man who came here every Sunday knew it was there and he had his own key, although neither the doorman nor Bill knew how he had come by it. This was only one of the faintly sinister things about him.

The chairs had to be lined up for the girls, neat rows facing the velvet-draped table. Bill and the doorman usually took down the stackable chairs from the upstairs meeting room. And, eeriest of all, every light bulb had to be removed and the special low-wattage, red-tinted bulbs put in place. Bill ordered them in bulk from the same suppliers Raymond's Revuebar used. It was cheaper that way. The meeting began at midnight exactly and ended an hour to an hour and a half later. No refreshments were served, but a decanter of brandy and a glass had to be left on the table, and it had to be the good brandy as well.

Neither Bill nor the doorman himself had ever questioned what would happen if the room was not ready one night or if the preparations deviated from the instructions, quite simply because it must never happen. The man who paid for the room's use, and who entered through the low door in the wall and sat at the table each Sunday night and drank the very good brandy was not someone either of them wanted to risk angering. This was remarkable in itself when you remembered the doorman's Navy and boxing years and the fact that Bill had grown up in one of the roughest parts of the East End.

They always told one another that one of these nights they would creep down and hide somewhere and see exactly what went on at the meetings. They were both becoming very curious indeed about the identity of the man who came under cover of darkness, and whose name nobody seemed to know, but who apparently wielded such authority in the neon-lit demi-world of Soho's night streets.

Putting the final touches to the room tonight, the doorman straightened up and looked about him. Like this, with the sulky lights burning, you might almost mistake it for a stage set – something from one of those slightly raunchy, sometimes bizarre shows in the sixties and seventies, where fantasy and fiction and reality all overlapped a bit. The rock musicals like *Hair* and *Oh Calcutta!* and *Jesus Christ Superstar*. Or that curious dark fairytale musical that had been such a cult at one time – the *Dwarf Spinner*. The doorman was familiar with the *Dwarf Spinner*; when he had left the Navy he had got a job at the Harlequin for a time, scene-shifting and carpentering, and he could remember helping to set the stage for the eerie scene where the twisted evil genius, Rossani, made his first appearance.

Looking about the red-lit cave that was the Greasepaint's deepest cellar, he was reminded very strongly of Rossani. Which was the outside of absurdity.

He shook his head to dispel the clustering shadows, and went back up the stairs.

Chapter Five

The dwarf's power is only to be broken if his name can be discovered.

Classic Fairy Tales, Iona and Peter Opie

Leila and Gilly normally went to the Sunday night Greasepaint meeting together. It was not precisely that they were fearful, but Leila said and Gilly agreed that the man they all knew as the Shadow was not someone you really wanted to face on your own. They usually met up with a few of the others on the way – there'd be Lori and her lot, and there might be Danilo if his stint at the club finished early enough. It generally did, because Danilo did not want to get on the Shadow's wrong side. Nobody did.

They all had to sit in a row like at school or the theatre. People made jokes about it, but the jokes were a bit shrill. Nerves, of course. Silly when you thought that most of them walked the streets by night and picked up men who might be anything from Jack the Ripper reborn to Frederick West, but there it was. Danilo said the Shadow was a hypnotist: he'd seen it done in clubs and he'd got them all hypnotised. Some people agreed with this, but some thought it was something to do with drugs and insisted that the Shadow had found a way of pumping speed or E through the walls of the cellar. Others said it was neither of these things, it was that the Shadow knew too much about them all. Nobody quite believed any of these theories, but nobody quite disbelieved them either. Gilly sometimes thought that the Shadow could see into people's minds, that he could see into hers, and that he knew how much she hated having fallen into this horrid, sordid way of life. Once or twice she had even thought that he sympathised with her, although this was probably being fanciful in the extreme.

It was remarkable how the tension built as they all assembled. They came in in threes and fours, the girls clicking down the stairs in their high heels, calling ribald greetings to one another as they sat down, comparing notes, telling how it had been a good week or a bad one, or a better week than last. People shrugged off coats if it had been cold outside, and shook out their hair so that a new colour could be noticed, or displayed a new outfit. Danilo was usually straight from a club gig, which meant there were sequins falling off him all over the place, to say nothing of false fingernails. If you were wearing leather that night you didn't sit next to him because there was nothing worse than getting scarlet and silver sequins stuck to leather. Leila said he did it deliberately.

And then one by one they fell silent, and turned to look up at the big clock on the wall, above the velvet-draped door. As the silence lengthened they all watched the minute hand crawling its way to midnight. Tick-tick . . . You almost felt his approach before you heard it. Tick-tick . . . He was almost with them. People seated nearest the thick red curtains behind the table sometimes caught a snatch of tune being hummed very softly: the theme from the old seventies musical the *Dwarf Spinner*. It still got played sometimes, and most people knew it.

O never go walking in the fields of the flax
At night when the looms are a-singing;
For Rossani's at work and he's hungry for prey;
He'll melt down your eyes and he'll spin them for gold.
He'll peel off your skin and he'll sew him a cloak.

O never go walking at Samhain at dusk
In company of one whom you know not to trust;
Rossani's a-prowl and he's looking for fools;
He'll cut out your heart and he'll weave it to gold.
He'll grind down your bones and he'll shred up your soul.

Samhain was Hallowe'en – the man who wrote the musical was Irish or married to an Irish wife or something – and the song had become a bit of a Hallowe'en anthem at discos and in wine bars and clubs. It was grisly and gory, and it could be sung with relish at Hallowe'en parties. But it was very creepy indeed to hear it softly whistled just as midnight was striking, just as the Shadow approached.

The minute-hand whirred the last few seconds, and clicked onto the twelve, and in the distance a church clock somewhere – most likely St Martin's-in-the-Fields – chimed dully.

There was a whisper of sound – silk against velvet – and the curtains shivered and parted and he was there. Gilly, who had had a bit of dance training and had got a few tiny parts before running out of money and ending up in the Soho clubs, thought it was as effective an entrance as you could get. Whoever the Shadow was, he had a terrific sense of theatre.

A stir of unease went through the room when he appeared, but every eye was on him. Once he was here, you simply were not aware of anyone or anything else. Sometimes he'd be wearing a black silk mask so that you only saw his eyes glittering through the slits, and other times he'd have on a deep-brimmed hat – the kind you saw old villains wearing in late-night black and white films. Tod Slaughter in *The Face at the Window*, or Bela Lugosi in *Dracula*. They were good for a laugh, those old villains, but nobody wanted to meet the real thing. Once or twice the Shadow had appeared with long black hair obscuring his face – like Michael Jackson's dreadlocks only much thicker – and dark glasses. He was not very tall and as far as anyone could tell he was quite thin. Gilly said he was slightly deformed, but opinion was divided about this.

He sat at the table, and switched on a strong desk light that shone onto them all, so that the pouring smoke of people's cigarettes showed blue in the beam, and he stayed behind the light so you only ever saw him as a black silhouette. And one by one they had to go up to the table and pay over the five per cent of the week's earnings.

It was quite a lot, five per cent, but it was not so bad for what you got in return. Protection, that was what you got. Nobody ever beat up one of the Shadow's girls and got away with it, and nobody ever tried to charge any of them extortionate rent for a flat or a bedsit. And if you had a grievance or a trouble you brought it along, and you spoke up when it was your turn at the desk, and although the Shadow seldom said much, he listened and nodded, and the next thing you knew the cheating landlord, or the sadistically-minded punter had received his come-uppance. It made you feel safe; it made you feel that you had someone fighting in your corner.

But for all that, he was still a sinister figure to them; a thin, crouching spider sitting at the centre of a black, sticky web. Nobody quite knew who his people were and who his spies were. It was not thought that he had any friends, but it was certain that he had a great many spies. This was the trouble; you did not know when you might be sitting next to one of them. They were probably in the room tonight.

Leila had said before tonight's meeting that she had had enough. It was a greedy, unfair system, and she was going to break out of it tonight. She had had a very good week, with a windfall on Friday night: a group of businessmen had taken her back to their hotel and between them they had given her six hundred pounds. The Shadow could not possibly know about that, she said, and she was not going to tell him. And if he started any of his scary tricks, she had another card up her sleeve, she said, and paused. It was Gilly who said, 'What?' and Leila smiled smugly.

'I think I know who the Shadow is,' she said. 'I think I've found out his name.'

'How?' demanded Gilly.

'Never mind how. But he's got a bloody arrogance, thinking he can come and go and give orders, and no one so much as asking a question.'

For once this was a reasonable thing for Leila to say. London had its share of weirdos, of course, and Soho took a large part of that share, but the Shadow was in a class by himself. Gilly even wondered if it was a bit naive of him not to realise that more people might notice him than he realised. But it was oddly uncomfortable to find this chink in the Shadow's defences, and so she asked Leila what she was going to do.

Leila smiled and said, 'I'm going to tell him tonight that I know who he is. And then we'll see about paying five per cent to bloody faceless pimps every week.'

Infuriatingly, she would not say any more about the Shadow's identity, not even when Lori jeered and said Leila was a piss-artist and it was all lies. Danilo bet Leila twenty pounds that she would chicken out when it came to it, and Leila took the bet. Gilly was in agonies, but you could not stop Leila from doing something she had set her mind on and Danilo and Lori were as bad, egging her on.

The meeting took its usual course. People went up to the table one by one. The Shadow addressed them all by name. He said, 'A good week, Lori?' or Michelle, or Gina, whoever it happened to be. His voice was low and soft, and there was a slurred, blurry note to it. Danilo, who read books and had ambitions to break into the real theatre, once said it was as if he had had to learn human speech because it was not natural to him, but this was such a grisly idea that everyone had told Danilo to shut his row.

There were several street musicians here tonight – people still called them buskers sometimes. Gilly pointed them out to Leila and Danilo, and Leila said at this rate the Shadow would end up owning half of London, never mind Soho. The buskers had their own community, and they sat together, not mixing with everybody else. They worked the tube entrances – Tottenham Court Road and Oxford Circus and Piccadilly – and the theatre crowds in Shaftesbury Avenue.

When it was Leila's turn she went up defiantly, tossing back her hair, and clopping her heels loudly on the floor. Gilly and Danilo moved to a front seat to see and hear better. Gilly thought Danilo was beginning to regret making the bet. He was very good-hearted underneath, Danilo.

Leila was handing over a wad of banknotes and the Shadow put them to one side, not counting them, barely even looking at them. He sat back and looked at Leila – just looked, raking her from head to toe, so slowly and so fixedly that Gilly remembered how she had thought he could see into people's minds.

Then he said, in his soft voice, 'Is this all, Leila?'

'Oh yes. Yes, that's all.' She was over-doing it; Gilly could hear that from where she sat. 'Oh yes, that's everything.'

The Shadow said, 'Are you sure about that? Wouldn't you like to think again, Leila?'

The silence lengthened. He knows, thought Gilly, in growing fear. He knows about the evening with the businessmen, because he's got spies everywhere that tell him. She glanced nervously around the room and then looked back at the table.

Leila placed her hands palm-down on the table, and leaned forward. There was a moment when Gilly almost thought the Shadow flinched, but this was not really believable. Leila said something to him in so low a whisper that even Gilly, straining her ears, could not catch it.

The quality of the silence was suddenly and frighteningly different. The Shadow remained motionless, but it was as if he had suddenly changed; as if his whole being had altered and he had turned into something quite different. Like the wolfman in the old film changing from man to wolf, or one of those creatures from a child's fairy story. Gilly shivered.

And then the Shadow made a brief dismissive gesture, and Leila shook back her hair again and straightened up, and looked round the room triumphantly.

A sigh of something that might have been regret, but that might as easily have been fear, stirred the room.

As Leila walked back to her lodgings after the meeting, she thought she could feel pretty pleased about tonight. She had shown the Shadow where he got off, and she had done it in front of everyone! She had stood up to the stupid tosser and she had defied him and told him she knew who he was. She was going to tell them all his name, she had said; this silly nonsense would be over then, and there would be no more five per cents and no more creepy meetings with them all forced to attend like school children. As for all this talk about spies and people in hotels and bars being in his pay, it was just a load of old balls! she said.

It had knocked him for six, Leila had known that at once. She had felt the shock go through him like an electrical current, and triumph had surged up. Got you! she thought, looking straight into the hidden eyes. He had been wearing the dense black glasses tonight, and the wide-brimmed hat, and the lower part of his face was covered by a kind of scarf-muffler. But she had disturbed him; she had upset the cold control.

Her stock would go up no end after tonight. Danilo and Gilly and that spiteful cat Lori would all treat her with a bit more respect now. Gilly and Danilo were good pals, and of course Gilly was not really one of the working girls, not properly. She had had some rotten luck, Gilly; Leila did not know all the details, because Gilly was not the kind to moan.

But that Lori jeered at Leila behind her back and called her the walking pox (which was bloody unjust, she had never had the pox in her life), and told everyone she was a slack old has-been. Vicious little bitch.

What was really good was that Leila would keep the whole of the six hundred quid. This was only fair as well, because she had bloody earned it with those four businessmen, three of whom had been so soddenly drunk they could not get it up. She had had to work on them non-stop for half an hour but she had managed it in the end. They had all felt very macho as a result, and had ordered up a huge supper from room service on top of the money. Leila had been so pleased she had told them to ask for ice-cream with the supper, so that she could give them all an ice-cream dick-lick as an extra, which none of them had ever heard of. The ice-cream had been flavoured with cherry brandy and tasted very good indeed.

She had even begun to have visions of moving out of Soho and setting up in a classy house, with a maid to answer the door and punters coming in by appointment. No need to drag out in the depths of winter; no need to pad the streets any more. She was a bit older than the rest, although there was no call for Lori to be so hurtful about it, and she felt the cold. She remembered the word vulnerable. You felt vulnerable as you got older, especially in this game.

She felt very vulnerable tonight. She ought to have gone with Gilly and Danilo or someone. There was never a great deal on at this time of a Sunday night, and they often went back to Danilo's place or to one of the all-night bars. It was quiet and a bit deserted out here; Leila's flat was in one of the tall old houses among the warehouses. It felt lonely tonight. Still, there might be a punter or two around. It sounded as if someone was following her now, in fact. Yes, she could hear soft footsteps coming along behind her. She slowed down to see what would happen, and it was then that she caught the sound of someone singing very softly. The tune was vaguely familiar. Leila frowned, trying to place it, and then with a thrill of icy fear, she knew what it was.

O never go walking in the fields of the flax
At night when the looms are a-singing;
For Rossani's at work and he's hungry for prey;
He'll melt down your eyes and he'll spin them for gold.

Rossani's song from the *Dwarf Spinner*; the eerie melody that almost always preceded the Shadow's meetings. He was following her.

Leila glanced fearfully over her shoulder, and as she did so, she saw the slight figure with the deep-brimmed hat coming towards her out of the darkness.

As Christian followed Leila through the dark streets, the shadow-world of Tod Miller's brilliant macabre character was waking and coming to life all about him.

He *was* Rossani; he was the dark, brilliant dwarf-magician whom he had seen on a lit stage fifteen years earlier and who had haunted him ever since. He had taken on Rossani's twisted, hate-filled persona: the persona who had prowled the Samhain night and taken his victims, and who had spun the magic for the miller's daughter when she could not spin it herself.

Rossani's at work and he's hungry for prey . . .

The words were singing in his head as he followed the bitch to her shoddy flat, and the London streets were dissolving all around him, giving way to the strange, hag-ridden, goblin-haunted realm that lay beneath, and that was only occasionally visible, and then only to madmen and drunkards. But it was in that dark nether-world that Rossani lived and ruled and had his lair. Christian could almost see the fields of the flax that Rossani spun out of human skins, and he could almost hear the looms singing.

It was easy to catch up the raddled, raucous female who had threatened to name him to her sleazy friends, and easier still to pretend he wanted to talk to her. He felt her initial bolt of fear, but he softened his voice, infusing it with the low, caressing note that had taken so many years to master. It was rare these days for him to slip back to the ugly, formless, distorted speech of his childhood.

A deal, he said. A deal with just the two of them knowing about it. If she really did know who he was, they could perhaps discuss an alliance. Could they do that? Just the two of them together?

The unexpected intimacy of his tone disconcerted her, but he knew at once that it intrigued her. Despite her bluster Leila was afraid of him, as all these girls were: Christian was amusedly aware of the fear, and he had deliberately allowed his legend to grow up in this part of London. He could sense the fear in Leila now, but he could sense the interest beneath it as well, and he knew that she had experienced a stir of attraction bordering on the sexual. She was intrigued by the thought of getting closer to him, physically and mentally.

Once in her flat it was as easy to overpower her as it had been to send out the subtle snake-thread of sexual beckoning. He waited until she turned her back to fill a kettle for coffee and then stunned her, using a marble paperweight he had brought with him for the purpose. He tied her up and sat her in a chair and then waited for her to regain consciousness. He needed her tied up, but he needed her conscious before he could do to her what Rossani had done to his victims.

As he sat waiting for her eyes to open, he was humming Rossani's song.

When Leila did not turn up at the sandwich bar where she and Gilly usually met for a bit of lunch on Mondays, Gilly dragged Danilo along to Leila's bedsit to find out if anything was wrong.

It was unusual for Leila not to show up. It was worrying to find that her curtains were still closed as well. She had what the landlady called the garden flat and everyone else called the half-basement, and it got pretty dark if you didn't keep the curtains open.

Danilo tried to say that nothing would be wrong: Leila might have flu or a sprained ankle or simply have slept in late. He said this several times, chewing his lower lip before he remembered that it would look scabby through lipstick and he had a club gig tonight.

The landlady lived on the first floor, and to start with was not going to open Leila's door, not for Gilly and Danilo, nor the Emperor of China, nor anyone else who might ask. Privacy was privacy, and Leila paid her rent regular, you had to say that for her, even though the men tramping in and out were a pain in the bum at times, never mind the nosy-parkering social workers who came around giving out free condoms. In the landlady's youth they'd been called johnnies or rubbers, and there'd been none of this AIDS thing. There was none of this rubbish about 'working girls' neither. You were a street-girl or a tart, or, if you felt a bit poetic-like, you could be a lady of the night. That was what you were, and you didn't pretend different. But whatever you called yourself, providing you paid your rent regular and didn't bring fights into the house, interfering folk couldn't go barging into private rooms for the asking.

There was quite an argument about it, with all of them standing in the narrow hallway, and a couple of the other tenants, attracted by the noise, came out to join in. Somebody said that Leila had brought home a punter last night, and somebody else agreed with this. There was some suggestion that the punter might still be in there with her, and the landlady said that if that was the case she was not going down there for the Chief Rabbi or the Pope, on account of not knowing what they might be interrupting.

In the end Danilo, who was getting quite successful on the club circuit and not short of a pound or two, slipped the landlady a twenty-pound note which settled matters. She plodded down to unlock Leila's rooms and everyone crowded after her.

For a moment Gilly, who was at the front, thought that Leila had simply nodded off in the chair. She experienced a huge relief, because after all nothing had happened: the Shadow had not done anything and they had all gone over the top about the whole thing.

Leila was sitting in one of the slightly worn, but very comfortable armchairs she had picked up cheap last summer. She was slumped down a bit; it did not look a very comfortable

61

way to sleep. The small gas ring that she had for heating soup and beans, and that she sometimes used to cook spaghetti bolognese for Gilly and two or three of the others, had been moved alongside the chair, which was odd, because it usually lived in the cubbyhole kitchen. It was the first thing that Gilly identified as being out of kilter.

And then gradually, with a creeping feeling of sick distortion, Gilly knew that it was not just that that was out of kilter here; it was everything, and in just a minute her mind would manage to get hold of the terrible wrongness and understand. At her side Danilo had drawn in his breath sharply and muttered, 'Oh, Jesus,' and there was the sound of the landlady tottering back into the narrow hall.

Leila would not mind the uncomfortable position in the chair because she was dead; that was why she had not got up when they came in. And even if she had not been dead, she would not have got up because she would not have been able to see.

Her eyes had been cut out of her face, leaving deep, dark, bloodied holes with a jagged frill of flesh. A trickle of blood had run down over the left cheekbone and dried there, brownish and crusted. On the little gas ring was a small pan, and in it was a glutinous mass, partly congealed, but still a bit jelly-like. It held a recognisable shape. Two recognisable shapes, each one about the size of a cherry, but with a whiteness like tiny poached eggs. Gilly felt sickness rising up from her stomach, and swallowed hard.

Lying alongside the two glutinous things was a sprinkling of something light and frivolous and something that struck such an incongruous note that for a moment the sickness receded, and Gilly frowned, trying to make sense of it . . .

And then Danilo spoke and everything clicked dreadfully into place. Danilo said, 'It's gold dust.' And then in a voice of extreme disbelief, ' *"Rossani's at work and he's hungry for prey. He'll melt down your eyes and he'll spin them for gold . . ."* Christ Almighty, he's dissolved her eyes over the gas, and he's sprinkled gold dust over them.'

Gilly tumbled out of the room and dived into the lavatory at the end of the corridor just in time to be violently sick.

Chapter Six

[Witches] steal young children out of their cradles,
ministerio daemonum, *and put deformed ones in
their rooms, which we call changelings . . .*

The Anatomy of Melancholy, Robert Burton

Fael had the curious sensation that as she worked in the quiet music room with the underwater light from the garden, her mother was very near to her.

This was strange; Aine was the dimmest of dim memories to Fael. A gentle, lovely lady with a beautiful voice and hair like rippling ivory silk. But Fael had barely been five years old when Aine died, and you only brought a few threadbare memories with you from that age.

Even so, she thought she could almost feel Aine guiding her hand when she took down the first of the old books of Celtic legends, and as she opened the pages, she thought that mingling with the scent of old leather and foxed parchment was a drift of remembered perfume. Something sweet and sad and evocative. Rose-leaf memories, pressed between the pages of an old, forgotten book, or reminiscences folded between leaves of tissue-thin silk, so that when you unwrapped them, they came up as clear as the day you had put them there, only a very little dimmed by the years, only a very little faded and creased. I believe you're with me, Aine, thought Fael, her skin prickling with delight and sadness. I can't see you, but I almost believe that if I turned my head I might catch a blurred glimpse of you.

Aine's books were all here; the leather-bound legends and tales of myth and evocative Irish folklore. Fael thought Irish mythology was like no other mythology in the world: it was eerie and chilly and it had its roots in lost peoples and creatures not quite human, and in dazzling heroes and giants and warrior queens. Or is that because I'm half-Irish to start with?

She turned the pages, making notes as she went, her mind lighting up with delight at the pouring blue and green world that was letting her into its misty depths. Battles and quests and mountain palaces. And inhuman faery beings who lured unwary human travellers into their lair . . .

And all the while, a tiny secret part of her mind was racing ahead to the night . . . To when *he* would slip through the night garden and sit silhouetted against the firelight of her room, and pick up the thread of her ideas, and spin them into something solid and real, and something that could be contained within a spotlit stage.

Christian always waited until darkness shrouded London, and it was possible to slip through the streets unnoticed.

There was starting to be a treacherous pleasure in the midnight sessions in Fael's room, twice or three times a week. Tod Miller had regular patterns to his evenings, and Christian only ever went to the house when Tod would be out. But there had been a couple of occasions when he had unexpectedly stayed at home, and those couple of occasions had been very interesting indeed.

'My father's at home tonight,' Fael had said, unlatching the garden door and speaking very softly.

Christian paused. 'Where is he?'

'In his bedroom.'

They looked at one another for a moment. 'Then I should not be here,' said Christian very softly. But he did not move back, and after a moment, picking his words deliberately, he said, 'We shouldn't be doing this, Fael.'

The low whispering conversation accentuated the secrecy, and Christian's words, so calculatedly chosen, drew them deeper into intimacy. We shouldn't be doing this! We're sharing something forbidden – something potentially dangerous! Christian saw Fael's eyes darken, and thought: If I reached for her now she would not repel me. With the thought came a sexual charge so strong that it almost overpowered him. I believe she would let me into her bed tonight, he thought. She would do so not out of fear or cupidity or curiosity as all those hired women do, but quite simply for what I am.

And then he remembered what he was, and he turned away and took his accustomed seat in the shadowy corner with the firelight behind him. But the accent had shifted, and a barrier had been let down, drawing them closer, not just mentally – the mental intimacy already existed – but physically. And one day, Fael . . .

He quenched the feeling at once; he had learned control in a harsh school, and turned to the notes she had made that afternoon. It was totally outside his experience to sit like this, discussing ideas and plans, and it was absorbing. Christian found it astonishingly easy to take up the threads of Fael's storylines and plait them into strands until the strands became ropes and the ropes became the weft and weave of a story. There were nights when he could almost see the glittering sphere that was their creation spinning back and forth between them, gathering strength and substance as it went.

He found it easy, as well, to thread his own music through the unfolding story; working alone in the Christchurch Street house, most of the music his own, but some of it based on discarded or unfinished fragments that his father had composed. On the nights when Tod was out at one of his theatre clubs, Christian played cassettes of what he had written, using Fael's stereo player.

But once he said to her, 'Open the music room tonight, Fael, and let me play this to you properly.' And saw her eyes darken in the way he was coming to know. If Tod comes back early we could be caught! The knowledge shivered between them, edged with excitement, laced with sexual anticipation.

But she said, 'All right. You'll be fairly quiet though, won't you?'

'As quiet as the night, Fael.'

It was after that, after he had played for over an hour on the well-tuned piano overlooking the dark garden, that she said, again, 'Won't you tell me who you are? Who you really are?'

'No.'

'Why not? Can't you trust me by now? Why won't you trust me?'

'I don't trust anyone, Fael.' *Don't push me, my dear*, said his tone, and Fael heard it and let the matter drop.

She was receptive to the music he wrote, and although she had not achieved the technical level that the professor had instilled into Christian, they were both pupils of the same master and she understood enough. Sometimes she talked about Roscius, half-affectionately, half-respectfully, and several times she referred to musical evenings in the Chelsea house, mentioning names that she clearly expected him to know. Christian found this unexpectedly disturbing. She's probing, he thought; if I'm not careful she'll realise that I don't know any of these people.

Once Fael said, 'There were areas of Roscius's life that he kept extremely private – times when he simply vanished for several weeks, and the Chelsea house was shut up.' And then, as Christian made no response, she said, 'It made him rather a man of mystery. But I suppose at times he had to have some kind of retreat where he could get away from his pupils.'

'I suppose all men of genius have to have that,' said Christian, deliberately off-hand, and the dangerous moment passed.

Once or twice she made suggestions for the music on her own account. Could they have a serenade, a *Ständchen*, for the opening scene where the stage was first dark and then gradually lit by threads and curls of turquoise and violet, portraying the ancient magic of long-ago Ireland stirring? And then there should be a march heralding the entrance of the legendary army of the Irish kings: a huge, awesome fanfare, played *con brio* – with vigour. And for the greedily sexual hermaphroditic spirits who drag the heroine down to their caves – something light and silvery but subtly laced with menace.

Fael called these uncanny water-spirits the *sidh*, and told Christian how they were to be found in several of the old tales and the legends of Ireland's west coast. They appeared in several guises, she said, her face flushed with delight and absorption, the leaping firelight from the hearth turning her hair from silver-gilt to rose and gold, as she tumbled the old books from the shelves and read sections to him. The *sidh* were a kind of *bean sidh* – a banshee, although some stories told how they were fallen angels. 'Too good for hell,' said Fael, softly quoting. 'Some fell to earth and dwelt there long before man was created, as the first gods, but others fell into the sea.'

'Go on,' said Christian, never taking his eyes from her face.

'They made the sea-caves their own, and they filled them with unearthly magic,' said Fael, her eyes filled with dreams and her voice faraway. 'And it's there they imprison their victims.'

'How?'

The other-world look vanished at once. 'By their music,' said Fael, sitting up. 'Like the sirens of the rocks who lure sailors to their doom. Listen, we have to have the *sidh* in this – I've made them evil but sexy and intriguing, and I've drafted a kind of siren song for their first appearance in Act One. This is when they're plotting to kidnap the Irish queen Mab – that's the nub of the plot, of course. This is it, here. See if you can conjure up something to fit it.'

Christian did not take the typed notes. He said, 'Read it to me, Fael.'

'Oh, but— Oh well, all right.'

As she started to read Christian felt as if his skin was being lightly scratched by a velvet-sheathed claw.

Temptation we are and desire we are.
Sin we are, and lust we are.
But beautiful we are and there is no resisting us.
We shall take your soul and drink your senses . . .
We shall feed on your heart and bathe in your love.
For the hunger's upon us.

See if you can conjure up something to fit it, she had said . . . The music would write itself; it would very nearly form itself on the air without him even trying to compose it. Light and silvery, Fael had said. Debussy-like, or Chopin, perhaps. Yes, he could write for those words, and the music he would write would have every female in the audience on the edge of her seat.

Fael grinned at him, and the slightly ethereal quality she so often possessed was suddenly and disconcertingly replaced by a glint of mischief.

'The *sidh* are led by their prince, Aillen mac Midha,' she said. 'That's a whale of a part for the right actor, by the way. I don't suppose we'll get a say in the casting, and even if we did, I can't begin to think who could play him. He ought to look very nearly sexless – in the way medieval angels do: grave and austere – but of course he's very sexy indeed. Not macho or butch, in fact he might even have a hint of homosexuality. And there's this immense magnetism just under the surface. Mab – the Irish queen – can't resist him, even though he isn't quite human.'

'Perhaps because he isn't quite human.'

'Well, yes. Yes, there's something intriguing about that, isn't there?' Fael looked up at Christian, and he waited, not speaking.

After a moment Fael said, 'I've written this for him. I thought he could sing it on a deserted stage, maybe seated on a rock with a single blue spotlight on him.' She passed a sheet of paper across to him, and Christian read it aloud, the words and the sentiments rasping across his mind, raking at his emotions.

I will melt your soul with longing, human,
And I will burn your heart with belonging, human.
With dreamful eyes I will lure you,
And with doomful lures I will trap you.

For the hunger's upon me and the spell is about me;
I am the lodestone and you cannot resist me.

Under the floods and over the seas;
There lies the path you will take to reach me.
Through fire and storm and famine, my love;
Along the paths that wolves fear to prowl, my love;
I will lure your mortal soul,
I will feed on your mortal dreams.
And in the cool green caverns I will trap you.
And you will never walk in the world of humans again.

I am the lodestone, and the hunger's upon me . . . Christian put

68

the single sheet of paper down, and remained sunk in thought.

Fael said, cautiously, 'Well? Will it do? He's a kind of sexy Puck-figure, you see. But he's also dangerous. We can have the earlier scene, where Aillen's *sidh* creatures dance around the two comic characters – that's the tarty old woman like a Doll Tearsheet or Mistress Overdone, and the fat lodge-keeper – and where they snatch at their groins and mock-rape them and throw the tarty woman's skirts over her face and everything— That's all for laughs. It's almost pantomime stuff.'

'Playing down to the groundlings.'

'Yes. *Yes*. But Aillen's scenes—' She paused, and then said, 'There've been dozens of famous productions of *Midsummer Night's Dream*, but I'm visualising one in particular. I think it was directed by Peter Brook.'

'I know of it. I didn't see it.' Pointless to say that to enter a theatre and hope to go unnoticed was impossible for him.

Fael said, 'When Titania was finally led to her wedding night with Bottom, the fairies – Cobweb and Mustardseed and the rest – lifted her shoulder-high on a draped litter, and carried her in a ceremonial procession. But as they went, one of them thrust his forearm up between her legs from beneath and clenched his fist, so that the audience saw it as – hum – as a huge jutting phallus. And if you join that up with something like Mendelssohn's *Wedding March* – not the perfunctory jangly thing you get at most weddings, but the real thing—'

'Indecently triumphant and blatantly randy.'

'Yes. *Yes*. That's what we want for Mab's kidnapping. Because once Aillen appears – really appears – the audience needs to be frightened but intrigued. When he carries Mab down to the under-ocean realm where he rules, we want everyone knowing precisely what's about to happen – visualising what's about to happen, for God's sake! – and we want the men envying him and the females swooning.'

Christian said, 'Even though they know once Mab submits she's lost for ever.'

They looked at one another. 'Yes,' said Fael after a moment. 'Once she submits, she's lost, isn't she?'

'Oh yes,' said Christian, very softly. 'Because once he's taken her, Mab will never again be free, will she? She'll be his, body and soul and blood and bone for ever.'

There was a pause. Then Fael said, a bit too briskly, 'But you understand what's wanted? The music—'

'Oh yes,' said Christian, again. 'I understand what's wanted.' To himself he thought: I understand, because that's how I want you, Fael. I want you to be frightened and intrigued – I think you already are – but when you do submit, I want you to do so more completely and more entirely than you can possibly imagine.

One day soon I'm going to beckon to you, Fael, and when I do you won't be able to resist me.

Because I am the lodestone, and the hunger's upon me . . .

As Christian walked back to the Chelsea house that night, his mind was working on a number of different levels.

It had been ridiculously easy to compel the street girls and the drag queens and the theatre-fringe, club-denizen people to accept an anonymous, slightly sinister master who would look after them and fight their battles. He had done all of that for them, but he had also learned a great deal about them from the spies he had planted in their midst. He had planted spies among the fringes of the theatre world as well, which was how he had learned of Tod Miller's newest venture with the northern factory-owner. He smiled the twisted smile. That had been money well invested. It was all money well invested, of course.

And even when there was the odd rebel, the occasional threat, it could be dealt with. That bitch Leila . . . Would she really have named him? Had she been speaking the truth or only taunting him? The risk was not one he could take. You were damned in that first instant, Leila, and you had to serve as an example to anyone else who might try the same trick. He wondered if her body had been found yet, and if so, by whom. The little red-head, Leila's friend Gilly, perhaps? Or Danilo, who was wasting his youth and his considerable gifts by singing in drag in night-clubs where nobody saw beneath the raunchy suggestive lyrics to the strong core of genuine talent? Danilo . . . Something stirred at the back of Christian's mind. Had Danilo the strange androgynous magnetism that Fael had described for Aillen mac Midha? Was it worth planting a few hints through the spy network when the time came, ensuring that Danilo auditioned for the new Harlequin show? He began to consider how this could be done, and was aware of cynical amusement that he could wield such power.

He turned towards the river, pulling his coat collar up to hide his face, wondering if the situation he had created in his corner of Soho could have been created anywhere else in the world. Chicago, perhaps, or Sicily, where protection rackets and gangster kings and Mafia networks were rife. Where people understood about revenge.

Revenge . . . Yes, it was about revenge, this. And when he had made that long-ago vow to destroy Tod Miller, and when he had conceived the present surreal plan, he had thought he had allowed for everything. But there was one thing he had not allowed for, and that was the astonishing closeness with Tod's daughter. It had happened without him realising it, and it was still happening and alongside it was a growing sexual awareness.

Christian knew about sexual awareness and sexual gratification; you could get those in any city if you were prepared to pay enough. He knew about the dark sensuality of bloodlust as well – that bitch Leila last night! And he knew about mental domination and the 1,000-volt charge you received when you entered a room full of people who were all in thrall to you. Tod Miller, twenty years previously, had given Rossani the famous, at the time slightly shocking, line: *I get my sexual kicks above the waist, my dear*, and Christian, setting himself up as a kind of demi-world overlord in the section of Soho he had mapped out, knew precisely what Miller had meant, even while he was conscious of surprise that so shallow a mind as Tod's could grasp such a concept.

But to share thoughts and ideas with another human being as he had done with Fael was totally new. Fael was fighting against being dominated – there were times when Christian could feel her fighting him, but there were times as well when he felt her mind yield, and it was sweeter than anything he had ever dreamed possible.

I get my kicks above the waist, my dear . . .

Christian had never learned about ordinary relationships, because he had never been allowed to experience them. Neither

Professor Roscius nor Christian's mother, during the few years of his life she had lived, had been able to visualise their son having any kind of relationships at all. The best that could be hoped for, they had said, was a solitary but scholarly existence. Not unrewarding, not without interest: something academic, something to do with writing, perhaps. Or even music, if he was found to have inherited his father's gifts. The professor, carefully balancing his time and husbanding his energies so that his pupils and his London and Galway theatre work did not suffer, so that he still found time for his protégé in Connemara, the young fatherless Flynn Deverill, had yet managed to map out a rough-and-ready blue print for his own son's life.

An academic existence, with all its gentle, often worthwhile benefits – yes, there were genuine and potentially happy possibilities there. He had himself considered entering the groves of academe when he came down from Oxford, but there had been a quirk in his nature that had sought excitement, and he had ended not in the scholar's ivory tower, but the Harlequin's motley one. He had not lived sufficiently long to discover that there was a quirk in his son's nature as well.

As Christian reached Christchurch Street and let himself into his own house, he smiled wryly, because of the two young men who had come so firmly under James Roscius's influence – Christian and Flynn Deverill – it was Flynn, the rebel without a cause, who was pursuing a more or less conventional career, while Christian – the academic recluse – was travelling down darker and more macabre paths than even the widely read, widely travelled professor could have imagined.

The irony of his present life amused him. He had broken out of the doorless tower his parents had tried to build around him; as soon as they were both dead he had escaped, shutting up the remote house on Ireland's west coast and living first in Dublin, and then in London. There had been sufficient money: the professor had invested his not inconsiderable earnings, and Christian's mother had come of a well-to-do family. Christian had inherited it all, including the rambling old Irish house, overlooking the wild and darkly beautiful Cliffs of Moher.

And there was an eerie coincidence in the fact that Fael had lit on the uncanny *sidh* spirits for her plot. The people of the small Moher community still quarter-believed in the *sidh*, and double-locked their doors on certain nights of the year and told how the *sidh* still walked the land looking for human prey . . . And how at times they stole away human babies and left in their place changelings, not quite human, wearing not quite human form. You could hear the *sidh* keening their chill faery music on those nights, they said nervously, and you did not walk abroad on Samhain, not if you had any sense, and certainly not if there was a newly-born child in your house.

Christian had been born in the clifftop house on the night that the Irish still called Samhain, and that the English called Hallowe'en. Had he been born to the sound of chill music, intended to blind the humans and deafen them, so that the human child could be stolen away and something else left in its stead . . . ?

The Moher house had been built by and intended for, a large family, whose lives were overflowing with people and happiness; with dogs and children and friends and music. Its huge, high-ceilinged rooms could fill up with the wild brilliant light from the lashing Atlantic and, even when the stormy skies plunged it into premature night, lights glowed in all the rooms and fires kindled in the hearths, and warm yellow beacons of welcome shone from all the windows. The house was called Maise, which was a distortion of an old Gaelic word for happiness, but while Christian lived there he had never known any happiness, only loneliness and deep misery. The house had belonged to his mother's family, and he was five when his parents took him there, and turned Maise for him into a sealed, living tomb.

Maise was the place where the small Christian was shut away between the spells in discreet private nursing homes, and between the attempts at what was called reconstructive surgery. His childhood had been bounded by pain – bad pain, sometimes barely-endurable pain. Pain that was not always alleviated because in those days he had not mastered speech, but pain that was so bad he had fought the doctors, screaming through his nose because it was the only way he could make sounds and beg for help . . .

Later there had been the hours upon hours of speech therapy,

73

and also what he now recognised as psychiatric sessions. 'To help him to come to terms,' someone had said. He had understood that, because he could understand speech by then. And running in and out of it all, like black spider-webs of misery, the whispers about mirrors. 'For the love of God,' they all kept saying, 'keep all mirrors locked up.'

It was not until he was seven that he had seen his own reflection in the surface of a polished saucepan in the Maise kitchen, and he had run from the room, not crying because he did not know how to cry, but with the blood pounding frighteningly inside his head. He had hidden himself in the attics for hours, curled into a tight, tiny ball in the darkest most inaccessible corner, because if people could not see him – if he pretended he did not exist – then the thing he had seen reflected fathoms down in the coppery depths might not exist either.

Later, after his father's death, he had hidden behind anonymity, deliberating cultivating it and deliberately setting up his own legend. If people did not know his name, that name could not become synonymous with hideous and repellent deformity.

But he was never to forget that first sight of his own face. Because it was not like other people's; it was not like his father's, which had clever eyes and a short neat beard framing a gentle sensitive mouth, and it was not like his mother's, whose features he could just remember, and which had been thin and worried, but with lovely, long-lashed green eyes and soft, creamy skin.

He understood now why he had been made to repeat words into a tape-recorder or a cassette-player, over and over until he got them right. He understood why no mirrors were allowed in Maise. His eyes and forehead were ordinary and normal. His eyes were his mother's: a clear hard green like a cat's, and his forehead was broad and white under glossy thick hair that grew in a widow's peak. But his face had scarcely any nose-bone, only two nostrils surrounded by thickened flesh, and although the upper lip was fully formed, it curled upwards to half-fuse with the nostrils like an animal's.

Where all other humans had a jaw, a mouth and chin, there was nothing save a thin, nearly transparent membrane like a sac to act as a food-trap. The sac was veined with thin fibrous gristle that might have been the cartilage and the bones that had not developed.

He had barely half a face.

Chapter Seven

Gerald Makepiece packed his suitcase happily and prepared to have an early night. Mia had set off for London ahead of him, catching the 9.45 train, and Gerald would follow her tomorrow. He would book in to his hotel and meet up with Mia, and in the evening he would go along to the Greasepaint Club for a meeting to discuss the show.

He was beginning to feel quite metropolitan by now; he had had to travel to London for several meetings, some of which had been in the Greasepaint, and some which had been in the rehearsal rooms in St Martin's Lane, and he was getting to know this corner of London quite well. Everyone seemed very pleased with progress, and everyone was very pleased indeed with the show, which Tod Miller had produced in what was apparently a remarkably short space of time.

Sir Julius had said solemnly that they had a sure-fire hit on their hands, and Flynn Deverill, who lounged in to most meetings, had said, 'Almost too good to be true, isn't it? Who would have thought Toddy to have had such talent all those years when he was writing baked bean adverts?'

'No, but what do you really think of it, Flynn?'

'I think it's very unexpected,' said Flynn, and Miller had smiled faintly and studied his fingernails.

Tod Miller's musical was called *Cauldron* and Gerald had already read it. Proper bound copies were being prepared by printers, but Gerald and Sir Julius and Simkins of the bank had been given preliminary copies of the typescript, which was really very nice of Miller.

Gerald thought *Cauldron* an unusual and very remarkable piece of work. He thought it was beautiful and funny and moving. He had furrowed his brow over several of the scenes as he read, because some were really quite disturbing, and they made you think a bit more deeply than perhaps you liked. A sure-fire hit, Sir Julius had said, although Simkins had cautiously observed that a modest success would suit very nicely.

Gerald thought there was nothing modest about *Cauldron*, but he thought there would be no half-measures about it. Either it would become a legendary and overnight success, or it would sink without trace. A turkey, didn't the Americans call it? He hoped, a bit uneasily, that he was not backing a turkey.

And to look at Tod Miller and to talk to him, you would never guess he was capable of conjuring up this remarkable fantasy world of Celtic mythology and legend, where people went on quests, and braved dangers and were carried off by half-human beings for sinister and sensual purposes. Nor had it previously occurred to Gerald that it was possible to draw parallels between such legends and the modern-day world, but that was what had been done. When the ill-starred hero was sent out to find for the Irish warriors the magical cauldron – 'Which is never without meat and always has enough to feed the whole world' – there was an extremely clever echo of the famines of Third World countries, for which Gerald himself sent regular donations, even though Mia had pouted and said it was not necessary.

When the legendary armies of the High King set out to storm the under-water realm of the strange inhuman *sidh* and rescue the kidnapped Irish queen, they might almost have been modern-day paratroopers or SAS men storming a beleaguered embassy. Some of the battles they fought along the way were clearly meant to suggest the fight for independence and justice for humanity that still went on today and Gerald thought there were one or two lightly-sketched depictions of people like Nelson Mandela or Lech Walesa. The royal armies were called the *Fianna*: Gerald had learned the pronunciation along with the pronunciation of *sidh*, which sounded like sheeth, poring over a Gaelic dictionary bought for the purpose. The *Fianna* were the kind of dashing hero-figures schoolboys had revered in Gerald's youth, and his romantic soul was thrilled to its depths by them; when he read the roistering swashbuckling captain's

77

speech, 'I have a dream,' (Martin Luther King's legendary words, of course), he could very nearly see audiences standing up and cheering.

Tomorrow evening, or the day after, they would all hear some of the music for the show. Tod Miller's daughter, Fael, had apparently recorded it onto a cassette, and it would be played over to them all. It would be unaccompanied piano music, and the final thing would be a full orchestra, of course, but it was hoped that everyone would be able to visualise the finished product. It had been explained to Gerald that a professional company was being engaged to transcribe or transpose the music (Gerald was not very sure of the difference) for the full orchestra. Violins and violas and cellos and trumpets.

This was all being done under the supervision of the musical director, Maurice Camperdown, whom Gerald had not yet met. Somebody said he was very good and they were lucky to get him, and somebody else said he was nearly as good as James Roscius had been in the Harlequin's heyday. Julius Sherry at once went off into several long anecdotes about Professor Roscius, and people suppressed yawns, because while everyone quite liked hearing about the professor, who had been charismatic, but – it had to be admitted – given to caprice at times, once Julius got on to the 'Ah me, I remember the days –' it could go on for some time.

And Mia was going to take the part of the Irish queen, Mab; Gerald hoped this would go without saying. She had protested to Gerald about the idea, saying she had become a little plump lately; her voice was a bit rusty, and perhaps she was a trifle old for the role, but Gerald had quelled these frivolous quibbles at once. Mia was not plump, she was nicely rounded, and gentlemen liked nicely-rounded figures. Her voice was not in the least rusty, either, and she was going to have a marvellous success as Mab. He did not say that this was what the whole project was about, but instead dwelled with pleasure on the picture of Mia as the queen. There was a song about her at the beginning of the show, sung by her court, all about how her name really meant mead, and how a sip from her lips would intoxicate a man for ever. Gerald was looking forward to hearing the music for that. It was this song that the strange inhuman creature,

78

Aillen mac Midha, overheard, and it was the reason he resolved to kidnap her. (And here again, Miller had been clever, just hinting at a hostage situation, the kind you so often heard of where terrorists kidnapped journalists or held embassies to ransom.)

Gerald was secretly a bit anxious about the young man they would get to play Aillen. You heard such tales about these actors and their leading ladies – well, you had only to read the newspapers! – so it was no use Mia telling him he was a jealous old silly and people did not behave like that. Gerald could remember the tales his grandfather had told (roistering old boy he'd been, what that generation had called a gay dog although you had to be careful about using the word 'gay' nowadays). But he'd had one or two lady-friends within the theatre, and Gerald could remember him telling how it was a long-standing theatrical tradition for actresses to go to bed with their leading men. Othello with Desdemona, Petruchio with Katherina and so on. Some Portias, said Gerald's grandfather, chuckling gleefully, slept with all three of the suitors, and not necessarily separately either, although that depended on the suitors' inclinations. Sometimes the suitors preferred each other to Portia, you could never tell.

But of course, Mia could be trusted absolutely.

Fael had gone to bed early tonight, because she had felt tired after recording *Cauldron*'s music onto the tape for her father's meeting with the Makepiece rabbit and Julius Sherry tomorrow. She had not played it all, but she had played quite a lot and it had taken most of the day. And then, over supper, there had been one of the exasperating conversations with her father, who was in one of his irritatingly vague moods and would not be drawn into a discussion about who had really written *Cauldron*. He said it was vulgar to talk about such things, and Fael had lost her temper and said he was a selfish, inconsiderate plagiarist, which instantly sent Tod into a tantrum. He said he saw that he had been nurturing a viper in his bosom all these years and obviously it had been expecting too much when he had asked his only daughter for a bit of help. At any minute he would start quoting Othello and saying, *O, who would be a father.*

Tod said, '*O, my female offspring*,' which was Rossini and was just as apt.

'Oh for heaven's sake!' said Fael, exasperated.

'All I wanted was a little help. I don't think that's too much to ask.'

'A little!' shouted Fael in disbelief. 'A *little!*'

Tod descended at once from grand tantrum to melancholy. He could not bear discord, he said, pained. It was inner agony to him. He would betake himself out, although it was a sad world when a man was driven from his own house and forced to seek solace in the company of strangers. And now he did say, *O, who would be a father*.

'Oh stop hamming it up!' rejoined Fael.

Tod switched from melancholy to self-pity. It was extremely inconsiderate of Fael to bother him with these trivial matters when he was so busy, he said. There was a great deal to be done, and he was bustling back and forth between the rehearsal rooms and Pimlico; soon he would be bustling between Pimlico and the Harlequin, and he really had no time to be worried about Fael's concerns. He certainly had no time to sit down to what sounded suspiciously like a family committee meeting.

Fael said, 'I don't know how you think we could hold a committee meeting with only the two of us. But shouldn't we at least talk about who's going to respond if there's a call for "author" on *Cauldron*'s first night?' And thought: That sounded greedy and hard. I don't care for myself, but there's *him*. *Scathach*. No, be honest, Fael, of course you care for yourself.

Tod said, airily, 'We've been into all that. I shall have a speech ready, of course. Nothing elaborate or fancy. But just a few words, in case—'

'Exactly,' said Fael. 'In case there's a call for "author". And will your few words acknowledge me?'

'I shall touch on it, of course. Of course I shall.' He had in fact jotted down a couple of phrases, in which 'pay tribute to the support of my daughter', and 'enthusiastic encouragement' figured. This was surely sufficient.

'I don't trust you,' said Fael, glaring at him. 'I don't trust you an inch. You know quite well that *Cauldron*'s mine.' Mine and one other's, said the inner voice. And if that other one suspects

I've cheated . . . She said, 'I wouldn't put it past you to claim it as your own. And it's not the slightest use looking grand and huffy, because we both know it's in your mind.' She studied him. 'I'm going to be listening to your speech with extreme interest.'

'Well, I shall tell you about it afterwards, naturally—' Tod stopped and then said, 'What do you mean, you're going to be listening to it?'

'You didn't think I'd miss the first night, did you?' demanded Fael. 'Yes, I see you did. Well, imagine that.'

'Oh, well, I don't know what you do half the time,' said Tod. 'But I'm far too busy to talk about it now.'

'Auditions?'

'Yes, we're having trouble finding Aillen mac Midha.'

'I thought you would,' said Fael. 'Can I come to them? A couple of them at least?'

Tod had been ready for this, and he said, cannily, that Fael could come, of course, but Julius Sherry – stupid old *poseur* – had apparently a very strict policy that only the director and the pianist be present at auditions.

'*I* think it's pretentious of him,' said Tod, grandly. 'But there it is.'

'So it is.' Fael studied her father thoughtfully, and then said, 'But I hear you've done quite well with the dancers and the *Fianna* captain.'

'Yes, we've managed to get— How did you hear about the auditions?' demanded Tod.

'Flynn Deverill told me about them when he phoned you the other day and you were at that sleazy Greasepaint.'

'Well, he had no right to discuss them with you.'

'Don't be silly.'

'And anyway, the Greasepaint isn't sleazy!' shouted Tod, and banged out of the house.

Fael had wheeled her chair crossly into the kitchen, even though it was really the time she should be devoting to exercises to strengthen her leg muscles. She had been so furious with Tod that she had dropped a vegetable tureen on the floor and of course it had to be one of the good ones, which was monstrous of it. She left the pieces for Tod to sweep up when he returned, because if he had not made her so angry it would not have happened.

She poured a very large gin and tonic, and banked up the fire in her room, seating herself in the deep armchair near the window. She could manage to get in and out of this chair without too much of an ungainly struggle now, and if he came tonight, he would see her out of the wheelchair for once.

If he came tonight . . .

She had not meant to topple into sleep, but she was actually quite tired tonight. It might only be the gin, or it might be reaction from the quarrel, or it might simply be tiredness from all that piano-playing into the cassette. It did not matter which it was, because it was good sleep: soft and alluring. Fael slid down and down, until she was fathoms below the oceans of the world, with smoky green waterlight rippling all about her, stirring her hair, and inhuman, beautiful creatures peering slyly through the cloudy waters, and lyrical music tapping like silver fingers against water-smoothed rocks.

The music was forming a soft regular rhythm. Tap-tap-tap . . . In another minute it would form into one of *Cauldron*'s songs. Was it the march that ushered in the royal armies of the *Fianna*? No, that was much more pulsating and modern. It might be Aillen mac Midha's beckoning song to Mab or the *sidh*'s cool, sexy siren-music. They were having trouble casting Aillen, Tod had said. Tod should be here now, because if Aillen was anywhere, he was in this drowned under-sea world, peering through its depths with his compelling eyes and his hidden face . . . No, that was *Scathach*. It was *Scathach*, the nameless one, who walked in the dark places and averted his face . . .

The tapping came again, more insistent now, and Fael blinked and sat bolt upright, abruptly and fully awake. There was someone outside her room. Or was it only Tod blundering back, half-drunk and maybe rushing to the loo to be sick?

But whoever it was was being very stealthy indeed, and Tod was not even stealthy when he was sober, let alone when he was half-drunk. The sound came again – a light, quick tapping, fingertips against solid oak. Fael's heart gave a huge bound. He was here. He had found the unlatched garden door, and for the first time he was entering the house without being invited, and he was coming in to her room.

Her heart began to race. He had never yet approached her physically, and he had certainly never indicated by the slightest gesture that he intended to. But what about those sizzling darts of mental intimacy? thought Fael, frantically. What about all those discussions we had, chock-full of double-meaning and unmistakable signals!

We shouldn't be doing this, Fael, he had said, his voice like a silken caress. And, *Once Mab submits she'll be lost . . . Once he's taken her, she'll never again be free . . . She'll be his, body and soul and blood and bone for ever. . .*

You fool! cried Fael in silent anguish. You knew quite well that he didn't mean Mab's submission, you knew quite well that you didn't mean it either! And he never did tell you what he'd do if you reneged on that bargain, but that's because he didn't need to! You know what he'll do, because you struck an unholy alliance, you made a midnight pact, and only the unholy pacts are struck at midnight, Fael . . . And, said her mind, still working at top speed, you'd better face it, girl: once he's had you, it's highly likely that you'll never again be free . . .

But when he came into the room, the fear dissolved at once, and he was the familiar companion of the secret midnight hours.

The soft voice said, 'Not asleep, Fael?'

'No. Come in.'

He crossed the room and took up his familiar place in the shadowy recess of the chimney breast. 'Tod's out, isn't he? Yes, I thought he was. I wanted to talk to you.'

'Well, I wanted to talk to you, as well.'

'About our alliance?' he said, and this was so horrifyingly in tune with Fael's panic-stricken thoughts, that for a moment she could not speak.

And then she said, 'Yes.'

'Yes. They like *Cauldron*, don't they?' he said. 'Your father and the backers. They're delighted with it, in fact. And so I think it's time to remind you about our deal. Acknowledgement on *Cauldron*'s opening night, remember?'

'I don't need reminding,' said Fael. 'I promised and I'll keep my promise. There was no need to come creeping in like this in

83

the middle of the night to remind me.' She nearly said, 'And frightening me half to death in the process,' but swallowed this, and said, in a deliberately prosaic voice, 'Would you like a glass of brandy or a cup of coffee or something?'

'No thank you.'

It had been a test question, of course, to see if he would trust her enough to remove the mask, and if tonight would be the night when he would venture out of his strange shadowland into the ordinary world of kettles boiling, and coffee percolating or wine being uncorked. But he did not, and it had probably been ridiculous to think otherwise. He refused the casual offer of a drink, or coffee, as he always had done. He sat in his old place in the chimney recess, the cloak falling in black silky pools about his feet.

After a moment, Fael said, 'I'll do my best to keep our bargain. But I think you ought to know it might not be possible.'

There was no apparent movement from him, but Fael thought he became very still, in the way a hunted animal becomes very still, hoping to escape detection. And then something in the quality of his stillness sent a scrape of fear across her mind, and she thought: No, you fool! He's not the hunted, he never has been! This is the stillness of the hunter, not the quarry!

At last, he said, almost to himself, 'So Tod Miller will cheat us, will he? It doesn't surprise me so very much.'

It did not surprise Fael either, but she said, 'I'm sorry. He's even making stupid excuses to keep me away from the auditions.'

'Ah yes, the auditions,' said the soft voice, thoughtfully. 'But there are ways of manipulating auditions, Fael.'

'I don't understand you,' said Fael. And then, as he did not respond, she said, 'But you do see I can't guarantee that Tod will even acknowledge me, let alone you. But I'll try to talk to him again.'

He stood up, and for the first time Fael had the impression that he was not so slight or slender as he appeared. He moved towards her chair, and Fael thought: Here it comes. In another minute he'll lean over, and maybe he'll lift me in his arms and carry me over to the bed . . . And maybe he'll remove the mask and maybe he won't . . . A fresh tremor of terror went through her, but beneath it was a rising excitement. If I yield, I'll be his body and soul and blood and bone . . . No, of course I won't, I'll never be anybody's, body and soul. I wasn't before the accident, and I'm damned if I will be now!

He was wearing silk gloves tonight, as well as the silk mask. What would it feel like to be caressed by hands wearing silk gloves . . . ? What would it feel like to be kissed through a silk mask . . . ? But what does the mask hide?

And then he straightened up and the moment passed. *Scathach* said, 'I can deal with Tod, Fael.'

He stepped back and the shadows twisted about him again. There was a whisper of sound as he went through the bedroom door, and then a soft, sad click as the outer garden door opened and then closed behind him.

Chapter Eight

Tod climbed the stairs to the rehearsal rooms and wished he had not agreed to renting the third floor, because the stairs were steep and he was getting out of breath. They were nearly fully cast now, but as he had told Fael, they were having a bit of trouble getting the right person for the *sidh* prince. There was a young man coming along today – nobody had ever heard of him, but somebody had said that somebody else had said the young man might be exactly right. Somebody had rung up the boy's agent – Tod did not know all the details, which sounded complicated. Still, if he was a complete unknown they would get away with basic Equity rates, which was worth thinking about.

Tod had been rather pleased with his cunning device to keep Fael away from auditions; he flattered himself that he had sounded really very convincing, and very plausible. It was as well, however, that Fael could not see the crowd that would be coming along today, because that would have given the lie to his words at once, by God it would!

Sir Julius Sherry was coming along to the audition, because he wanted to hear the boy sing Aillen mac Midha's 'Lodestone Song', which he liked, and Flynn Deverill was coming as well for some reason which Tod had forgotten. Flynn would probably be late, as usual, and he would probably be rude when he arrived, as usual.

Tod was not going to take any rudeness from anybody. He had presented Fael's really remarkable work to the small nucleus that formed the managing board of Mia Productions – an irritating name it was, even a touch twee, but the Makepiece rabbit had insisted, and anyway, what was in a name? But all of them, little Makepiece and Sir Julius, had been lavish with praise. There were two other Harlequin trustees, but they were so ancient they said what Julius told them to say and therefore did not really count, but they had been lavish with praise as well. Really, it was as well that he was keeping Fael at a distance from this entire thing.

Simkins of the bank had been a bit cautious as bank people always were, but the general atmosphere had been one of unqualified approval. Tod had basked in it, because when you came to think sensibly, Fael had not done so very much work. Tod had given her his own notes to work from and his musical jottings after all, and the ideas had all been there. He was sure of it. Anybody could work up a storyline from someone else's ideas. You could in fact say that Tod had given Fael the skeleton of the show, well, more than the skeleton. All she had had to do was flesh it out a bit. So much for that fit of temper the other evening!

Makepiece had already signed several cheques, beaming as if they were all doing something enormously exciting. Everyone knew that he was expecting the appalling Mia to play the part of Mab, and nobody had yet thought of a way to tell him that she could not get within ten miles of it, although Stephen Sherry, good old dependable, unflappable Stephen, would probably end up doing it, and Morrie Camperdown might help him. The trouble was that they were all afraid Gerald might stop signing cheques. Simkins of the bank had even said that he might put a stop on the cheques not yet cleared, but this was ungracious, even of Simkins. Tod had had another uncomfortable meeting with Simkins, who had summoned Tod to his office in the City – as if Tod was no more than some paltry overdrawn client, for goodness' sake! – and had outlined the bank's intentions. They would continue to honour the calls on the account, said Simkins, but only the ones relating to what they considered essential items. Mortgage interest payments naturally: *both* mortgage payments, said Simkins, as if to stress the second charge on the Pimlico house, which Tod had taken out eighteen months earlier.

'Against the bank's advice, you recall, Mr Miller?'

Tod did recall, but he would just like to know what a man was supposed to do when his income had dropped to virtually nothing at all, on account of jealous plotters and spiteful vendettas. And if the bank had been a bit more accommodating Tod would not perforce have approached a firm of private lenders who had seemed so gentlemanly at the outset, but had turned out to be nothing of the kind, and had levied the most shocking rate of interest on the loan. It made Tod feel quite ill to think of how much was owed to the company who had seemed so friendly, but who were now sending hectoring letters all because Tod had overlooked a couple of payments, and were even – bloody cheek! – following their letters up with unheralded visits to his house.

Simkins, working through his nasty little list – as if he was a character from a Gilbert and Sullivan operetta for goodness' sake! – next said the bank would of course honour payments relating to such things as electricity and gas and water rates, and reasonable sums for food and provisions. They were not about to turn him and his daughter homeless and starving onto the streets, said Simkins, with what Tod thought a very ill-timed attempt at black humour. He glared at Simkins and heard with horror that Simkins and his bloodless colleagues had had the temerity to work out for him what they thought a reasonable amount for weekly living. There was even a list – another list! – itemising amounts to be spent on food and tube or bus fares and so on. Tod said, sarcastically, that he saw that a small amount for entertainment had been included, and Simkins said, Oh well, the bank was not wholly without humanity. But until such time as receipts began to come in from the show – and he would remind Mr Miller the bank had a lien on the percentage agreed – he must insist that a degree of restraint was exercised.

Tod had made as dignified and disdainful an exit as could be achieved under the circumstances, and defiantly took a taxi to the rehearsal rooms for the afternoon's audition.

As he climbed puffily up the stairs he was thinking that this audition would have to be decisive. They could not afford to delay the decision about Aillen any longer; the orchestral parts would be delivered next week, and rehearsals were starting in ten days' time. If today's contender was no good they would have to settle for somebody they had already auditioned. There was a short list in somebody's office somewhere.

Probably this afternoon would be a waste of time, but they might as well go through with it.

Danilo had told Gilly the whole thing was almost certain to be a waste of time, but they might as well go through with it.

The trouble was that these huge glitzy West End things were often cast before even the agents got to hear about them. But it was worth a go. It was worth a go for Gilly as well, who was going to try for an understudy: Danilo had said this might be the break she needed to get her off the game. She was a good dancer and her voice was not too dusty either. And she had an up-to-date Equity card, even though it was only up-to-date because of the Christmas thing he had managed to get for her at one of his club gigs.

Anyway, why not give it a go? he said, and Gilly was going to do just that. If nothing else, it would put a bit of distance between her and Leila, poor silly cow. Gilly was going to take a long time to get over what had happened to Leila, and Lori had told Danilo that she was thinking of taking a job as a night-club check-out girl, because if that was where being on the game led you, you could shove it.

Danilo said his agent could shove it as well, because not a bloody whisper had there been about this new show, not a solitary murmur from him. *Cauldron* it was called, and the word was that they'd got the Harlequin for it. A very prestigious house indeed, the Harlequin, ever since James Roscius had made its name for it. Danilo had once sung chorus at the Harlequin, and it was a real gem. But there had not even been a whisper of a hint from Danilo's agent that it might be worth going along and trying for a part; in fact if it had not been for one of the buskers telling Danilo about it at last Sunday's Greasepaint meeting he would have been none the wiser now. The busker, who worked the Piccadilly tube, had been surprisingly well-informed. A couple of juicy good parts for young men who weren't too butch, he had said. Strong singing voices were needed, but nothing too bass. Danilo had not in the least minded being described as not too butch, and his voice was certainly not bass. He had wanted to know where the busker had heard about the new show, but the busker had only said vaguely that it was a friend of a friend of a friend – Danilo knew how these things worked. But worth a go, he thought. In fact, he'd even suggested he and Danilo meet for a drink before next Sunday, just so he could hear how Danilo had got on, which was unusual because the buskers tended to keep to their own little circle as a rule.

Anyway, here they were. Gilly had come along partly for support and because a few understudies were being tried out straight afterwards. The stage director's job that would be, said Danilo. Somebody had said it was Stephen Sherry. He was not a ball of fire, Stephen, but he was dependable and approachable.

Flynn Deverill had come to the rehearsal rooms, partly because he wanted to see if this final audition would turn up someone suitable for the *sidh* prince, and partly because he had arranged to show Julius and Stephen – and Tod, of course – some of the preliminary set designs. He had not got as far as balsa and plywood mock-ups in small scale yet, but he had sketched a number of colour-washed ideas, and he wanted to get Julius and Tod's approval.

He was going to enjoy designing *Cauldron*. He had read the script a week ago, and last evening he had listened to the tapes of the music which Fael Miller had apparently recorded. He had been so fired by the music that he had telephoned her this morning to tell her. She had rather a nice voice, Fael, and she had made some intelligent comments about the show. Flynn remembered that she was supposed to be a bit of a stunner, and he found himself thinking it would be interesting to meet her.

But the music had only coalesced the ideas that were already in his mind. The whole concept of *Cauldron* had fired him before he had got a quarter of the way through the script, and the images had cascaded through his mind so quickly, that he had barely been able to get them down on paper. He had shut himself away in the studio flat where he lived in North London, moving between the untidy living room and the immaculate workroom, oblivious to the outside world. He had fallen fathoms deep into the curious, fey world that *Cauldron* embodied, and walked hand-in-hand with the creatures who dwelled in the misty realm of half-human beings and stolen-away princesses and ancient thrones and hazardous quests. Because I'm Irish, is that it? Or simply because I recognise quality without having to think about it?

And this was the disturbing thing: this was the other reason why he was following the auditions more closely than usual. *Cauldron* was quality. It was very high, very gold-tipped quality indeed. But Tod Miller was not. The puzzle nagged at Flynn's mind, shaping itself into a syllogism. *Cauldron* was quality. Tod Miller was not. Therefore, Tod Miller could not have written *Cauldron*. *Cauldron* was a magical, spell-binding play, with marvellous, beautiful music. Tod Miller had never been a spell-binder in his life. Ergo, someone else had spun the enchantment.

As Flynn went lightly up the stairs to this afternoon's audition, he was thinking that it might be interesting to probe a little during rehearsals. He did not believe Tod Miller had written *Cauldron*, and he would give a great deal to know the name of the person who had.

He thought he might telephone Fael Miller again.

Gilly was nervous, but not paralysingly so. She thought that when they got to the understudies she would be able to give a fair account of herself.

It was nice of the *Cauldron* people to invite her to sit in on Danilo's audition. She had expected to stay inconspicuously outside, but a thin-faced man, who turned out to be Stephen Sherry himself, had said that of course she could come inside, they did not like to have people standing around on landings, it was unfriendly.

Tod Miller was here, of course, and also a timid little man called something-or-other Makepiece and a red-haired lady wearing a sweater that was slightly too tight for her bust, which was large, and trousers that were slightly too tight for her bottom, which was even larger. A fur jacket was draped over the chair she was sitting on. Gilly, who only put on her low-cut sweater, mini-skirt and high heels in the evenings, was wearing a denim skirt and denim bomber jacket, and she had a sudden hideous doubt that she might be wrongly dressed. But Danilo would have tipped her the wink about that, and anyway Danilo was wearing the most ordinary corduroy trousers and a sweater, with scuffed loafers. And surely to goodness nobody in the theatre wore fur jackets for theatre rehearsals these days! Starlet complex, thought Gilly. Nineteen fifties starlet complex. Whoever this female was, she was eyeing Gilly with dislike. Too bad.

Julius Sherry – actually Sir Julius himself, for God's sake! – patted Gilly's hand and said she should sit next to him, and later on they would hear her sing, how would that be? Gilly thought that would be fine. She intercepted a dagger-like glare from the red-headed large-busted-and-bottomed female and resisted the urge to stick up two fingers.

She did not in the least mind Sir Julius patting her hand; she was perfectly used to portly gentlemen, who started with hand-patting and worked up to more intimate exercises. She desperately wanted to get off the game, and if things went well here she might manage it, but she would not mind making an exception for Julius Sherry (think of name-dropping amongst Lori and her lot!), although he would have to pay top whack.

Danilo looked as cool as if he did this kind of thing every day of his life. He had listened absorbedly to the explanation of the part he was trying for, and he had been given a couple of sheets of music score. Gilly felt panic well up at that, because if they were expecting her to sight-read music, she might as well leave now.

Stephen Sherry had produced a cassette player, so that Danilo could listen to the piece first. It was strange music; not quite the stuff you heard in the pubs and clubs, but not quite the stuff people went to Covent Garden or the Royal Opera to hear either. It made you think of lost loves and forbidden passions and dark, dangerous creatures who would suck out your soul or your blood or both . . .

Danilo was studying the music score, and asking if it would be possible for him to hear the music again at a slightly slower pace. He said something about more *andante*, and Gilly remembered that he had received a proper musical training. You tended to forget that, especially if you were more used to seeing him togged up for one of his drag acts. It took guts to make such a request in such company as well, but it seemed to have gone down all right. Sir Julius said of course it would be possible, they had the piano to hand, and Mr Miller would not mind. Everyone looked at Tod Miller, and Gilly turned round to see better.

For some reason the request had flustered Mr Miller. There was a peculiar silence, and Gilly saw that Danilo was about to say it did not matter, he would sing with the tape as backing.

And then the black-haired young man who had arrived after everyone else and who had been sprawling untidily across a sagging chaise-longue at the back of the room, got up and came towards the group.

He said, 'There you are then, Toddy; there's the piano and there's the request, and it seems a fair one to me. Your man wants to hear it slower, and why not?' He paused deliberately, and then said, 'Will you play it for him, or will I?'

The silence came down again, and lengthened embarrassingly. The red-haired woman sighed and studied her nails in a bored fashion, and then pulled the fur jacket around her shoulders pettishly.

Stephen Sherry said, 'I didn't know you could play, Flynn.'

'And I a protégé of James Roscius? Come on now, Stephen. Would the professor have turned me untutored and unharmonic into the uncaring world? I'm a bit out of practice, but if Tod's declining, I can probably get us through it.'

Miller said at once, 'Oh you play it, if you don't mind, Flynn.' His voice was very off-hand, as if this was really a very minor thing indeed. 'A touch of my old trouble, I'm afraid,' he said, and rubbed his hands together, smiling ruefully round the room.

'Is that Portnoy's Complaint, Toddy, or just miser's cramp?'

'It's rheumatism!' shouted Tod, angrily. 'Will you please stop making these disgusting remarks, Flynn. I know quite well you only do it to rile me!'

'And,' observed Flynn, 'I appear to succeed.' He crossed to the piano and sat down, flinging the trailing skirts of his disreputable greatcoat out behind him. 'I really am out of practice,' he said, speaking directly to Danilo. 'But they say it's like swimming or riding a bike or screwing a woman—'

Danilo, straight-faced, said, 'Once you've done it, you never lose the knack.'

'Whether you get this part or not, you're a man after my own heart,' rejoined Flynn. He tried a few chords, and then said, 'At least the thing's in tune, you can never guarantee it in these places, and when it's Toddy paying the bills—'

He bent forward, frowning in sudden concentration at the music propped up in front of him, and the flippancy and the insolence seemed suddenly to dissolve. Gilly saw for the first time that Flynn Deverill cared very deeply about this show. She wondered what his part in it was. Not a musician, clearly. He might be one of the backers; he looked about as scruffy as it was possible to look without actually being a tramp, but that was no indication. Padding the Soho streets taught you that.

Flynn grinned at Danilo. 'This is going to be the blind leading the halt,' he said. 'But at least it's not the rheumatic leading the dumb, which it nearly was. Wait now, till we see—' He played the music through once, frowning as he did so, hitting a few wrong notes, but making (Gilly thought) a pretty good job of it. It was remarkable how much better it sounded even on this worn-out honky-tonk piano than coming out of a tinny cassette player. This was a beautiful piece of music.

'Ready?' said Flynn Deverill, his hands poised over the keys.

'Ready,' said Danilo, and straightaway launched into Aillen mac Midha's 'Lodestone Song'.

For every person present the song sent a different message.

For Julius Sherry it was the lingering regret of a lost youth which had not been nearly as mis-spent as it might have been. This young man, wherever he had come from, whatever his sexual persuasion might be (he looked as if he might be just a touch ambiguous), had an extraordinary voice. Not quite tenor, certainly not soprano. Sexless but somehow chockfull of sex, thought Sir Julius in some surprise at his own epigrammatical wit. He wondered what Stephen was thinking of it; he was a bit of a cold fish, Stephen. No real private life; no life at all in fact outside of his work.

Sir Julius was very nearly right; Stephen Sherry was listening with detached appreciation to the music, and he was hearing the gilt-edged notes of chart-toppers and rave reviews, and he was seeing the glittering visions of House Full notices outside the Harlequin. It would be good to have a genuine West End success, although it was vaguely irritating that once again his father would be involved.

Gerald Makepiece sighed with unaffected pleasure in the music. Lovely, it was, and made you feel honoured to be having a part in all this. He had listened to quite a lot of the tapes now – Fael Miller was clearly a gifted pianist and Gerald was looking forward to meeting her – and the haunting quality of the songs and the music came across very clearly indeed. Some of it had quite made the hairs stand up on the back of Gerald's neck, although Mia had pouted a bit and said it was very difficult to follow; she was not sure she could manage such high notes. This was just her modesty, however; when the young man had finished singing, Gerald would politely suggest that he and Mia might try the duet. She would enjoy that. He glanced at her, and was pleased to see that she was watching the young man with rapt attention. It was grand to see her recognising his quality, just as Gerald had recognised it. He sighed happily, delighted to find himself so completely in accord with her.

Flynn was still playing, studying Danilo without appearing to do so. Neither quite masculine nor wholly feminine, this one. The husky voice, the slightly tip-tilted eyes – Italian? – were filled with implicit promises, but they were promises that might well be very slightly off-centre. The phrase, *One of the third sex* slid through Flynn's mind. He wondered if any of the others saw it, and thought they did not. It doesn't matter in any case, thought Flynn, although it wouldn't be my taste. But he'll cause a flutter among the females – yes, and the men backstage. God, he's got to play the prince or there's no justice in the world! I'll give him a slinky, sensual outfit of turquoise and violet – like the drowned evening light that creeps inland on Ireland's west coast – and a cloak of iridescent green over it all. He'll trail it arrogantly in the dust as he walks. His scenes will have to be very carefully lit as well ... Pouring purple shadows and the outlines of half-glimpsed, not-quite-substantial buildings: under-sea fortresses ... I'll revamp them a bit now I've seen him. I wonder could we somehow pump one of those heady, sexy perfumes into the auditorium while he's centre stage, or would that be classed as tampering with the senses of the audience? It would be bloody effective, though.

Only Tod Miller, cross with Danilo for putting him into an impossible situation and furious with Flynn for making the situation even worse, missed the husky allure of Danilo's voice. Ugly, thought Tod, resentfully. You could almost believe the boy has a bad cold. Well, we can't let this one loose in the theatre, that's for sure!

Chapter Nine

*Often the changeling would be an ancient, withered
fairy, of no more use to the fairy tribe . . . cherished,
fed and carried about by its foster-mother, wawling
and crying for food and attention, in an apparent
state of paralysis.*

Medieval Chronicles of Ralph of Coggeshall and
Gervase of Tilbury, *A Dictionary of Fairies*,
Katharine Briggs

The suspicion that Tod Miller had not written *Cauldron* or
even had much of a hand in any part of it grew on Flynn as
rehearsals progressed. But it was not until just before the
company moved from the rehearsal rooms into the Harlequin
for the final stretch before opening night, that he picked up any
real clues.

Flynn liked the Harlequin better than any other London
theatre he had worked in. He had no idea if it was because it
was here that he had received his first real break, or if it was the
Harlequin's long and colourfully ignoble tradition, or if it was
simply the theatre's particular atmosphere, which was generally
agreed to be unusual. Parts of it were very old indeed, and
romantically-minded actresses were apt to say that if you stood
in a particular corner backstage, or near the stair where the old
tiring rooms had been, you could imagine the ghosts quite close
to you. You could almost see the past stretching back and back,
all the way to the days of the notorious Scaramel Smith, who
had bought the land with her father's money and built the
theatre's fame on the strength of her mother's reputation – her
mother having been one Frances Smith, a player of small parts

at His Majesty's Theatre Royal in Brydges Street, her father having been one Charles Stuart, a man of many parts at His Majesty's Court in Whitehall.

By the time the Theatre Royal had metamorphosed into the Theatre Royal, Drury Lane, the Harlequin had become famous and Scaramel had become infamous, flaunting a cheerful immorality across half of London – a legacy, said the disapproving, from her amoral father and her immoral mother. Irritated rivals recalled that Frances had been known as Fivepenny Fan in her Hounsditch days, and said once a guttersnipe always a guttersnipe, and what was in the meat came out in the gravy.

Flynn enjoyed Scaramel's legend, and he never passed through the Harlequin's Green Room without tipping a wink to the portrait which hung there, and from which the lady herself regarded the world with mischievous delight. One day, if he could find the right writer, Flynn was going to piece together the snippets and the tag-ends of legend and disentangle which was myth and which was fact and which was plain jealous gossip, and stage a huge, raunchy musical here of Scaramel's life. It would be a kind of *Moll Flanders* meets *Tom Jones* meets *Forever Amber*, but it would be lively and fun and it ought to be very promotable indeed. Not for the first time, he paid silent tribute to James Roscius who had been instrumental in bringing him here eight years earlier.

Roscius had resigned as the Harlequin's musical director by then, and he had been living that curious life, spending half his time in Ireland, but he had been invited back as guest director for the Christmas play, and he had suggested that Flynn submit designs for it. The Harlequin did not put on pantomime but it remained, as Scaramel had intended, a people's theatre, and there was a long tradition of lively Christmas shows for children. The play that year had been Hans Christian Andersen's *The Tinder Box*, and Roscius said that although nothing might come of it, it would be interesting to see what kind of settings and costumes Flynn could conjure up.

There were few people from whom Flynn would accept either criticism or help, but James Roscius was one of these. He thought – when he thought about it at all – that it was because the professor had for so long been a part of his life: there was some kind of distant connection with Flynn's mother and Roscius had possessed the Irish clan-instinct.

Flynn had poured his heart and soul into that first Harlequin project, basing his designs on the evocative Gothic-flavoured work of the Victorian illustrators: Andrew Lang and the amazingly grisly work of Gustave Doré, which had been considered suitable for children's books in the nineteenth century, a fact that never ceased to amaze Flynn.

He could still remember how Roscius had studied them in silence, and then had said, 'Flynn, you're very talented. If you behave yourself, you could go very far indeed in the theatre.' And for some reason, his eyes had been shadowed, almost as if Flynn's talent caused him a deep sadness.

The *Tinder Box* designs had been accepted; the show had received considerable acclaim and Flynn had shared in it, which for a young man barely out of university was heady stuff. He had gone on to design other Christmas shows for other houses on the strength of it – light, frothy stuff – and then shows that were not quite so light and frothy. There had been a couple of seasons with the RSC and a couple more with Chichester and a summer at Glyndebourne. He was not quite at the stage where he could pick and choose work, but the nerve-wracking periods of unemployment had been amazingly few. Before Roscius died he had nominated Flynn as one of the Harlequin's trustees, which brought a small quarterly income, and a large degree of involvement and prestige.

Flynn did not care about the prestige, but he enjoyed being part of the Harlequin's administrative board, and he liked the idea of continuing to carry out Scaramel's designs for her theatre, in accordance with the will, made, it was said, on the lady's unrepentant deathbed. The will stated with arrogant assurance that if the Harlequin ever ceased to be a theatre, it should be burned down rather than used for some other purpose. Flynn suspected that Scaramel had enjoyed laying this imperious demand on future generations of theatre managers; he thought she had derived great enjoyment from her flamboyant reputation. Flynn enjoyed being flamboyant as well; he liked puncturing the pretentions of the pompous and denouncing ridiculous back-scratching award ceremonies – that meaningless Inigo Jones thing last year! – and he got an immense kick from playing the prima donna before people like Tod Miller. But designing *Cauldron* had been a joy and whoever had created it possessed genuine brilliance. Which brought him full circle to the nagging question of *Cauldron*'s real creator.

The early rehearsals intrigued Flynn, and he noticed that Tod seemed to be delegating a good deal of the actual direction to Stephen Sherry. But it was not until the week preceding the dress and technical rehearsals, when the company was preparing to move from St Martin's Lane, that he had his first glimpse of the slight figure standing in the upper circle, its face in shadow, but seeming to watch the stage with the fiercest concentration Flynn had ever seen.

And then, as he started forward, puzzled rather than anything else, there was a whisper of sound, and the figure melted into the shadows and was gone.

Entering the Harlequin once more was a bitter-sweet experience. Christian had timed his visit carefully, waiting until just before Tod Miller's company would be taking up residence, and when the place – especially the backstage areas – would be inhabited only by a handful of maintenance men or carpenters. He had chosen the late afternoon, the time of half-shadows, when daylight was draining but no one had yet switched on lights, and he had gone quietly through the small sub-basement door, which had been the original stage door, and which even in his father's day had never been used. Christian thought very few people had ever known it was there.

He was taking a bit of a gamble, but not much of a one. The door had once opened directly into the Harlequin's original brick and wood structure, and it was inconvenient and difficult to find if you did not know exactly where it was. It opened now onto a dank, brick-walled corridor with a cobblestone floor which might have once been part of an old inn-yard. There was no electricity, and there were not even any of the old gas mantles, which were still evident in parts of the building. He switched on a thin pencil torch and went cautiously forward. But he did not think he was likely to be heard or seen; no one

was, that a plan began to form in his mind.

This corridor was almost level with the great well that lay beneath the stage. There was a brick wall, with two or three alcoves that were sealed-off doors, but that would once have led straight to the under-stage area. He paused, staring at the alcoves. Three of them – no, four.

He glanced up and down the passageway, trying to fix his bearings. The stage had been lifted in his father's time, and sufficient space had been allowed between the new stage and the old for storage and mechanical scene-changing, and for trapdoor entrances. But the old stage had never been removed: beneath it was a vast, dark cavern, dipping far down into the Harlequin's foundations, and it was that cavern that lay on the other side of these walls.

The Harlequin had a curious, mixed history; Christian knew a good deal about it. He knew about the robust, raucous years of Scaramel Smith, with her mother's guttersnipe impudence, and he knew about the gentler years, when the house was filled with player kings and queens, with music and brilliance. Gala performances and benefit nights, and nights when all London came here and the Prince Regent and Mrs Fitzherbert might be seen in the royal box . . .

He knew, as well, about the darker years towards the end of the nineteenth century, when the Harlequin had fallen on evil times, and been disparagingly dubbed as a blood-tub, a gaff, a theatre where fifth-rate melodrama was staged, and the poorer sections of the community could pay tuppence to enjoy the gruesome spectacle of murder and rape, and see blood and guts strewn all over the stage.

The under-stage area would have been utilised for those blood-tub plays. The stage-hands would have crouched in the dark, ready to operate the machines that caused fake blood to gush onto the stage, probably using some kind of hand-pump which would have sprayed the entire stage, and very likely the front row of the stalls into the bargain. This was where Maria Marten would have screamed her way out of the Red Barn, and where Sweeney Todd's victims would have been precipitated into the sinister cellar, there to wait their transformation into man-pies. Because once upon a time, the Harlequin had been a place where people had been slaughtered, publicly and messily, by way of warning and revenge.

Revenge ... Wasn't that what this entire thing with Tod Miller was all about?

Christian bent down, examining the brickwork more closely. The mortar was very old indeed; in places it had crumbled, leaving what was almost a drystone wall. How easy would it be to knock through? And what would be the advantage? A hiding place? A deep, deep chasm, that might go down and down and never end ...

And where, if you kept going down and down, you might easily find yourself entering strange, subterranean worlds, where faceless creatures prowled dripping, cavernous halls, and where vengeful not-quite-human beings made their secret lair ...

Rossani's song began to form itself in his mind, for this was the kind of dark underworld that Rossani understood; it was the world he came from.

The difficult smile twisted Christian's incomplete mouth.

Chapter Ten

Twilight is not good for maidens;
Should not loiter in the glen
In the haunts of goblin men.

Goblin Market, Christina Rossetti

Mia Makepiece was feeling very pleased with life.

It had taken all the coaxing and cajoling she was capable of to persuade old Gerald to back a play, but now that the deed was done, he was as pleased with himself as if it had all been his own idea.

It was good to be back in London. A girl got screamingly bored stuck up in the north with nothing to do and she had told Gerald so, winding a finger in his hair (the bit he had left), and saying he could have no idea how much she missed her life in London. She managed to make it sound as if she had walked away from a string of glittering West End successes and abandoned a dazzling career in order to marry him, and as if she had turned her back on a social life crammed to overflowing, instead of that rotten, shoddy house in its rotten, shoddy backstreet, and no offers of work except provincial tours with fifth-rate companies.

And so Gerald, who could not bear to think of his dear one being deprived of anything, had started to make cautious forays into the fringes of the theatrical world. There had been a few consultations with agents – Mia had enjoyed that, because of course she had insisted on going along, and of course Gerald would not have dreamed of leaving her out of it. She had enjoyed sweeping into offices where once she had sat for hours on hard chairs waiting to be told there was nothing doing at the moment, except maybe chorus in panto at Christmas. And the end of it all had been the introduction to Tod Miller and the explanations about the show he was apparently so keen to put on if only he could find a backer or two. Really, you had to be swept along by the man's enthusiasm, said Gerald, and Mia suppressed a yawn and said she supposed so.

Finally Gerald had agreed to put up some of the money, and Sir Julius Sherry had agreed to put up a bit more, and Tod Miller's bank had some kind of involvement as well (Mia had never found out what that was, because it was nothing to do with her and boring anyway), and the Harlequin had somehow been available as part of the deal. And they were all set for a smash hit, which meant that Mia was set for a smash hit which was the important part, and everyone was prophesying that *Cauldron* was going to have the longest run in history.

Mia could not see why they were all going so raving mad about *Cauldron*. To Mia it was a weird old thing, full of peculiar creatures and situations that were supposed to be one thing but somehow changed into another. People going on quests for cauldrons filled with food to feed starving peasants, and people being spirited away by inhuman creatures with unpronounceable names.

And the music! Well, mournful was the only word for most of it. Music ought to be bright and loud so that you wanted to get up and dance. Proper music was lively songs with catchy tunes, or it was raunchy with a good, strong beat so that it got played in discos and on Radio One. This belly-aching row was not going to get within a million miles of any disco. And as for the settings – all Mia could say was that if drab blues and greens, and sets filled with pouring violet smoke were people's idea of beauty, they were not hers! You could not see your hand in front of your face in some of Flynn Deverill's settings! Dreary, that was the word for them; in fact this was the dreariest show she had ever been in, and the sooner they opened and got the thing recognised as a hit (and Mia herself acknowledged as a star), the sooner she could move on to something better.

The dreariness was considerably lightened when, ten days before the first night, the anonymous note was delivered to her.

It was very intriguing indeed. Mia read it as soon as it arrived

108

by the second post, and then tucked it quickly into her pocket because if Gerald saw it he might very easily get the wrong idea.

Cara Mia, it began, which was a rather nicely-turned compliment about her name. *You must by now be aware how much I admire you. You have made me believe that my feelings are returned. I think that the time has come for us to explore our emotions a little further. I shall be in the theatre at nine o'clock on Tuesday evening, and will wait there for you. Come in through the stage door, wait just inside and I will come to you.*

I have booked a table for two at Marivaux's – but that is not until eleven. How we spend the intervening two hours is entirely up to you, but I am certainly yours to command for those hours . . . I will not write now of the physical sensations you have aroused in me ever since I saw you, but will hope to demonstrate them to you.

There was a scribbled initial that might have been anything at all, and the writing was a rather decorative slanting hand that she had never seen before.

Well! Well, as a love-letter it was peculiar. A bit old-fashioned, as if the author was not very used to writing such notes, or as if he had got the phrases out of some old book. But people did not often write love-letters these days; they phoned, or they simply asked you out and you went on from there. But the intention was unmistakable.

Mia studied the indecipherable initial again, and felt a tingle of pleasurable anticipation as she ran over the possible identities of the letter's author. Danilo sprung instantly to mind: he and she had exchanged a great many smouldering looks during their scenes together, and there was a tradition of leading ladies and leading men having it off. Method Acting, some people called it, although why they could not admit to it as plain, honest bonking, Mia could not see. She would certainly not object to it being Danilo who had sent the note, although as an ordinary member of the company Danilo would not be very likely to have a key to the Harlequin, which was prudently and thoroughly locked up each evening at six. Also Mia doubted whether he could afford Marivaux's.

Flynn Deverill could almost certainly afford Marivaux's, for all that he went around dressed like a disreputable drop-out most of the time. And he was one of the Harlequin's trustees as well as being *Cauldron*'s design director, which meant he might very well have a key. Mia found herself hoping that the note was from Flynn. It was true that he had not, so far, appeared to respond to the signals she had thrown out, but that might be just his way. It would be extremely gratifying if it did turn out to be Flynn; Mia would make sure that it became known within the company. It would be necessary to keep it from Gerald, but Mia had had considerable practice at doing that.

It was just possible that Sir Julius Sherry had sent the note, but it was not very likely that he would write about it being time for them to explore their emotions, not when they had explored them pretty thoroughly on four occasions already. It was a promising situation with Julius, of course, although it was a pity he was so portly, and an even greater pity that he was apt to get out of breath at the wrong moment. But he was richer than Gerald and he lived in London and it would be very nice indeed to be Lady Sherry, although Mia was not going to ditch Gerald quite yet; a girl could fall between two stools that way, and end up with nothing. And now that she thought about it, romantic secrecy was hardly Julius Sherry's line. As for his son writing the note, the idea had only to be examined to be dismissed; Mia had never come across such a cold fish as Stephen Sherry, and hoped never to do so again.

There was one other contender for that scribbled initial, and that was Tod Miller. Was it possible that Tod had conceived a romantic passion for her? This seemed not beyond the realms of possibility. On balance Mia would prefer to find Flynn Deverill waiting in the shadowy theatre, but a girl had to be practical and you could not have too many strings to your bow. Beaux to your string. At least Tod Miller seemed fitter than old Juley-boy, and less likely to succumb to revolting fits of spluttering bronchitic breathlessness when he reached the short strokes.

There were over twenty-four hours to get through before she

would know. There were two boring rehearsals, both with the musical director, Maurice Camperdown, who was taking them through the kidnapping scenes. Mia had decided that if there were any more sarcastic remarks from him about hitting bum notes, she would complain to Gerald, and he would tell the stupid old bandleader where he could stick his baton. She was not hitting bum notes at all and she was doing her best, in fact she was working bloody hard, and a whole lot harder than some of the others! Those irritating understudies, for instance! Mia had seen that common little red-haired tart who was under-studying for Mab watching her – yes, and now she came to think about it, she would not be a bit surprised to find that the creature was egging Camperdown on! Probably she was giving him a few free bonks on the side and very likely they had cooked up a nasty little plan for Mia to throw up the part in a tantrum, so that the red-head could step in. Over my dead body! thought Mia, angrily.

She would get through their silly rehearsals and she would not be irritated into losing her temper. And she would tell Gerald that there were some extra bits of polishing to do on her scenes which would give her a good excuse for going out by herself.

She began to plan what she would wear, with due attention to the practicalities of undressing (or, better still, being undressed, especially if it was Flynn), but then of looking suitably dazzling afterwards. You did not want to walk into Marivaux's (*Marivaux's*, for heaven's sake!) looking creased and dishevelled.

Tod Miller? Danilo? Flynn Deverill?

It had been simplicity itself to break through one of the bricked-up arches.

Christian had kept watch for four nights, until he was reasonably sure of the security arrangements. The Harlequin was patrolled by a company who specialised in night watches for large buildings, and checks were made at ten o'clock, midnight, two a.m. and four a.m. when two men, armed with intercoms and mobile phones, went into the building – one through the stage door and one through the box office entrance – and checked each floor in turn, and then the backstage and dressing room areas. Between those hours the place was deserted, and Christian thought the two men worked to a fairly strict timetable, covering several buildings in the vicinity and allowing a set time for each.

He entered the theatre just before eleven, which was a time when the streets were still sufficiently crowded for him to pass unnoticed, but which was safely between the ten p.m. and the midnight patrol. He had brought two powerful torches with him, and although he was fairly certain that no light would penetrate up to the main theatre, he switched both on, and walked into the upper passages, testing the range of the light. Not a glimmer. Good.

He retraced his steps, and positioned the torches so that their beams shone directly onto the smallest of the arches, where the brickwork looked weakest. Actually breaking through the wall had exercised his mind considerably: he had turned over ideas for bringing some kind of drill down here, but he had no idea what sized drill would be needed, or whether it would be possible to operate one without electricity. And then, on one of his forays into the Harlequin, he had come upon a pile of scaffolding poles – probably part of a dismantled gantry left by electricians or scenery painters – and he had picked one of them up to gauge the weight. The poles were all very heavy indeed. They were so heavy, in fact, that with a reasonable degree of luck, one of the shorter ones could be used as a battering-ram to break through the old brickwork. To make assurance doubly sure, he brought with him a large, heavy-headed hammer.

In the end, the hammer was hardly needed. Christian found it possible to use the pole like a battering-ram, simply swinging it against the brickwork with all his strength. And whoever had bricked up these old stage entrances had made a very cursory job of it indeed; several bricks yielded almost at once, crumbling like chalk and tumbling inwards, smashing on the cobbled floor with a sound that ricochetted through the tunnel like the crack of doom. Christian jumped and felt his heart leap. He waited, prepared to meet an attack, but there were only the shadows and the ghosts, and ghosts did not worry him.

He worked doggedly at the small hole, chipping at the bricks around it with the hammer, careful to stop at the times when the guards would be in the theatre. Several times he thought he heard movement, and he stopped at once, turning sharply to scan the shadows. Something approaching? Someone coming down to investigate? Once he thought footsteps approached and once there was the sound of a door being slammed. The security guards coming in at a different hour after all? Deliberately altering their schedule to fool burglars who might have kept watch and be timing a break-in? He waited, ready to make good his escape through the old sub-level door, but the footsteps – if footsteps they had been – ceased and there was no sound other than the occasional creaking of old timbers as the wood contracted in the cold night air.

And then a little before three a.m. a much bigger section of the brickwork suddenly collapsed, and sour dry air gusted out to meet him with a little sighing sound, as if something that had long lain buried had drawn breath once more.

Christian picked up the nearer of the torches and shone it into the yawning gap. The beam picked out amorphous shapes, swathed in layers upon layers of cobwebs: ancient skips and tea-chests, and pieces of discarded scenery and props; rotting costumes and old stage weights and canvas flats. There was a scent of extreme age now as well – old timbers, and mildew and sadness.

After a moment, he stepped through into the ancient cellars that lay below Scaramel's theatre, and felt the crowded history and the soaked-up memories of three hundred years close about him.

Mia wore black for the rendezvous. A very smart Vivienne Westwood black two-piece, it was, with silver buttons on the jacket and a very short skirt, trimmed with silver lace. Gerald had expressed innocent amazement that such a small garment should be so expensive. With it she wore shiny, black, high-heeled boots, and black stockings with a scarlet silk suspender belt. All men were turned on by stockings and suspenders. She would be taking the two-piece off (at least, she hoped she would), but she would be keeping the stockings and suspender belt on. And the boots – yes, keeping on the boots would be a terrific turn-on. She put on the stockings in the bathroom of the hotel room, so that Gerald would not see them, and she had put her scarlet coat over the whole thing. Scarlet and black always took the eye, and she did not intend to go unnoticed in Marivaux's.

She was feeling quite tingly with anticipation as she paid off the taxi and approached the Harlequin. It reared up against the night sky, black and bulky, and Mia glanced up at it and thought you could almost say it looked menacing. But this was a silly fancy; she stood for a moment longer, and imagined how it would look in a week's time: the show's title in lights along with her own name. Her name in lights . . . Oh yes, it was a good feeling. It was worth a dozen tedious marriages to boring old men, and it was worth all the nights spent coaxing a stubbornly flaccid manhood to a semblance of stiffness. And poor old Gerald, poor old sod, was always so bloody grateful when that happened!

Come through the stage door and wait just inside, the note had said, and Mia went carefully around the side of the building and down the narrow, cobbled alleyway. The Harlequin was so old it had quite a few traces of a much older London; everyone kept saying this with a kind of hushed awe, although Mia could not see what was so wonderful about antiquity. In buildings it meant draughts and cold floors, and in people it meant indigestion and impotence. She pushed the stage door and felt it swing inwards. He was keeping to his promise, then; he had left it open for her, and he would be waiting somewhere inside.

Wait just inside and I will come to you . . .

It was darker than she had been expecting, and it was suddenly a rather nasty darkness; all clotting shadows and slithering black shapes. Like those old films where the stupid heroine was lured into the deserted old house, miles from anywhere, and then torn to pieces by a raving maniac. Mia wished she had not thought about that, because you could almost say that she had been lured here, and that this was a deserted old house, although it was certainly not miles from anywhere; if she stood still she could hear the traffic from the road. And far from the rendezvous being with a raving maniac, it was with a cultured and distinguished gentleman of the theatre who had harboured a passion for her ever since he had seen her, and who had contrived this romantic and exciting meeting, and who, moreover, was going to take her to supper at Marivaux's afterwards. Cheered up by these undoubted facts, Mia went deeper into the dark Harlequin, her high-heeled boots tapping against the stone floor.

Wait just inside and I will come to you . . . He was taking a bloody long time about it. It was to be hoped he did not expect her to hang about by this draughty stage door for too long. Mia shivered and wrapped the scarlet coat around her a bit more tightly. Behind her the door closed very softly, almost as if of its own volition, and there was a click as the catch slid home. Mia whipped round, peering into the darkness, fear prickling her skin, but there was nothing to be seen. Very likely a gust of wind had blown the door, because it was a draughty old barn, the Harlequin. She moved away from the door, and remembered that there was a row of light switches somewhere on the right. She went forward, feeling her way cautiously, trying to remember if there were any steps or uneven bits of floor.

It was then that she became aware that there was someone standing quite near to her.

For the space of three heartbeats panic engulfed her, and then she almost laughed aloud.

'So there you are – you gave me quite a scare.' She managed one of the laughs which Gerald always said fondly were musical, but which, even to her own ears, sounded a bit hollow now.

'Of course I am here.' He spoke softly and a bit blurrily, as if he was disguising his voice, or as if he was wearing a scarf over his mouth. It was impossible to identify him from that. 'Did you not expect me to be here?'

'Well yes, but you made me jump, creeping up like that. Aren't you going to let me see you?' said Mia, and at once the indistinct figure moved away.

'Not just yet, Mia.' Yes, he had a smooth, caressing way of saying her name. As if he enjoyed it. As if he was savouring it. 'Come away from the door,' said the figure, and Mia felt another tingle of anticipation, because had there been a suggestion of Irishness then? Flynn Deverill after all? This was beginning to be an excellent evening. Herself and the startlingly good-looking, hot-tempered Flynn! They said hot-tempered men made tremendous lovers – all that mental passion. Mia was very glad indeed she had responded to the intriguing invitation, instead of staying in with Gerald and watching boring old telly.

'Follow me,' said the man. Yes, he *was* wearing something across his mouth; Mia could hear how the words came out muffled.

'Where are we going?' She went after him, her boots clattering on the stone floor again. Her companion moved almost noiselessly, like a cat. A black cat, slinking through the darkness . . . As long as he's a tomcat I don't much mind, thought Mia. I wonder where we're going? It would be rather fun to end up in one of the old stage boxes; the Edwardians had been famous for the things they had got up to in theatre boxes, drawing the curtains and banging away with their girlfriends. Like the Mile High Club today.

Wherever they were going tonight it did not look as if it was a box. Mia followed the dark figure obediently, although he was moving so quickly that she could not quite catch him up. There was not much light in here, but there was just enough to see your way, and her companion did not hesitate. He looked as if he was wearing a cloak, which was unusual, although cloaks might be making a comeback for men. Mia found herself stumbling a bit because of the high heels. It would be a screaming irony if she tripped and sprained her ankle.

They were in the backstage part now, which was a bit unexpected. But perhaps there was a set of offices somewhere – a hospitality suite. Yes, that would be it.

'This way, Mia . . .'

And now down a flight of stairs and through a narrow door. Mia had lost all sense of direction by now, but she knew she had never been in this part of the theatre. There was a light up ahead, though, which was something, but her companion seemed to have vanished. If this turned out to be a stupid practical joke she would have something to say about it in the morning! She would just let them know that she was not someone to be played jokes on like this! She started to say, 'Now look here, Mr Whoever-You-Are—' and was stopped by the sound of his voice again.

'In here, Mia . . .' The words sang a silly little rhythm in her head. In-here-Mi-ha . . . In-hia-Mere . . .

There was the flicker of a torch being played over old brick walls – where was this, for God's sake? – and Mia stood irresolute for a moment. And then the torch shone again, seeming to come from inside some kind of arched opening. He was behind the light – Mia could just make out the dark shape. This had bloody better be worth it! She ducked her head and went through the opening.

And now it was no longer vaguely frightening, it was the real thing. Wherever this place was, it was spooky and very menacing indeed. Mia glanced over her shoulder, and saw the blurry outline of the brick opening. If something started to happen that she did not like she would just run hell-for-leather through that opening, and she would run all through the theatre, screaming bloody murder as she went. And then she would run out into the street and scream bloody murder as well, and that would teach this creep to treat her a bit better!

She was just thinking that maybe this was what she would do anyway, when there was the soft laugh again, and the voice came whisperingly through the shadows. 'Oh Mia,' it said. 'Don't you trust me?'

And of course it was all right, and of course it was a wildly romantic game after all, and there was probably a secret love-nest down here, and in a very few minutes she would know who her companion was. (And wasn't it looking more and more as if it was Flynn Deverill? You could never, in a million years, imagine Julius Sherry or Tod Miller setting this up.)

Mia began to move forward through the old rubbish and the tattered bits of scenery and props. Smelly old things, they were. The whole place smelt. Damp and dirt and mice. Her eyes were adjusting to the light, and she could see the shrouded outlines of furniture. That one looked like a sofa, and there were several large chairs, and over there was a dismantled four-poster. They were all draped in dustsheets and covered with cobwebs, and in the gloom they were extremely eerie. Mia bit her lip and glanced back. How far to the brick opening? Yes, but if it really was Flynn . . . ? She could not see him any longer, but she could feel that he was quite near.

And then she heard something that was so soft and light she might almost have imagined it, but something so filled with trickling menace that her mind reeled with terror.

A soft, soft voice singing . . .

O never go walking in the fields of the flax
At night when the looms are a-singing;

The pale thick dustsheet draped over the nearest sofa suddenly reared up and a dark shape emerged from it and began to walk towards her. The mocking singing came to her again.

For Rossani's at work and he's hungry for prey;
He'll melt down your eyes and he'll spin them for gold.
He'll peel off your skin and he'll sew him a cloak.

Mia began to scream.

Christian had stunned the screaming, stupid creature in the same way that he had stunned the bitch Leila in Soho. Enough to shut her up for a while but not enough to render her unconscious for very long. Certainly not enough to kill her.

He dragged Mia's inert body across the dusty floor and laid her out on the small area he had cleared earlier, and then bent to feel for a pulse. Yes, there was a little beating hammer at the base of her throat. Good.

The silly, vain bitch was wearing leather boots. Christian studied them for a moment, and then bent over, preparing to unzip them and drag them off. The scarlet coat had fallen open, and he saw that she was wearing a short, tight, black skirt which had ridden up, exposing the tops of stockings, held up by scarlet suspenders. In different circumstances it might have been immensely arousing, but looking down at the thick, fleshy thighs and the clinging mini-skirt, Christian was aware only of deep contempt. This creature to attempt to play Mab, to attempt to portray the magical, fey, Irish queen that he and Fael had created!

The memory of Fael brushed against his mind for a moment, and with it came a breath of something from a different world:

something that was scented with autumn rain and spring meadows, and crackling applewood fires and the sun dissolving into the sea on Ireland's wild western coast . . . A world where there were no dark shadowlands and no tormented minds etched with the need for revenge. The thought: *I could still turn away from this; she could still be revived*, started to frame.

And then the moment vanished and there was only the angry darkness again, and the driving need to remove this travesty who would spoil *Cauldron*.

There was only the deep swirling awareness that he was again in Rossani's world; he had fallen down into it once more, and his mind was merging with Rossani's.

And this was the night when Rossani was hungry for prey . . .

He stripped the garish clothes off the creature who had walked so easily into his trap, and stood looking down at the pale, exposed flesh for a moment.

And then he reached into the deep pocket of his cloak and drew out the narrow-bladed scalpel. As he bent over the unconscious Mia, Rossani's eerie song was thrumming all about him, and he was no longer aware that he was singing it in a soft, mad, crooning little voice.

O never go walking in the fields of the flax
At night when the looms are a-singing;
For Rossani's at work and he's hungry for prey;
He'll melt down your eyes and he'll spin them for gold.
He'll peel off your skin and he'll sew him a cloak . . .

Chapter Eleven

Sir Julius Sherry seated himself at the head of the table in the Harlequin's Green Room and looked round at the small group of people assembled there.

It had really all been rather distressing. A police inspector had been and gone; he had asked people a great many apparently unrelated questions about the missing Mia Makepiece, mostly concerning her movements prior to the time she had left her hotel at 8.30 on Tuesday evening. He had irritated most people by his casual attitude, and he had incensed Gerald by suggesting, in barely veiled terms, that ladies sometimes disappeared for a couple of nights to pursue their own clandestine activities. Stephen Sherry and Morrie Camperdown had had to restrain Gerald from physically attacking the man at that point, and Sir Julius had produced his hip flask, with the idea of administering a couple of tots to Makepiece. Unfortunately, Gerald had swigged almost the entire contents without anyone (least of all Gerald himself) realising, and was now judged to be in a stage halfway between abject misery and a drunken stupor. It was anyone's guess whether he would burst into tears all over again (which would be embarrassing), be sick on the floor (which would be messy as well as embarrassing), or fall asleep, which would mean they could make a few sensible decisions without him.

It was thought that the inspector's men had made some kind of a search of the theatre, but it was not thought it had been particularly detailed. As Sir Julius pointed out, Gerald Makepiece had already made his own search of the Harlequin, scurrying up and down, muttering anxiously to himself as he went, and opening doors to the unlikeliest of places. He had even distractedly plunged into the ladies' cloakrooms and insisted on opening every cubicle in case Mia had fainted and was lying behind a door undiscovered. Nobody had yet found a way of telling him that so far as any of them knew, there had not been a rehearsal of any kind anywhere on Tuesday night.

The inspector had taken himself off half an hour ago, saying he was very sorry, gentlemen, but there was not really much more that could be done and he dared say they would be wanting to discuss the lady's replacement in their play.

Since Sir Julius had taken the head of the table, Tod, after a prolonged stare which should show the pompous old fool where he got off, walked deliberately to the other end and sat down. Gerald, hiccuping with misery and brandy, sank wretchedly into the nearest chair and stared disconsolately at his feet. Clearly he was not going to be of much help to anyone at this meeting, but he had had to be included as one of the board of Mia Productions, and at least the brandy had stopped him from filling up with embarrassing masculine tears every five minutes, or dashing off to search broom cupboards. Sir Julius thought he would not have offered his flask at all if he had known the silly little man was going to down the lot, and remembered with annoyance that it had been a rather good cognac. And it looked as if they were going to have trouble with Tod Miller, who had tried to take the head of the table and only been prevented by Sir Julius nipping in first. It was typical of Toddy to stump sulkily to the other end of the table, and sit there glowering, the hammy old braggart.

Stephen Sherry and Camperdown took places approximately in the middle, and Flynn Deverill, who had been summoned as a Harlequin trustee, lounged untidily in the window seat with the air of one disassociating himself from the entire proceedings.

Sir Julius drew breath to embark on a little speech, in which commiseration (for Makepiece) and bracing, forward-looking good humour (for everybody else) were going to be nicely blended. He was forestalled by Tod, who leaned forward, linked his hands earnestly together, and said, in his most impressively sonorous voice, 'My friends.'

'Oh Jesus save us all, he's about to be intense,' said a bored voice from the window seat.

Tod said loudly, 'My friends, the thing we must all remember

121

this afternoon is the famous adage of our beloved profession—'
He paused for effect, and allowed his eyes to roam over
his auditors, coming to rest, more or less at random, on
Camperdown.

'Yes?' said the musical director, politely.

'The words that were coined by a better mummer than I—'

'He's going to get it wrong,' observed Flynn conversationally
to Stephen. 'Unless he's thinking of *Hamlet*, of course.'

'Dammit, Flynn, I am not thinking of *Hamlet*!'

'Whatever you are thinking of, I wish you'd get on with
saying it,' said Sir Julius testily.

'I was going to say,' said Tod, huffily, 'that the show must go
on. That's what I was going to say.' He sat back, looking jowly
and responsible.

Flynn promptly said, 'Stephen, you owe me a tenner.'

'A fiver,' said Stephen, glancing at his watch. 'You said he'd
say it in the first *three* minutes—'

'Skinflint,' said Flynn amiably, pocketing the five-pound note
that Stephen handed over.

Tod glared at them both, and did not know what things were
coming to when vulgar bets were taken about what people might
say, especially when there was such a serious situation before
them. 'Very serious indeed,' he said. 'We must all stand together.
The play's the thing.'

'I told you he was thinking of *Hamlet*, Stephen.'

Gerald Makepiece emerged from his torpor to say brokenly
that Mia would have wanted the show to go on. 'Wherever she
is, she'd want *Cauldron* to go ahead,' he said, reaching into a
pocket for his handkerchief again.

There was an uncomfortable silence.

'Amnesia,' said Sir Julius, suddenly, and looked brightly
round the table. 'Mark my words, that'll be the answer. And it
can happen to anyone at any time. I remember I had a great-
aunt once—'

'Or she might have had a bit of a fall,' put in Camperdown.
'A touch of concussion, and been detained in a hospital
somewhere—'

'Any advance on amnesia or concussion? Stephen? Toddy?
What about a hostage situation? Or a threat by a secret

organisation to blow up the entire western world unless we pay ten billion dollars into a Swiss bank account? Or – listen, here's a really good one, now – a consortium of rival theatres wanting to sabotage *Cauldron*—'

Tod said, frostily, that it was incumbent on them all to behave in a responsible and serious-minded fashion in this crisis, and to treat people's feelings politely.

'Angels and ministers of grace defend me from Toddy's serious politeness,' said Flynn. 'Stephen, have we the understudy outside?'

'We have. Danilo's here as well.'

'And,' put in Maurice Camperdown, who was trying very hard not to appear pleased, but was secretly thanking whatever fates might be responsible for the unexpected disappearance of Mia Makepiece, 'in my opinion, Julius, Toddy, the understudy can go on.'

'Ah. Indeed?'

'Gilly Blair. The little red-head, Julius. You might remember her?'

'Of course he remembers her, the priapic old goat.'

'Well, since you mention it,' said Sir Julius, studiedly off-hand, 'I believe I do remember now. Dear me yes. Pretty little thing.'

'Stephen, what's your opinion?'

'She'll need extra rehearsals,' said Stephen cautiously. 'But we've got time for that. She's seemed competent at the understudy run-throughs.'

Somebody muttered that they did not want competence, they wanted brilliance, and Tod demanded they consider bringing in a big name. 'Could we not think who might be available?' he said, in his best I-dine-with-the-rich voice. 'Between us we must have so many contacts and friendships in the profession. One meets with people. The Groucho Club, and the Garrick, you know.'

'Toddy would like us all to think he has lunch with Elaine Paige every Tuesday and Lesley Garrett every Friday—'

'I'm inclined to agree with Morrie about the understudy,' Stephen, the peace-maker, put in hastily.

'—not to mention supper with Lloyd-Webber—'

'You don't know Andrew, do you, Toddy?' said Camperdown, surprised.

'Not intimately. Hum.'

'But listen, I think we can bring the understudy up to concert pitch in the time. There's just over a week left.'

'And in any case,' said Flynn, getting up from the window seat, 'the budget won't run to superstars, Toddy. Let's hear what the red-head's like before the little fowl tips over into unconsciousness.'

'Don't expect too much,' said Stephen, warningly.

But in the event, Flynn thought the understudy was not as bad as he had been fearing. She was not brilliant, but she had a degree of stage presence which he had not expected, and her voice was certainly sweeter and truer than ever Makepiece's had been. She was naturally graceful as well, and she looked the part. Slender and slight, but with a faint street-urchin look, so that you suspected that beneath the graceful fragility she might be quite capable of abusing you in gutter language. It was rather an attractive quality; Flynn thought it was a quality that Mab might well have possessed. This was not someone who would set the town alight, thought Flynn, studying Gilly from his seat in the stalls; but she would do. Yes, put her in the frock and light her a bit, and she would do.

It was as Stephen and Morrie took them through Mab's scenes with the *sidh* prince, that Flynn heard a faint sound from the dress circle. A door closing, had it been? The inspector's men still searching? He glanced at the others. Julius and Tod were watching the stage – Julius was nodding approvingly at the red-haired Gilly, and Toddy was looking glum. Little Makepiece was slumped in his seat; Flynn felt a twist of sympathy for the poor little man.

After a moment he got up and went softly and stealthily to the back of the theatre, and out into the foyer. It was already dark outside, with the depressing afternoon darkness of early November, and rain was lashing against the huge plate-glass doors. Flynn shivered, and turning up the collar of his coat crossed the foyer towards the curving stair leading to the dress circle. Probably there was no one up here at all. But it would not hurt to check.

But as his feet trod soundlessly across the thick, dark-red carpet, he felt a prickle of unease. There *was* someone up here. There was someone up here who was being very furtive and very stealthy. In Flynn's mind there formed again the image of the dark-clad figure he had glimpsed before; the watcher who had vanished into the shadows. A prowler? Even a spy, as he had suggested to them in the Green Room? It was a bit far-fetched, but it was not completely out of the question. Espionage was rife in all professions, and it was just believable that a rival house was trying to find out what the Harlequin's new show was about. But it was not terribly likely.

The dress circle was cold, as if the heating had not been switched on up here, or as if one of the exits had been left open. Flynn went quietly in and stood for a moment, his eyes adjusting to the dimness. There was a faint overspill of light from the stage, but it was still very dark up here. On stage the little red-head and Danilo were singing the duet in which Mab pleads for mercy, and the prince overpowers her. Their voices blended well. Wherever Mia Makepiece had gone, she had done *Cauldron* a favour by going. And that's odd, thought Flynn, because I'd have wagered half a king's ransom that Mia would never have bowed out of *Cauldron*. Yes, but did she bow out willingly, or was she made to bow out? said his mind. Was that likely? Could someone have cooked up a plan to remove her for *Cauldron's* good, and if so, who? It was surely too subtle for Tod Miller. Yes, but supposing you were right about Toddy having a collaborator? Supposing there really is a fine Italian hand somewhere in all this? Almost at once Flynn caught a flicker of movement on the rim of his vision, as if his thoughts had taken substance in the shadowy theatre and evinced an abrupt response. He stood very still for a moment, and then very slowly he turned his head, scanning the darkness.

In the far corner, standing near to the exit that led down to Burbage Lane, was a dark figure. Whoever it was was standing so still that he – or even she? – melted into the shadows so that it was impossible to see where the figure ended and the shadows began. So much part of the darkness was the figure that for a moment Flynn distrusted his own eyes.

But no! – there was someone standing there, and it was someone cloaked and wearing a deep-brimmed hat. Flynn found this unspeakably sinister. But whoever this was, it was unquestionably the same person he had seen before. He's watching the stage with exactly the same intensity, thought Flynn, and he's listening with fierce concentration. This is absurd. This is *Phantom of the Opera* territory. He moved then, deliberately making a noise, and at once the figure swung round. Flynn had a brief fleeting impression of darkness where the face should have been, and the figure flinched, and threw up a hand as if to ward off a blow. And then it turned with a swirl of silk and darted towards the exit. Flynn heard its footsteps echoing on the old stone steps that led down to the lane, and then bounded across the floor after him.

Christian was furious at having been so nearly caught, and he was even more furious that it should have been Flynn Deverill who had so nearly caught him.

He went down the steps to Burbage Lane, the cloak billowing out around him, his mind working at top speed. He would never outrun Flynn; the evening rush hour was in full flood and the streets were teeming with people. And to run full pelt through crowded London streets, with someone in pursuit, would be to attract attention. His mind flinched from it.

If he could have been sure of picking up a taxi, he thought he might have gone out into St Martin's Lane, but he could not be sure. He could not be sure, either, that Deverill would not be able to hail a second taxi and follow him; Deverill was the kind of man who would always attract a taxi driver's attention. He would attract waiters' attention in restaurants as well, and he would attract females like a magnet. Christian was aware of a deep hatred for Flynn who was good-looking and talented, and who had been held in high regard by Christian's father. The son he wanted! thought Christian, bitterly, as he slipped around the side of the building and into the narrow alley that led to the Harlequin's sub-basement entrance. He paused, listening. Was that someone running hard after him? No. Most people assumed that this was a blind alley; it was only when you went right up to the end that you saw the jutting spur of brick and realised you could get through.

He took a deep breath, fighting for control, hating Flynn who had been the cause of his loss of control. Flynn's suspicions might have been aroused in earnest; he might even mount some kind of search. Christian reviewed everything he had done. He had not been able to re-brick the opening in the old tunnel – he had not even bothered to try – but he had managed to smear sufficient dust and rubble around to make it look like a natural cave-in. He thought a cursory search would not show anything untoward.

But supposing Flynn reported seeing a prowler, and supposing the police connected it with the disappearance of the Makepiece woman? Was there anything that could lead them to the Christchurch Street house? Was there anything to implicate Christian himself? He thought there was not. He thought he was safe.

But the anger against Flynn, who had so nearly seen him and so nearly caught him, solidified into a cold hatred. Flynn was not quite indispensable, because Flynn was *Cauldron*'s designer, and from what Christian had seen so far, he had caught the mood very exactly indeed, and he had understood the subtleties and the imagery that Fael had wanted to depict.

But once the show was running, Flynn would no longer be necessary.

The Harlequin thrummed with excitement and shone with anticipation.

Flynn, strolling through the Green Room, a large whisky and soda in his hand, arrayed for once in the sharp formality of evening clothes, felt the invisible flame of the place start to burn. Remarkable. Is it the players, churning up their inner emotions, unleashing their controlled passions, or is it the theatre itself, waking with delight to another first night? I could reach out and slice a layer of the atmosphere tonight, he thought. And if I did, what should I find in those layers? Fear, certainly, but excitement as well, and probably envy and greed and vanity.

Yes, all of those things were present tonight; they coursed through the old theatre, feeding the strange, inner lamp that glowed just out of sight and just beyond awareness. Flynn finished his whisky and headed back to the bar for a refill. All the emotions were here tonight: the vanity of players, the selfishness of showmen. A greedy breed, showmen.

Gilly was feeling all of the emotions that Flynn had identified and several more besides. It was all very well for people to say she would be absolutely fine; she was to go out there and knock them in the aisles, and wasn't this a chance most of them would give their back teeth for? Gilly knew all of that. She had known she would be nervous, as well, but she had not bargained for this paralysing terror. She thought she would probably feel better if she could stop reminding herself that she had only had a week of rehearsals. A week was plenty long enough, everyone had told her that, and it had been a very concentrated week indeed.

Once they got going it would almost certainly be all right, but every time she thought about stepping out onto that legendary stage, with that huge audience waiting, ready to criticise or devour, her stomach cramped with panic and her pulse-rate went through the roof. She was beginning to feel as if she was here under false pretences, and she thought that at any minute somebody would recognise her for what she was, and denounce her, and they would all suddenly realise that it was only Gilly Blair after all: a street-girl, who had been padding the hoof through Soho barely a month ago. And had only rehearsed for a week. They would throw her out and she would end in the sleazy world of half-drunk tourists who could not get it up and thought it was your fault; she would be back with the Sunday evenings at the Greasepaint, paying the Shadow his bloody five per cent! And this wonderful opportunity, this marvellous world would vanish.

And I awoke and found me here on the cold hill side . . .

That was a line from one of Mab's songs; the one she sang at the end of the second act, when she had escaped from Aillen mac Midha and was struggling to find her way back to her own world, and when the gallant *Fianna* captain found her and took her with him on the quest for the cauldron, not realising her true identity.

It was a lovely song, achingly sad, and Gilly had to sing it alone on the great stage, with the marvellous, swirling, violet mists that Flynn Deverill had managed to create everywhere, and the tantalising, smoky vision of her lost palace glimpsed through a thin gauze scrim at the back. One or two of the cast had said, a bit scathingly, that the words of the song were a shameless pinch from a poem by Keats, but Gilly had gone to the public library and looked it up, and she did not think it was a pinch at all. Whoever had written the song (Tod Miller, presumably) had simply loosened one or two threads of the poem, and woven them with his own threads to make a different tapestry. It conjured up something misty and a bit chill, and something that might occasionally turn back a corner of a magic veil to let you see through to strange, inhuman worlds . . .

As Gilly began to make up for the opening scene, she thought again how much appearances could deceive. She would never have believed Tod Miller capable of writing such wonderful music.

The rest of the company were succumbing to their own brand of nerves.

Danilo studied himself in the mirror of the dressing room he shared with the *Fianna* captain, and felt an inward twinge of amusement. Well, and what would the club circuit say if they could see me now? From drag queen to inhuman prince, and that's a leg up the ladder if ever there was one! Off with the sequins and the false eyelashes, Danny-boy, and on with the motley instead.

He was churning with nerves, but beneath it he was aware of a feeling of being where he belonged at last. Finished with the appalling tedium of the clubs, and done with the nail-biting, shoulder-hunching jealousies and spiteful gossiping. The jealousies were here as well, of course; human nature was human nature the world over, but they were different jealousies. They were somehow larger and easier to tolerate. Like Gilly, he thought: I'm finished with those macabre little meetings every Sunday night, and he wondered suddenly what happened to the Shadow's people when they broke away from that odd world and entered new ones.

He leaned closer to the mirror, lengthening his eyes with dark liner, and then brushing on green and blue to give them a slanting, inhuman look. A 'beckoning' look. He had not yet decided who he would beckon to once *Cauldron* was up and running, or if he would in fact beckon to anyone, but there were several possibilities.

The *Fianna* captain, applying his own make-up at the other mirror, thought it was going to get bloody hot in all this armour. It was a very strenuous part, the captain. But it was a brilliant part to have landed. Second lead, really. And it was great to only have to share a dressing room with one, instead of lumping in with half a dozen others, which you often had to do, putting up with sweaty armpits and stupid rituals that had to be followed to ward off disasters, never mind queuing for the loo because of people having a nervous pee every five minutes. The captain had not quite made up his mind about Danilo's sexual proclivities, but at least he did not smell of sweat and he got on with things quietly and without fuss. Still, it might be as well to just mention to him that the captain was considering his chances with the girl playing the sorceress who guarded the magic cauldron.

Tod Miller was still being very busy indeed. He had arranged that the press should be brought to the hospitality suite at the first interval, where Tod would himself dispense drinks. It was a good thing he had got in before Julius, who liked to buttonhole critics in the most embarrassing way, and could not be trusted not to tip them off about snippets of information that would be better kept from them. Tod would not be surprised to learn that Julius was in the pay of gossip columnists, in fact, and he was certainly not having that. He straightened his bow tie in the mirror and went down to the circle bar, where he solemnly drank a pint of the tipple called Black Velvet, which was half Guinness and half vintage champagne. The very young barman had never heard of it, and so he was very grateful to Tod for telling him that it had been Prince Bismarck's drink. Tod set down the empty glass and took himself off, feeling pleased. The very young barman would have been flattered at Tod's talking to him in such a friendly way. It paid to take trouble over these little details; the boy would tell everyone that Tod Miller was a man of the people.

The barman washed up the empty glass thoughtfully. He did not give a toss what people drank so long as they did not expect him to put it on the slate, and actually he had thought Bismarck was a ship (you saw it on the old black-and-white films on the telly). In any case, he was more interested in deciding whether he dare invite Danilo to come out for a beer. He would not do it tonight, because there would be the usual first-night bash and then they would all be waiting for the papers to read the reviews. But he might try tomorrow. He checked the stores for Guinness and champers, in case that pretentious old fart, Tod Miller, asked for it again.

The *sidh* manoeuvred for the best positions at the two long mirrors they shared in the chorus's dressing room. The more experienced were very blasé in front of a couple of newcomers, whose first West End show this was. Same old cramped dressing room, they said. Same old treadmill. There was a minor altercation over a pair of green tights which had unaccountably vanished, and then an anxious discussion as to whether a new hair colour, tried by one of them that morning, and disastrously streaky, would show up too blonde under the lights. Somebody said that Flynn Deverill would play merry hell if the *sidh* did not have the right appearance, and the streaky-haired one looked terrified and calculated whether there was time to shampoo it out before Beginners was called. People began to warm up at the wooden barre at the far end.

Stephen Sherry padded conscientiously round the dressing rooms, wishing good luck to those who were not superstitious, and saying 'break a leg' to those who were. For the *sidh* dancers, he remembered to say '*Merde*' which was a ballet tradition. He kissed the females and shook the men's hands, and everyone said what a nice chap he was, good old Stephen, never forgot anyone's name, never forgot a single detail. Shame he never married, probably married to his work, though.

Morrie Camperdown arranged his music, pocketed a handful of loose soda mints, and drank a glass of milk very slowly because first-night nerves always attacked his stomach.

Sir Julius Sherry cunningly arranged things so that the press should be brought to the hospitality bar in the second interval (which was the longest), so that he could hand out drinks. He would have preferred to make it the first interval, because of getting to the press before Toddy – you never knew what the old buffoon might say, and Julius would not put it past Miller to feed them with indiscreet snippets about the company, which would never do. But the first interval was traditionally taken up with touring the dressing rooms and boosting the cast, and telling them how well things were going and how much the audience were loving the show. Sir Julius hoped that he would be able to say this with truth tonight, because sometimes you had to lie just to keep the actors' spirits up.

Gerald Makepiece got quietly and miserably drunk in his hotel room, and tried to think how to get through the evening without breaking down at the sight of another female playing the part that had been his beloved Mia's.

And Fael Miller, at exactly six-fifteen, discovered that her father had locked her in the house and taken away the wheelchair.

Chapter Twelve

Fael had bathed and changed in good time; her bath had a swivel-chair which meant she could get in and out without anyone having to help her, which she would have found intolerable. She was going to wear velvet trousers, the colour of moss, with a cream silk shirt with full sleeves and deep cuffs. There was a matching, moss-velvet waistcoat, cut like a man's. She had washed her hair that morning, and it was like a shining silver-gilt cap. She would have liked to grow it long, but it was too awkward to manage while she was still using the wheelchair. Her mother had had hair the same colour, but it had rippled past her shoulders, and when it was loose she had looked like a water nymph or a gilt-haired pre-Raphaelite. Fael put on the huge jade ear-rings that had been her mother's and the matching moss agate ring. Pretty good for a cripple, Fael. Not perfect, but not bad.

It was when she reached for the phone to ring up the taxi firm she always used that she saw her chair was not in its normal place. This was so odd that she stopped halfway through tapping out the number. When she was not using the chair it was always, but always, in the little alcove just outside her bedroom door. This was its logical and sensible place, because Fael could reach it easily and it was tucked away so that people coming through the hall could not fall over it. It was never moved. But somebody must have moved it, because it was not there now.

Fael felt the start of a flutter of panic. Don't be ridiculous, probably Tod shunted it farther down the hall because he was looking for something. But what? There was nothing else in the alcove, except for a couple of framed flower prints on the wall.

Using her stick she managed to get all the way along the hall, and she managed to look in each room as she went. It was a long and exhausting process; the hall was a large L-shaped arrangement with the sitting room and the dining room and study opening off the long leg of the L, and the kitchen and downstairs cloakroom and the old pantry opening off the short one. Fael's own two rooms were at the very back, at the foot of the L. By the time she had finished she was drenched in sweat, which meant she would have to change the silk shirt if she was to appear at the Harlequin looking halfway decent. This was a nuisance because it was already twenty to seven. Her arms were aching unbearably and her leg muscles felt as if they had been torn with red-hot pincers. Not good. She was supposed to increase the exercises by a little each day, and a little meant about five minutes, not half an hour spent in a panicky search. But she might still make it. The taxi people were very good, and the Harlequin was only a quarter of an hour's drive. If she could find the wheelchair she would make it.

The wheelchair was not here. It was not anywhere on the ground floor. Fael sank into a chair in the front half of the hall and leaned against the small hall table which held letters and a phone extension, and considered the situation. It was possible that the chair was upstairs, and although she might just about manage the stairs, it would take a very long time. And it would not really advance the case much, because even if the chair was there, she would never get it down unaided.

She was avoiding the main issue, of course, and that was the issue of who had deliberately moved the chair out of her reach. Her father. Fael admitted this at last, and it was just as nasty as she had known it would be. Her father had calculatedly and furtively taken her chair away so that she would not get out of the house tonight. Hard on its heels came another thought: if Tod had done that, he might also have locked her in. Her handbag was sitting on the hall table next to the phone. She checked it for her keys. They weren't there. They weren't in her coat pocket. The spare set wasn't on the hook in the kitchen. Fael dragged painfully along the hall once more, going to check the garden door first. Yes, locked. And that door had an old-fashioned deadlock which meant that without the key you could not open it from within. That left the front door. Fael summoned her strength again and after what felt like a lifetime, managed to reach the front of the hall. The door was a massive late-Victorian affair with complicated coloured glass in a fanlight, and interlacings of thin metal wires so that enterprising burglars could not break the glass and get in.

She stared at the shiny brass door knob. This was a bad moment, because if this door was locked— She shook her head impatiently and reached for the knob. It resisted at once, and Fael's heart sank. Locked. In fact double-locked; the knob would not turn at all, which meant that whoever had locked it from outside had engaged the extra spin of the key which was meant to be yet another precaution against burglars. That extra turn of the key meant the door could not be opened from the inside, and it was the last turn of the screw as well. It was the final straw. But it was no good standing here like a wimpish Victorian heroine wringing her hands; her father had locked her in. The bastard had actually taken away her chair and stolen her keys and locked her in.

Tod had never intended her to be present at *Cauldron*'s first night, and he had intended all along to grab the acclaim for himself. Unless Fael could think of a way of getting to the Harlequin he was going to get away with it as well.

She returned to the hall chair to review the situation. She could ring the taxi company, who would certainly come out, but short of breaking a window she could not get out of the house. The anti-theft precautions were working both ways. The taxidrivers at the company all knew her, and they were always cheerful and friendly about helping her into the car and about folding the chair away, and then unfolding it at the other end, wherever the other end happened to be. But she thought she could not expect a taximan to help her to break a window and climb out. She probably could not climb out anyway.

She looked back at the phone. Was there anyone she could ring? The names of various people came to mind, and most of them would help but none of them had a key and all of them would take at least half an hour to get here. Also, a number of them were theatre people and working, and would therefore be unreachable at this hour. Fael glanced at her watch. Five past seven. She cursed her father all over again.

The obvious thing was to ring Tod at the theatre, but Fael

dismissed this idea almost at once. There was just under half an hour to curtain up and whoever answered the phone would probably be unable to reach Tod. And even if he was reached he would simply refuse to speak to her, and even if he did not, he would never in a million years come all the way out to Pimlico now. He would not send anyone out with the key either, because that would mean admitting what he had done.

But unless she could somehow get to the Harlequin before the final curtain, she would have broken her promise to *Scathach*. Fael sat very still. The central heating was humming through the pipes and the hall radiator was warm, but she suddenly felt as if she had been plunged neck-deep into black, icy water.

The thought of facing *Scathach*'s anger was very frightening indeed.

Tod was feeling very pleased with himself. Nowhere in the world was there any thrill to equal the thrill of a first night, and when it was your own first night – when you were at the centre and at the humming, spinning heart – ah yes, that was the greatest thrill of all. He had come home. He was in his rightful place once more.

Act One had gone splendidly. It had been brilliant, and there was no other word for it. The *Fianna* had erupted onto the stage, recognisable as the half-legendary, half-historical royal armies they were, but now and again showing glimpses of their modern-day counterparts: paratroopers or SAS men or the allied troops in Bosnia. Flynn Deverill had been very clever and very subtle over the costumes and the settings; Tod would give credit where it was due. Of course, Deverill had only worked to the directions that he, Tod, had given.

And the first appearance of the *sidh*-creatures had almost brought the house down. The *sidh*'s first foray into the world of humans, and their raunchy gangbang of the comic lodge-keeper's wife, had erupted across the stage in an explosion of burlesque hilarity. The audience, until now still in a mood to suspend judgement, had been instantly won; they rocked with helpless laughter, and people in the stalls cheered and catcalled as half a dozen of the *sidh* chased the lodge-keeper's wife around the stage, and then half a dozen more tumbled her onto the ground, leaping on and off her, until she was shrieking with glee.

It was a remarkable scene: Tod thought it might very easily have been over-explicit and possibly even embarrassing or offensive, but somehow it was not any of these things. It was not suggestive like sleazy men touting for porno sex clubs or offering dirty postcards; it was bawdy in the way that the Elizabethans had been bawdy, and it was very funny indeed. The eight girls and eight men playing the *sidh* were extremely good, which helped. They all wore sinuous blue-green costumes, with sometimes-clinging, sometimes-floating draperies, that deceived you into thinking they were transparent, and that were spattered here and there with shining fishtail iridescence. Tod had jibbed a bit at the high fees for the *sidh*'s choreographer, but he hoped he was large-minded enough to admit that he had been wrong, because it looked as if it had been worth the money.

The lodge-keeper had given a terrific performance as well; wringing his hands and wailing to the gods to rout the mischievous *sidh*-creatures or at least render the evil little creatures impotent, because his wife would never after this be satisfied with what he could give her. The mournful lodge-keeper's song – '*I'm only a once-a-week man*' – had been cheered, and when the wife had joined with the sly rollicking counterpart – '*He's a weak man once a week*' – which was their duet, several people had shouted 'Encore!' Tod had been quite annoyed that Morrie Camperdown had ignored that; he would have to have a word with him.

Tod was saddened to think that Fael was missing all this, but of course the risk had been too great. It had hurt him to carry the wheelchair out to the greenhouse and hide it behind an ancient mower while Fael was in the bath; it had actually given him a physical pain in his stomach to do it, so that he had had to pour a large brandy afterwards. It had hurt, as well, to steal her keys and secure all the doorlocks, and then sneak away from the house before she realised. Tod had felt quite ill all the way to the theatre. But there had really been no other course open to him. Fael was quite capable of making a public scene at the final curtain, in fact she was quite capable of enjoying it.

Tod still shuddered when he remembered the very narrow escape he had had just before the *Dwarf Spinner*, when Fael's mother had lost her temper and made several very melodramatic threats. It was only her death that had saved him from a distressing and embarrassingly public scene – an unpleasant business that whole episode had been, but he had done what had to be done. He could not have risked Aine in the theatre that night, and he could not risk Aine's daughter in the theatre tonight, either.

He went happily down to the hospitality suite where the press would be waiting to congratulate him on a cracking first act. Life was very good.

Gilly and Danilo hugged one another just before the second act curtain and agreed that things were looking good. People had come round to tell them how terrifically well it was all going – Sir Julius Sherry had been the first, which they had thought very nice of him; he had hugged Gilly a bit closer and a bit longer than was perhaps strictly necessary, the old goat, but she had not really minded. Stephen had been next, saying quietly that he thought they were in for a long run, and to remember about keeping up the pace, and then Mr Camperdown, still awash with indigestion tablets and milk of magnesia, poor Campers, saying he hoped everyone had understood about not taking up the call for an encore, but they would all know that it was something which was absolutely never done so early on a first night. Gilly had not known this at all, and she was glad she had not said anything that would have shown her inexperience, which could easily have happened. She remembered her fears about being unmasked as an impostor, and sobered up a bit. There were still three acts to go.

Flynn Deverill had wandered into most of the dressing rooms, a glass of whisky in his hand, his grey eyes liquid with delight (and probably also with whisky). He was indecently good-looking when he smiled. He was indecently good-looking when he was scowling as well, of course. He said hadn't they the greatest hit ever, and weren't they all making their fortunes, and they would be celebrating all night. One of the *sidh* girls told Gilly that bets were already being laid in the *sidh* dressing room on who Flynn would go to bed with tonight, because the story was that he always had at least one female on a first night and often two, and not necessarily separately either. In fact, they were thinking of putting numbers in a hat and drawing for it, said the *sidh*, who appeared to have been dipping into the whisky herself.

Even poor little Makepiece had come round to the dressing rooms, dabbing his eyes and spicing the air with brandy, but saying how happy he was for them all, and how thrilled Mia would have been – oh dear, they were please to forgive him, he was just a silly old fool. Gilly had not known quite how to respond to this so she had given him a hug.

As the audience settled down for the second act and the front-of-house staff drew the thick curtains over the exits, a dark-clad figure, wearing a deep-brimmed slouch hat hiding its face, slipped through into the back of the dress circle and stood unnoticed, watching the stage.

Fael thought they must be just about starting the second act. Damn! This was where the tension really started to build: it was where the *Fianna* captain set off on the quest for the cauldron that would save his starving people, and where Aillen first caught sight of Mab and vowed to spin an enchantment around her and carry her off to his eerie under-sea world. She remembered how strongly she had identified with the half-spellbound Mab, and how she had tried to put across the feeling of being imprisoned.

Because I've been imprisoned by a wheelchair for over a year myself, or because I was half-spellbound by a mysterious stranger when I wrote that? There was no point in following such a profitless line of thought.

It was half-past eight. If she could get out of the house, she could be at the theatre before the third act started. She reviewed all the possible exits yet again, this time feeling less exhausted and irresolute because of her earlier exertions. Most of the windows were double-glazed because of keeping out noise and keeping in heat, but the garden door – the door that *Scathach* always used – was a long, single pane of glass. Could she smash it and push out sufficient glass to climb through? Could she even climb through? And if she could, what then? Be blowed to asking pointless questions, thought Fael, angrily; if I think I really can get out, I'll phone for a cab and get it to meet me by the front gate.

She was no longer sure whether her churning anger was against Tod, or whether it was simply against being cheated out of seeing her creation brought to life. She had a swift, vivid image of her father walking onto the lit stage and holding out his hands to a theatre awash with cheers and applause, and of herself shouting, 'Impostor!' from the back of the hall. What would happen if she did that? Would a sudden hush fall and every head turn to her? Or would her voice simply go unnoticed? Maybe – this was a nasty thought – maybe a couple of the front-of-house people would even come quietly in and escort her out.

Whichever way you looked at it, it was a daunting vision, in fact it was absolutely terrifying. I don't know if I can do it, thought Fael, aghast. I really don't think I can. But I'm blowed if I'm going to sit here with my hands folded and do nothing. I will break the glass in that wretched door and I'll see if I can crawl through. I'll take the cordless phone with me and then I can call the taxi firm there and then. She grasped her walking stick again, and levered herself upright. Her thigh muscles screamed in protest, and Fael gasped aloud at the sudden cramping pain. But it had to be coped with, and she took a deep, shuddering breath and began to inch painfully back through the house towards the garden door.

She had no idea how she would get from the taxi into the Harlequin or how she would get up the theatre steps without help. But she would worry about that if she got there. The first thing to do was get out of the house.

Christian had gone out of the dress circle shortly before the end of the second act, using the exit stair that came out into Burbage Lane. He would have liked to hear the audience's reactions to the 'Lodestone Song', but it was too near to the end of the act and he dared not risk being here when the house lights went up.

The first interval had been relatively short, and he had simply concealed himself in the exit, crouching halfway down the stair. If anyone came out early he could whisk down the steps and be lost in the teeming streets within minutes.

But this was the main interval; people would be collecting the drinks they had ordered before the curtain went up, and the press would probably be invited to drinks with Tod Miller and the management. People would be milling all over the place. He went swiftly around the side of the building and in again through the old door. There was an odd sense of homecoming, as if whatever ghosts lurked here knew him and welcomed him. He passed by the brick opening, and the difficult smile twisted his mouth.

It was then that he became aware of sounds overhead. Footsteps were approaching – someone was coming quickly and lightly along one of the old corridors. Someone was pushing open the disused door and pausing at the head of the steps. Christian froze, his heart pounding with panic and anger. Someone entering my domain!

He pressed back against the wall, melting into the shadows, knowing he could not be seen from above. A faint spill of light came from the half-open door, and silhouetted in the light was the figure of a youngish man with black hair tumbling over his brow. Flynn Deverill. Hatred scalded through Christian afresh. Flynn was looking for him! He was stalking him as if Christian was vermin and Flynn the hunter! And if he found him, he would drag him into the light and denounce him, and everyone would know him for who he was, and everyone would see him for what he was— And Fael, who was probably in a prime seat in the stalls, would see as well . . .

It was not to be borne. The gloved hands curled into talons, and as Flynn placed a foot on the topmost step Christian began to move out of the concealing shadows. He would let Flynn reach the bottom stair and then he would be on him. Flynn was taller and stronger, but Christian would have the advantage of surprise. He would have the advantage of this surging hatred as well. He felt larger than life, as strong as a lion. He could overpower Flynn and he would kill him. Deep within his mind, a tiny voice said, between you, you and Rossani could kill him with ease. Oh Flynn, thought

141

Christian, this is my domain, and you should never have come walking down here . . .

O never go walking at Samhain at dusk
In company of one whom you know not to trust;
Rossani's aprowl and he's looking for fools;
He'll cut out your heart and he'll weave it to gold.

You've come walking at dusk, Flynn, thought Christian, starting to creep towards the stairs. You've come walking and you're about to meet the one you never must trust . . .

His shadow was going ahead of him, grotesque and slightly hunched over, the cloak swirling about his ankles. His breath was coming faster, and he was aware of the beginning of sexual arousal as well. I get my kicks above the waist . . . No, that's Rossani.

Come nearer, Flynn, because I should like to curl my fingers round your unspoiled throat, and I should like to claw out your eyes with my nails, and tear the flesh of your handsome face into bloody tatters . . .

Flynn began to walk along the brick tunnel.

Chapter Thirteen

Flynn had managed to search a good part of the theatre without anyone realising what he was doing, but there was no sign of the dark-clad figure.

Damn, thought Flynn, angrily, I know he's here! He eluded me last time, and he's eluding me tonight. But he's here – I can feel that he's here. And I want to know who he is and what he is, and what he's up to.

Flynn had been into each of the dressing rooms at the first interval under the pretext of congratulating the company – although he would have done that anyway – and he had wandered through the two Green Rooms, and the three bars. Nowhere was there anyone who appeared in the least suspicious. He had also looked into the hospitality suite, where Tod Miller was holding court to the press. Toddy was well away; he was waving his arms and getting red in the face with excitement and brandy, and if he was not careful he would irritate the critics into giving the show dubious reviews.

Flynn paused in the door of the long, carpeted room, half of him wanting to go in and counter whatever rubbish Miller was feeding the press, the other half mischievously wanting to leave Toddy to hoist himself with his own petard. But Julius and Morrie Camperdown would probably smooth things over at the second interval, and in any case *Cauldron* was good enough to stand or fall by its own brilliance. And of course it will stand, thought Flynn. It's a brilliant show; it's far too brilliant for Tod Miller to have had a hand in. The memory of the cloaked figure who had stood watching the stage brushed his mind again. If there really had been a collaborator wouldn't he have watched with just that hungry concentration? But why the secrecy? Why would anyone need to keep quiet about having created such a marvellous thing? If I had written *Cauldron* and composed that magical music, thought Flynn, I'd want to shout it from the rooftops. Why would stealth be necessary? Half-jumbled, half-serious ideas of Tod Miller having some poor, wretched composer or writer in his power darted across Flynn's mind, only to be impatiently dismissed.

He retraced his steps, going towards the seldom-used stairway that led into the old part of the theatre. There were a couple of rather dismal corridors, a little below street level; they echoed with his footsteps, and then there was a door giving onto a narrow flight of stone steps. At the foot of the steps was a brick tunnel, more or less shut off now. It was taking the thing to the extreme end of absurdity to search down here – if the figure he had seen was in the theatre at all, it would be upstairs, hiding out in one of the lurking backstage holes, or mingling unnoticed with the audience. But he might as well look.

Very few people knew this sub-basement tunnel existed; Flynn only knew because James Roscius had loved the Harlequin and its history, and during his spells in London he had taught his protégé to love it as well. He had brought Flynn down here, and Flynn had never forgotten it, because he had never forgotten the professor's glowing enthusiasm as he conjured up the theatre's past, showing Flynn where the tiring rooms had been and the bricked-up stage door, and the ghost-outline of the old entrance to the original platform-stage with the cellar beneath.

Wonderful, Roscius had said, his eyes going over the dim, dusty walls. The Harlequin had suffered a bit from settlement, he added, but all old buildings suffered from that. It only meant that the foundations had slipped, leaving the structure that Scaramel Smith had known below street level. But this was the heart of the theatre, said Roscius, his eyes faraway, his voice with the faint Irish lilt taking on the hypnotic once-upon-a-time story-teller's rhythm. If Scaramel walked anywhere, she would walk here: in this vaguely eerie, subterranean place that was filled with resonances and echoes. There were tales told of cloaked ladies with Restoration hairstyles and panniers being seen down here, and of bewigged gentlemen with satin breeches. Occasionally snatches of unknown songs and music were heard.

It was probably all imagination; these stories drifted through the fabric and the folklore of most old buildings. Look at Drury Lane with its famous eighteenth-century gentleman ghost. It would be nice to think that the Harlequin had a ghost or two of its own, said Roscius, wistfully.

Flynn had never decided whether he believed in the Harlequin's ghosts, but he was sufficiently Irish to not quite disbelieve. He approached the door to the tunnel. It would almost certainly be locked because this part of the building was deemed unsafe, and it would be quite dark as well, because there was no electricity down here, and no gaslight, even. I'm descending into the candlelit world of Scaramel and her glittering ragtail company, thought Flynn. There'll be nothing to find, except maybe a tramp, or a few ghosts. I don't think I mind ghosts, although I'm not sure about tramps. But now I'm down here I may as well go on.

The door was not locked. Flynn pushed it open and looked down at the steps, hesitating. He could just hear Aillen mac Midha's 'Lodestone Song' beginning and Danilo's voice soaring through the theatre, spinning its enchantment around Mab. This was momentarily disconcerting, until Flynn realised that he must be almost on a level with the old stage void.

He descended the stairs slowly, waiting for his eyes to adjust to the dimness. It was not so very dark here after all; there was a spill of light from above. Flynn thought he would just look along the tunnel and then go back upstairs. He reached the foot of the stair and stood for a moment, scanning the shadows. Nothing. It looked as if it had been a waste of time, after all. He might as well go back upstairs – the dress-circle bar was serving a very good malt whisky.

He had half turned back when a dark figure bounded out of the shadows and knocked him to the ground. Flynn swore, and hit out at once, feeling his fist connect with bone and flesh. His attacker flinched and there was a swirl of dark silk. Flynn, half-dazed but recovering, thought, the cloaked figure! I've got him! Triumph surged up and he lunged forward, and Christian, caught off-balance, fell backwards. Flynn launched himself forward, and the two men crashed to the ground, struggling against one another and locked in a grim embrace. The cloaked figure was much smaller and much thinner than Flynn had thought, and there was a frailty about it. Flynn pushed away the sudden disconcerting thought that he was maltreating something small and vulnerable.

And then gloved hands reached for Flynn's throat, and steely fingers tightened about his windpipe. The impression of frailty vanished at once. Crimson stars wheeled across Flynn's vision and a huge suffocating weight pressed down on his lungs. He was forced onto his back, and as he fought wildly to dislodge the iron grip, his attacker half-knelt over him, tightening his hands around Flynn's neck. Flynn could hear the other man's harsh, ragged breathing, and he could sense the excitement coursing through him. The pressure on his throat increased unbearably, and Flynn, his lungs bursting, his mind spinning into suffocating unconsciousness, brought his knee sharply up in a last desperate attempt to escape. It slammed into his assailant's groin, and there was a muffled grunt of surprise and pain. The stranglehold slackened at once, and Flynn, gasping for air but blessedly able to breathe again, struck out with both hands. His aim was almost random and his left hand flailed uselessly through the air, but his right hand, better co-ordinated, smacked against the black silken mask, touching flesh and bone beneath.

The instant Flynn's hands touched his face, the man recoiled like a scalded animal, releasing Flynn properly, and throwing up his hands in the instinctive protective gesture Flynn remembered. He felt a surge of triumph – Got you, you bastard! And although he was still breathing as if he had run a mile at speed, and his throat felt as if it had been scraped raw with sandpaper, he dived forward, reaching for the mask.

The man flinched, but Flynn snatched at his face, and felt the silk tear free. The figure stumbled back, pawing at the air with a dreadful defensiveness, covering its face with both arms and cringing into the shadows. Flynn went after him, grabbing him by both arms, forcing him to turn around so that they were face to face. He thought he started to say, 'I'll know who you are, you bastard, if I have to beat your name out of you—'

The words died in his throat. He stared down at the dreadful, incomplete face that had been so well hidden by the mask, and that was now so mercilessly exposed, even in the dark, and his mind spun with disbelief and horror.

There was a moment when they held one another's stare, sharing the appalling knowledge, and Flynn felt painful compassion scald through him. He drew breath to speak, although he had no idea what he was going to say. He had no idea what anyone could have said in such a situation.

And then Christian ducked his head away with the pitiful, defensive gesture again, and pushing Flynn back against the wall, snatched the mask out of his nerveless hands, and fled into the shadows.

'Well, I don't know what you expect me to do about it,' said Tod, irritably, thinking it was exactly like Flynn to cause problems when everyone ought to be looking forward to celebrating a wonderful success. They were all going on to Marivaux's later, and Tod would be wearing his new dinner jacket because a person of his standing could not be seen at Marivaux's looking shabby. He had been looking forward to wearing the new jacket and to receiving the congratulations, and to waiting for the papers to appear, and it was too bad of Flynn to spoil it all.

He said, 'Even if there was an intruder down there, I don't see that we need to involve the police. I daresay it was no more than a tramp. Some poor creature looking for a place to sleep.'

Some poor creature with a face so unbelievable that it flinches from the light, and hits out like a trapped cur at anyone who tries to unmask it . . . Hell and the devil! thought Flynn, angrily, I don't want to feel pity for the thing. It nearly bloody throttled me!

But when Tod said, 'Did you recognise him?' he said at once, 'I did not. It certainly wasn't anyone I knew.'

'Well, could you give a description to the police?'

Could I give a description . . . *Deform'd, unfinish'd, sent before my time/Into this breathing world scarce half made up* . . . The words of Shakespeare's tormented, warped Richard formed in Flynn's mind and he scowled and said, 'Not a description that would be of any use. But we could have the theatre properly searched after the show.'

147

'Why? Why should we do that?' Tod did not want the police crawling all over the place again, poking into corners and upsetting everyone. There was the question of it all being leaked to the papers as well, because these things always did get leaked. And then before they knew it, people would be muttering about runs of bad luck and old curses waking, and the next thing would be everyone saying that *Cauldron* was doomed and the Harlequin was an unlucky house. And the box office receipts would plummet. Tod felt quite ill at the thought. He felt positively sick when he remembered the bank's chilly attitude and the second mortgage, to say nothing of phrases like 'lien on the receipts', and even 'repossession of the house'. So he said, very sharply, 'The intruder isn't still down there, is he?'

'I don't think so. I think he got out, although I don't know where he went; I wasn't in a mood to be taking notes.'

'Well, did you find anything else down there?'

'Nothing much. Charles II's Letters Patent to Drury Lane – the original, of course, which means the one the present incumbents keep in the vaults is a fake. I expect Killigrew mortgaged it or Scum Goodman auctioned it, or somebody seduced it out of Garrick. Oh, and there was the mouldering body of an actor-manager down there as well, and a couple of mummified money-lenders, still waiting for their pound of flesh.'

'Oh, stop it,' said Tod, crossly, because the reference to money-lenders had flicked him on the raw. 'I mean anything that would provide a clue to the intruder.'

'Only a cobweb-draped corpse, clutching a Shakespearean first folio in its fleshless fingers—'

'For heaven's sake—'

'At the very least won't you alert the security firm for later on?' said Flynn, angrily. 'Remember Mia Makepiece?'

'Oh, blow Mia Makepiece,' said Tod, who was so pleased with the little red-haired understudy he had almost convinced himself he had planned the entire thing deliberately. 'She went off with a man,' he said. 'Anyone knows that.'

'I don't know it. Makepiece doesn't know it.' Flynn studied Miller through narrowed eyes. 'What about it, Toddy? Will I ask Stephen to phone the security firm?'

'Oh well, I suppose so. All right then. I daresay Stephen would do it. *I* haven't time,' said Tod, grandly. 'I've got far too much to do. The supper party at Marivaux's for one thing – I suppose you're coming to that, are you? Yes, I thought you would. Well, make sure you brush down your evening suit beforehand. You look as if you've been rolling about in the dust.'

'I have been rolling about in the dust,' said Flynn. 'I've just told you so.'

'And then there's my daughter arriving at any minute – I could have done without that, I don't mind admitting, but there's some garbled story about her having trouble getting out of the house and missing the first two acts – I don't know why, and of course the office never gets any message right. It's all very annoying.'

It had been extremely annoying to be sought out by some officious female, with a message that Fael would be arriving at the front entrance in about fifteen minutes, and could some arrangements be made to meet her, please? There were any number of people who could have met Fael's taxi and helped her into the theatre, but Tod did not dare risk letting anyone else do it. He could not trust Fael not to make some ridiculous public accusation, which would upset the entire applecart and even mean that Tod might have to rewrite his author's speech for the curtain-fall. So he was going to meet Fael himself, and he was going to whisk her into a vacant box after the third act curtain had gone up, and he would jolly well see to it that she did not get the chance to spill any embarrassing beans!

And so he said loftily that what with one thing and what with another, he really had no time to be worrying about stray down-and-outs; Flynn had his permission to do whatever he thought best, providing the police were not called in. And now if Flynn would excuse him, there was still a roomful of journalists upstairs and they would think it very odd indeed if no one from the company was present.

Flynn said, with malicious pleasure, 'I'll go and talk to your journalists, Toddy.'

'No, you will not,' said Tod, crossly, and banged out of his office to discover how Fael had got out of the house and down to the theatre.

Fael thought she had managed pretty well. She had smashed the large pane of glass out of the garden door using a small hammer, and then she had wrapped a thick towel around her hand and knocked the splinters through, dropping the towel over them. She was pretty sure she could half-crawl, half-drag herself through without too much difficulty. The door would have to stay like this until tomorrow when a glazier would have to be called out, but she could prop a board over the hole to keep out the cold. A board would not keep a burglar out, of course, but Fael was not in a mood to care if the entire underworld broke in and loaded up a pantechnicon. She was a little horrified to discover how angry she still was with Tod, but only a very little.

She went back into her own room, discarded the sweat-soaked silk shirt, donned a clean one, sloshed on some *Ma Griffe*, and phoned the taxi firm and the theatre. She was quite brief with the Harlequin, explaining that she had encountered a problem, but her father was expecting her, and please could they get a message to him to meet her in fifteen minutes' time? The theatre staff were helpful and friendly. Certainly they would get a message to Mr Miller, they said. No, it was no trouble at all. And they would have a wheelchair ready as well; they always had one or two to help people who fainted or sprained their ankles on the stairs. Fael had forgotten how committed theatres and concert halls were to the disabled these days, and she thought it was nice of whoever was on the other end of the phone not to actually use the word disabled. It was not particularly nice to have to rely on wheelchairs and other people, but at least she would get to see some of the performance.

It was annoying to find that it was Tod himself who came down the steps, and pushed the small chair through the foyer and up a steep ramp. He said, shortly, that there were no seats left – or none that Fael could get to without making a disturbance – and so he was taking her up to one of the boxes. They could use the small maintenance lift, and could get her settled before the third act curtain went up, he said. He was off-hand and over-grand, which meant he was feeling guilty. Fael considered this as they went up the ramp and then into the small rattletrap lift, and saw that there would be no point in forcing a show-down now; her father would simply walk away. She would wait until they could be face to face.

The Harlequin had only eight boxes, and they were all rather small, but they were pretty plush. The one that Tod trundled Fael into had six velvet-covered seats, three at the front and three behind, and there was a thick curtain across the back. It was not as private as it had probably been when there would have been a wall and a door to the outer foyer, but the heavy curtain would shut out quite a lot of things and it was quite private.

Tod said, 'I suppose you'll be all right here, will you?' It was not really a question: he was avoiding her eyes and backing away, glancing anxiously at his watch. Fael said, 'Perfectly all right, thank you,' and then, just as he was turning away, said, 'By the way, you'd better let me have my keys to get back in to the house later.' And saw the hot flush stain his neck. The bastard!

Tod made a little show of searching his pockets, saying, rather elaborately, that he was hopelessly impractical, always losing keys and not understanding how locks worked. Fael said, 'Or wheelchairs either?' at which Tod found the key at once and handed it over.

'Thank you. I'd better take it, hadn't I?' said Fael. 'We might arrive home separately.'

Tod threw out his chest a bit and said that was very probable indeed, because there were any number of things he might become involved in later on. In fact it might be better not to expect him home too early. Presumably he could safely leave her to find her own way home? he added.

'Oh yes,' said Fael, cheerfully. 'Especially now I've got my key back,' and Tod went thankfully off.

It was like her father to tuck her away somewhere where she could not cause trouble, but she would think how to deal with Tod later. For now it was enough – oh God, yes, it was more than enough! – to simply be here, to feel the marvellous warmth of the old theatre ebbing and flowing all about her, and to know what was ahead. I've missed a good half, thought Fael. But I refuse to feel cheated or disappointed; I'll just make jolly sure to come back tomorrow night and see it all. And anyway, there are still two acts to come.

She manoeuvred the chair to the front and slid carefully onto one of the velvet-covered seats. This instantly made her feel stronger and more confident. She was sitting in an ordinary seat like an ordinary person, and she could lean over the ledge and look down on the stalls and across to the upper and dress circles. If people looked up they would only see somebody seated normally in a box. Fael wished she had not had to discard the cream silk shirt, but she was wearing a pale green one which was nearly as good, and she had kept the jade ear-rings on.

The interval bell had not sounded yet and the house lights were still up. But quite a lot of people were in their seats, and Fael could see them, studying their programmes, leaning forward to talk to one another. A warm buzz of conversation and of pleased anticipation lay on the air, and Fael experienced a sudden feeling of immense well-being. Because I managed to get here against all the odds? Because I've routed my father's petty little plot? Or because I can feel that everyone's enjoying *Cauldron*? Yes, of course it's that. This is all mine, thought Fael, with sudden delight; I've caused all this. And with the thought came a stir of fear and a little breath of coldness, as if someone had brushed icy fingers across the back of her neck. I didn't create quite all of it. I had help; I had a collaborator, a dark satanic familiar.

Despite the theatre's warmth she shivered. He's here, of course – *Scathach*. Is he? Yes, of course he is, you fool, he's somewhere in the theatre; watching and waiting.

So strong was the feeling of *Scathach*'s presence, that the soft footfall beyond the box's curtain sent her heart leaping up into her throat, and she half twisted round, expecting to see the cloaked and masked silhouette framed against the fall of dark blue velvet. And if it is him, if he really is here, I'll have to do whatever he tells me, thought Fael, wildly. Even if he tells me to stand up at the end and denounce my father to the entire theatre, I think I'll have to do it. I won't be able to help it. That's the curtain at the back being pulled aside now. He's here, he's in the box with me . . .

Her heart was knocking against her ribs, and she saw with annoyance that she was clasping her hands so tightly together in her lap that the knuckles had turned white. But when she did turn completely round she saw that it was not him at all. It was a young man, five or six years older than she was, wearing extremely well-cut evening clothes which did nothing to conceal a distinct air of raffishness, and the kind of slender whipcord strength that suggested he might be a good person to have on your side in a fight. He had untidy black hair and the most startling good looks Fael had ever seen, and he was regarding her with unashamed interest.

'Fael Miller,' said this unexpected young man. 'Isn't it? I'm Flynn Deverill. I was there when your father had the message about you arriving, and since I'm the only person with nothing to do just now I thought I'd come up to see if you wanted any company.'

Fael said, 'That's nice of you. We spoke on the phone, didn't we?'

'We did.' He came into the box. 'If you'd rather be on your own say so and I'll vanish.' He appeared to look round the box as if he might be searching for something. 'You don't look like your voice, by the way,' he said, absently.

'Neither do you.'

'No, it's one of my greatest assets, although my voice is a bit husky just now on account of a little difference of opinion with an intruder.'

'What are you looking for?'

'Oh, the theatre ghost, or the theatre cat, whichever I can find.'

'Or the intruder you encountered earlier?'

He glanced back at her as if to say: One up to you. But he only said, 'The intruder's long since gone. But ghosts have this unpleasant habit of stealing into places where people are alone and unprotected.' He looked about the box thoughtfully, and then glanced back at Fael. 'I don't think there are any ghosts up here,' he said, and grinned suddenly. Fael blinked. 'I've brought you a drink,' said Flynn, holding up a bottle of wine and two glasses. 'This is a great show, you know. And it had a brilliant designer.'

'You,' said Fael.

'Me,' said Flynn. Again the grin. 'D'you know, a man could get drunk on this show without touching a drop of wine,' he said. 'But we could drink the wine anyway. We'll dispel the ghosts and the chill—'

'And the intruder.'

'And the intruder,' agreed Flynn. 'And we'll pile the logs upon the fire and pour with generous hand the old wine from the Sabine jar—'

'You sound as if you've already poured several Sabine jars fairly freely.'

'I have,' said Flynn at once. 'It's wine that has played the infidel and robbed me of my robe of honour— Not that I ever had much honour to begin with, you understand, and I never knew what robes had to do with it. And although this isn't strictly speaking a Sabine jar, it's a pretty good claret. Will I pour you a glass and put it here for you?'

'Yes. Thank you.' The wine was already uncorked. 'What would you have done if I'd refused?' demanded Fael.

'Drunk it all myself, what do you think? And you don't mean "thank you", do you? You mean, "sod off, I can pour my own wine." '

'I wouldn't have been quite so direct,' said Fael, watching him fill the two wine glasses. 'But the sentiment's the same.'

'You hate being dependent.'

'Yes. How did you know?'

'I'd hate it as well. Is it permanent? That wheelchair?'

'You do go straight to the point, don't you? No, it isn't permanent. Only a rather long gluing-together process. Oh, you're right about the wine, it's very good.'

'Of course it's good, I chose it myself,' said Flynn. 'If we'd relied on your father we'd both have been as sick as cats after one mouthful. There's no need to glare at me; he's your father, you should know how mean he is.'

Tod was as mean as a waggonload of misers, but Fael was not going to admit it to a stranger. She said, coldly, 'Do you think you ought to talk about your employer like that?'

'Oh, everyone knows what Toddy is.' He topped up his own glass, and set the wine bottle on the floor near her chair. 'That's the second bell. I'll leave you to enjoy what's left of the show,' he said. 'You'd rather watch it on your own, wouldn't you?'

'How did you know?'

'You have a look,' said Flynn, studying her. 'And it's a look of mental hunger. As if you want to concentrate very intensely indeed.'

'Well I do, rather.'

'Yes,' said Flynn, thoughtfully. 'I thought so. I've seen that look once or twice before.' He frowned, and Fael thought he was about to say something that was neither flippant nor vaguely insulting. But when he did speak he only said, 'Will I see you at Marivaux's later on?'

'I don't think—'

'For once my motives are pure,' said Flynn. 'I'm thinking of the ghosts and the intruders.'

'Knight errantry, in fact.'

'Yes. If I was going to seduce you, I wouldn't be so devious. Well?'

Fael took a quick sartorial inventory. Green velvet trousers and waistcoat, black Gucci boots – yes, good enough. She said, 'All right. Marivaux's it is.'

Flynn made a mock salute and vanished through the rear curtain, and Fael turned to the stage.

The curtain was going up on the magical twilight world of the *sidh* and there was a spontaneous burst of applause at this the first sight of Aillen mac Midha's eerie domain. Fael caught her breath at the soaring rock formations that might simply have been coral reefs, but that could as easily be shimmering palaces, drowned in ancient enchantments. There were silvery swathes of cobweb-fine mesh that might have been nets to catch fish, or even nets to snare human souls. Or, look again, and they might be fifteenth-century chain mail, or even the computerised circuit boards studded with silver pin-points that you saw inside a television when it went wrong. But the entire stage was bathed in a rippling twilight, so that you could not be entirely sure what was intended and what was only hinted, and what was in your own mind. Clever, thought Fael, delighted. Oh God yes, Flynn Deverill, you're clever!

The triumphant, sumptuously sexual music that Fael had visualised and *Scathach* had created poured into the auditorium, and Aillen mac Midha entered, arrogant and imperious and sizzlingly charismatic. He was followed by the *sidh*, in joyful procession, carrying aloft the captive Mab. Fael registered that Mab was small and thin with a pointed face like a cat's and wide-apart eyes. She's not quite what I visualised, thought Fael, studying Gilly critically. But if she can belt out the music she's near enough.

And she's almost lost, thought Fael, her eyes on the stage. He's lured her away from her own world, and he's about to possess her – he'll do it now, in front of the audience. And once he's done that she'll be his, body and soul and blood and bone.

As the exultant march soared up to its jubilant zenith, Aillen began to walk slowly towards Mab, casting aside the iridescent cloak as he did so, and unbuckling the immense silver belt. His eyes – huge, inhuman eyes, black and opaque and very nearly insectile – never left her. Good, thought Fael, leaning forward and resting her chin absorbedly in her cupped hands. Oh yes, very good. Slow and measured and exciting beyond words. That's a clever piece of casting – he's giving off a sexuality that's neither quite male nor female. There's a link between them as well, it's unmistakable. I wonder are they lovers in real life?

As the *sidh* prince stood over the mesmerised Mab, a shiver of delighted anticipation went through the theatre, and Fael felt herself tumbling at last into the world she and *Scathach* had created.

The world she had never, until tonight, seen.

Chapter Fourteen

Tod had not stayed to watch the seduction scene between Aillen and Mab, because it made him feel a bit uncomfortable. So much naked lust – there was no other word for it! – and so much raw emotion flashing across the stage. He had thrashed the matter of this scene out with Stephen Sherry, saying that they should take a responsible attitude: they did not want to find themselves labelled voyeurs by the tabloids, or *Cauldron* dubbed 'pornographic' by the tourists; they did not want to find that the Harlequin had become the butt of nasty sniggers and elbow-diggings by furtive-eyed men, and the subject of shrieking amusement by giggling females.

Stephen, rather unexpectedly, had disagreed; in fact he had argued quite vehemently against diluting the scene. He said it was a powerful and very moving part of the story; it was beautiful and evocative and although it would certainly lift a few eyebrows, it was not in the least bit offensive. They had planned it carefully and with great tact, he said, and it did not come within a million light years of being pornographic or snigger-worthy.

'And surely,' Stephen had said, studying Tod rather curiously, 'you of all people wouldn't want to cut any of *Cauldron*, Toddy?' and Tod had remembered just in time that if he really had written *Cauldron* he would not have borne to have a single syllable altered.

But still, watching Danilo slowly take off his cloak and unbuckle the huge silver belt made him feel hot under the collar, and when Danilo parted Mab's robes and slid between her legs, he felt downright uncomfortable. The music did not help either: pounding swelling music it was – you might very nearly say the music was indecent on its own. Tod did say it, although not out

157

loud, and it occurred to him to think that a parent never really knew his own child. Imagine Fael conjuring up all this!

And to top it all, Flynn Deverill must needs create a throbbing, beating light-effect, a kind of strobe disco-lighting that pulsated and shivered all around the stage, until it exploded in what was quite obviously intended to depict a sexual climax.

Tod could not cope with watching folk have sexual climaxes (all right, *simulated* sexual climaxes!) on stage in front of several hundred people, and he shut himself away in his office and poured a very large brandy and soda. He was joined for a while by little Gerald Makepiece, who could not cope with watching this scene either – who in fact could not really cope with watching any of the show at all and was only here because it was less lonely than his hotel, and also it would look bad to stay away on the first night.

Tod poured Gerald a nip of brandy – just a nip, because the little man had already had more than was good for him, and lso it was Tod's private supply and he was not handing it out to all and sundry. Gerald said, disconsolately, that he was pleased that things were going so well, blew his nose and mopped his eyes, and thought that Mia would have been so happy at the show's success. Of course, she had not really cared for one or two of the scenes, said Gerald; the *close* scene with Aillen mac Midha had been particularly difficult for her. But that was not to say that the scene was not well written, said Gerald, suddenly remembering his company; it was a beautiful scene. Tod, who thought the scene was anything but beautiful but could not say so, stared awkwardly into his brandy, and when Gerald said with a sigh that Mia had been a very sensitive and fastidious lady, Tod murmured, ah yes, that was very true indeed, because he could hardly say what he and the rest of the Harlequin company really thought, which was that Mia Makepiece had been a tough old bird with the sensitivity of a harpy and the fastidiousness of Messalina.

He breathed a sigh of relief when Gerald eventually took himself off, and went back to the drinks cabinet to refill his glass. He was just thinking that they would have reached the discovery of the magical cauldron by the *Fianna* captain, and that the noisy battle between the captain and the cauldron's sorceress-guardian might be a good time to slip into the audience, when the door was pushed open and someone came quietly in.

It was a very peculiar moment. Tod had had his back to the door, and he was in the act of reaching for the soda siphon. Any one of the company might have come in to his office for any number of reasons, although it was to be hoped they would have had the good manners to tap on the door first. But there was a disquieting sensation of being watched and of being coldly assessed and it was a sensation that drew icy shivers down a man's spine. Tod turned round sharply, prepared to see Julius or Stephen, or somebody from front of house with a message.

Standing against the closed door was a slender figure wearing a long black cloak, a deep-brimmed hat, and a dark face-mask with narrow slits, through which eyes glittered coldly. Tod started to say something, and the figure reached down to turn the key in the lock.

'We don't want to be disturbed,' said the stranger, coming forward into the room.

Tod said, blusteringly, 'Look here, who are you? What the devil do you want?'

'Do you really not know who I am?' said Christian. 'I'm *Cauldron*'s creator, Tod.' And, as Tod opened his mouth to protest, he said, 'Its real creator. Your daughter and I wrote *Cauldron* between us. And I'm here for justice.'

Christian had not intended to beard Tod Miller in his den quite so soon. He had intended to see what happened at the curtain-fall, to see whether Miller would acknowledge Fael, and whether Fael would acknowledge Christian himself.

They had never actually talked about the precise form the acknowledgement should take, but there were a number of ways it could be done. In ordinary circumstances Tod could have called Fael onto the stage and introduced her as the writer and librettist and Fael could then have called upon Christian as the composer. But the circumstances were not ordinary; Christian would certainly not have gone out onto the lit stage, and he thought Fael, more or less tied to the wheelchair, would not have wanted to do so, either. He thought they had both been

159

assuming that some kind of announcement would be made without either of them needing to make an appearance, certainly without Christian being named. The idea of being the anonymous composer of *Cauldron* was immensely alluring. He thought that Fael had found it so as well, and he thought she had been attracted by the idea of telling people she had had a secret collaborator. And on a purely cynical, materialistic level, the publicity would have given *Cauldron* the boost of a ten-million-volt charge.

But he knew now that none of it was going to happen. He did not trust Tod Miller, and he was not sure that he trusted Fael any more, either.

Christian had been watching from the shadows when Tod met Fael outside the theatre, and he had heard Miller telling Fael that he was taking her to one of the boxes. His heart had given a sudden leap at this unexpected sight of Fael; he had been visualising her in the stalls, surrounded by people; but plainly something had gone wrong with the arrangements and she had arrived late. And if she was being taken to a box to watch the show, that meant that if Christian himself was very stealthy and very careful, it might be possible for him to slip into the box, and watch the remainder of the show with her.

Fael and himself in the privacy of one of the Harlequin's velvet-lined boxes, shut away from the rest of the house ... Close together, sharing the sight of the marvellous world they had created; watching it unfold in front of them. The thought of the physical and mental intimacy sent sensuous ripples of pleasure across Christian's skin, and a little warm flame of anticipation burned up.

The rear of the boxes gave onto a small, more or less private, foyer: Christian thought they had probably been used specifically for royalty, or for notable figures who wanted to visit the theatre unrecognised, or who wanted to be private with female companions. There was a small washroom and lavatory, and a narrow room with a sink and cupboards, that had probably once been used to prepare drinks or even an *entr'acte* supper. He had stolen up to the deserted foyer, and slipped unseen into the old kitchen, leaving the door open a chink so that he could see

swam in and out of his vision, absorbed in its grisly work, and Tod struggled against the gag and tried to cry out again. But he could not, and in any case the pain was screaming all by itself now, it was raging through his head, and uncontrollable sickness was welling up from his stomach . . . He could feel flesh parting and muscle tearing, and it *hurt*, *it hurt*, there could not be so much pain in all the world . . .

There was a sudden, violent pulsing in his chest as his heart was exposed, and he was aware of retching and trying to be sick but meeting only the gag. There was the truly appalling sensation of being forced to inhale his own vomit and of fighting for breath before the blessed blackness closed down.

He did not feel the final wrench as the dwarf-magician cut his heart from his body and held it triumphantly aloft, dripping and steaming.

Marivaux's had been delighted to put the large supper room at the disposal of the Harlequin company, and charmed to provide the food and drink specified by Sir Julius Sherry and Mr Gerald Makepiece.

'They'll all be ravenously hungry,' said Sir Julius to Gerald, who knew nothing of such gatherings. 'They'll have been living on their nerves, poor sods, for at least a week, and now they'll be suffering the reaction, d'you see. Which means we'd better be lavish.'

It had been nice of Sir Julius to arrange this party, and even nicer of him to invite Gerald to accompany him to the restaurant to make the arrangements. Gerald felt quite overcome when he thought how very kind people were being.

Marivaux's was a very posh place indeed. Not rubbish, Mia would have said. Oh dear. But in the discussion as to the rival merits of lobster and marinated salmon by way of a starter, to the possibility of rack of lamb roasted in claret (a speciality of the chef) along with Beef Wellington (Sir Julius's own favourite), Gerald was able to stop thinking, Oh dear, how am I to cope? He was even able to put forward a tentative suggestion as to whether it mightn't be rather attractive to have the tables got up in blue and green, by way of compliment to the show. This was well received, and apparently perfectly possible. Orchids and delphiniums, said the catering manager, with the aplomb of one who has scant knowledge of horticulture, but who knows that anything can be got in any season, provided the customer can pay. Orchids and delphiniums, and maybe trailing periwinkle plants. No, it would be no problem at all. They would use dark blue damask table napkins on green damask cloths, and they had a very nice stock of blue glassware for the wine. A very attractive idea indeed, said the catering manager deferentially.

It would have been too much to have said that Gerald's feelings for Mia were changing, but incredibly he discovered a curl of anger against her. Logic dictated that if something bad had happened – a road accident, for instance – Gerald would have heard about it. Logic also threw up the traitorous memory of Mia pouting when Mr Camperdown had suggested extra voice rehearsals and of retorting, when Gerald had tried to suggest that this was not a good way to behave, that Camperdown was nothing but a finicky fart-arse, and Gerald himself a pernickety old meddler. Oh *dear*. The tiny suspicion that after all Mia might not have been up to the part of Mab – and that she might have realised it and taken off of her own accord – took a firmer hold of Gerald's mind. Alongside it was anger, because she might have considered the company a bit, to say nothing of Gerald himself.

And so he was very pleased to help with the supper arrangements, agreeing with Sir Julius that Beef Wellington would go down very well, but that the catering manager's suggestion of a good vegetarian dish in addition should be considered. The chef's special mushroom stroganoff would fit the bill nicely, it seemed, and it could be accompanied by rice pilau and French bread and salad. Cherries Jubilee or Victorian Tipsy Cake by way of pudding, and then coffee. A very well-chosen meal indeed, said the catering manager approvingly, and Gerald downed the generous measure of liqueur brandy which it was Marivaux's custom to offer to all customers making large bookings, and felt resentful towards Mia who had very nearly spoiled what should have been such a wonderful night.

It was not spoiled at all. It was a wonderful night. The company had put on their best clothes, because you did not often get the chance to dine at Marivaux's and at someone else's expense, so nobody was going to run the risk of being thought shabby. In any case, they were all set for a long and successful run; everyone was saying so, and therefore startling new outfits could be afforded.

The *sidh*, collectively, were being very startling indeed, making an entrance *en masse*, and causing the diners in the public restaurant to look round in astonishment. Skin-tight silver satin and black leather trousers figured heavily, along with laced boots and diamanté-studded velvet waistcoats. The girls were mostly wearing heavy jewellery and high heels, but that was about the only way to tell them from the men.

The *Fianna* captain had shared a taxi with the sorceress-guardian, with whom he was already becoming entwined. The sorceress, true to character, was wearing a plunging scarlet silk dress and very little else so far as anyone could see, and it was to be hoped there was no explicit footsie under the table or rendezvous in the loo because Marivaux's were a bit old-fashioned about that kind of thing. Also it spoiled people's appetites.

Danilo came in with Gilly, the two of them sticking together because both of them were nervous. It was one thing to step onto a West End stage and act your boots off to a packed house, but it was another thing entirely to enter a swish restaurant and sit down to supper with people like Sir Julius Sherry and Maurice Camperdown; you suffered a whole new range of stage fright. Danilo said it was even worse than attending one of the Greasepaint's nasty midnight gatherings with the Shadow presiding, did Gilly remember those?

'I'm not likely to forget,' said Gilly, shuddering. 'I shouldn't think anyone who was there ever would forget. We've come a long way in the last six weeks, haven't we? Like making an exciting journey and you're not sure of your destination.'

Danilo said it was to be hoped the destination was fame and fortune, and it was to be prayed for that the journey had been via a one-way street because he was not going back to the old days any more than Gilly was. After all this glitter and pzazz he could never face the night-club drag circuit again, or the half-world of hookers and pimps and drug-dealers. It felt a bit odd, didn't it, to think that the Shadow's world was still going on, only half a mile or so away?

'But we've got out,' said Gilly, who still had nightmares about the Shadow's sinister spider network finding them and some macabre kind of vengeance overtaking them. She had nightmares about Leila as well, and about what kind of monster could have butchered her that night. She had never contacted Lori or any of the others to find out if the killer had been caught, but she thought he had not. She thought she would have heard, because it would have been splashed all over the papers.

To dispel the memories she said, firmly, 'We're in a different world now, and we're going to stay in it. You've found the new flat in Belsize Park and I'm moving out to Notting Hill Gate next week. I think we're safe.'

They were safe and they were going to enjoy *Cauldron*'s run; it was a cracker of a show. And they were going to enjoy this evening. Danilo was wearing his first-ever real evening suit, and Gilly had gone into Bond Street the previous afternoon and bought the kind of dress you really wanted to wear inside-out so that everyone could see the label. It had cost the earth, but if you were poised on the brink of stardom, you might as well dress up for it and stuff the overdraft. When she saw what the *sidh* girls and the sorceress were wearing, she was very glad she had spent the money. She almost wished she had gone for the backless Jasper Conran, but when she discovered that somebody had put her at Sir Julius's table she was glad she had not, because the skirt had been slit to the thigh, and Julius Sherry was the kind of randy old devil who would touch you up between the main course and the pudding.

The lodge-keeper and his wife were sitting with the orchestra's wind section, and the lodge-keeper had embarked on a series of jokes which he had picked up in Amsterdam. It was a fair bet that the wind section would turn this into a joke-telling competition at any minute, and it was a racing certainty that this would end up as the noisiest table in the room. Maurice Camperdown was going to have a quiet word with the wine waiter to see if a limit could be discreetly imposed on the amount drunk at that table. The wind section were apt to get a bit drunk at first-night parties; in fact they usually got more or less legless. Maurice did not in the least mind people getting legless, but he did mind having a quarter of his orchestra hungover for the second performance. It looked as if the lodge-keeper and the actress playing his wife had better be included in the arrangement as well, or they would never get beyond Act One tomorrow night.

Everyone agreed vaguely that it was a pity that Tod Miller did not appear to be joining the party, and then forgot all about it. A few people – most notably Julius Sherry and Maurice Camperdown – told one another that it was distinctly odd that Toddy had not answered the call for 'author' at the end. An ASM despatched to find him had reported breathlessly that Mr Miller was nowhere to be found, but nobody had taken this literally because he was bound to be somewhere. You never knew which way Toddy was going to jump, egocentric old Toddy; he might have cooked up some plot of his own to gain extra publicity. Sir Julius, in a mood to be pleased with the whole world in general and Gilly Blair in particular, said indulgently that it was not unlikely that the dear boy had gone off to enjoy a quiet supper with a friend somewhere. He emphasised the *friend* rather heavily, and winked at Simkins from the bank who had been invited by somebody or other, and who appeared to have struck up an unlikely alliance with one of the *sidh* girls.

Gerald Makepiece thought it more probable that Miller had simply suffered an attack of exhaustion after such a gruelling few weeks, and had gone home to bed, but this was not a view supported by anyone else. Sir Julius, boozily proposing toasts, randily pleased that Marivaux's staff had put Gilly next to him as he had privately requested, said that at any event they had Fael with them and she was much better-looking than old Toddy any day! He was even prepared to be polite to Flynn Deverill tonight, he said, and by way of proving this sent an extra bottle of claret over to Flynn and Fael's table.

Chapter Fifteen

Flynn was rather pleased to be seen entering Marivaux's with Fael. The wheelchair, borrowed from the theatre, did not matter because she was striking enough to render it almost unnoticeable, and she would turn heads in any company; Flynn saw a few heads turning tonight as they arrived, and his masculine ego was flattered.

As they took their places Fael spun the wheelchair offhandedly into place at the table, and introductions were made and glasses filled. Conversation buzzed everywhere, and as the wine circulated, the decibel level began to rise. People were laughing, and waiters were bringing round plates of smoked salmon and extra ice buckets for the wine. Fael's eyes narrowed when she smiled; they were pure, clear green like a cat's, and Flynn thought: She's not in the least beautiful and she's certainly not pretty. But she's got something that I don't think I've ever encountered in any other female. Something elusive like moonlight or quicksilver. 'Melting the Moonlight' – yes, of course, Toddy wrote that to her mother; I remember the professor telling me about it once.

Fael suddenly turned to face him as if she had caught this last thought and their eyes met. Flynn looked at her steadily over the rim of his wine glass, and something strongly sexual thrummed on the air between them. Flynn smiled at her lazily and raised his wine glass in a mock salute, and Fael stared at him. The moment lengthened and it deepened as well, and something stirred that was deeper and stronger than anything physical. Mental intimacy in the blink of an eyelash, thought Flynn. Jesus God, there's a thing now. That would be the devil of a complication! I don't want to get into anything that deep, do I? Or do I, though?

And then from Sir Julius's table somebody tapped the side of a glass, and Julius was getting to his feet to make a speech of some kind, and half-serious, half-drunken toasts were being proposed from several of the tables, and everyone was laughing and the moment passed.

It was probably just as well. Flynn returned abruptly to reality, and was aware of someone at the table saying something about Tod: wasn't it odd not to see him here, and did anyone know where he was?

'Probably hassling a Broadway producer into buying the show,' said Flynn, draining his glass.

'No, but it is strange that he's not here.'

'Does Tod actually know any Broadway producers?' asked the *Fianna* captain hopefully.

'Of course not, but he'd like us to think he does. He's probably giving an interview to an obscure journalist in some steamy nightclub,' said Flynn. 'And getting drunk in the process. Talking of getting drunk, will I refill everyone's glass with this Traminer?'

Christian waited until he was sure that everyone had left the theatre, before venturing out.

The stench of Miller's blood was already tainting the small, windowless room, and the desk where Miller had been sitting was in an appalling state, with blood soaking into the polished surface and staining the litter of papers.

Miller's eyes had rolled up showing only the whites and there was a stale wet smell from the expulsion of urine in the death spasm. As Christian looked at Miller's blank dead stare with exultant hatred his own soaring finale music reached him faintly, and then there was frantic applause and cheers, and shouts for 'author'.

For a wild moment Christian toyed with the idea of going out there; of carrying this contemptible figure to the forefront of the stage so that the entire house could see him. '*Here is the creature who would have had you believe him* Cauldron's *author and composer and librettist . . . Here is the sly greedy cheat who would have basked in your praise and given never a thought to the real authors . . . Because one of them is up there in the*

171

stage box, and here before you is the other one . . . !'

It could not be done, of course; it was *Svengali* stuff, *Phantom of the Opera* territory, and there would have been stunned embarrassed silence before Christian was dragged away and unmasked. But for a moment a fierce desire to be recognised – to have his work acknowledged and complimented, and to take part in the happy exultant discussions about the show – seized him, and a violent tremor shook his whole body. He felt Rossani's dark evil begin to uncurl deep within his mind, and he quenched it almost at once.

A cursory search had been made for Miller half an hour or so after curtain-fall; Christian heard people coming along the corridor outside, and somebody trying the door. He remained absolutely still, and heard a voice say, 'Locked. Then he's not here, that's for sure.'

A second voice said, 'Oh, he's probably already on his way to Marivaux's. Which is where we should be if we don't want to miss everything.'

The footsteps started to move away, and Christian began to relax.

And then the first voice said, 'Did you notice Flynn Deverill keeping up to his reputation?'

'What—? Oh, the first-night legend. Who's he going to be laying tonight?'

The footsteps were fading, but Christian just caught the reply.

'Fael Miller by the look of it,' said the voice. 'Not that I blame him – she's a cracker, isn't she?'

Fael, thought Christian as the footsteps went out of hearing, and somewhere at the back of his mind Rossani's mesmeric claws unsheathed and flexed. The gore-splashed office with the fetid stench of Miller's blood blurred, and beyond it he glimpsed the nightmare wastelands of Rossani's dark realm.

He forced it back – dive thoughts, down into my soul! – but it stayed with him, and the insidious thoughts stayed as well.

Fael. But not just Fael: Fael and Flynn together. Are you with him now, Fael? thought Christian in silent anguish. Are you at Marivaux's, enjoying the food and the wine and the company? – stunning them all with the way you look – because they think you're a cracker, Fael, they're all saying so . . .

And what about afterwards? Will Flynn take you home with him, and from there to bed with him, Fael? Because that's what he does, my dear, that's his reputation and he'll surely live up to his reputation tonight of all nights. Images of Fael and Flynn together scalded his mind, and he was aware of Rossani's world pulling him in more strongly than it had ever done before. He could hear the claw scratchings and the slitherings of the faceless shades that walked in that strange underworld; he could feel the beating of leathery wings on the dark lowering skies . . .

You shouldn't have gone off with him, Fael. You shouldn't have let people link the two of you. You're *mine*, Fael; you're mine body and soul and blood and bone, just as Mab was Aillen mac Midha's, just as the rainbow-haired heroine of the *Dwarf Spinner* was Rossani's . . .

Rossani . . .

The evil twilight of that other world closed over his head. Oh Fael, you shouldn't have betrayed me with Flynn, thought Christian.

It was almost midnight when he unlocked the door of Tod Miller's office, and went swiftly through the dark hallways and landings, lit by low security lights. He moved as quietly and as insubstantially as the shadow that the Soho call-girls had named him, his eyes scanning the corners for movement, his ears straining for the least sound that would mean he was being followed. But no eyes watched from the darkness and no creeping footsteps came after him, and he descended to the lower levels and went through the old door and down to the brick tunnel.

Christian had no idea if the same security arrangements held; it was possible that now the show was running the timing of the patrols had been altered. But even if they had, it was unlikely that the security men would come down here. And even if they did he would hear them and have time to hide. It might take some time to do what Rossani had whispered, but he would do it.

As he went through the opening he had made a week ago, he caught the sickly sweet gust of decaying flesh, and Rossani's smile curved his incomplete lips.

* * *

And now he was alone with the ghosts and with his own victims.

But as he worked, Rossani was at his side, chuckling throatily as he painted the dark images on Christian's mind. It was time to display their cunning, whispered Rossani. It was time to let these fools see the extent of their cleverness.

Isolate Fael, said Rossani; isolate her, not only from Flynn, but from the entire world. Cut her off from all contact, shut her away. And then she really would be mine, thought Christian, and his heart began to race as he remembered the closeness they had shared and the way her mind had flowed into his. Something wholly unfamiliar fastened around his heart, because was it possible, was it remotely conceivable, that after all there might be something good in the world for him . . . ? Oh God, he thought, oh God, if I could believe she would not shrink from me . . . Would she?

And now the images were changing; they were no longer images of Fael with Flynn, they were of Fael by herself in the Moher house. Living there, driving back the shadows, bringing back the light and the happiness.

He thought: *And supposing there could be a child?*

A child . . . A little girl, perhaps: mischievous, elfin-eyed with slanting cheekbones . . . Or a slender supple boy, gilt-haired, with ears set just a fraction too high to look entirely human . . . But in either case, beautiful and complete. *Unmarred . . .*

And would the chill inhuman *sidh* covet it? Would they steal it away because of its beauty, and replace it with the changeling of the old beliefs: the ancient withered thing that was of no more use to the tribe, and that constantly cried to its foster-mother for attention . . . ? The age-old superstition reared up anew to taunt him, and even though he knew it for the dark fantasising of a mind soured and embittered, it was still very real to him.

Fael, and a child – a child so lovely, so filled with brilliance and beauty, that the *sidh* might indeed attend its birth, they might indeed slyly sprinkle their intoxicating music into the eyes and ears and senses of the humans. They might covet such a child so greedily that they would be prepared to strike a bargain. Take this one but in return you must give back the unmarred unflawed babe you stole all those years ago . . . I'm suffering a spell of madness, he thought. I really am.

But people had bargained with devils and demons before now and not been necessarily mad, even though some of them had been dragged down to hell, there to suffer endless torment, and even though others had been torn apart by the greedy cohorts of Satan. But there had been those who had beaten the devil at his own game, and yoked the demons and harnessed the devil's power for a time. The idea, once seeded, lodged a little more firmly in his mind; it snaked little silken roots into his brain. Fael and a child who would be born in Maise, as Christian had been born in Maise. A child who could be used as a pawn, as bait.

And in return, I will have the semblance of humanity that was my birthright . . .

The party at Marivaux's, which had been sinking into torpor, revived magically, when Stephen Sherry and two of the ASMs burst through the door with armfuls of early editions of the morning papers.

'Distribute them all round,' shouted Sir Julius, and for several minutes the room was filled with the sound of pages being turned, and mutterings of, 'Can't find the theatre page,' and, 'Well, *I* shan't pay any attention whatever the critics say,' and, from the lodge-keeper's table, 'Of course, dear boy, I've been reviewed by Harold Hobson and Kenneth Tynan, you know.'

And then everyone who had a newspaper suddenly found the theatre page, and an abrupt silence fell. Fael, who was sharing the *Daily Mail* with Flynn and the *Fianna* captain, felt her heart start to bump alarmingly. Because this was it, if the critics liked *Cauldron* people would go to see it and it would run, and she would have scored a success, and *Scathach* would have scored it with her. The print danced in front of her eyes, and she forced her mind to concentrate.

And then Flynn said, ' "The stunning, eerily beautiful new show at the Harlequin . . ." ' and at the same moment, Sir Julius said, ' "Absolutely not to be missed . . ." ' and somewhere else in the room somebody was saying, ' "Music that will haunt you for days and settings that will stay with you for ever . . ." '

And then from all round the room, the acclaim was coming like soft sweet rain falling on an upturned face . . .

'Spell-binding . . .' 'Raunchy and tender . . .' 'Will have you laughing at one minute and crying the next . . .' 'Aillen mac Midha sizzles across the stage . . .' 'Newcomer Gilly Blair a delight as the beleaguered Irish heroine . . .'

And it was all true, it was really happening: *Cauldron* was a success, it was a huge smash hit, and Fael was having to tell herself she would not cry, she absolutely would *not* . . .

Flynn took Fael home in a taxi shortly before four a.m. The taxi was the old type where the driver was separated from the passengers by a glass partition, and the interior was dark and close and intimate. There used to be jokes about what people got up to in the back of taxis, or maybe they weren't jokes at all.

The idea of asking Flynn in for a nightcap flickered across Fael's mind again, only to be reluctantly dismissed. He might see it as a direct invitation, which would look blatant after meeting him for the first time tonight. People in wheelchairs could not get away with being blatant. She had learned that when Simon did his vanishing act at the time of the car crash.

There was also the fact that bringing Flynn into the house – no matter how unblatant the intention – would emphasise her disabled state, and he might think she had only done it because she needed help.

But it would be rather nice – well, it would be better than nice – to sit talking over the evening with Flynn, discussing *Cauldron*, and perhaps laughing over the supper at Marivaux's. They could sit in the music room, and she could switch on the low desk lamp and maybe even bank up the fire . . .

Oh sure, said her mind sardonically. And what about *Scathach*? Or are you really going to kid yourself that he'll stay away tonight? Tonight of all nights he'll be with you, and let's be fair about this, let's give the devil his due: he's the one you should be discussing *Cauldron* with. So how would you deal with that situation? Introduce them? Flynn, this is the guy who wrote *Cauldron* with me, only I don't know his name, and I don't know what he looks like. Oh, and this is Flynn Deverill, who I think I rather fancy – who I should think half of London fancies . . . And supposing Tod blunders in halfway through, or starts noisily throwing up in the loo because he's had too much to drink again?

For the first time, Fael thought crossly: Oh damn *Scathach*! and she was still weighing up the pros and cons when Flynn resolved it for her by asking the taxi to wait while he saw her to the door. Serve you right! thought Fael, manoeuvring the horrid chair down the path and up the ramp leading to the front door. There you were, planning it all out, and he wasn't interested after all! Probably he had been sorry for her and it had not occurred to him to think of her in a sexual capacity. Probably he was going straight on to a rendezvous with someone who was capable of performing the entire works of the *Kama Sutra* all the way through without pausing for breath. One of those beautiful, sensuous *sidh* girls, for instance. I hope he enjoys it, thought Fael, crossly. No I don't; I hope she was eating garlic all evening so that he gets a faceful of it, secondhand, when he wakes up next to her tomorrow morning!

She thanked him for helping her, and for the great evening, and added, as if it had just occurred to her, that he would always be welcome to drop in for a drink any time. This was the kind of thing you could say without anyone reading anything much into it. Flynn said, 'I'll do that,' which was the kind of rejoinder you could give without it meaning a thing. He waited until she was in the house, and then went back out to the waiting taxi and presumably on to whatever else might be waiting for him.

The house was in darkness, and Tod was not home yet. Fael checked the downstairs cloakroom where he always hung his outdoor things and kicked his shoes off. Nothing. And the answerphone on the hall table was registering two unread messages, which was a sure sign that he was still out; Tod could not resist finding out who had phoned him, no matter how late he arrived home, or how drunk he was when he got there.

Fael played the messages in case there was one for her from Tod himself, but there were only a couple of 'good luck' calls for *Cauldron*: one from Tod's agent and one from someone whom Tod frequently drank with at the Greasepaint Club and who sounded sloshed. Fael scribbled a note of them on the pad for whenever Tod got home, reset the machine, and wheeled down the hall to her own room. The theatre had told her to keep the chair for a day or two, which had been nice of them. It was a bit awkward to manipulate, but it would be a godsend until she could find her own.

The house felt a bit cold, in fact it felt downright chilly. That would be because of the smashed garden door, of course. Actually it felt peculiarly unfriendly as well as chilly. Fael found herself glancing nervously over her shoulder and suddenly wished she had asked Flynn in after all, and be blowed to what he thought. She went determinedly into the kitchen, switching on lights along the way. She would make a cup of tea and drink it while she got ready for bed. She banged cupboard doors and clattered crockery deliberately loudly because they were friendly, everyday sounds. The singing of the kettle as the water started to boil was friendly as well. Ridiculous to have been so nervous earlier.

The evening had been wonderful but it had been tiring; Fael was not used to being out until the small hours, and there had been the terrific tension of watching *Cauldron*. Well, all right, of watching the last two acts of *Cauldron*. A smile curved her lips as she poured water into the teapot. *Cauldron* had been good, it had been tremendous. Everyone at the party had said so, and Fael thought they had meant it and were not just being polite. The critics had said so as well, and they had certainly not been polite.

It would be luxuriously good to stretch out in bed, sipping the hot tea, and drift into sleep thinking about it all. And just for tonight she would not think about recognition or rightful attributions, and people snatching credit. Nobody had snatched anything tonight, in fact the person she had expected to do most of the snatching seemed to have vanished before the final curtain.

Fael considered her father's absence as she stirred milk into her tea. She was puzzled, but not wildly alarmed. They had agreed to make their separate ways home, and when her father had given her her key back, he had hinted that he might have other fish to fry later. This was not at all out of pattern; in fact it was not unknown for Tod to stay out all night or come home

178

with the milk. It was usually better not to question him too much on those occasions, although sometimes he proffered information of his own accord, hinting boastfully at some new conquest or some new important business deal struck in exalted surroundings.

It *was* cold in here. Fael started to wheel across to the hall once more, and for the first time saw that the board she had propped across the garden door was not where she had left it. A faint thread of alarm slithered through her mind. She had wedged the board quite tightly, although it was just conceivable that it could have slid to the floor of its own accord, or been dislodged by a gust of wind. If Tod had come home earlier he could have banged a door somewhere and unseated it. But Tod had not come home, and gusts of wind or slamming doors would not have put the board where it was now, which was against the larder, three feet away from the door.

Fael stared at the board, and thought: Someone's been in the house. Someone's been in here while I was out. Tod? No, Tod would have used his own key and come in through the front door. The nape of her neck began to prickle with fear, and a chilling picture formed of someone pushing the board away from outside and squeezing through. It would be the easiest thing in the world to walk around the side of the house unseen and get in. There had not seemed to be any signs of burglary anywhere, but Fael had not really checked. It was necessary to check now, and perhaps phone the police. It was vital not to panic.

Fael was just deciding that she was not anywhere near to panicking when a sound from beyond the kitchen sent her heart bounding up into her throat. Someone was in the cellar.

She shrank back into the chair, one hand going to her mouth. Someone in the cellar! Someone walking slowly across the old stone floor of the basement directly beneath the kitchen! Her father? She grabbed the thought. Could it be Tod after all? Perhaps taken ill in the theatre – something trivial but debilitating like violent earache, or something embarrassing like sickness and diarrhoea – and quietly getting a taxi home so as not to upset anyone's enjoyment.

But Tod had never considered anyone else's feelings in his

entire life, and if he had come home because of illness he would certainly have made sure that Fael knew. He would have sent for her in the theatre, or phoned through to Marivaux's, and he would have demanded her attendance along with hot-water bottles and aspirin, or whisky in warm milk, and consultations about the desirability of summoning a doctor. And the only reason Tod ever went into the cellar was to bring up a bottle of wine or mend a fuse.

Fael remained very still, listening intently. Yes, there it went again. Someone was walking stealthily across the cellar.

The thought that it might be *Scathach* brushed her mind and for a moment hope bounded up. But I don't believe he would hide and lie in wait like this, thought Fael, her mind working frantically. He'd wait in the garden like he always does. He wouldn't know if my father would be with me, or if we might have brought someone back for a drink. Oh, why didn't I ask Flynn to come in? Someone's in the cellar and he's creeping up towards me, and I'm trapped. No, of course I'm not trapped, I can get out, or I can get help. Can I get through the garden door and out into the night and yell for help? No, of course I can't. Police then – can I ring the police? Where the hell is the phone? She looked frenziedly about for the cordless phone that she normally kept to hand. Nowhere to be seen. Never mind it, there's the ordinary kitchen extension on the wall. She began to inch the chair across the floor, trying not to make any sound. Her heart was hammering and the palms of her hands were slippery with sweat.

She was halfway across the kitchen, when there was the abrupt click of a heavy switch being depressed and at once every light went out. Darkness, immediate and overwhelming, closed down.

And now terror swept in unchecked, because Fael knew exactly what had happened. The intruder, whoever he was, had deliberately thrown the mains electricity switch from below, and plunged the entire house into darkness. Unless she could get out, she was absolutely at his mercy.

She could hear the characteristic creak of the wooden steps that debouched into the hall, just beneath the stairs. Then he's coming up to get me, thought Fael, backing towards the smashed

180

garden door, her heart racing with terror, icy sweat sliding between her shoulder-blades. He's creeping up the stairs – yes, that's the door at the top opening. That means he's in the hall now.

And now she could hear him plainly; he was moving slowly towards the kitchen, and there was the sound of his breathing. Harsh, slightly too-fast breathing, like warped sexual arousal. Oh God. But by now her eyes were adjusting to the darkness a little, and she could see the phone on its wall bracket, tantalisingly near. Could I get to it and summon help? Because if I know the police are on their way – if he knows it as well! – I might manage to fight him off until they get here. I'll find a weapon – a knife, yes, that's the thing. If I can get to the drawer under the sink and get the breadknife I'll stick it in his guts the minute he touches me . . . I'll hate it, but I'll do it. As she gripped the sides of her chair, she heard the soft pad of footsteps coming towards her, and the dreadful aroused breathing. There was a whisper of silk.

And then a soft, familiar voice said, 'Hello Fael.'

Chapter Sixteen

It was a slightly jaded Harlequin company that assembled for the second performance of *Cauldron*.

Gilly and Danilo arrived together and separated to go into their adjacent dressing rooms, having wished each other luck for tonight. Gilly was trying to avoid Sir Julius Sherry, randy old sod, and was hoping that an awkward situation was not going to develop there, what with Sir Julius being a person of importance.

The *Fianna* captain and the sorceress-guardian of the cauldron came in looking complacently pink-eyed from lack of sleep, talking loudly about the pizza they had sent out for at midday, and the curry they were going to be ordering for later. A fresh lot of bets were at once taken in the *sidh* dressing room as to how long that would last, since it was well known that the sorceress was anybody's. One of the male *sidh* dancers, who had bet that the sorceress would specifically be Flynn Deverill's last night, was in a bad temper because Flynn had gone off with that smashing Fael Miller, which meant the *sidh* dancer had lost five pounds.

The orchestra's wind section was noticeably subdued, and there was much passing round of Alka Seltzers and earnest discussion as to the efficacy of prairie oysters as opposed to a nauseous mixture made up for the flugelhornist by a little man in a chemist's in the King's Road. It was doubtful if any of the woodwinds would manage to achieve the correct flutter-tonguing trill for the sorceress's solo in Act Two. The flautist said, morosely, that it looked as if the sorceress had been achieving a certain amount of flutter-tonguing herself, because she looked like death warmed over and it was to be hoped the make-up would cover it.

Julius Sherry and Gerald Makepiece partook of a light supper in a wine bar that catered for early theatre-goers, and then walked companionably along to the theatre. Gerald had drunk more wine than perhaps was good for him, and Julius, at bottom a kind-hearted soul, tried to ensure that the poor little rabbit at least ate a good plateful of the wine bar's excellent chicken and ham pie.

As they went in at the stage door, Sir Julius remarked that it was to be hoped that Tod would put in an appearance tonight because it had been rather rude of him to have disappeared last night. He added irritably that you could never tell what Toddy might be getting up to and thought, but did not say, that it would be just like Toddy to have spent the night with a lady somewhere – and to be smugly public about it this evening – whereas Julius had been tactfully but firmly fobbed off by Gilly Blair. He was feeling elderly and disconsolate as a result and was likely to be touchy with anyone who had spent last night in the arms of Venus, or in the arms of anybody, really.

Gilly thought the first act had gone as well as it had last night. It was a marvellous feeling to know you were achieving all of this, especially after only a single week of rehearsal. Not bad for a hooker! She might even agree to have supper with Sir Julius after the show; he was a persistent old bugger, but he could be quite interesting to talk to, and he had actually sent yellow roses round to her dressing room tonight. Roses in November!

She stood at the side of the stage, waiting for her cue for the court scene, and beneath the stomach-churning stagefright, she felt a sudden, huge, all-embracing happiness and an awareness of every sense becoming heightened. I'm invincible, and I can do anything, thought Gilly, in delight. I'm going to have supper with a baronet after the show, and it's not impossible that very soon now I'm going to be rich and famous. I'm not actually loaded with talent, of course: I do know that. I do know that all of this is because of a freak stroke of luck. But I think I'm getting by. And no one has noticed that I'm a masquerader; in fact a couple of the reviews actually singled me out for praise. The piercing happiness sliced through her again, so that her face kept wanting to smile.

Danilo would say it was dangerous to feel like this; he would say it was what Celtic folk called fey – the false euphoria that the gods sent down just before tragedy struck. But tragedy was not going to strike.

She concentrated on the stage. They were coming up to the scene in which Mab enters imperiously and berates the *Fianna* captain for losing a battle. By way of punishment, he must seek out and bring back the magical cauldron. As the order was given, the royal armies poured onto the stage like paratroopers of World War One armies marching out to the sound of cheering and flag-waving. Jingoism, that had been the word they had used.

It was an elaborate scene. Flynn Deverill had designed an extravagantly beautiful set, all glittering crystal pillars and spun-sugar columns. There was a small dais at the centre, with Mab's throne, and great swathes of shimmering silver silk framing it.

As the *Fianna* prepared to set out on their quest, the palace dissolved and gave way to the outskirts of the dark, dangerous forest through which they would travel, and as the eerie and sinister trees were wound up from the shallow under-stage area, a soft, scented wind blew gently across the stage and out into the audience. This was a remarkable and startling effect and it had caused quite a stir last night; people had apparently talked animatedly about it during the intervals, and nobody could remember anything quite like it being done in a London theatre before.

Flynn had worked closely with the backstage staff to create this scented wind, losing his temper several times with spectacular abandon and cursing the carpenters and the two stage managers in a mixture of what most people thought was fluent Gaelic, punctuated with what was unmistakably plain Anglo-Saxon. In the end they had achieved what he wanted by disinterring the old-fashioned wind machine from the back of the prop room and adapting it.

The wind machine was a monstrous Heath-Robinson affair; a hand-operated machine standing on squat legs and set into action by crank handles and flywheels. There was a rotating drum attached to it; in the old days this had been filled with dried beans or pebbles and then turned to give the sound of heavy rainfall or hail. Flynn had had the machine adapted so that the drum was mounted above a kind of industrial fan – the sort you saw in factories – and driven by an electric motor. The drum was filled with shredded but strongly-scented pot pourri, so that once it was set turning, the pot pourri was forced into the fan which blew it across the stage. There had been much muttering about the use of this contrivance, which the carpenters had dubbed Deverill's Mincing Machine, and several unions had been consulted. But once the thing was built it worked marvellously, everyone was agreed on that.

Then there had been more head-shaking and disapproval by some department of health and safety who had had to be called in, and who apparently harboured dark suspicions of the pot pourri being spiked with sinister substances by evil-minded people plotting to drug the entire Harlequin audience. Flynn had lost his temper all over again, damned everyone within range for a bunch of amateurs, and threatened to resign. But in the end the safety people had been placated by Stephen Sherry setting up a system of very stringent checks, and issuing half a dozen complimentary seats.

Gilly thought the transformation of the palace into the forest outskirts was a very good scene indeed. It was achieved by what was called the rise-and-sink, which was an old-fashioned but effective mechanism that lifted the silken drapes on their wooden frames up into the flies, and simultaneously wound up the forest from the cellar directly beneath the stage. Sir Julius had told her last night that the Harlequin was so old, there were several cellars under at least three stages: 'The old place has sunk,' he said. 'Building settlement, they call it. So there are layers because they built new stages smack over the old ones. If you went pot-holing down beneath the present stage, you might find all kinds of priceless fragments.'

The wind machine was even creakier tonight than it had been at rehearsals. Gilly could hear the crank handle groaning, and she could hear the stagehands muttering on the catwalk overhead as they prepared to fly the silken drapes up to the grid and wind the forest up from the under-stage. This took place about five minutes after Mab's entrance, and it had gone down very well last night.

Here was her cue. Gilly took a deep breath and walked out

onto the stage, feeling the instant warmth from the audience. There were only a few lines of dialogue – the chastising of the *Fianna* captain, and then the summoning of the royal armies to capture the cauldron at the forest's heart. The wind machine was taking a long time to get going – Gilly wondered fleetingly if it had given up the ghost. Would they have to ad lib to cover the hesitation? Flynn Deverill would be pacing the floor and swearing if he was out front. Here came the faint rumbling vibration from beneath the stage, indicating that the enchanted forest was being brought up. The lighting plot dimmed, and the ancient twilit wood began to take shape all around them. Deep violet light poured in from overhead, purple-tinged and sinister, and Flynn's trees were so ancient and so nearly human-looking, that even Gilly, who had seen them in the cold light of a ten a.m. rehearsal and knew that they were plywood and painted polystyrene, felt a shiver of atavistic fear. For a moment it felt as if she really was standing at the edge of an old, dark forest with evil magic stalking through the night.

Evil, creeping up . . . Edging nearer . . . Gilly gave a shiver that was not entirely simulated, and prepared to embark on the speech which would send them all off to brave the assorted dangers and various adventures. She had got as far as the first few words when the last section of the forest came up into its appointed place, and a gasp and then a shudder of horror went through the audience. There's something wrong, thought Gilly, faltering. Something's gone dreadfully wrong. What? Where? Something to do with the mechanism – the rise-and-sink? And there's something wrong with the wind machine as well – it's screeching like a banshee, but it isn't working yet. There's a smell as well – something foul and sickish. Like decaying fish, like meat gone off in hot weather . . .

Several of the actors were stumbling back, their hands flying to their faces in half-protective gestures. Odd how ugly real horror looked as against the acted sort. It's the backdrop, thought Gilly, panic starting to rush in. There's something wrong with the backdrop. She had been half facing front, the *Fianna* captain on one knee before her, but in another second she was going to have to turn round.

People in the audience were getting to their feet, and there was the sound of the seats tipping up, and cries of fright. Women were screaming, and exit doors were being pushed frantically open. There would be a stampede in a minute. From the wings a furious voice was shouting to bring down the bloody curtain, for Christ's sake bring it down you bunch of tossers!

As the curtain descended, Gilly at last turned to face the back of the stage, and the rising panic at once switched to stunned horror. Impaled onto Flynn Deverill's eerie fantastical forest, pinned there in a macabre X-shape, and lit to nightmarish clarity by the woodland dusk, were two of the most gruesome objects Gilly had ever seen. They're dead bodies, she thought, staring helplessly. They're skewered to the backcloth like – like monstrous human butterflies in a collection. This is dreadful, it's *dreadful*. It's not believable. I can't fit this into anything sane.

One of the bodies was recognisably that of a partly naked man. His head hung forward, but it was possible to see his features, and it was to him that Gilly looked first. Tod Miller, she thought, appalled. Is it? Oh God, yes it is. He's partly wrapped in something – I can't quite see what. Something thin and dry-looking. There was a huge jagged-edged wound on the left side of Miller's chest, with white splintered rib bones protruding. Blood had run out of the wound and dried in dreadful smeary patches, and whatever it was that was hanging over Miller's shoulders had had its edges dabbled in the blood.

Gilly looked then to the other shape, and saw why she had been trying to avoid this one even more strenuously.

The second body was nailed to the backdrop in the same way, but Mia Makepiece had been dead for a week, and it was only the improbable chestnut hair that gave Gilly the clue to identification. But it looks as if he's left her a face, thought Gilly, as the hair swung forward. That's a mercy.

But although Mia's killer had left her face alone, he had not left much more. Great sections of skin had been peeled away from her thighs and from her shoulders and stomach, leaving huge livid patches like raw meat. The image of a butchered carcase, the hide imperfectly removed, was impossible to avoid. Except that when you saw carcases in butchers' cold stores, they did not have the beginnings of putrefaction . . . They did

187

not have this bloated, decayed look, and they did not give you the impression that at any minute they might start to leak their terrible juices all over the floor . . .

He's skinned her, thought Gilly, sickness welling up, so that she clapped her hand to her mouth to force it down. Oh dear God, whoever killed her skinned her and sewed the bits of skin into a cloak – *sewed* them, for heaven's sake! – and then wrapped the cloak around Tod Miller. She tried to stumble back, but her legs did not seem to be obeying her.

As if on cue, from the other side of the stage the wind machine suddenly tore out of its sluggish coughing mode and shot uncontrollably into top gear. There was a wet slopping sound – appalling, intolerable! – and gobbets of Tod Miller's gouged-out heart rained across the stage.

Julius Sherry said, 'Half the audience thought it was a sick publicity stunt and the other half thought it was a surreal twist of the plot.'

'Some twist. Some plot,' said Stephen.

'Has it been confirmed that it was – hum – Mia Makepiece and Tod?' asked Maurice Camperdown.

Julius glanced with embarrassed pity at the mute figure at the foot of the table. 'Yes,' he said, and Gerald Makepiece gave a moan of anguish.

'They've been – well, identified?'

'Oh, for the Lord's sake, Morrie,' said Flynn, who was standing at the window staring moodily into the street, 'do we need the gory details? We could all see who they were! And the police are looking for a maniac,' he added, in a preoccupied voice.

'Will they close us down? The police?' This was Camperdown.

'They'll have to close us temporarily at least while their forensic team crawls all over the whole theatre.'

'What about advance ticket sales? Tonight's performance?'

'Oh God, I don't know. I don't think anyone's had time to think about anything like that, yet,' said Stephen.

'Well, somebody's got to, and very quickly,' said Maurice.

Sir Julius cleared his throat, and said, 'Mr – ah – Mr Simkins,

I don't quite know the bank's exact procedure in a case such as this, but—'

Simkins said dryly that there was no exact procedure, because the bank had never before been faced with quite such a situation. The words, 'And hope never to be again,' were not spoken, but they hung heavily on the air.

'Then,' said Julius, heavily, 'we should tell the company what we know so far. Reassure them if we can. Stephen – Morrie – will you come with me now? They're all assembled in the upstairs Green Room. Flynn, I don't know if you want to be present—?'

'No, I don't want to be present.'

Julius said, 'Your beautiful set, Flynn. My dear chap, I can't imagine how you must be feeling—'

'I'm not your dear chap, and of course you can't imagine how I'm feeling,' said Flynn, tersely. 'Isn't it astonishing how bloody murder churns up insincerity? If you've finished being polite, I'm off to see the police. There's no need to look so alarmed, Julius. I'm only going to tell them about the intruder we saw on opening night; if you've been fiddling the takings, nobody's found out yet.'

Gilly sat in a cold and miserable little huddle in a corner of the Green Room, her mind churning with bits of the evening's events and fragments of the show, and how after all it was dangerous to be too happy too abruptly. Underneath it all was a faint warning that it would not take much to make her physically sick. She had not actually been sick yet, which was God's mercy, but it still might be touch-and-go.

Most of the *sidh* had been sick, and several of the *Fianna*. Some of them had not made it to the cloakroom, which had been unfortunate, and, as Danilo said, had added to the mess on the stage. He had said this a bit defiantly, and nobody had been quite sure if it was a ghastly attempt at black humour or a clumsy attempt to draw attention to himself. Only Gilly had understood that Danilo had said it deliberately in order to churn up anger in people's minds and blot out the gruesome thing they had seen.

The sorceress-guardian and her two attendants, who had been standing in the wings waiting for their cue for their first entrance, had actually been hit by one of the bits of flesh. The sorceress had gone into strong hysterics and had had to be given a sedative by a doctor who had been in the audience. Gilly had nearly gone into strong hysterics herself when the front-of-house manager had gone out onto the stage and said, 'Is there a doctor in the house?'

The sorceress and the attendants had now had scaldingly hot showers and were dressed in jeans and sweaters. Gilly wished someone would give her a sedative and tell her to go and stand under a hot shower because she was beginning to think she would never be warm again. It was therefore a bit of a shock – although it was not entirely unpleasant – when Julius Sherry put his hand on her arm, and said, in a soft voice, 'My dear, here's a large brandy for you, and if you want to go home, I will drive you.'

This was a tiny core of warmth and friendship. Gilly sipped the brandy gratefully, and said she thought she had better stay on for a while; they were all going to be questioned, and anyway, she was beginning to feel better.

'Good girl,' said Julius, nodding to the others, and then going off with a heavy tread and serious expression to high-level discussions. It had been very kind of him to think about her. He was actually rather nice when you thought about it sensibly. Gilly sipped the brandy and resolved to think about it very sensibly indeed. If Mia Makepiece – oh dear, it was better not to think about her – but if *other* girls could marry doting elderly gentlemen with money, there was no reason why Gilly could not.

Although she would much have preferred *Cauldron* and overnight fame.

Flynn seated himself opposite to Sir Julius Sherry's desk, which had been temporarily allotted to the detective inspector in charge of the investigation and said, 'We'll cut the preliminaries, inspector, because I should tell you I saw your man a couple of times and I can give you a description.'

'Did you indeed, sir?'

'I did, and what you've got to look for is a creature with a deformed face who wears a dark mask to hide it, and a black cloak.'

This was received with stony-faced courtesy. The inspector, who had been told that theatre folk were apt to be flamboyant, and who remembered Flynn Deverill's extraordinary denouncement of the Inigo Jones Award last year, said, 'That's a very interesting statement, Mr Deverill. Would you happen to know any more about the person than that?'

'I would not. But I've seen him twice now; in fact on the opening night of *Cauldron* he damn nearly killed me.'

'*I* see,' said the inspector, and wrote down the words, 'intruder seen on first night of play'. 'Can you give a more precise statement, Mr Deverill? Where exactly did you see this person?'

'In the old part of the theatre. The haunted part,' said Flynn, impatiently. 'And don't say, "*I* see" again. All self-respecting theatres have ghosts, inspector. There's a couple of interconnecting brick tunnels near to the stage void. He was down there.'

'And you say he had a deformed face? Would you mean an injury? Or some kind of abnormality?'

Flynn said, 'His face was incomplete.'

'Ah. Incomplete?'

'Jesus God, man, I wasn't in any state to be taking notes! He came at me like a raving maniac, and it was all I could do to fight him off! But I'd guess that at some time he'd had extensive surgery—' He stopped abruptly as the intruder's appalling face swam before his vision again, and dug his fingernails into his palms. I won't be sorry for that creature! After a moment, he said, flippantly, 'Would you like to hear any more, inspector, while your men are scraping Tod Miller's heart out of the crankshafts of the wind machine? Or will I show you the precise spot where the monster reared up out of the shadows?'

The inspector exchanged glances with his sergeant, and then said, 'Have we been down there yet, Williams?'

'No, sir.' The slab-faced Williams seemed to imply that it was scarcely within the duties of respectable officers of the law to go burrowing around in haunted brick tunnels.

'I expect we'd better see it, however,' said the inspector, resignedly.

'Oh, you must see it,' said Flynn, at once. 'You don't know

what else might be lurking down there, or what other corpses might be mouldering in a dusty corner.'

'Would you be winding us up by any chance, Mr Deverill? Because if so, it's called wasting police officers' time, and it's quite a serious offence.'

'Inspector, I am an experienced, industrious, ambitious and often picturesque liar, and my second name is Ananias. But,' said Flynn, 'on this occasion I am telling you the truth.'

'Then we'll take a look at this tunnel of yours, Mr Deverill.'

'Of course you will,' said Flynn, standing up. 'I'll give you the guided tour so that you don't miss a shred of the atmosphere while you're here. And afterwards, unless you want me any more, I'm going out to see Fael Miller.'

'You'd be a friend of Miss Miller's, perhaps, sir?'

'There's no need for heavy innuendoes, inspector. I took Fael home last night, but I didn't get into bed with her. I'm going to see her because no one's been able to reach her by phone yet, and because I think she might need a friend when she hears about her father's murder.'

Stirring up the disapproval of Julius and the police had been the only way that Flynn had been able to hide his feelings.

The gruesome things that had been done to Tod Miller and the Makepiece female had been shocking and appalling and an affront to every sense. But it was what had been done to *Cauldron* that had gouged down into Flynn's deepest feelings and seared his mind.

But this was something that must be quenched and it was something that no one must guess existed. He would hide the feeling under a veneer of cynicism and disrespect in the way he always did hide his real feelings. He would even hide it from himself by focusing on seeing Fael, on making sure she was all right, on finding out as much as possible about what had happened tonight. If I pretend it's not there, that furious pain, when I look for it again it may even be gone, he thought, alighting from the taxi outside the large, rather ugly house in Pimlico.

There was a policewoman standing outside the door, which presumably meant they had still not been able to get any reply from the phone and that they had come out here to wait until Fael returned from wherever she had been for the evening. But I don't believe she's been anywhere, thought Flynn, going up the narrow path. If she was going anywhere tonight she would have gone to the theatre; she would have wanted to see the first half of the show, because she missed it last night. There's something wrong about all this. There's something *planned*.

It came as a severe shock to learn that the main reason for the police presence was because the house had been broken into, and that there were signs of a struggle in the downstairs rooms.

And Fael Miller had vanished.

To return to his own flat – with the *Cauldron* designs and bits of the scale model sets still lying around the workroom – was unthinkable. The underground had stopped running by this time, but Flynn kept walking through the night streets, and finally picked up a taxi near Vauxhall Bridge, directing the driver to take him on to Soho.

He got out in Greek Street, and from there plunged deep into the seething, red-lit streets. It was like entering another world, but it was a world of garish neon lights and smoke-filled bars, and strident-voiced prostitutes of both sexes, and thumping rock music . . . The contrast with the world that someone had created for *Cauldron* – that Flynn had brought to life for the Harlequin's stage – was painful, but tonight Flynn derived a perverse satisfaction from it.

Because those worlds where smoky dusklight filled up the stage, and where dangerous, beautiful, androgynous creatures prowled and spun magical music that would melt your soul and fuse all your senses, did not really exist. They were dreams, chimerae. Their inhabitants were beings glimpsed in a shadowy mirror, or seen through a glass darkly . . . In fact the whole world's better seen through a glass, thought Flynn, and turned into the nearest bar.

Time blurred inside the clubs and the bars, and alcohol dulled the pain and forgetting could be bought or at least rented by the hour. But was the pain because of Fael or the show? How did you come to terms with bloody fragments of human bodies smeared across that ethereal, visionary landscape? How did you cope with the dream-world when it crossed over into a nightmare?

I'm damned if I know any longer, thought Flynn, sitting moodily in a bar just off Brewer Street shortly after three a.m., a half-finished glass of whisky in front of him. What I do know is that wretched play slid under my skin and stuck there and I'm not sure if I'm going to be able to scrape it off. Skin . . . Scrape . . . Had they really had to scrape Tod Miller's heart out of the cogs of that appalling machine? Had they had to peel away the travesty of a cloak that had been draped around Miller's body?

Flynn shuddered and drained the whisky, setting the glass down unsteadily. He supposed he looked pretty disreputable by this time; his hair was tumbling over his brow and he had not shaved since early morning. He had dragged off the black evening tie and stuffed it in a pocket, and loosened the collar of his dress shirt. The long overcoat he had worn over his evening suit fell open, the skirts trailing on the ground. He probably looked like the archetypal drunk, or an irreclaimable drop-out. He could not have cared less.

It was half-past three when he made his way onto the street once more. Sober enough to walk? Yes, just about. And with luck drunk enough to fall into the sleep that knits up the unravelled sleeve of care. It was as he turned the corner and began to scan the street for a cruising taxi that he realised he was near the Greasepaint Club's side entrance. He stopped, considering. Bill or the doorman would still be on duty, and there would probably be some coffee brewing. Was that better than going home to face *Cauldron*'s debris and remember how the Harlequin stage had looked tonight, and wonder all over again about Fael's disappearance?

Anything's better than that, said Flynn to himself, and turned in through the side door.

Bill was on duty at the door tonight, and glad of a bit of company because there was never much doing at this time of the morning.

But although he was pleased to see Flynn, he deplored the state he was in. Drink was the ruin of many a good career. It would be a great pity if Flynn's career was ruined because of it;

Bill kept his ear to the ground, which you could do in a place like the Greasepaint, and he knew that Flynn Deverill as a designer was very highly regarded. Difficult, of course; in fact downright bloody rude at times, if you wanted to be accurate. He'd thrown away one or two good opportunities because of it, so the word ran – that scandalous speech he had made at the Inigo Jones Award ceremony! Bill could still remember the uproar that had caused, even though it had been reported that the BBC's viewing figures had gone into orbit that night as a result. But weren't all genuinely creative people temperamental at times?

But it was more a question of too much intelligence than of temperament with this one, thought Bill shrewdly. Impatient with the slower-witted and intolerant of fools, that was Flynn; Bill had seen it before. The right female could go a long way to curing it, of course, but there you were again: this one could have the pick of the females, and according to the gossip, often did. It had made him too particular. Not that the boy looked as if he had been very particular tonight, in fact he looked as if he might have been indulging in just about every excess Soho could offer. But he hauled Flynn into his private lair reserved for off-peak times – very cosy, he and the doorman had made it – and set about making very strong, very hot coffee.

Flynn half fell into the sagging comfortable chair by the glowing electric fire, and said, 'I'm bloody pissed, Bill.'

'So I see. A woman, is it?'

Flynn accepted the coffee, and thought: Is it? What about Fael Miller? He said, angrily, 'Is it hell, a woman. In any case I'm drunk beyond the point of capability tonight.'

'Whisky,' said Bill, nodding.

'Whisky it is. It provokes the desire but takes away the performance, did you know that, Bill?'

'Oh yes.'

Flynn grinned. 'It's not a woman,' he said. 'It's that sorry bloody mess at the Harlequin. Did you hear what happened tonight?'

Bill said he had heard, indeed he had, in fact it was a safe bet that the whole of London had heard by now. 'People talk, you know, Mr Deverill. Even here—'

'Especially here, I should think.' Flynn drank the scalding coffee gratefully. 'This place could tell a few tales.'

'Well, that's true. Mind, so could the old Harlequin. It'll all be in the papers tomorrow.'

'Oh, God, don't remind me.'

'Murder at the Harlequin,' said Bill, shaking his head. 'You can't expect the tabloids to pass that up. Cracker of a headline, that.'

'I saw him, you know,' said Flynn, suddenly. 'The murderer.'

Bill paused in the act of drinking his own coffee, and set it down carefully. 'Is that a fact, Mr Deverill?'

'Yes, it is a fact. It's not the ravings of a soused imagination, although you might be forgiven for thinking it.'

'Did you tell the police?'

'Yes, of course I did. They wrote it all down, and they were very polite, and they didn't believe a bloody word I said.'

'Why not?'

'Why not?' Flynn drank his coffee, frowning. 'Oh, because I was anything but polite to them. Because I was extravagant and flippant. And because I told them a bizarre story about a poor sod of a creature who wears a black silk mask to hide the most appalling— What's the matter, what have I said?'

'A poor sod of a creature who wears a black silk mask,' said Bill, staring at Flynn. 'Is he the Harlequin murderer?'

'Well, he damn near murdered me. Yes, almost certainly he is. Why? Do you know who he is?'

'No,' said Bill. 'Nobody does. But unless there're two masked men stalking London, he comes here every Sunday night at midnight.'

'Every Sunday?'

'Regular as income tax.'

'And he wears a mask? Black silk with eye-slits?'

'Black silk with eye-slits.'

They looked at one another. 'Boil the kettle for another round of black coffee, will you, Bill,' said Flynn. 'While you're doing that, I'd better put my head under the cold tap in the cloakroom. And then when I've sobered up a bit, we're going to have a talk.'

'We are?'

'We are.' Flynn stood up and tested his stability. 'Because if the police aren't going to take our masked stranger seriously, then it's down to me to do something,' he said. 'Or maybe it's up to me. Which do I mean, Bill?'

Bill grinned. 'You really are soused, aren't you, Mr Deverill?'

'I know it. But listen now, first off, you're going to tell me about the masked man and the midnight meetings.'

'And then?' demanded Bill, suspiciously.

'I might see it differently when I'm sober,' said Flynn. 'In fact I hope I will.

'But I've got the strongest feeling that what I'm going to do is ask you to let me in on the next meeting so that I can find out a bit more about this elusive masked gentleman.'

PART TWO

*The changeling ... is often tormented or exposed,
to induce the fairy parents to change the [human]
child back again ...*

A Dictionary of Fairies, Katharine Briggs

Chapter Seventeen

As the large car disembarked from the ferry at Rosslare, Fael's sense of unreality increased.

Just under two days ago I was sitting in the Harlequin, watching a lit stage with my own characters on it. Everything was good in life and everything was opening up for me, and I'd met Flynn Deverill, and the only real problem was how I was going to get my father to acknowledge *Cauldron*'s true creators. And now I'm being driven across Southern Ireland, and night's approaching, and I have absolutely no idea where we're going or what's going to happen to me.

I suppose I'm really quite frightened, she thought. But I don't know that I feel frightened, not properly; there's too much of a dreamlike quality about this to be out-and-out terrified. And I'm with someone I know very well indeed, I'm with the person I shared all those soft, secret nights with. She risked a glance at the silent figure behind the wheel. How could I be afraid of someone who knew what I was thinking before I did – whose tormented loneliness I felt as if it was my own?

But she knew that she was actually very frightened indeed. She thought she was not frightened of the shadow being who had written *Cauldron* with her; she was afraid of the person who might exist behind the shadow. I don't know him at all, she thought.

She felt a shiver of panic when she remembered how easily he had overpowered her in the dark kitchen. She had fought like a wildcat, using her fists and clawing and yelling, but she was unable to get out of the hated wheelchair and she was virtually powerless. In the end he had simply moved round to the back of her chair and gagged her with a silk scarf to keep her quiet. After that he had twisted her arms behind her back and tied her wrists together with a second scarf. He had been swift and skilful and there had been a lack of brutality, although there had been no lack of emotion; the quickened breathing had slowed as if he had deliberately banked it down, but excitement blazed from him, and Fael found this a million times more frightening than any physical threat. Because of course he's mad, she thought helplessly, as he carried her out of the dark house and into the waiting car. But he isn't so mad that he hasn't planned all this very cunningly indeed, retorted her mind. It's the small hours of the morning – there'll be nobody about.

He had deposited her on the back seat of the car, and then activated what Fael thought were electronic child-proof locks. The click as they were all secured was a very bad sound indeed.

He leaned over then and untied the scarf gag, and before she could draw a shaking breath to speak, he said, 'We're driving to South Wales where we're catching the early ferry to Rosslare.'

'Rosslare?' said Fael, staring at him in disbelief. '*Ireland?* You're taking me to Ireland?'

'I am. The drive takes about four hours at both ends, but we'll stop for petrol and a break. I put some things in a suitcase for you before we left. It's in the boot.' He glanced at her. 'I was in the house before you came home.'

So he had riffled her wardrobe and dressing table while she was at Marivaux's with Flynn. He had taken out sweaters and jeans and presumably underclothes. This was unspeakably unpleasant, but Fael concentrated on it, because it was immeasurably better than trying to think why he was abducting her. In a minute I'll ask him. No I won't, not yet. Instead, she said sharply, 'I hope you remembered toothbrush and hairbrush and shampoo.'

'Of course.' He swung the car towards the west-bound M4, concentrating on merging with the traffic. There were very few cars, but there were some, and several heavy lorries. As the car gathered speed again, Christian said, 'If you behave sensibly this will be a relatively pleasant and quite companionable journey. Don't we know one another well enough now to be companionable, Fael?'

'I don't know you at all,' retorted Fael. 'I don't even know your name.'

'You don't need to know it.' The eyes behind the mask slits glittered coldly. 'Listen, Fael,' he said, 'if you try to get away or spin crazy stories to anyone about being kidnapped I will render you even more helpless than you are now. Be very sure that I can do that and be very sure that I will do it.'

Fael said, furiously, 'You're mad. And if you really believe I won't yell for help the first chance I get—'

There was a flicker of emotion at that. 'Have you forgotten that your father didn't come home tonight, Fael?' said her companion, softly. 'Don't you think you should be wondering what happened to him? Or even – what might be about to happen to him?'

Fael had been trying to see how the door-locks worked. But even if I *could* open the door we're doing seventy miles an hour, and if I did get out, how far could I run? About six feet? At his words she said shakily, 'What do you mean? What's any of this got to do with my father?'

'A great deal. If you try to escape me,' said the soft voice, 'how can you be sure that Tod won't suffer?'

There was an abrupt silence. Then Fael said, very carefully, 'Are you saying that you've – that you've got my father? That you've somehow abducted him and that you're using him as some kind of hostage? For goodness' sake, that's every bad thriller plot ever written!'

'I don't know that I'd have been quite so obvious as to use a bad thriller plot device,' said Christian, thoughtfully. 'I don't think I would have put it in quite that way, either. But since you've said it for me—'

'Do you really mean that my father's – that you've got him locked up somewhere?' demanded Fael, incredulously. 'And that unless I do what you want—' She took a deep breath, and said, 'What is it you want? Why am I here?'

He half-turned his head. 'Don't you know?'

'No. But whatever it is you want of me I won't do it.' And then, as he did not answer, she said, 'Have you really got Tod?'

'You tell me. But he didn't come home tonight, did he? And he vanished quite abruptly from the theatre. Everyone was commenting on it.'

'How do you know that?' demanded Fael.

'How do you think I know it?'

'You were there?'

'Oh Fael,' said Christian, and there was unmistakable affection in his voice. 'Did you really think I would have stayed away? Of course I was there.'

Fael stared at him. 'You really have taken him, haven't you?' she said, at last. 'My God, you really have. What did you do – set some kind of trap?'

'Some kind of.'

'And he walked straight into it?' said Fael, furiously. 'Yes, of course he did!'

The gloved hands lifted from the steering wheel for a moment, in a deprecatory gesture. 'You know Tod,' said her companion.

'Oh yes,' said Fael. 'It would be just like him to blunder head-first into a trap. And,' she added, grimly, 'to drag me in after him. Where is he now? What have you done with him?'

'Oh, he's quite safe. You don't need to worry about him. He's not going anywhere,' said Christian, and incredibly there was a note of amusement in his voice. He glanced at her sideways. 'You'd much better face the fact that you're in my power, Fael.'

'For a brilliant composer you're dragging out all the old clichés,' said Fael, caustically.

'So I am. But you know, you haven't a hope of getting away from me; no one's going to challenge me. No one's even going to question me.'

Fael felt panic rising all over again, because the appalling thing was that he was right. No one was going to question him and certainly no one was going to challenge him, because he carried with him that astonishing aura of authority and power. People in motorway service stations, or on the ferry, would see that his face was covered and that he wore a deep-brimmed hat, and they would think nothing more than that he had been in a bad road smash, or maybe a fire. They might feel a bit embarrassed, in the way people did feel embarrassed when faced with deformity or mutilation, but that would be all. I'll have to go along with it, thought Fael. And if he really has got my father – Oh, curse Tod!

But the night's events were starting to take their toll and

the nervous energy that had driven her to fight him was draining so that she felt weak and a bit shivery, like the onset of flu. But beneath the physical exhaustion, her mind was still working, not thinking – not daring to think! – of what might be ahead, focusing instead on the enigmatic character of her abductor, on the strangeness, on the continual insistence on anonymity. Did he extend that anonymity to all levels of his life? Fael leaned her head back against the head-rest, her eyes half-closed, considering this. If he did, how did he cope with practical things – shopping and medical things and money? Yes, money – what did he live on? And how did he manage about buying or renting a house or a flat? He can drive, she thought; glancing across at him. In fact he drives very well: the car looked like a Jaguar when he threw me into it, but whatever it is, it's big and very powerful and he's handling it with a sort of careless expertise. This was unexpected, but Fael thought that was only because you did not associate anonymous midnight beings with such mundane things as coping with motorway traffic and tax discs, or checking tyre pressures. But there was also an inescapably sexual allure about a man – practically any man – handling a fast car efficiently. Blast him, thought Fael, staring crossly out of the passenger window. Blast him, I don't want to see any sexual allure in him at all. I need to think of him as evil and cunning so that I can hate him and fight him.

She wondered how he had acquired the car, which did not appear to be a hired one. Had he simply walked into a car showroom and said, 'I'll take that one,' and handed over a wad of cash for the correct amount? Or had he stolen a suitable model from a garage forecourt? There would be an enormous irony in discovering that this enigmatic Svengali was a common or garden car thief, although it was not very likely; petty crime was hardly his line. I suppose he might have paid for it with a bank draft, thought Fael, beginning to feel overwhelmingly tired now, and wondering if she dare give way to sleep. Yes, a bank draft would be anonymous enough. But then if you had enough money not to have to work you could presumably arrange things however you wanted. Money was the answer to most things; it would certainly let you buy a Jaguar . . . Her eyes were growing unbearably heavy, and it was probably safe to give in to sleep for a short while. She would need all her wits about her when they reached Ireland, but even Svengalis could not do anything to their victims while they were hurtling along a motorway at seventy miles an hour. She would probably be all right on the ferry as well. Having assured herself of this, she fell gratefully into soft, smothering sleep.

It was not until they had disembarked at Rosslare that she finally managed to ask precisely where they were heading. And when I know that, then I'll ask again what he's going to do with me – or should it be going to do *to* me?

They stopped at a small, nearly deserted restaurant, and Fael ate what was either a very late lunch or a very early supper. Her companion ate and drank nothing, simply sitting at the table with her, his back to the room, his eyes behind the mask unreadable. Fael remembered how he had steadfastly refused all her offers of coffee or wine when they had been together. Because it meant removing the mask, you fool, said her mind. Then when does he eat and drink? Presumably when he is completely alone.

When they took to the road again the drowned evening light was stealing over the countryside, and the masked figure took on the remembered air of dark romance once more. Fael shivered. This was the persona to be wary of; this was the creature who could exert that silvery magnetism. But if ever there was a moment to find out what was ahead, this was it, and so she dredged up her courage and said, 'Exactly where are you taking me?'

'To the Moher cliffs on the west coast,' said Christian, and now Fael heard the definite Irish lilt in his voice. A little like Flynn's voice. Oh God, *why* didn't I ask Flynn into the house that night?

'We're going to a very remote part of Ireland, Fael,' said her companion, and this time there was no doubt about the difference in his voice. Because something within him was waking and responding to his surroundings? And whatever this place – Moher – was, it clearly held some deep significance for him.

'It's a strange place,' said Christian, and Fael had the feeling

206

that he was barely aware of her presence now. 'It's a place where the villagers and the crofters still double-lock their doors at Samhain and Beltane. And where people whisper fearfully about hearing strange, haunting music when the Purple Hour falls on the land.'

'The Purple Hour?'

'They use the old terms in Moher,' said Christian. 'The Purple Hour is what you call twilight.' He sent her another of the sidelong looks.

And now I really could almost believe that he's some kind of masquerade knight, thought Fael. Galloping off into the sunset with me flung across the saddle, unravelling dark tales of myths and legends as we go . . . Scheherezade's masculine counterpart . . . Don't be ridiculous, Fael, he's a cold, selfish monster, he's probably doing it deliberately and getting a tremendous kick out of it!

'They believe the old stories out here, as well, Fael,' said the soft voice, and Fael caught the purring note, and frowned, because he was doing it again, he was deliberately setting the spell working again. It was important to close her ears to the seductive beckoning in his voice, and to set a guard over her senses. It was important to remember that he had forcibly brought her here – he had tied her up and gagged her, for heaven's sake! – and he had trapped her father as well, and was using him as a hostage.

Christian said, 'The people of Moher believe that there are times when evil prowls the world – real evil, not the watered-down substance of the Christian church.'

'Catholic Ireland?' said Fael, forcing her voice to sound hard and even a bit jeering.

'Oh, you'd still find traces of paganism in Ireland if you scratched the surface in some parts,' said Christian. 'And the community where we're going is a very old one indeed; some even say the people are the direct descendants of one of the lost tribes of Ireland.' He sent her a quick glance. 'The Cruithin,' he said. 'The little, dark, elfin people who ruled Ireland long before the Gaels or the Celts came. They once walked these cliffs, Fael, and they spoke the untainted speech of Ireland's golden age. The druids would have been here as well then, and the

Pretani and Qretani who traded with the East and were called the people of the misty blue and green northern isle.' He looked across at her again. 'How do you know I'm not one of those lost races, Fael; how do you know I'm not something not quite human?' His voice was a low, menacing purr.

Fael shivered, and then said, 'I can cope with lost races, but if you start on leprechauns and will o' the wisps, I warn you I shall be sick.' Her voice held the right note of sarcasm.

'No, I won't do that.' She heard the smile in his voice and felt the dark menace recede a little. 'But out here they believe that there are nights when the chill, inhuman beings, who once lived beneath the ocean, wake and creep onto the land, scouring the barren hills for human prey and human souls.' He paused, and then said, half to himself, 'And human babies to steal away . . .'

Fael stared at him, and then said, 'Changelings.'

'Yes.'

There was silence. Fael had the sudden disquieting feeling that she was being drawn deeper and deeper into a dark unknown world; a macabre realm that existed invisibly alongside the real world, and that was inhabited by fearsome half-beings and soaked in old, old magic, and where hobgoblin creatures and eldritch spirits might prowl.

And where hungering, soulless beings patrol the desolate shores, setting snares to catch human souls, and stealing away human babies . . . ? She pushed the clustering images away sharply, because surely it was only in fiction – and a very particular kind of fiction at that – where those things happened?

At last she said, 'Why are you taking me to this place? Moher?'

'I'm taking you to my house, Fael. To the house that has been in my family for many generations, and that my father re-named in the hope that it would bring some happiness into his changeling child's life. I'm taking you to Maise.'

Fael stared at him, and thought: But he still hasn't answered my question.

When twilight stole over the cliffs, and the great oceans that lashed the shores turned black, and when the calendar showed certain significant dates in the year, the farmers and the crofters of the Moher cliffs did indeed double-lock their doors and huddle by their own firesides.

They kept to the old ways in Moher, and they believed the old beliefs. They believed that Samhain – what the English called Hallowe'en – was a time when the ancient music might be heard: when cold, beckoning cadences might drift eerily through the darkness, and a strange masked figure be glimpsed prowling the night.

He had not been seen for two or three years now, but one day he would return; there would come sightings, perhaps by a couple of bold girls giggling their way back from Flaherty's Bar, or perhaps by Seamus O'Sullivan returning home the worse for drink, like he did most nights, the shame of it.

When he was there, there was a tendency for people to gather together; to assemble in Flaherty's Bar, or Seamus O'Sullivan's big, comfortable farmhouse where Sinead would bank up the fire and Seamus would hand round the drinks. Their ancestors had done exactly the same, and the only difference was that in those days the drink had come from the poteen jar, and now it came from a bottle, distilled in Galway or Cork. Most of them drank whiskey, except the women, who liked a glass of wine, and Father Mack, who enjoyed a nip of gin outside of Lent, and providing the bishop was not visiting.

The trouble was that the older people of the community had known a time when the house on top of the cliff had not been called Maise, but something darker, something that meant demon. Mera, it had been known as, said the people of Moher, flinching from the word. Because although you might alter the name a thousand times over, you would never alter the legend. Mera was sometimes pronounced and spelt *mara*, and it had long since found its way into the English word nightmare. But in Moher people had long memories, and they knew that *mera* had been one of the names for the sea-demons of Moher, the malicious and evilly beautiful *leanan-sidhe*.

Everyone in Moher knew the legend of the *leanan-sidhe*. It had been against them that their ancestors had double-locked their doors and barred their windows, for all of the old stories told how the *leanan-sidhe* had the way of creeping up onto the land, and snatching away human children and leaving their own warped, wizened offspring in their places. They did not really believe that any longer, they said, half-defiant, half-shamefaced. No one believed in such things these days. Sinead O'Sullivan's grandmother had a tale about how a poor, dumb thing had been born in Moher back in the eighteen-nineties, and how it had been burned to death by officious neighbours who had believed it a *leanan-sidhe* creature, and had put it on a red-hot shovel in the expectation of it flying up the chimney. Sinead's brother, Liam, told how you could still hear it shrieking in agony on the anniversary of its terrible death, and Seamus said wasn't that very true, and it the most heart-rending sound you ever heard. No one actually believed any of this, because Liam would tell a good tale if it would inveigle a girl into bed with him, and Seamus would go along with anything he was told after he had taken a few drinks at Flaherty's Bar.

It was all superstition, of course. But still, it did not hurt to be a bit watchful, especially at Samhain and Beltane. It did not hurt to take the long road home on those nights and so avoid Maise and the famous stone, with the sinister eyehole at its tip. Seamus O'Sullivan insisted that it was a Self-Bored Stone, and if you climbed up to the very top and looked through the eyelet at dawn – or maybe it had to be at midnight, no one was quite sure on that point – you would glimpse dark underworlds you had never dreamed existed. They ought to publicise it as an attraction to rival the stone at Blarney, said Seamus firmly, and then the tourists would come and they would all make a lot of money. He had been saying this ever since anyone could remember, and it was a safe bet that he would never get around to doing anything about it.

It was towards the end of a damp, chill November that the message came from London – a phone call to Flaherty's, it was – that Maise was to be cleaned and aired; provisions were to be delivered to the house and left in the scullery, and the fridge was to be switched on and left running. Beds were to be made up and fires laid in the main rooms. Flaherty's daughter did this faithfully, making sure to take along a friend, because Maise was the scariest old house for a person to enter alone.

Partway into the bleakest December any of them had ever known Father Mack saw and then Seamus saw, and then everybody saw, lights burning in Maise's windows.

He had come back.

Chapter Eighteen

Fael's first sight of Maise set her heart racing with a mixture of fear and awe.

They had rounded a curve in the narrow cliff road, and the car was climbing a steep incline. *Scathach* – the name seemed to fit him even more strongly than ever out here – was leaning forward over the wheel, concentrating on negotiating the treacherously winding road. On their left huge black crags rose upwards, blotting out what was left of the failing daylight. Fael, leaning forward, made out one in particular: a thin, towering crag like a monolith, easily thirty feet high, tapering towards the top, but with a round aperture at the pinnacle.

Christian glanced at her, and as if sensing her curiosity, said, 'That's what the local people will tell you is a Self-Bored Stone.'

'What on earth is a Self-Bored Stone?' The rearing black mass with the single circular hole was somehow menacing, like a one-eyed giant straddling the cliffs and staring down at the little scattering of houses at his feet.

'It's a stone believed to possess magical powers,' said her companion. 'The hole is bored through by some natural process – constant dripping of water or weather. You have to climb to the tip at dawn or midnight on certain nights in the year, and look through the aperture.'

'You'd need nailed boots and mountaineering equipment,' said Fael. 'It's over thirty feet high.' She stared up at the stone. 'If you got to the top and looked through the hole, what would you see?'

'Other worlds. One legend tells that you would be able to read the ancient chronicles listing the names of creatures bound by the *sidh*'s dark enchantments.'

For some reason this struck a familiar note. But so many

folk tales and legends had a common root; Fael thought there was probably an English version of the story. She glanced uneasily up at the rearing mass, and then the car rounded another of the sharp bends, and the stone dropped from view behind the crags. On their right the ground fell away in a terrifyingly sheer drop, and the bottom was the ocean. It lashed wildly against the rocks at the foot of the cliffs, throwing up pale spumy spray that seemed to rise and shroud the road in soft, clinging whiteness.

And then the house was there, looming up out of the mist, a stark silhouette against the darkening sky. Fael stared at it and felt ice close about her heart. There was surely never a more desolate, forbidding place anywhere in the world. And that's where he's taking me, she thought. He's going to carry me inside and shut me away and I still haven't found out what he intends. And once in there, I could scream until my lungs burst and no one would hear me.

She said, abruptly, 'Is this where my father is?' and felt a stir of amusement from him.

'Oh no,' he said. 'He's not here, Fael. There'll only be the two of us here.'

So. So, he had tricked her over that. Tod was very likely perfectly all right, and stomping about London demanding to know where his daughter was. Fael felt bitter anger at her own gullibility well up, but beneath the anger the icy fear was becoming nearly overwhelming. Is this the reckoning I thought would never come? Because I promised him recognition for his music, there's no dodging that, and it didn't happen. It wasn't my fault that it didn't, but if he's mad it might not weigh with him. Of course he's mad.

As they went up the steep, rutted drive leading to the house, she was dimly aware of several clusters of lights scattered about the landscape. Farmhouses, thought Fael, trying to fix their position. Farmhouses and cottages, and possibly small, remote inns. It looks as if there's some kind of little community out here. Does that make me feel any better? She thought it did not. The little pinpoint clusters of lights looked a long way off. And even if she could escape, she would never drag herself down the uneven cliff road.

As he unlocked the immense front door and pushed it open,

Fael received the impression of a cold unfriendliness from the old house. She felt as if it was studying her as *Scathach* carried her in, and as if it might be saying: What are you doing here? What right have you to come in here like this? This is a house for ghosts and wraiths and the dark, drifting creatures of Irish legend. You have no right here. The feeling of falling deeper into a blurred, cracked-mirror world increased.

There was a massive hall beyond the front door, with rooms opening off on each side, and a wide, shallow stairway that wound up to a shadowed landing. Fael shivered and felt her abductor's arms tighten. Fear sliced through her again, but after a moment he carried her to a straight-backed chair just inside the door and set her down before going back out to the car for the wheelchair.

'So you're allowing me some freedom?' said Fael, angrily.

'Some.' He moved around the hall, flicking on switches, and warm yellow light sprang up at once. Fael drew a deep, rather shaky breath. Better. Extraordinary how light dispelled terror. But she thought she was hiding the terror pretty successfully so far. She waited until *Scathach* had gone back to the car to unload boxes of provisions, and wheeled tentatively across the hall to explore the ground floor.

Maise was a large, rambling, old place but Fael, peering into shadowy, high-ceilinged rooms where huge furniture draped in dust-sheets loomed like monstrous squatting beasts, thought that once it might have been a happy house. Once it might have been filled with people and the kind of large, slightly undisciplined, slightly untidy family that had lots of children and friends and dogs all tumbling over one another.

But there was no happiness here now; now there was only grief and agony filling up the silence, and the lingering aura of mental and physical misery like thick choking silt on the air. Because this was where he grew up? Because it was where he spent a lonely childhood? Damn, now I'm feeling pity for him again.

He took her into the room on the right of the hall, twitching aside the dust sheets, revealing dark, rather heavy Victorian and Edwardian furniture. Velvet curtains hung at the windows and there was a massive fireplace with an iron grate and the kind of tiles that were considered ugly until about fifteen years ago, when people started to decide they were fashionable and hunted for the originals in street markets. Somebody had laid a fire: a neat arrangement of concertinaed newspapers and what Fael guessed was turf or peat.

The fire had been laid before they arrived. Fael registered this and then registered as well that although the rooms were dusty they held only the surface dust of a few days. Then someone had been here before them. Someone had come into the house and dusted the rooms and laid the fires. And the fridge in the large, stone-floored kitchen had been switched on and running, and it had held milk and butter and cheese and eggs and bacon. There had been two large boxes of provisions in the back of the car, but Fael was fairly sure those things had not been among them. She considered this new piece of information carefully. Setting aside wild notions of invisible servants who swept and garnished the master's house like something out of Kipling or Tolkien, and who could only be seen if your eyelids had been streaked with fairy-juice or you had swigged down hallucinogenic drugs for the occasion, it was a rather warming discovery. It looks as if there's some traffic between this house and the local community, then, thought Fael. Maise isn't quite as enisled in the sea of life as I was fearing. I'll get free, she vowed, silently. I'll think of a plan and I'll find an ally. I'll bribe someone or blackmail someone, and I'll get free.

'The electricity's a bit unreliable out here,' said her captor, indicating the wall sconces, which were of elaborately-wrought but rather tarnished silver. 'It's often necessary to resort to a primitive way of living: candlelight and cooking over the old kitchen range.'

But Fael, watching him set a match to the fire, thought there were worse things than eating by candlelight and curling up with a book before a peat fire. It depended on who you were sharing the candlelight and the firelight with, of course . . .

Scathach took the deep, wing-backed chair on the other side of the fire, his eyes behind the mask slitted and remote, and Fael met them and felt her heart begin to race. This is it. This is the moment. He's about to tell me what he's going to do to me . . .

215

And then: he's about to tell me who he is, she thought. Or, if not that, then he's going to tell me where we are – where we *really* are. She almost had the feeling that she did know where they were, or if she did not know, that she ought to be able to work it out, because all the clues were in front of her. But it was as if she had all the pieces of a puzzle except one, or as if she had one piece too many and it was throwing the whole pattern out. Or maybe I'm just too plain frightened, thought Fael.

The fire was burning up strongly now, washing the room to a warm glow, but the velvet curtains did not quite shut out the night, and little sighing winds stirred the heavy folds from time to time, as if they were trying to find a way into the house. It was easy to imagine that it was not the wind at all, but someone standing silently in the deep window bays, listening and watching . . . Fael shivered and at last *Scathach* spoke.

'I brought you here because of the promise you made, Fael. Because of the bargain.'

'You think I reneged on our deal, don't you?' said Fael at once. 'You think I broke the promise, and now you're calling it in.'

'In a way.' He leaned forward, and Fael felt the familiar magnetic tug. 'But now you're going to redress the balance,' he said.

'How?'

He rose from his chair and came to stand before her. He moves like a cat, thought Fael, feeling the coiling strands of sexuality snake around her mind. 'You're going to share my bed,' said Christian. 'Didn't you guess?' His voice brushed her senses like velvet sliding across naked skin.

'That wasn't in the bond,' said Fael, forcing a defiance she was not feeling into her tone.

'Wasn't it?' He paused, and when he spoke again, his voice was cold and hard. 'But I'm not the hero of the piece, Fael,' he said. 'I'm the villain. Never lose sight of that. If you wanted a hero you should have encouraged that insolent devil in London.'

Flynn. Fael said, 'So you saw him?'

'Oh yes.'

'And hated him.'

'Yes.'

'Why?'

'Because he has everything I have not.' The words came out unemphatically, but the raw emotion behind them etched itself on the quiet room. He shook his head as if to clear it, and bent over to pick her up. As he did so, he said, softly, 'You surely didn't forget that all villains like to have the beleaguered heroine in their power and their beds?'

'Supposing I fight you? Supposing I scream for help?' They went out of the firelit room across the dark hall, and Christian paused and looked down into her face. The shadows twisted about him, so that it was difficult to tell where the mask ended and the shadows began.

'Scream away,' he said. 'Out here there's no one to hear.'

The shadows were trickling up the stairs as well. They seemed to come stealing out from their corners as he ascended them, and to half-form themselves into grotesque, reaching shapes. Fael had the frightening idea that they were acknowledging him: *Scathach*, who could command the darkness. And who could call spirits from the vasty deep . . . ? But supposing we're actually in the vasty deep already? Supposing we've passed into some kind of forgotten underworld, and supposing it's a world peopled with demons and shadow-creatures, and supposing he really can call to them?

Yes, but any man can call to spirits, she thought, her mind a jumble of panic and a wild singing excitement. Any man can call to them, but it's a question of whether they will answer him. But what if this is the one man to whom they will answer? And what if the feeling of familiarity with Maise is because it's the dark beckoning mansion of everybody's deepest nightmares . . . ? What if the nightmare mansion exists, and always has existed, and what if this is it?

I think I'm becoming light-headed, thought Fael, struggling for calm. I certainly think I might be bordering on the lunatic fringe on my own account now. The long journey here, and his presence . . . The strange tales about hungering sea-creatures, and timeless and invisible fairy chronicles . . .

They had reached the wide landing on the first floor and turned along a corridor that stretched into the darkness. At the far end was a second staircase; a narrow set of steps that looked as if it led away from the main part of the house. Servants' quarters?

'I hope,' said Fael, speaking loudly to chase the lingering fears away, 'that you aren't taking me up to some wretched kitchenmaid's room.'

'My mother used the rooms up here,' he said, and his voice was as remote as the black cliffs overlooking the ocean beyond Maise.

'Oh, I see. I'm sorry.'

'There's no need for sorrow. She's dead.' Again it was the flat, touch-me-not voice. But then he said, 'I wanted you to have her rooms.'

'Why?'

'I wanted to see you there.'

He went up the stairway carefully but with unmistakable familiarity. It wound sharply to the right several times, like a spiralling turret stair, and thin cold moonlight spilled in from several small windows set high in the walls. As they reached a tiny, square half-landing and Christian leaned down to depress the handle of a door, Fael looked about her in panic.

'If I'm really to be up here, I won't be able to—' She stopped.

Christian said, 'You won't be able to get up and down those stairs unless I carry you? That's what you were going to say?'

'Yes.' She looked at him. 'That's what you want, isn't it? You want me to be a prisoner here?'

'Oh yes,' he said, softly. 'But didn't you expect that? Didn't you know I intended you to be mine, body and soul and blood and bone?'

The rooms were strung out over one floor, and as the door swung open there was a faint ghost-scent of lavender, and Fael had the sense of the past looping forward to join the present.

There was a large, L-shaped room, with one limb furnished as a sitting room and the other, shorter one, as a bedroom. A small bathroom opened off it. There were more wall sconces up here as well, and whoever had laid the fire downstairs had done the same up here, and had also made up the bed.

Scathach went out, closing the door behind him but not

locking it, and Fael thought wryly that he did not need to lock any of the doors. These rooms were on the second, or more likely the third floor, and although she would manage to get from room to room, she would never be able to negotiate the stairs. Even with the wheelchair, which he had carried up after her, she was hopelessly imprisoned.

The rooms were lovely in a faded, rather sad way. There was a square window facing the fireplace; in the daylight it probably overlooked the sea, and there was a padded seat built into it. Fael propelled the chair across so that it was resting against the seat, facing the room, and stayed very still to see if there were any ghosts up here. But if ordinary human ghosts haunted Maise they were shy ones, and there was nothing except the fragile, will o' the wisp drift of the lavender, old-fashioned and evocative of a gentler world. She thought: But once, when this house was a lot younger, somebody used to sit up here and weave dreams in the soft summer twilight, and perhaps that somebody planted a lavender bush somewhere in the tangled gardens outside, and dried sprigs of it to bring indoors and fill open-mouthed bowls up here. His mother? Yes. I think she used to sit up here, thought Fael, and I think she was very unhappy indeed.

But, *I wanted you to have her rooms*, he had said. *I wanted to see you in here . . .*

She's left an imprint here, thought Fael, in the way that all strong emotions leave an imprint. She shivered and spun the chair across to the hearth.

A box of matches had been left on the narrow mantel, but it took several attempts to get the fire going, partly because it was awkward to get sufficiently low enough to reach it, but also because the peat was difficult to fire. But eventually she managed it, and a friendly little curl of flame licked up. Fael watched it for a moment and then wheeled through to the bathroom to wash.

The bathroom was as old-fashioned as everything else in Maise, but it was serviceable and the water was hot, with the silky feel of genuinely soft water. Fael washed, brushed her hair and cleaned her teeth, and then made her way back to the main room. After a moment, she deliberately opened the door leading out to the stair. Because I want to hear if he comes? Don't be ridiculous, Fael, of course he'll come. You'll share my bed, he had said . . . You're mine, body and soul and blood and bone . . . Oh no I'm not, thought Fael, defiantly. But I'm leaving the door open.

The fire was burning up well now, and the flames were leaping on the walls, turning the room into a fire-drenched cave. It was beginning to rain, and Fael could hear the patter of raindrops against the window panes. She stayed where she was, the chair facing the fire, staring into its depths and seeing pictures in the flames.

It was midnight before she heard the soft footfall at the foot of the stairs and her heart gave a great bound, and then resumed a too-fast beating. There was the acrid scent of a candle flame as well, drifting up from below. Fael turned her head to watch the door.

As he came up the narrow stair, the flickering candle he carried cast moving shapes onto the wall, so that she saw his shadow before she saw him: menacing and larger than life. As he came nearer, the current of air caused the candle-flame to dance wildly, and there was a moment when it seemed as if other shadows joined him: prowling, prancing shapes with greedy, snatching hands and shifting, changing outlines. Why candles? thought Fael.

And then he was in the room, turning off the electric light and placing two candles on each side of the bed and two more in the wall brackets. The tiny flames leapt up, mingling with the firelight, sending the shadows dancing across the ceiling. Fael drew in a deep, shaking breath and thought: Well, he sets a good scene, at least; I'll give him that.

When he finally lifted her and carried her to the bed, his hands were curiously gentle, although she found to her anger that she was starting to tremble. But when he began to undress her, his touch roused such instant and fierce emotion, that she felt as if her skin would scorch the sheets with passion. The surgeons had said it wouldn't make any difference . . . They said the feeling wouldn't have gone, that I could have a partner like anyone else, even before I was able to walk properly. I didn't believe them, not really, but I do now . . . And I'd forgotten

– oh God, yes, I'd forgotten how good the feeling is . . .

A tiny, detached part of her mind held back for a moment, saying that what she was feeling was almost wholly due to the curious compulsion of his mind, and that it was the natural culmination of their weeks of immense mental closeness. The body expressing what the mind had already experienced . . . Because let's face it, Fael, let's be absolutely honest, mentally you've already done this; you've already locked minds and this is only a by-product . . . Some by-product. Oh God, yes, I'd forgotten what it felt like . . .

When she reached up to touch his face, he resisted at once, and a hand came up to imprison her wrists. 'Don't—' said Christian, and Fael heard for the first time that his voice was breathless and ragged with emotion.

'But won't you let me see you— Won't you tell me your name now—'

'No!' It was torn from him in anguish. 'No,' he said, softly.

So he was still keeping the barriers between them. Fael registered this with a return of the anger, because surely like this, surely with this mounting intimacy he could have trusted her . . . There was a whisper of cloth and then he was lying alongside her on the bed. He's not undressing, said her mind. Not properly, not fully. Only enough to— I'm going to hate this, she thought, abruptly. I'm going to feel used or raped . . .

But when at last he moved inside her, he did so with a kind of helpless, blind need, that wrenched her defences aside. There was an unguarded moment when she felt the brush of the black mask against her cheek, and there was a dark, shivering sensuality about the brief contact.

She felt the moment when his body spun out of its iron control, and in the same instant his mind melted into hers – lonely and anguished and desperately unhappy. Fael's senses spiralled with pity and the agonising need to comfort him, and there was a blazing, bone-melting fusion, so that she could no longer tell the difference between mind and body, and she could no longer tell where his mind and his body ended and hers began.

As he shuddered in climax, she felt his anguish and his need stream into her own consciousness.

There was a sort of timelessness in lying in the deep, soft bed, drifting in and out of half-sleep. Fael watched the moonlight slide through the windows of the sad, faded room, touching the dim furnishings with silver.

I don't know what I feel, she thought, staring up at the ceiling. I certainly don't know what he feels. She turned her head and saw him seated in the deep window, his head turned away from her. But at her movement he looked across at the bed. The mask was still in place.

Fael sat up in the bed, linking her hands about her bent knees (yes, I can do that more easily as well now!) and said, 'What are you looking at?'

He turned sharply as if the sound of her voice had surprised him, and Fael understood that what had happened between them was totally outside his experience. He knew, technically, how to make love (How? Street women? Oh God, how appallingly lonely for him!), but he had no concept of the pleasant, drowsy closeness afterwards, where you might both drift into sleep, still half-coupled, or you might decide to get up and cook bacon and eggs together, or simply just get up and go home.

He looked back at the window, to where the darkness was pressing against the glass. 'Listen,' he said, softly. 'Can't you hear them, Fael?' and Fael felt as if icy fingers had traced a path down her spine.

'What? Hear what?'

'The *leanan-sidhe*,' he said. 'They're quite near tonight. I've been watching for them.'

There was an abrupt silence. Then Fael said, '*Leanan-sidhe*? What are *leanan-sidhe*? Is that another word for the *sidh* we used in *Cauldron*?'

'They were another branch of the legend. The *leanan-sidhe* of Moher were far more malevolent and far more powerful. They were water demons who possessed the ancient flame that inspired writers and musicians and poets,' said Christian. 'The legend is that this house is directly over an ancient subterranean water cave, where they held their strange court.'

Fael shivered and drew the sheets more closely about her.

'It's told that although they could bestow the mantle of creativity,' said Christian, his voice still far away, 'they did so maliciously, giving it only in its pure elemental state. The recipient burned up in the fires of his own genius and died young, and the *leanan-sidhe* presided over his deathbed, shrieking with glee.' He paused, and then said, 'Yeats believed that version, by the way.'

Fael said, almost to herself, 'It's an explanation of why true genius hardly ever reaches old age. Writers and composers – Keats and Shelley and Mozart and Byron.'

'Yes. You might want to warm your hands at the flame of genius a bit, but you wouldn't want that flame to consume you. Of course it's all only a myth – embroidered a bit, because the Irish love to embroider a story.'

'Have you ever – seen them?' said Fael, carefully. 'The *leanan-sidhe*?'

'Not properly. I've glimpsed them beyond the house – blurred shapes darting across the dark garden. Sometimes I've thought I've heard them gathering under my window, plotting and laughing with their heads together.'

This conjured up an unspeakably nasty image for Fael.

'But twenty-nine years ago,' said Christian, 'they were certainly inside Maise.'

'The night you were born,' said Fael, staring at him.

'Yes. Very few people have seen the *leanan-sidhe* materialise – they say in the village that it's a terrible sight – but my mother witnessed it that night. She saw them struggle into their human form, Fael, here in this room, and once they had formed, they gathered about the bed, and they waited to see what would be born.'

'This is mad,' said Fael, after a moment. 'You're talking as if we're in a fantasy world. The *leanan-sidhe* aren't real, they're legends, myths.'

'Are they?' He came back to the bed, his eyes on her, and despite herself, Fael felt the familiar tug. He's setting the spell working again, she thought.

'They were real on that night,' said Christian. 'They sprinkled their music everywhere, so that the humans were blind and deaf; and so that they could watch for the human child being born.

And then, when the long birth was over, they took the child and left in its place—'

He stopped, and Fael said in a whisper, 'A changeling.'

'Yes. One of their own kind.' He was pacing the room now, driving one clenched fist into the other. 'And that is why I am condemned to live this half-life, Fael, this non-existence. That is why I have to walk in the shadows, and why I have to go masked and cloaked, and avoid human contact.' Fael could feel the bitter torment pouring out of his mind, as if it was black silt. He's mad, of course, said her mind. And then – but how much is madness and how much is that anguished desolation I felt earlier?

She said, 'But why would the *leanan-sidhe* come back now?'

He stopped pacing the room and turned to face her. 'Because you're here, Fael,' he said. 'Because we're going to have a child – you and I.' He looked down at her. 'The *leanan-sidhe* are greedy, you see,' he said, softly. 'They can never resist first-born children.'

Understanding was flooding Fael's mind now, but with it, cold sick horror. But she said, 'You're taking a lot for granted, aren't you?' and was pleased to hear the anger in her voice. 'In any case, it's pretty rare to conceive on a single encounter—' And stopped, because of course there was not going to be just a single encounter – he would keep her here until she really did become pregnant.

She said, 'But even if there were to be a child—'

'Yes?'

'It wouldn't be a first-born,' said Fael.

The silence closed down at once, and white-hot currents seemed to ebb and flow between them. After what seemed to be a very long time, he sat down on the bed and said, 'What do you mean?' One hand came out to imprison her wrist.

'It wouldn't be a first-born,' said Fael again, managing to meet the narrow eyes levelly. 'There was a – a child that was—' For some reason the word, miscarriage, was unacceptable. Because it was too intimate? Or simply too modern? Or was it because it reduced that never-to-live scrap of humanity to medical and clinical levels? Fael said, 'It was born before its time because of the road crash.'

For a moment she thought he would strike her, but he remained perfectly still, the fingers of his hand still circling her wrist. When eventually he spoke, the words came out with such extreme difficulty that Fael only just understood them. He's lost all control, she thought. He can't discipline his speech.

'Oh God, you cheating bitch,' said Christian. 'You gilt-haired, silver-voiced bitch!' He stopped, breathing raggedly, and Fael was acutely aware of the hard bone and muscle beneath his skin; she thought she could nearly feel the fight he was waging for mastery of his emotions.

When he spoke again, his voice was almost normal once more. 'A human child,' he said, and the bitter desperation in his tone scraped against Fael's senses. 'A human baby, Fael, to use as a pawn – that was what I wanted. For a long time I didn't see it – I didn't realise what I should do. And then I saw it all, and I saw that it was the only way. And I wanted it to be yours, Fael,' he said. 'But it had to be a first-born – anything else would have been of no use to them—'

Fael said, in a voice of horror, 'You were going to use a new-born child – *my* child – to *bargain* with a legend? For – for—' She stopped, unable to find words.

'Children have been used as pawns before. And a human child – a beautiful unflawed human child – offered in return for the humanity they stole from me—'

Humanity. So that was how he saw it.

'And they would have honoured the bargain, Fael,' said Christian. 'Because the child – your child – would have been so very beautiful that they would never have been able to resist—' He broke off, turning away from her, his hands going up to the thin, concealing mask. 'There was no other way,' cried Christian in an anguished voice. 'It was the only way I could have any hope!'

Fael felt anew the aching desolation, and pity sliced her afresh. But behind the pity another, much darker emotion was welling up: a need to know, to share, to see . . . Humanity, he had said. They stole my humanity.

Before he realised what she was doing – almost before Fael realised what she was doing herself – she had reached up and pulled the silk mask aside.

He sprang back from her at once, flinging his hands up in the gesture of defence that had scalded Flynn Deverill's mind with compassion, and cowering into the shadowy corners of the room.

Fael stared at him, her mind tumbling with disbelief, her throat closing chokingly so that she could not even scream. Because even though he was holding his hands up protectively, and turning away from her, she had seen what the mask had hidden: she had seen that he had thick dark brown hair, and clear, long-lashed eyes . . .

But above all that, had been the single terrible moment when the candleglow had burned up, showing with pitiless clarity his face, *his face, HIS FACE . . .*

There was an appalled moment of frozen horror, and then he went from the room, and Fael heard his agonised footsteps running down the stair like a wounded animal in search of a place to hide.

Chapter Nineteen

Fael woke in the deep, old bed and for a minute could not remember where she was. And then as she turned her head, she saw the square window with the padded velvet seat and the unfamiliar furniture, and remembered.

Maise was shrouded in muffled silence, pale damp mist pressing in on the windows. Fael made a slow, careful way to the window seat, considering her situation. She had absolutely no idea how she was going to face her captor this morning.

She washed and dressed in the bathroom, and felt marginally better. Since the situation had to be faced at some point it was better to at least face it properly dressed, with your teeth brushed and your hair combed, and a dab of make-up to hide the dark rings under your eyes. When *Scathach* kidnapped her he had at any rate put her handbag in the car.

By daylight, the L-shaped room was attractive in a faded, elegant fashion and it was comfortably furnished. There were button-backed sofas and chairs into which you could probably sink in fair luxury, and there were several small tables inlaid with ebony and rosewood. The walls were hung with silk-striped paper, patchily faded to pale straw, and here and there were marks where pictures or mirrors must have hung. No, not mirrors. There would be no mirrors in Maise.

There was a desk between two of the windows which might well be Regency: it had an inset oblong of dark green leather, and pigeon-holes for notepaper, and envelopes and the little embossed wafers people had once used to seal envelopes. Fael was examining it when a movement from the stair sent her heart thumping with apprehension. She turned to face him.

'Good morning,' he said, and even though he had donned the

mask again, the familiar voice gave a freakish tweak of distortion to the situation.

'Good morning,' said Fael, warily.

He stayed by the door, not attempting to approach her. He's finding this difficult, she thought. He's unused to human contact and he doesn't know what to do or what to say. He only knows about threats and cold bargaining. Bargaining . . . Oh God, did he really think he could bargain with those myth-creatures . . . ?

When he spoke again, she heard at once that their relationship had entered a different territory. His voice was cold and distant, and there was a bleak touch-me-not quality about him.

He said, 'I'm returning to London later today.'

Fael stared at him. 'But we've only just got here.'

'That's not your concern. I'll be back on Monday night.' His tone set her beyond all the barriers.

'But the mist—' Fael looked towards the window. 'You're surely not going to drive through that?'

'Weather conditions don't bother me. In any case, it's local only. Maise is enclosed by mist for most of the year.'

Fael said, 'But – what about me?' and was annoyed to hear a pleading note in her voice. 'You're surely not going to – to just leave me here on my own?' In this huge, dark, old house where the shadows might be something more than shadows . . . Where human-hungry beings gather under the window, chuckling and plotting—

'You'll be quite safe,' he said. 'It's only for three days. I'll bring up food and an electric plate and a primus stove from the kitchen. There are peat turves in the box by the fire. Even if the electricity supply fails you'll be all right.' He studied her for a moment. 'I shall lock you in.'

'I thought you were going to say that,' rejoined Fael. 'How do you know I won't escape?'

'You can't.'

'I might. I might burn the house down. Or I might knot sheets together and climb out of the window.'

'If you burn the house, you will burn with it. And if you try to climb through the windows up here you will assuredly be dashed to pieces on the rocks,' said *Scathach* unemotionally. 'If the mists clear later on you will see for yourself that there is a sheer drop all the way to the cliff-face. Your prison is a very secure prison indeed.'

'So,' said Fael, softly, 'it is a prison after all, is it?'

'Oh yes. I thought that was understood.'

'I don't think I altogether understood it,' said Fael. And then, without letting herself think too long about what she was saying, 'Why did you run from the room last night?' she said.

She thought a flicker of bitter anger showed in the narrow eyes, but he only said, 'Have you never heard of the primitive belief of the interdependence between identity and safety?'

'I'm sorry, I don't understand you— Oh,' said Fael. 'Yes, I think I do understand. Safety reliant on identity. You mean that your only safety lies in remaining anonymous – at least, that's what you believe. And last night I—' Impossible to say, 'I saw you.' Fael said, 'Last night, I came too close, didn't I? I came too near to knowing who you are.'

'Yes.'

'But,' said Fael, 'you know, I don't know who you are. I truly don't.'

'Don't you?' said Christian Roscius, and turning, went back down the winding stair.

It had hurt more than Christian could have believed possible to see the recoil in Fael's eyes last night, and the horrified pity. It hurt as well to remember how they had sat together last evening, with a fire burning in the hearth and how the sad, dark, old house had seemed to grow warm and to unfurl hesitant little shoots of happiness. I was right about her lighting up Maise, he thought, going through to the sculleries; she would have chased away the darknesses and the memories and the lingering sadnesses and Maise might have regained a very little of its former happiness.

But the bitch had cheated him. There had been someone she had loved – that was to have been expected, and probably there would have been more than just one. She was beautiful and intelligent and clever, and she had not always been tied to a wheelchair. Yes, there would have been a lot of men who would have wanted to take her to bed and some of them had probably done so. But there had been someone special, someone with whom she had shared the ultimate intimacy of making a child, and then, perhaps, shared the torment of its loss.

Violent jealousy of this unknown man seared Christian's mind, and for a moment he bent over, feeling it lance his whole body. But overriding the jealousy, was the far deeper pain of knowing that the mad, wild dream he had spun of luring the *leanan-sidhe* into Maise, of striking that unreal, surreal bargain with them, was dead.

I didn't believe in it! cried his mind. I didn't believe it would work, not really, not truly! It was only—

It was only that it had been something to cling to: a dream, a shining Utopia, a land of heart's desire – oh God, yes, a land of heart's desire, where nobody ever gets old and bitter of tongue ... Where I should have had peace, because it's there that peace comes dropping slow from the veils of the morning ...

But Fael cheated me.

And now none of it would happen. Rossani had been right all along; Rossani was the only one worth listening to. Remember how good it felt to punish Tod Miller? said Rossani's hoarse, chuckling voice in Christian's mind. Remember the charge you got out of killing him, out of bending over him and gouging the knife deep into his flabby chest, snapping back rib bones, until you could plunge your hand in and feel the flaccid heart and feel the fluttering pumping suddenly falter ... *Get your kicks above the waist, fool!* said Rossani's voice. Like I always did ...

But I killed *Cauldron* when I killed Miller! thought Christian in anguish, and at once Rossani's hateful voice said: But what did you expect? You can't have it all ways. You carried out your plan to punish Tod Miller, and the revenge was satisfying.

But had it been Rossani, or had it been Christian himself who fed Miller's heart into the wind machine, because he deserved a ridiculous death, he deserved to have his naked body displayed for all London to see, and he deserved to have his heart spewed out over the stage ...

Christian bent over the scrubbed top of the kitchen table, his breath ragged and too fast. Miller had deserved to die – he had deserved every ounce of agony and every shred of fear and every grisly fragment of the last humiliation. The Makepiece female had deserved to die as well. But—

But I didn't expect to feel like this afterwards! he cried. I didn't expect to feel this remorse – not at killing Tod or Mia, that was part of the plan – but at ruining *Cauldron*!

It had been black bitter gall to realise too late that he might have dealt *Cauldron* a disabling blow that night, and for a time he had known murderous rage against the sly insinuating Rossani who crept so easily inside his mind, and who dictated, so arrogantly, his emotions. Rossani would not have expected Christian to care so much about *Cauldron*.

He had not expected to care so much about Fael, either. But he would have to kill her as well now. It would tear his own heart out to do it, but she had cheated him, and last night she had come too close. *And the only safety lies in complete anonymity*, you know that, don't you? said the hoarse, chuckling little voice in his mind. Never forget it.

Fael's death would be swift and painless, though. It would not be like Miller or Makepiece; not like the bitch Leila in Soho.

Soho . . . It was annoying to have to return to London and tomorrow's Sunday night meeting at the Greasepaint, but it had to be done. He had to cover his tracks in all directions; if he had simply vanished it would have caused comment, it would have set up scurrying little pockets of speculation and rumour. Therefore he would preside over one final gathering, and he would end the strange, dark syndicate that had been so satisfying and so rewarding. But it would be positively the last appearance of the creature that the street girls and the buskers and the rent boys knew as the Shadow.

As he took food from the kitchen cupboards and the fridge to carry up to Fael, he felt no fear at returning to London, to where investigations into the three deaths would still be going on.

He mounted the turret stair, and the twisted smile touched his lips briefly as he visualised the police investigations into the deaths of Tod Miller and Mia Makepiece. They would turn up nothing, of course, absolutely nothing. He was entirely safe.

* * *

Sir Julius Sherry was not best pleased at the news that, thus far, the detective inspector in charge of the murder enquiry had turned up absolutely nothing of any value.

Julius had been very shocked indeed at what had happened to poor old Toddy and Mia Makepiece. He was inclined to think kindly of Toddy now, silly old fool, shocking old ham, because Toddy, despite everyone's dubious predictions, had come up with the goods: he had produced this marvellous magical show that was going to make them all so rich.

Mia Makepiece, however, was another pair of shoes entirely. Sir Julius would not, naturally, speak ill of the dead, but he thought that Gerald Makepiece might count himself well rid of the greedy little cat. It could not be denied that Mia had been a ruthless little gold-digger, and Sir Julius would not have been surprised to learn that she had pursued the career of a tart at some point, because she had certainly never learned her tricks in Gerald's bed! A most astonishing sexual appetite she'd had, and amazingly inventive – in fact almost downright avant-garde. Julius remembered certain incidents involving lit candles and king-sized cigar-holders with a touch of embarrassment and an uncomfortable suspicion that he might nearly have got himself into blackmail territory once or twice. Perhaps he had been a touch imprudent over that liaison. Yes, perhaps just a touch. Not that it mattered now, however.

They had all had a very unpleasant time since the spectacularly gruesome appearance of the two bodies on the Harlequin's stage, and Sir Julius himself had had the most unpleasant time of all.

He had held several interviews with the police – which had been tedious – and had resulted in him privately damning Flynn Deverill from here to kingdom come, because it turned out that Flynn had taken the inspector on a private tour of the Harlequin's nether regions, culminating in the discovery that somebody had tampered with the ancient brickwork leading to the old under-stage area.

It had been at this point that everything stopped being merely tedious and accelerated into disaster. The police had opened up the entire under-stage area – 'Got to be done, sir, can't have murderers roaming about the place' – which was true, but which

felt uncomfortable and inadequate when confronted with dramatic and good-looking young men. To counteract this, he took a seat next to Gilly Blair who was always so nice to him and so very pretty. They had had several discussions about Mia – of course, Gilly had been Mia's good friend. It had been nice of her to come out to lunch with him yesterday; they had had a very good meal at a nice restaurant in Knightsbridge, and Gilly had said it had made her feel better than she had felt since the appalling second night of the show. Gerald had thought she really meant it and was not just being polite.

Julius rustled his notes importantly, cleared his throat, and said, 'Now, you will be wondering why I have called you all here like this, and—'

'And it a Sunday,' said Flynn, 'but then a man can be sacked as well on a Sunday as any other day. If that's what it is, Julius, say so at once, and those of us with religious inclinations can go off to pray for salvation and another job. The rest can go down to get drunk in the bar – you and your man there can pay.'

'Oh, I say,' began Gerald.

'We're not here to sack you!' said Julius, crossly. 'If you'd come to the trustees' meeting on Friday night, you'd know that.'

'Oh God, you weren't expecting me to come to a meeting, were you? Didn't I tell you I never go to meetings?'

'You're at this one,' pointed out Stephen.

'No, I'm here to lead a rebellion if Julius and the little fowl and the money-lender look like cheating the down-trodden peasants out of their dues. We'll be manning the barricades and tipping boiling oil down over the battlements.'

'Don't be absurd,' said Simkins, who disliked being referred to as a money-lender and thought Flynn irreverent.

'Also,' said Flynn, ignoring this, 'somebody's got to make sure that no more bits of actor managers fall into a wind machine and get spattered across the stage. Are you in trouble with the Health and Safety people because of that, Julius?'

There was a rather shocked silence, and then Maurice Camperdown said, 'Flynn, that's an extremely tasteless remark.'

'It is, isn't it?' said Flynn, pleased. 'Give me another couple of minutes and I'll come up with a description of how the pathologist's men scraped the bodies off the scenery.'

This time the silence lasted even longer, because nobody could think of a response. Flynn grinned and walked across the stage to sit on a piece of scenery.

'Shall we get to the point of the meeting,' said Gerald, at last. 'Time is getting on, you know.'

Julius cleared his throat and said, 'Well now. Most unfortunately, the results of the police investigations have turned up some – hum – structural problems in the Harlequin's foundations—'

'Somebody fell through the stage?' demanded Flynn. 'It was bound to happen one day.'

'As a matter of fact, nobody fell through anywhere,' said Sir Julius, resolutely quelling the memory of the architect and the unsound section of floor. 'But it appears that some rather major work is needed before we can re-open.'

'Extremely expensive major work,' put in Simkins, dourly.

'Which is a fairly large obstacle,' said Julius.

'We will find a way to overcome it, though,' put in Makepiece, and to his credit, managed not to say, anxiously, 'Won't we?'

'Oh, we shall find a way,' said Julius airily, 'although at the moment I have to tell you it's proving beyond our reach.' He tucked his chins into his neck and regarded the company with the air of a man being immensely sensible in the face of insurmountable odds.

Flynn said, ' "When we mean to build/We first survey the plot, then draw the model".'

'I don't see what that's got to do with—'

' "And when we see the figure of the house/Then must we rate the cost of the erection". Are you telling us that the cost of your erection's proving beyond reach, Julius?'

'Flynn, if you're being pornographic again—'

'Henry the Fourth, Part Two,' said Flynn blandly. 'When was I ever pornographic?'

'Anyway,' said Julius hastily, 'Gerald Makepiece and I have been in consultation and we have come up with rather a good scheme.' He paused, and then said, 'I should like, at this point, to formally and publicly thank Gerald who has been very helpful indeed at a number of difficult discussions.' He paused so that this could sink properly into people's minds, because it was all too easy to overlook little Makepiece's unexpectedly astute business sense. The trouble was that people tended to forget that the little rabbit had made a great deal of money manufacturing whatever it was he manufactured, and to remember only what a besotted idiot he had been over his terrible Mia.

Everyone except Flynn made vaguely appropriate noises, and Julius beamed round the room, and said, 'Now. What we have decided is that since the *Cauldron* company has no longer a London home—'

'Being doomed,' said a muffled voice from the corner.

'Being temporarily dispossessed of its theatre,' said Sir Julius, loudly, 'we propose doing what our forbears did.' He paused for effect, and several people looked bewildered. The sorceress was heard to demand of the *Fianna* captain what the devil the old boy was talking about.

'Search me. If you ask me he's been at the sauce.'

'I mean,' said Julius, pretending not to hear this, 'that we are going to take to the roads!' He beamed round the stage. 'We shall don the mantle of the strolling players of Shakespeare's day: the vagabonds and the minstrels, peddling our trade in tilt-yards and barns and inns—'

'I hope nobody expects *me* to peddle anything in a barn—'

'Or sleep in one, dear.'

'I should say not.'

'The results of our discussions,' said Julius in the tones of a man driven to the far point of extreme endurance, 'are that we shall open *Cauldron* in a theatre that was very close to the heart of James Roscius, the man responsible for so many Harlequin successes.'

He waited, but a listening silence had fallen on the company now. In his corner, slightly removed from the rest, Flynn Deverill was motionless.

'Professor Roscius,' said Sir Julius, 'had several theatrical involvements in his later life, and one of those involvements was with the Gallery Theatre in Ennismara, just outside Galway. We – that is, Gerald and I – have talked with the management of the Gallery, and the upshot is—' He paused for effect. 'The upshot is that we are taking *Cauldron* to Ireland and the Gallery.'

In the surprised silence that followed this announcement, Flynn's voice was heard to say, 'The home of the worst raff and scaff of Victorian theatre. The festering blot on the landscape of Ireland's escutcheon. Well, Julius, you and the little fowl have surpassed yourselves.' And, as Sir Julius made to speak, Flynn said, 'Mother of God, couldn't you have found a better home for us all than that tumbledown slum!'

Chapter Twenty

Flynn had not derived the usual satisfaction from taunting Julius Sherry and the others this time. Damn, he thought, walking home after the meeting; damn and blast, I'm giving way to something I really don't want to give way to. Fael. Is it Fael? If I could stop remembering that vivid moment of mental intimacy at Marivaux's it would be easier. If I could stop remembering the flare of sexual attraction that followed it, it would be even better. I wish to God I knew what's happened to her, he thought in sudden anguish.

It was better to think about something else – to think about what was happening to the Harlequin company, and to concentrate on *Cauldron* transferring to the Gallery.

He wondered, did Julius and Stephen and little Makepiece not know the Gallery Theatre's reputation? Did they not know it was the shabbiest, most dismally unsuccessful theatre in all Ireland, for God's sake? But it appeared that they did not. Professor Roscius had tried to revive the Gallery's failing fortunes shortly before his death – Flynn thought there had been some idea of setting up an exchange system with the Gallery's company playing London audiences, and the Harlequin company playing Ennismara. He supposed this was what had given Julius and Makepiece the connection to set up the present scheme.

But a great many people had tried to revive the Gallery's fortunes, and none of them had succeeded. The Gallery was irredeemably caught in its twilight world, on its own half-acre of half-slum, in the wrong part of the Ennismara suburbs. It was the haunt of tramps and winos, said the people who lived near to it; it was the meeting place of squalling cats and brawling females, if it was not a secret hideout for the provisional IRA and maybe the neo-Nazi movement, not to mention half the terrorist organisations in Europe. It was dangerous and immoral and a bad example for innocent children, they said, crossly. As well as that, it affected property values in the area.

But even the energetic Roscius, optimistically planning revivals of Boucicault and Yeats and Behan there, had said that not all the perfumes of Arabia could sweeten it, and not all the oceans of Neptune could cleanse it. *Macbeth*, thought Flynn, wryly. Trust the old boy not to mind quoting it.

It was an irreclaimable old whore, the Gallery, for hire to any tenant who would make use of it, but between hirings it sank obstinately back into its raddled squalor. Not even that awesome force in Ireland, the Roman Catholic Church, had been able to do anything about the embarrassing old place. Whole benches of bishops had tried to have it razed to the ground, saying wasn't it a scandal and a disgrace, and any number of churchmen, from archbishops downwards and cardinals upwards, had put forward worthy projects for its usage.

The trouble was that at some stage somebody had discovered that David Garrick had appeared on the Gallery's stage (rumour said he had done several other things in the Green Room with a very prominent Irish lady who could not be named); and then someone else had discovered that Oscar Wilde had written something there (no one had dared speculate on any other activities he might have indulged in), and then that Bernard Shaw had written something there as well. They dragged out pretty much every famous Irish writer they could, thought Flynn cynically, very nearly in chronological order as well.

The thing had snowballed in a way that it probably would not have done in any other country in the world, and everybody had had a whale of a time discovering new and increasingly fantastical snippets of history, until somebody delving into mildewed papers somewhere came up with what appeared to be fairly indisputable proof that the Earl of Essex – Elizabeth Tudor's Robert – had actually been involved with the building of the place during his term as Ireland's lord-lieutenant. This was seized on and although it was hotly disputed in many quarters (for what would Himself of Essex be doing in a forsaken place like Ennismara?), by that time the Gallery Theatre's legend had grown all by itself and was flourishing like the bay tree in the wilderness. And incredibly, cautious preliminary investigation of the ugly, chipped, old facade did indeed reveal an Elizabethan frontage, with surprisingly sound timber-framing. Preservation injunctions and Listed Building orders of varying grades and severity were at once smacked onto the place and people talked excitedly about rivalling the Swan at Stratford and putting on plain, untampered-with Elizabethan plays. Couldn't you have a great old time doing that, and couldn't you restore the Gallery's fortunes and set up a grand tourist attraction as well? The pity had been that there had not been anyone prepared to take overall responsibility, let alone admitting to the ownership of the land on which the wretched place stood. Every attempt had been a resounding flop.

Flynn, walking back to his flat in the dark winter afternoon, thought it was almost as if the place had an albatross tied around its neck. And this was the place that Julius Sherry intended to use for the re-staging of *Cauldron*! Has he *seen* it, for God's sake? thought Flynn. Has he even seen a photograph of it? I suppose he simply seized on the tentative connection with the Harlequin, and I suppose the Ennismara authorities seized on the chance to have the place occupied for a time.

A sleety rain was starting to fall as he reached his flat and he went quickly up the stairs to his own floor, switching on lights and heating. He set the kettle to boil for a cup of tea, and went through to the studio. There were a number of hours to fill in before setting out, and there were designs to submit for *Peter Pan* for the J. M. Barrie festival in March. It would be a good commission; Flynn would be pleased to get it, and he would normally have sat down at the long work-table with enthusiasm. He had already started to rough out some ideas, thinking that the nursery could have a slightly sinister feel for the lost-shadow scenes when Peter first appeared ... And then Captain Hook and the pirate ship – that was something one could have a great old time with, providing one avoided that recent Robin Williams film, of course. And Never-Never Land – yes, you could weave in a few present-day analogies there if you were so inclined and if it chimed with what the director wanted. Flynn, trying to sink himself into the project, thought involuntarily that that was the kind of thing *Cauldron*'s creator would certainly have wanted. *Cauldron*'s creator. Fael Miller?

Fael. All roads led back to her, it seemed. And the trouble was that once he started thinking about her it was difficult to stop. It was ridiculous to feel this scalding anxiety because she had disappeared as completely and as unexpectedly as one of *Cauldron*'s wraith-like characters. It was the height of absurdity to draw parallels with the abducting of the Irish queen by the *sidh* prince.

The sleet was driving hard against the windows now; Flynn glanced out and repressed a shiver. It was a night for staying indoors in front of a good fire, with the curtains closed. It was not a night for stealing out to a raffish theatre club in the sleazier part of Soho to identify a murderer who looked like something from a *film noir*. But it had to be done. The arrangement had been made with Bill at the Greasepaint, and Flynn was not going to renege on it because of a blizzard – particularly when Bill had taken so much persuading.

'Because he's a weird one, this,' Bill had said that night, when Flynn, his hair dripping wet from the cold-water dousing, had outlined the plan. 'He's suspicious and secretive, and he don't like strangers.'

'He won't see strangers,' Flynn had said, towelling his hair and his face vigorously and feeling the whisky fumes clearing from his brain. 'He won't see me at all; I'll be in hiding.'

'Who's going to hide you?' Bill had demanded.

'You are.'

'Am I hell as like! Listen, Mr Deverill, this is a very weird bloke indeed.'

'You said that.'

'No, but even the girls and the pimps are frightened of him.'

'I'm not a street-walker or a pimp,' Flynn had said.

'Seriously, though. There was a girl got done in a few weeks ago – nasty affair, it was, and they never caught the man. She used to come here. Leila, that was her name. Bit older than the others.'

'Are you saying our man did that as well?'

'Bit of a coincidence, isn't it?'

'Yes, it is. All the more reason to find out a bit more. And

I'm not frightened – no, really I'm not, Bill. Show me the room now till we see where I can hide.'

In the end Bill had complied, but he had been reluctant. 'You'll think better of it when you wake up properly sober, Mr Deverill,' he had said.

But Flynn had known he would not think better of it. Because someone had killed Mia Makepiece and torn away half her skin to make a grisly cloak, and someone had dug out poor silly Tod Miller's heart. And it was more than possible that the same person had stolen out to Fael's house and overpowered her and carried her off.

I've got to find out who he is, thought Flynn, grimly.

Fael wheeled the chair through the rooms that *Scathach* had designated as her prison, trying to see if there was a way of getting out, but finding none. Of course not, said her mind angrily: did you really expect him to have left you an escape route? Did you seriously believe that he wouldn't have checked every crack in every floorboard and every section of every window and door before bringing you up here?

He had left a couple of hours earlier – Fael had heard the powerful car go snarling down the cliff road – but before that he had brought food up as he had promised. There was bread and butter, and cheese and eggs. A small cardboard box contained several large tins of soup and corned beef and tuna fish. There were also several vacuum packs of ham and bacon and a bag of pears and apples. In a second box was a canister of tea and one of instant coffee, and two sealed cartons of milk. He had added three half-bottles of red wine. About two glasses for each night. Elegant to the last, thought Fael. None of it comprised a feast, but it would certainly sustain her very comfortably for three days and probably longer. There was no fridge, of course, but the milk and the perishable stuff could be put on the bathroom window ledge.

And now she was alone in the silent old house; she was alone with the softly creaking floorboards that might almost make you think someone was creeping quietly up the twisty stairway, and she was alone with the clustering shadows that would certainly start to form as the light drained outside.

None of that now! said Fael determinedly. I'll make myself some lunch – yes, it's one o'clock already and I'm quite hungry.

She scrambled eggs over the small electric plate more easily than she had been expecting, buttered a slice of bread, and added a wedge of cheese and an apple. She ate sitting by the large window with the velvet seat, where it was possible to make out the looming shapes of the Moher crags through the mists. Was the curious, sinister, Self-Bored Stone on this side? It had been difficult to keep her bearings on the drive here, but Fael thought it might be on this side. If the mists cleared later she would look again.

It had been rather an unusual tale, the Self-Bored Stone one, but there had been that odd, familiar resonance about it. It would only be because all these legends and fairytales echoed one another. Look at Rossani, her father's *Dwarf Spinner*. Fael could remember her mother saying that Rossani had at least half a dozen other incarnations in various parts of the world. There had been a stack of different versions of the story on the shelves of the Pimlico house which Tod had presumably acquired when he was writing his musical. Fael could remember her mother reading some of them to her, and then later, reading them for herself.

Rossani had been the Italian name, of course, and Fael thought that the best-known – 'Rumpelstiltskin' – was the German version. English and Welsh folklore called the evil little creature Tom Tit Tot and Trwtyn-Tratyn and two or three other names, which she had forgotten. And he had been quite a widely-travelled dwarf; in France he had gone under the title of Robiquet, and in Hungary, Winterkolbe. Fael thought there had even been a Russian and an Icelandic version, although she could not remember much about either of them. The Icelanders had a terrific myth culture, of course. And in Austria he had been called something that sounded more like one of those marvellous Austrian gateaux, all chocolate and almonds, than a vengefully-inclined goblin. Kruzimugeli, was it? Fael grinned.

But in each story the theme was the same: the creature helped the heroine, extorted the grisly promise to either grab the heroine's first-born or her virtue by way of reward, and then

246

relied on his anonymity to preserve him from discovery or justice.

His anonymity ... Light exploded in Fael's mind. His *anonymity*. The nameless, unnamed creature helped the heroine, and then kidnapped her. And his power could only be broken if his name could be discovered. And: '*Have you never heard of the primitive belief of the interdependence between identity and safety?*' he had said.

Why didn't I see it before? thought Fael, sitting up very straight in the chair, her eyes bright with discovery. Why didn't I see the parallel before – it's very nearly exact. It's the *Dwarf Spinner* replayed, it's all those macabre fairytales come to life. Winterkolbe and Rossani and Tom Tit Tot alive and well and stalking the west coast of Ireland. How amazing.

Yes, and I'm the beleaguered heroine, which means he had to covet either the first-born child or my virtue. Well he's had the virtue, even though he wasn't the first to have it. He probably didn't expect to be; this is the permissive twentieth century after all, it's not some timeless myth-world.

But he certainly wanted the first-born child. Fael sat very still, staring through the mists beyond her window. Even Tod had never known about that poor half-thing, tipped out by the car crash, ending its poor little life in a hospital bowl ... Oh blast, I didn't know I still minded. Oh hell.

She finished her lunch and washed up the plate and knife and fork in the little bathroom handbasin, her mind turning determinedly to the enigmatic creature who had brought her here. Not for the first time, she wondered about his background. It was only in fairytales that the villain made his appearance fully grown, apparently with no past life, no childhood, no schooling or parents.

What had her villain's childhood been like? Had he been to an ordinary school, or a university? Because he was certainly no fool, in fact he was extremely intelligent and very widely-read. And there had been the music – someone taught him music to a very high standard indeed, thought Fael. Someone taught him about composition as well, in the way that Roscius tried to teach me, only I hadn't the spark of originality. But if he was one of the professor's students – which is what he tried to indicate that first night – that's not so very surprising. The feeling of hovering identification still lingered. I ought to know who he is, thought Fael, frowning. I ought to be able to make sense of all the clues. She could not do it. It was like trying to pin down an elusive memory; it was like trying to remember why a face or a snatch of music was familiar. You tried and tried, but it kept slithering through your grasp, and it was only when you gave up and stopped trying that the memory suddenly clicked into place and you knew.

Whoever her captor was he had been gone for over four hours now. Would he have reached Rosslare and boarded a ferry? Fael's mind conjured up the image of the slenderly-built figure driving through the countryside, driving on to the ferry, remote and withdrawn . . . The silk mask would be firmly in place, and the mental mask would be in place as well, concealing the cold, dark creature who had brought her out here and shut her away.

He was there all the time, she thought. That appalling face was there all along – I could almost have guessed at that, of course – but I could never have guessed at the complexity of that second self. There's more than a trace of the schizophrenic about him; in fact he's very nearly Jekyll and Hyde. The trouble is I think there might be a trace of the schizophrenic in my own feelings; I think I might still respond to the masked lover, she thought, with profound self-disgust. I might very easily respond as strongly as ever, even while I was shuddering from what's behind the mask . . .

And then, the thought she had been trying to force down ever since last night finally thrust itself up to the surface: what would *Scathach* do with her now that she could no longer provide the first-born child for his grisly bargain with the *leanan-sidhe*?

The Gallery Theatre in Ennismara was as appalling as Flynn Deverill had prophesied; in fact Julius Sherry and Gerald Makepiece, arriving in Ireland along with the stage manager and his electrician to reconnoitre the terrain, thought it was worse. Plainly there would have to be immediate discussions as to what was going to be done, because neither of them had visualised anything like this and both were secretly wishing they had taken more notice of Flynn Deverill, who might be exasperating beyond bearing at times, but who appeared to have told the truth on this occasion.

'Yards of peeling facade,' said Julius, staring up at the glowering exterior.

'Miles of rotting floorboards,' added Gerald, going back inside. 'And I heard the stage manager saying that the lighting's 1940s vintage.'

'We're probably lucky there's lighting at all, and not gas jets or limes,' said Julius, grimly. 'We can't possibly put *Cauldron* on here. We can't bring the company to this terrible place.'

But they would have to put *Cauldron* on here, and they would have to bring the company here, because the arrangements had been made and a lease had been signed for a three-month period of the Gallery, and individual contracts had been renegotiated with most of the actors for the out-of-London run. Sir Julius had a brief but sickeningly vivid image of the quarrels that would rage if those contracts were terminated, and felt ill when he tried to calculate the compensation that would have to be paid out, never mind braving Equity's wrath and that of the Irish authorities.

The negotiations for the leasing of the Gallery had been conducted in London, with a body which was based in Galway and which was called the County Arts Association. Simkins of the bank, lugubriously reviewing finances and gloomily aware of the bank's investment, had told Sir Julius that he thought this was the nearest thing to a governing board they would be likely to get.

'They're responsible for the actual letting,' he had said. 'And also for maintenance, although from the sound of things there isn't any too much money for that.'

'Of course,' said the official whom Julius and Gerald Makepiece ran to earth in a small office on the main Galway road, 'of course, there isn't any too much money for maintenance.'

'So we see,' said Sir Julius, acidly. 'The place is a disgrace and a scandal.'

'Oh, it is,' agreed the official, whose name was Flanagan, and who thought it a grand thing to be having this London company over here. 'It's a disgrace to us all, but we're in the hands of the *Dail Eireann*, you see, there's the problem.'

'Government funding,' said Sir Julius. It had a depressingly familiar ring.

'And then of course, there's Preservation Orders on the place till they're coming out of its chimney pots,' added Flanagan, cheerfully. 'You've to go through fifty different societies and have a hundred surveyors in from heaven knows where before you can so much as change a light bulb. We're tied hand, foot and whisker.' He eyed them hopefully. 'But if you could add your word to ours, I daresay we'd get a bit done to the place, you know. Just to spruce it up here and there.'

Gerald, possibly with the optimism of ignorance, suggested that it would not take very much to make the place inhabitable for the run of the show.

'Oh, it would not,' agreed Flanagan, pleased to find a kindred spirit.

'Because we don't want to undertake the entire restoration, you understand.'

'Of course you don't. Nor need to. It's good, sound timber in there, in the main.'

Gerald murmured something about rising damp and roofs, and Flanagan at once said what was a bit of damp, for God's sake; hadn't all old properties a bit of damp? You'd cure that in a week once the heating was running.

'And the roof's sound, I know that, for we had to have it seen to two years since. But a bit of re-rendering to the outside – providing you comply with the Preservation Order – and maybe a scrub-down of the interior plasterwork and a lick of gilt paint where it's peeled. That'd work wonders.'

'We'll consider it and let you know,' said Sir Julius, leading Gerald out of the office before he could say anything that might be considered as having compromised finances the company did not have.

'See here, Makepiece,' he said, as they sped back to the theatre in the car they had hired for the duration, 'see here now, we can't have any talk about putting the place to rights ourselves. The lease we negotiated isn't a fully repairing lease; that means we don't have to touch a splinter of that rotting old hulk—'

'I know what a fully repairing lease is,' said Gerald, who did not but was not going to admit it.

'—and the onus is all on the County Arts Association to make it – what's the wording? – habitable and suitable for the performing of public performances of drama and the furtherance thereof.'

'Yes, but they aren't going to make it habitable and suitable for the furtherance thereof,' pointed out Gerald. 'They haven't got the money to do it – you heard what Mr Flanagan said. They're in the hands of their government. The *Dail*,' he added, carefully pronouncing it as Mr Flanagan had, because when in Rome you had to do as the Romans did.

'Publicity,' said Sir Julius firmly. 'That's the thing we want. Publicity and sponsors. We'll get the press on our side, and we'll appeal to people's better nature – we could employ a press agent to do it for us, in fact. There're one or two very good ones over here—'

Gerald said he did not see the point of paying a press agent when it would be more straightforward to pay for the repairs.

'No, but it would be cheaper in the long run. And with good planning we'll have sponsors inside of a week, and very likely half a dozen specialist companies clamouring to do the actual work free.'

'Well,' said Gerald, doubtfully, 'I should prefer to just do the work ourselves. I think it would be more dignified.'

'Blow dignity,' said Sir Julius.

By the time they reached their hotel, the minor difference of opinion was starting to escalate, Sir Julius still insisting that a properly orchestrated publicity campaign was the answer; Gerald maintaining that a judicious lick and a promise would do wonders.

'Unfortunately,' said Sir Julius, haughtily, 'it is not customary practice in theatre circles to give a lick and a promise to buildings, especially when it is not the company's responsibility. And, Mr Makepiece, it would be very expensive.'

Gerald drew himself up to his full height, and said, just as haughtily, 'The expense, Sir Julius, need not weigh with me.'

They parted company, Julius telling himself he had reminded the silly little man that he was a person of some standing and prestige in his world; Gerald gleefully pleased at having emphasised his own superior wealth and open-handedness. He might even mention the fact to Gilly when she arrived here; generosity was an attractive feature – Mia had always said she liked a man to be generous. Oh, poor Mia. But life had to be lived, and it had been curiously comforting to find that after all Mia had not run off with another man, but had been killed by a calculating murderer who had coveted her. It made Mia seem doubly desirable and alluring: it almost made it seem as if she had driven some man mad with her charms, which was something Gerald could well believe, and which also reflected flatteringly on Gerald himself. He could almost imagine people pointing him out; perhaps saying, That's the poor man who was married to that famous actress – the one who was killed for her beauty. He's no Adonis, is he? they would say; but he must have something to have had a wife like that.

It had to be admitted that shocking as Mia's death had been, it was a whole lot easier to grieve for a murderer's victim than for a faithless wife.

Chapter Twenty-One

Flynn stood in the long, dimly-lit room beneath the Greasepaint Club, and felt the strangeness of the place ebb and flow all about him.

He had sufficient stage experience to know that a good deal of the atmosphere came from the setting – trappings, that's all these are, he thought. Take away the sultry lighting and replace it with ordinary 100-watt light bulbs; tear down those stifling curtains, and what would you be left with? A large half-cellar under a slightly raffish Soho club.

But he's a clever devil, whoever he is, thought Flynn. He's set the stage exactly right, and he's sold these people the idea of someone slightly mystical, slightly unearthly.

Even so, there was still something uncomfortable in here – something that had nothing to do with the macabre lighting or the velvet curtains and the solitary chair behind the long rosewood table. Rosewood, said his mind appraisingly. That didn't come out of the Greasepaint's ragbag lumber room. A bit of a hedonist, this villain. But he's got style, thought Flynn.

Bill and the doorman, who had had to be brought in on the plot, were still being determinedly pessimistic, Bill prophesying all manner of unpleasant scenes, and the doorman pointing out that this was the creature hardened Soho pimps shuddered from, and that the buskers and the tough little Piccadilly hookers had dubbed the Shadow.

'I don't give a damn what they call him,' said Flynn. 'I'm going to find out who he is, or die in the attempt – no, all right, I didn't mean that literally, Bill. See now, where will we have the hiding-place? It's a pity you didn't warn me the room hasn't a cupboard to its name, because a cupboard would have been great.'

Neither Bill nor the doorman thought that anywhere down here would be great at all. They repeated their admonitions all over again, and the doorman pointed out that they could not take any responsibility for anything that might happen if Flynn was discovered. Bill, mindful of his slightly longer service and slightly heavier responsibilities, added that the Greasepaint and the management could not take any responsibility either. They reminded one another of Leila, poor silly cow, and said that wherever Mr Deverill hid, he would have to be very still and very quiet.

'I'll be as still as the night and as quiet as the dawn,' agreed Flynn. 'I'll be as careful as a virginal nun with a— Will I be safe behind these velvet drapes, do you think?'

The drapes were the ones that were normally half-drawn across the door which was where the Shadow entered, and Bill and the doorman did not think that Mr Deverill would be safe behind them at all. They did not think he would be safe anywhere in this room tonight, in fact, although it was looking as if it was a waste of time to say so. And at least the curtains were thick and wide. The doorman explained worriedly about the Shadow's entrance: they could not be sure that the curtains would not be disarranged when he came in. A remarkable entrance he made, so people said, not that people said much at all, on account of being afraid of the outcome. The Shadow did not like these meetings to be gossiped about.

Flynn said, 'Oh, will you stop acting as if he's Jesus Christ making his entrance for the Second Coming and Satan incarnate rolled into one! Listen now, could we draw this left-hand curtain a bit further back so that it's across this recess here? If I stayed behind it I'd be able to see him come in and I'd have a fair view of most of the room as well, and I don't believe anyone would suspect anything.' He stood back, surveying the fall of the curtains critically.

'You'll hardly be a couple of feet away from him, Mr Deverill,' said the doorman.

'All the better. I'll get a good look at him. We'll have to cut a couple of spyholes in the curtain though – here and here, I should think, shouldn't you? If I sit on the floor I'll be below

254

people's eye-level. Bill, stand back and tell me if you can see me peering through.'

'No,' said Bill, after a suitable interval. 'But you'll have to be careful not to move.'

'I know it. Listen, fetch me a bottle of whisky before curtain up, will you? If I'm to be stuck here half the night I'll want something to keep me company.'

'I'll bring half a bottle,' said Bill.

'A quarter,' put in the doorman, lugubriously.

'Yes, or you'll be three-parts drunk by the time the meeting starts,' said Bill. 'I know you, Mr Deverill.' He went off to the main door that led to upper floors and his own domain, the doorman following, both of them agreeing that this was the wildest idea anyone had ever heard of, but that was the Irish for you.

The curtains smelt of stale cigarette smoke and cheap perfume, but they provided better cover than Flynn had hoped. There was sufficient space to sit on the floor in reasonable comfort providing he drew his knees up, and he could lean back against the wall. It was half past eleven. He unscrewed the top of the whisky bottle – at least Bill had made it a good malt even if he had only brought a quarter bottle – and took a long drink. The room settled into silence. Flynn could hear the steady ticking of the clock on the far wall. Tick-tick . . . Tick-tick . . . He was aware of his heart beginning to beat a bit faster than normal.

It was a quarter to midnight when the silence was disturbed by the first group of people coming in from the main part of the club. Flynn set down the whisky bottle, and froze into immobility.

The room filled up quite quickly, and in a much more orderly fashion than he had visualised. There was a low murmur of voices but it was a subdued murmur, and it was virtually impossible to hear what anyone was saying. None of these sounds were the sounds that Flynn had expected to hear, given the character of the people, given the nature of the venue. According to Bill this was a roomful of street girls and rent boys and street musicians. Probably there would be a few drug pushers as well. It was remarkable for such a gathering to be so quiet.

There were ten minutes to go. Flynn put his eye to the tiny spyhole, and saw that there were easily eighty to a hundred people in the room already. And they were still coming in. They were coming down the steps at the other end of the room, in twos and threes, the girls mostly in mini-skirts and low, clinging sweaters and high heels; the men wearing jeans or chinos, and leather or cheap velvet jackets. There was a sprinkling of drag artists and several people whom Flynn thought were professional buskers. They sat on the rows of chairs that Bill and the doorman had put out, some of them studiedly nonchalant, others quieter. The thought that this mysterious, hedonistic gentleman wielded a greater power than Flynn had bargained for, formed rather chillingly on his mind.

And then little by little, as the hands of the clock inched their way to midnight, the low murmuring died away and a waiting silence replaced it. Flynn could feel the blood pounding in his head, and he could almost hear his own too-fast heartbeats – damn, I'm as bad as the rest of them! But something very eerie was approaching. Flynn could feel apprehension filling up the low-ceilinged room; he could feel the silence becoming charged with nervous excitement. One minute to go, he thought, glancing across at the wall clock. Sixty seconds . . . fifty . . . There's someone coming . . . Is there? Yes, I can hear soft footsteps. Someone's just outside the door.

And then above the footsteps he heard a faint snatch of music – someone humming or someone singing very softly, so softly that it was as if the person was doing it unconsciously. This was so unexpected and somehow so bizarre that Flynn felt prickles of fear scud across his skin. The masked creature? Or only a stray passer-by, humming to himself as he wended his way home?

The tension in the room was so strong that the air was nearly shivering with it. And the footsteps were unmistakably approaching the door; they were in exact synchronisation with the ticking clock. Tick-tick . . . Pad-pad . . . Tick-tick . . . Tap-tap . . . They were in time with the low humming as well. Flynn frowned, trying to hear the melody more clearly, and then it came suddenly nearer, and he heard not only the tune, but the words.

O never go walking in the fields of the flax
At night when the looms are a-singing . . .

Flynn knew instantly what it was. He thought he should have been prepared, given the grisly nature of the Harlequin murders. The Shadow was singing the macabre lament from Tod Miller's *Dwarf Spinner*, the chant that the evil Rossani sang as he padded after his victims, and that the BBC had tried to ban on Radio One, not so much because of its gruesome content, but more because of the dwarf magician's exultant sensuality as he savoured his victims.

Rossani's at work and he's hungry for prey;
He'll melt down your eyes and he'll spin them for gold.
He'll peel off your skin and he'll sew him a cloak.

He'll cut out your heart and he'll weave it to gold.
He'll grind down your bones and he'll shred up your soul.

Flynn had never heard the original rendering, and subsequent recordings lost a good deal of the blood-thirsty voluptuousness. But on the opening night of the *Dwarf Spinner* this song had stopped the show, and even in the milk-and-water revivals it was powerful, sung by the tormented Rossani as he stood alone on a dimly-lit stage, spotlighted by a single crimson gel, the only musical accompaniment a sinisterly-throbbing bass-viol, and a rhythmic, low-key tapping of the base drum.

Heard like this, crouched in a dark corner of a dimly-lit room, the soft music thrummed with its own inner menace, and Flynn felt a lurch of fear again. But at least it proves the connection, he thought. This is the killer who butchered poor old Toddy Miller and that vain, silly Mia.

There was a faint movement in the shadows by the door, and as the chimes of midnight sounded, between one heartbeat and the next, he was there. Flynn had thought he was prepared and to some extent armoured, but his mind still jumped with surprise. It almost seemed as if the figure had materialised.

A little sigh ruffled the still surface of the room, releasing some of the nervous tension. He was here. Now the evening could be dealt with and forgotten until next week. It's as if he exerts some kind of hypnotism over them, thought Flynn, unable to take his eyes off the small cloaked figure as it moved to take the waiting chair. My God, this is one very clever gentleman indeed! He's just performed the subtlest, most brilliant piece of stage illusion I've ever seen! The door hardly moved – I can't quite see it, but I should certainly have heard it, for God's sake! He forced himself to concentrate. The stranger was studying the company and his whole manner was cool and unhurried. Flynn stared at him, forcing himself to remain absolutely still. Because if he suspects I'm here he'll probably haul me out and cut out my heart and weave it for gold . . . No, that was Rossani. And he's already done that with Tod. In any case, people don't do that kind of thing in the real world. No? What makes you think this one belongs to the real world? jeered his mind.

But he pushed this very disturbing thought away, and watched carefully as the orderly procession to the rosewood table began. He saw at once what Bill and the doorman had meant by calling it organised. It was very organised indeed; in fact it looked orchestrated. It's some kind of accounting, thought Flynn. They're all handing over money. Is that all he is, then? A high-gloss pimp? Is this only a souped-up protection racket? Perversely he felt a stab of disappointment because it would be something of a let-down if this charismatic gentleman turned out to be nothing more than a common-or-garden Soho racketeer.

If he'd turn his head a bit I could get a better look at him, thought Flynn. Damn! Maybe it wasn't such a good idea to be behind the curtain after all! I'm behind him and I can only see the back of him. But then, as if in mocking response, the man did turn his head, and Flynn saw with a little thrill of repulsion that he was wearing huge-lensed, thickly-black glasses and that the lenses caught the dull light, turning them into hard, shell-like growths that gave an eerie impression of sight. Like a giant fly's head, with enormous bulbous insectile eyes, thought Flynn, in appalled fascination. He's like a mutant creature – something out of a necromancer's crucible or an evil geneticist's laboratory. Flowing Rastafarian-type plaits hung from beneath the slouch hat, covering most of the face, but Flynn, inching as far forward as he dared, could not make out anything behind the plaits.

Several times he caught the low, soft voice as it spoke to the people trooping up to the table, but he was not sufficiently near to hear what was being said. And then, without warning, it appeared to end; the bizarre figure stood up and the rustlings and scraping of chairs – the little trickles of conversation that had broken out here and there – ceased instantly. The man said, 'I will bid all of you goodbye now,' and a stir of surprise went through the listeners. This is something new, thought Flynn, straining to hear. This is something different.

The soft voice said, 'Our association must end now. I am leaving. You will work for yourselves in future. You will look after your own interests.' He paused, and Flynn unknowingly shared a thought with Fael, who had noticed that her dark, satanic familiar often sounded stilted, and with Mia Makepiece who had thought her unknown lover wrote in an old-fashioned way. He's awkward with words! thought Flynn. He's no fool and he possesses that extraordinary magnetic power, but when it comes to addressing people in an ordinary way he's very nearly inept. Because he's unused to human contact, is that it?

The murmur of surprise had grown momentarily louder, and Flynn could hear people asking one another whether they had suspected this, and whether it was a good thing. One or two of the girls were being loudly nonchalant, tossing their hair and saying they would do better on their own anyway: you did not need a protector or a pimp these days, what century did the Shadow think he was living in, for God's sake? Several of the men told one another they would be bloody glad not to have to hand over five per cent every sodding week, never mind it got you a bit of security and a reasonable deal from landlords and such. You could sort your own landlords out, thank you very much! Who needed a protector?

The dark figure was stepping back unnoticed, going as silently and as dramatically as he had come. Hell and the devil, I nearly lost him! thought Flynn, and moving as swiftly as a cat, slipped unseen from behind the curtain and went out through the door in pursuit.

Even on a Sunday night this part of London teemed with life, and Flynn wondered what he would do if his quarry hailed a taxi, and whether it would be as easy as it looked on films to summon a second vehicle and utter the classic line, 'Follow that cab.'

But at length the cloaked figure turned into a quiet, tree-lined street near the river, and vanished into a tall, narrow house. Flynn stopped and looked about him, and for the first time since leaving the Greasepaint was able to focus on something other than staying out of sight.

Once or twice he had lost his bearings, but he had spotted several familiar streets or squares on the way, and now that he could look about him without fear of being seen, he knew exactly where he was. He knew this part of London, in fact he knew this very street, close to Christchurch Street. He thought cynically that if this villain could afford to live in this part of Chelsea, he must be a very well-heeled villain indeed.

But Flynn not only knew the street, he knew the house into which his quarry had vanished. He knew because when he first came to London, with scarcely a penny to his name, he had been made very welcome at this house at any time he cared to turn up.

'No need for warning,' the house's owner had said. 'Just arrive on the doorstep. There will always be a meal here for you; there will be a bed for you as well if you need it.'

There had always been a meal and there had often been people from the theatre and music world as well. It had been a tedious journey from the cramped basement flat which had been all he could afford in those days, but it was a journey he had always made with a sense of grateful anticipation. Sometimes there would be dizzyingly important theatre people there, which had been heady stuff for a twenty-one-year-old who had still to make his mark in this chancy world. On other nights impromptu musical evenings would start up out of nowhere, and a disparate collection of people would take over the entire ground floor of the house, and improvise or rehearse or simply flop on cushions on the floor and talk into the small hours. Flynn's mother, who belonged to a generation who believed that piano-playing was a useful social skill, had insisted that Flynn learn the rudiments of music, and as well as that he had the Irish ability to blend with any company. He had enjoyed it all: the musicians and the embryo conductors and the would-be composers, and the directors and the actors.

Most of all, he had been unceasingly grateful for the curious sense of security that he was always given by the owner of the house.

The owner of the house.

Professor James Roscius.

Chapter Twenty-Two

'... messengers were sent all over the land to inquire after the dwarf's name.'

German Popular Stories, Translated from the *Kinder und Haus-Marchen*, collected by M. M. Grimm from oral tradition, 1823

Christian had stayed behind the curtain in the Chelsea house, leaving the rooms in darkness, so that he could watch Flynn Deverill without Flynn knowing.

It was almost two a.m. when Flynn abandoned his watch, dug his hands deeply into his jacket pockets and went back down the road, and Christian smiled to himself. Exactly as he had predicted. Flynn was going back to wherever he lived, and he would spend what was left of the night mulling over what he had seen and what had happened, and he would almost certainly draw the exact conclusions Christian wanted him to draw. It had amused him to lead Flynn through London's streets, reaching Chelsea only when it suited Christian to do so.

He pulled the curtains tightly across and switched on lights, going quietly about the familiar rooms, packing things into boxes and suitcases. If he was to leave London for any length of time, it was vital to ensure that he left no trace of his identity behind.

It was not very likely that he would do so. Since his father's death five years ago and his own arrival in London, he had striven for complete anonymity and he had succeeded. The practical side had been the most difficult, but he had overcome it by opening a bank account under the name of Mr Christopher James at a large branch of Barclays in West London. The money that the professor had left had been invested by a broker operating from Dublin, and all income was paid directly into the bank. Gas and electricity bills were dealt with by standing order, and if a repair was needed to the house, Christian wrote to a building contractor, posting the key by registered post, and leaving London while the work was done. As a security measure he always had all the locks changed by a different company after one of these jobs. Ready cash had come from the Soho organisation, so that he had seldom even needed to cash a cheque. He smiled briefly at the memory of the Greasepaint nights. He had enjoyed those; he had enjoyed the power he had wielded over the girls and the street musicians and the rent boys.

Everything had worked, as Christian had known it would, and all that anyone knew about the seldom-seen Mr James was that he led a quiet life, paid his bills scrupulously, and took no part at all in the pleasant little social events that local residents organised and attended. He had not even been labelled a recluse or an oddity; he was simply a lone gentleman who had a house here but who was away a good deal, probably on business, probably at some country cottage. Anonymous. London was full of such people. His neighbours would probably not even notice he had gone for longer than usual this time.

Leaving this house empty for such a long stretch worried him slightly, but he could not risk trying to sell it – a sale would mean solicitors and signing legal documents for which the useful Mr James's name could not be invoked. He had spent some time considering whether it could be let. This was more feasible; he could write to the bank, instructing them to appoint an estate agent to find a suitable tenant, and it would give him an extra source of income; houses in this part of Chelsea were at a very high premium indeed. But after some thought he had rejected the idea; his father had died a relatively wealthy man, even by today's standards, and the Soho ring had been profitable while it lasted. Christian did not actually need the money. And even if the bank were given a power of attorney there would still be legalities to deal with and presumably a deed to be signed for a lease arrangement.

It could not be done. It would lay down too many trails and

too many clues to his identity and perhaps even to his where-abouts. He would leave the house as it was for the time being, and later he might arrange for one of those house-cleaning firms to come in once a month or so to keep the place aired, and tidy the garden. Payment could be made through the bank, and a doorkey sent with reasonable anonymity. At the back of his mind was also the thought that he might need the house as a bolthole at some future date. He did not foresee having to leave Ireland and Maise again, and he thought his plans were foolproof, but no plan was entirely foolproof, only a fool believed that. Yes, a bolthole in this part of London, where he was not known, would be a very good thing indeed.

As he locked the door and stacked the last suitcase into the car, he was smiling as he remembered Flynn Deverill. Had Flynn really not guessed that there would be spies within the camp; that there would be moles among the motley collection of people that the organisation had drawn in? Christian had known about Flynn's visit to the Greasepaint from three separate sources – none of them had been the doorman or Bill the barman – and he had known that Flynn was planning to watch the meeting from a hiding place and then slip out to follow him. He had known from these spies as well, that the police had not taken Flynn's statement about a masked intruder very seriously. Were you extravagant and rude with them, Flynn? he had thought in delight.

Even if the police started to cast about for the intruder, they would find no clues as to his identity. Christian had covered all his tracks and he was perfectly safe.

And now Flynn would follow him to Ireland; Christian knew this as surely as he knew the sun would rise tomorrow. Flynn's imagination had been caught and fired – possibly his chivalry had been fired as well and certainly his sexual ardour had been aroused by Fael. He would have added up all the clues he had – clues that in some cases had been deliberately left out for him to find – and he would guess at the link with Christian's father. He would come to Ireland and he would eventually come to Maise.

And then Christian would kill him.

As he swung the car out towards the west-bound motorway,

Rossani's spirit was filling him up once more, and the evil, erratic mind was in the ascendant.

O never go walking at Beltane at dusk
In company of one whom you know not to trust;
Rossani's a-prowl and he's looking for fools;
He'll cut out your heart and he'll weave it to gold.
He'll grind down your bones and he'll shred up your soul.

O Flynn, thought Christian Roscius, the dark exultant power surging through him; O Flynn, you're walking into the company of one you should never trust! You're walking into Rossani's lair, Flynn, and even though you think you've guessed Rossani's identity, you don't know the half!

The hatred he had so long felt against the dazzling, successful Flynn scalded through his entire body, leaving him gasping and half-blinded. He was the son of my father's heart! thought Christian, bitterly. My father stamped Flynn with his own likeness; he made Flynn free in a world that should have been mine! *I* should have been the one who was welcomed and made much of in the house in Chelsea: guided and sponsored and protected by James Roscius! *I* should have been the one at Fael Miller's side on *Cauldron*'s glittering opening night; the one she smiled at with that blend of interest and sexual awareness!

The agony of jealousy tore through him again, so that for a moment his hands clenched about the steering wheel, and the unwinding ribbon of road wavered before his vision.

And then it cleared, and in its place was the soaring triumph once more.

Because for all Flynn's cleverness, it would be Christian himself who would have the final victory. Flynn was walking into Rossani's lair, and once he was there, the balance would be redressed.

Gilly was a bit startled to find Flynn Deverill on her doorstep and receive the abrupt, off-hand invitation to supper. She was even more startled when he said, 'This isn't a ploy to get you into bed, Gilly – not that you aren't enormously beddable, you understand. All that red hair – the pre-Raphaelite look, very sexy. But I have a thing on my mind just now, and I can't spare the energy for seducing anyone.'

'Ah. Then the supper—'

'I need an ally,' said Flynn. 'There's a plot going on – at least, I think there is – and I have to uncover it. I don't want to do it, but I think I have to.'

'Is it to do with Tod Miller's murder? And his daughter's disappearance?'

'It is.'

'Oh. And there's a plot.' Gilly tried the word out, which seemed a bit melodramatic on the face of it, but not when you heard it coming from this extremely melodramatic young man. 'Why d'you want me as an ally?' she demanded.

'Because I need someone inside the company and I don't want the likes of Julius or the little fowl,' said Flynn impatiently, as if this ought to be obvious. 'I want someone who knows what's been going on inside the Harlequin – someone who really understands about the oddness of everything. Mia's disappearance just before the first night, and then her death and Tod's death.'

'And Fael Miller's disappearance.'

'Yes.'

He paused and a slight frown creased his brow. Gilly looked at him and thought: That's the motive. He doesn't want to admit it – he might not even know it – but that's what's really driving him. Fael.

Flynn said, 'I've reviewed all the others, and I think you're the person I want. I think you're a lady who can be trusted. I'd like Danilo in on it as well because he's another one you could trust, isn't he? Would he come out to supper, do you think?'

'I don't see why not.'

'Good. Have you his phone number because I'll ring him this afternoon.'

'He's got a new flat in Parkhill Road. Hang on, I've got the number somewhere – yes, here it is.'

Flynn wrote down the number, and then said, 'I'm not wanting to seduce Danilo either, I'd better say that as well, hadn't I? I haven't the taste for that. Should I say it to him direct, do you think, or would he be offended?'

Gilly said, a bit faintly, 'I'm not actually sure about Danilo—'

'No, I'm not sure myself,' said Flynn, and gave Gilly the sudden, blinding smile that threw a good deal of light on the indiscretions of some very surprising ladies indeed. I bet you've created some havoc in your time, thought Gilly, appraising Flynn with a shrewd professional eye.

'Can you eat Italian food?' asked Flynn.

'What? Oh – yes.'

'Good, so can I. Will we say Luigi's just off St Martin's Lane – you know where I mean?'

'I do. And we will say Luigi's indeed,' said Gilly, swept along by the moment and the company.

'So you see,' said Flynn, seated opposite Gilly and Danilo in Luigi's, and eating fresh pasta with industrious pleasure, 'I'm pretty sure the man I followed from the Greasepaint is the same one I caught in the Harlequin's cellars.'

'And he went into Professor Roscius's old house last night?' said Danilo, carefully. He and Gilly exchanged looks, the same thing in both their minds. Do we admit to knowing about the Shadow and the Greasepaint meetings?

'He did,' said Flynn, reaching for the pepper mill. 'As well as that, he apparently knew the secret way into and out of the Harlequin. I shouldn't think more than half a dozen people today know about that.'

'It couldn't conceivably have been Professor Roscius himself?'

'No, it couldn't,' said Flynn. 'I've already thought of that. I went to James Roscius's funeral five years ago and if you think it was faked—'

'Could it have been faked?'

'God, it's an alluring idea to think of half the music establishment of Western Europe walking mournfully behind an empty box,' said Flynn. 'But I shouldn't think it's very likely. I should think it's quite difficult to fake a full-blown funeral. And there was a memorial service at St Martin's as well.'

'You'd have to have an awful lot of people in on the fake,' agreed Gilly. 'Undertakers and medical people and whatnot.'

'Exactly. But I did think about it for all that,' said Flynn. 'I had all the wild ideas of Roscius being still alive – of having been mutilated in a road accident or a fire—'

'*Phantom of the Opera* stuff—'

'I thought somebody would say that. Yes, or even that he might have been the victim of some disfiguring disease – leprosy or one of those appalling face cancers. But I don't really think that's likely. And you don't come across many cases of leprosy in Chelsea these days, do you?'

He paused to take another mouthful of pasta, and Danilo said, 'How old was Roscius when he died?'

'At least fifty and probably a good bit older.'

'And the creature you saw?'

'Oh, barely thirty,' said Flynn. 'About my age, in fact. He moved like a young man, although I did wonder—'

'What?'

'If there was the faintest crookedness about his spine.' He refilled their wine glasses, and Gilly and Danilo glanced at one another, both remembering the Shadow. A faint crookedness described him exactly.

Flynn said, as if it had only just occurred to him, 'It's quite difficult to convey the – the strangeness of this Shadow creature to someone who hasn't seen him.' He drank more wine, looking at them both blandly over the rim of the glass.

There was a silence. Then Danilo said, 'You know, don't you? That we – that I was at some of those Sunday-night gatherings?'

'I do.'

'How?'

'As a matter of fact,' said Flynn, setting down his glass and reaching for a wedge of bread, 'the doorman at the Greasepaint told me.'

He glanced up, and Gilly said angrily, 'What? What did he tell you?'

'Only that there was a guy who had managed to get off the drag club circuit into the Harlequin company – deservedly so, he said. And that he had a girl with him who looked like something out of a Burne Jones painting. He's surprisingly erudite, that doorman.' Flynn grinned at Gilly, and then looked back at Danilo. 'It was you he meant, wasn't it? Yes, I thought it must be. Only someone who genuinely understood about cross-dressing and drag – in a stage sense, I mean – could have managed such brilliant characterisation of Aillen.'

Danilo said defensively, 'I was on the club circuit—'

'We were only on the fringes of that world—' chimed in Gilly, and thought: Well, you knew it would come out at some point. Here's the point. She said, furiously, 'I suppose that's the only reason you involved us. Because we already knew some of the story.' She glared at him, and pushed back her chair, ready to fling out of the restaurant in a temper.

'Listen,' said Flynn, putting out a hand to stop her, 'we'd better clear the air on this. I don't care where you were or what you did – well, short of murder or terrorism or drug-dealing, I don't care. All right?'

'Well,' said Gilly. 'I suppose so. Yes, all right.' She subsided into her chair.

Flynn said, 'In any case, I'm the only one allowed to throw fits of temper.' He looked at her for a moment and Gilly was unable to decide if he was being serious. 'The fact that you knew about the Shadow made it easier to explain,' said Flynn, 'but I wouldn't have approached either of you if I hadn't thought you'd be trustworthy. Or,' he said, speaking very deliberately, 'if I thought you were short on guts.'

'You think there's danger?' began Danilo, and then said impatiently, 'Yes, of course there's danger. He's killed twice that we know of—'

'Three times,' said Gilly. 'There's Leila.'

'God yes, poor Leila.'

Flynn leaned forward. He's forgotten about being rude and outrageous, thought Gilly. He's absorbed in this and because it's caught his interest he hasn't time to be bored or impatient. And he's concerned as well – is that for *Cauldron*, or for Tod Miller's daughter, I wonder? She said, 'OK, so we know about this Shadow, and we understand about his oddness and the hypnotic powers he possesses or whatever else they are – so what? What do you want from us?'

'I want you to help me to trap him,' said Flynn.

'That's mad.' Gilly stared at him. 'You're mad.'

'I know.'

'No, but look here, you should go to the police.'

'I did go to the police,' said Flynn. 'And they didn't believe me. In fact the inspector practically accused me of sensationalism.' He grinned, and said, 'Admit it now. It's pretty difficult to describe the Shadow to a police officer.'

'If you described him, I should think it sounded impossible.'

Flynn grinned, but said, 'The thing is that you've both seen him; you've talked to him.'

'Well, only briefly,' said Gilly, repressing a shiver.

'Yes, but you understand about him. That's why I asked you out tonight. You see, if the police won't do anything about this villain, then I must. And that means I've got to find out as much as I can about him. To do that, I need a couple of allies who won't think I'm in the first stages of insanity.'

' "Allies"?' said Gilly, pouncing on this suspiciously.

'Us?' said Danilo.

'Yes, but it's all right, you won't be asked to do anything dangerous. I'll explain about that in a minute.'

Flynn picked up his glass again, and Gilly said, absently, 'You'll be too drunk to do anything at all if you keep sloshing that wine back.'

'I know it.' Flynn drained his wine glass and set it down. 'Now listen. There's another aspect to all this that also has to be considered.'

'The real composer of *Cauldron*.'

'Yes.' Flynn looked at Danilo curiously. 'How did you know I meant that?'

'Obvious, really,' said Danilo. 'We all know that poor, stupid old bugger Tod Miller could never have written *Cauldron*.'

'What's that got to do with it?' Gilly was glad Danilo had added the word 'poor' to his description of Miller.

Danilo glanced at her with indulgent impatience. 'Gilly, my love, do you truly believe that Tod Miller wrote *Cauldron*?' he said. 'The man hadn't the – the depth. The subtlety.'

'Are you saying that – the Shadow wrote it?'

'I'm not sure,' said Danilo, looking to Flynn. 'Are we saying that?'

'I'm not sure either.' Flynn was pleased to find them both so perceptive. 'But if we add up all the bits of information we've got they make a remarkable total.' He leaned forward again, ticking the points off on his fingers. Sensitive hands, thought Gilly. Artist's hands. I'll bet he's dynamite in the sack.

'Think about what we know about our man,' said Flynn. 'For starters he looked as if he was living in Professor Roscius's old house.'

'He knew the secret way into the Harlequin,' said Danilo.

'And he was in the Harlequin the night Tod Miller was killed,' contributed Gilly.

'And,' said Flynn, 'the first time I saw him, he was watching *Cauldron* with a kind of hungry intensity.'

They stopped and looked at one another. 'You think he wrote it,' hazarded Gilly. 'But – would he be capable— The musical side—' She stopped and stared at Flynn. 'Oh,' she said. 'I've just seen what you're getting at. But I still don't see why he would kill Mia Makepiece.'

'If it's his show he'd kill her to stop her ruining it,' said Flynn at once. 'I'd have killed her myself at times if somebody had handed me the means.'

Danilo said, impatiently, 'Oh, we'd all have killed her for two pins. No, it's all right, Gilly, I don't mean it literally. But she was crap in the part.'

'Isn't killing her a bit – extreme?'

'Listen, Gilly, he's an extreme man, this villain,' said Flynn.

'Well, all right, I'll allow the Shadow Mia's murder – if he's mad, that is – but why would he kill Tod Miller?'

'Any number of reasons.'

'Name them.'

'Revenge is the likeliest,' said Flynn. 'If Miller refused to acknowledge the Shadow as *Cauldron*'s creator he could have flown into a rage and—'

'Chopped out his heart?'

'And Julius Sherry accused me of lack of taste,' said Flynn, eyeing Danilo with amusement and reaching for the wine again. 'But yes, that could be the way of it.'

'You really think he's linked with Professor Roscius?'

'He means more than that,' said Gilly, watching Flynn. 'Don't you?'

'I do mean more than that,' said Flynn. He looked at Gilly. 'You've guessed, haven't you?'

271

Gilly said, softly, 'He's Professor Roscius's son. That's what you think, isn't it?'

'It's a logical conclusion,' said Flynn.

'Wouldn't it have been known if Roscius had had a son? Wouldn't you have known?'

'Not necessarily. If he was disfigured to this extent—' Flynn stopped, remembering with an inward shudder the man's face. 'If he was born like that,' he said, 'Roscius might have kept him in seclusion, for the boy's own good as much as anyone else's.'

'But even if all this is right, I still don't see where we come in.'

'If I'm right,' said Flynn, 'the Shadow won't be able to bear letting his show go to the Gallery Theatre without him. He'll follow it – he won't be able to help himself. And that's where you come in.' He paused, and then said, 'You'll be there already – you'll be at the Gallery, God help you.'

'Is it as bad as all that?' asked Gilly, momentarily diverted.

'Oh God, it's worse,' said Flynn, with a return to his normal abrasive manner. 'It's a dismal, squalid slum of a theatre and you'll be fighting cockroaches in the dressing rooms and tinkers and hookers in the stalls.'

'I didn't think Ireland had hookers. I thought it was against your Church.'

'Believe me, Gilly, we have a great many things in Ireland that are against the Church. Hookers are only one of them.'

'So, all right,' said Danilo, 'we're in the squalid old slum-theatre, fighting cockroaches—'

'And keeping a watch for the Shadow,' said Flynn. 'That's what I want you both to do. To watch for him – see if he appears, or if anyone catches sight of him prowling around.'

Gilly and Danilo exchanged glances. Then Danilo said, slowly, 'OK. That seems fair enough. But while we're doing that, what about you? What will you be doing?'

'I'll be in Ireland with you. Did you think I'd miss out on a fight?' demanded Flynn.

'No, silly of me.'

'But I'll be scouring the west coast trying to find Professor Roscius's old house.'

'Oh I see. Can you – er – afford the time to do that? I mean,' said Gilly, a bit awkwardly, 'can you just go off and leave your work?'

'In the normal way, no,' said Flynn. 'Not any more than you can. But it so happens that I've just roughed out an initial set of designs for submission for the Barrie festival in March, and I won't hear for a while whether I've got the commission. I couldn't take a year off to search for our lost lady and our vanished villain, but I can spend two or three weeks in Ireland without going bankrupt. Wouldn't you know that for luck?'

'Wouldn't you just,' murmured Danilo, and Flynn smiled.

'Are you sure about Roscius living on the west coast?' asked Gilly.

'I am. I don't know precisely where his house is, because nobody ever did know – the old boy rather liked surrounding himself with mystery. But I do know it's somewhere just outside of Galway City, near the Moher cliffs. It oughtn't to be that hard to find – it isn't a very densely populated part of Ireland. And if I'm right then that's where we'll run our man to earth. That's where his lair is.'

Gilly shivered, and wished the word 'lair' had not been used. To counteract this, she said, half to herself, 'We don't even know his name.'

'First name your villain and then set a trap for him,' said Flynn, and sat back and surveyed the littered table. 'And now will we order some more of Luigi's ciabatta bread? And another bottle of wine to go with it?'

Chapter Twenty-Three

After *Scathach* went, Fael had finally faced the fact that she might not be entirely alone in Maise. This feeling had grown over the last two days and two nights, and now she was beginning to separate and identify the sounds; the stirrings and the night rustlings.

What had he said? 'The legend tells how this house is directly over an ancient subterranean water cave, where the *leanan-sidhe* once held their strange court.'

If you were going to be outrageously fanciful, if you really wanted to spook yourself, you would start wondering if that was true, and whether the creatures of the Moher legends sometimes found their way into the house, and even whether it was your own arrival that had woken them. Fael did not want to spook herself in the least – the entire situation was spooky enough already, for God's sake! – but it was impossible to stop her mind from looping back to those half-sinister, half-romantic fragments of myth and legend that her captor had fed her. It was impossible, as well, not to keep visualising a great dark void like a monstrous well somewhere beneath her, and to imagine wizened-faced, hobgoblin beings assembling there to plot evil.

She had no idea if her fears were because she was alone in an unfamiliar place, or if Maise's strange atmosphere was spinning a dark fantasy around her nerves, or if the sounds she heard once darkness fell were in fact real sounds, made by real, explainable creatures. Rats and bats and ravens and owls, thought Fael. But aren't they all part of a darkly sinister romance of their own? The spectral owl dwelling in his hollow in the old grey tower – night's fatal bellman, Macbeth had called him, and if Macbeth did not know about fate and its heralds, then no one did. And the raven with his dreaming demon's eyes trailing his own lamplit fantasies in his wake . . . Yes, owls and ravens were undoubtedly creatures loaded with the macabre. And bats and rats had never had a good press, of course.

And this is all the wild, nightmare imaginings of a disordered mind, said Fael, firmly. If there are owls and bats or ravens out here, they're simply going quietly about their lawful nocturnal occasions. They aren't converging on Maise, full of malice aforethought, unless it's aforethought to raid the larder – that's always a possibility, I daresay. So let's keep a sense of proportion here.

Yes, but you're in a land where magic once ruled, Fael, and there's no proportion in magic, or at least not the proportions that hold good in the ordinary world. Whether you like it or not – and on balance, you don't like it one bit – you've been carried deep into one of the forgotten pockets of Ireland and dumped there, and it's a pocket where the old ways are remembered, and where the creatures of the ancient myths are still sometimes glimpsed . . .

The first night after *Scathach* left, she had sat in the deep old window seat, trying to think of a way of escaping, wondering whether she could bargain with her captor in some way. The lamps had burned steadily and the fire had sent out a gentle, comforting crackle, and the turret room had been a little oasis of warmth and light and safety, so that it had been possible to ignore – almost not to notice – the unfamiliar creaking of the old timbers, and the occasional scutterings outside.

It was only when she finally tumbled into bed and felt the darkness settle all about her that the sounds seemed to change. They became little bony goblin-fingers tapping on the window-pane, and they became hoarse gloating chuckles outside her door, so that several times there formed in her mind an image of tiny, evil-featured creatures clustering together on the stair, plotting to snare her soul, or to steal away the human child that might be born here in exactly nine months' time . . .

It was all ridiculous. The tappings would be nothing more sinister than the wind outside, or the nocturnal birds and flying things indigenous to Moher's wild coast (flapping bats and spectral owls after all?), and the throaty laughter was most likely the water gurgling in the pipes. And to become pregnant after a single encounter was unlikely in the extreme. I'll keep telling myself that, thought Fael, determinedly.

She eventually fell into an uneasy sleep, only to wake to a cold light slithering through the curtains and the leaden knowledge that she was still here, still shut away miles from anywhere, miles from human contact, and that there was no escape. For a truly terrible moment she wanted nothing so much as to pull the clothes over her head and burrow back into sleep – hours and hours of sleep so that she would not have to face any of it and so that she would not wake up until it was all over. But this could not be allowed; that was something she had learned from the days immediately following the accident. If you once gave in to that kind of despair you were lost for always.

And so she got up, washed, brushed her hair and dressed, and determinedly made toast and a pot of tea. This was a comfortingly ordinary thing to do, and the hot tea acted like a charm against the muffled silence of Maise. The large, L-shaped room was already becoming familiar, like a hotel room did after a couple of days, or a holiday cottage. Fael drank a second cup of tea in her favourite window spot, trying to see through the fog to the black cliffs beyond. No good. There was nothing to be seen outside. There was not a great deal to be seen inside either, really. But there were books – presumably left here by her captor's mother. Fael eyed them thoughtfully. With food and drink and shelter, and something to read one could surely face out any situation.

Most of the books were old and rather dusty: the covers calf- or leather-bound, some with rubbed gilt lettering on the front, some with the spines splitting. It's almost all Irish folklore, by the look of it, thought Fael, sorting through them with interest. No, this one's a Shakespeare, a bit battered, and there are several volumes of Frazer's *The Golden Bough* as well. That's the classic definitive study of magic and ancient religions, I think. That ought to be interesting. Oh, and that's some of Yeats's work, and with it is something called *Ancient Legends of Ireland*, by Lady Wilde. Lady Wilde – would she have been Oscar Wilde's mother? The date's about right. Yes, she was his mother, there's a potted biography in the front. That looks intriguing as well.

She began to tumble the books open, dipping first into one,

then another. The *Ancient Legends of Ireland* turned out to be absorbing. I could almost write another musical out of all this, thought Fael, and with the thought her hand was arrested in the act of turning a page.

I could write another musical . . .

Excitement welled up at once, and with it a feeling of engaging in battle with *him*, with *Scathach*. I believe I'll try, thought Fael. Hell's teeth, I *will*! I'll start drafting something out right away, and when he returns – because he will return, of course, I do know that – I'll show it to him. And maybe he'll be so interested that he'll want me to finish it before he decides what he's going to do with me, and maybe he'll even want to compose the music again. I'll be like Scheherezade, spinning stories to ward off her killer, or the French writer Colette, who had a husband who locked her up and fed her bread and water in return for writing books. And even if what I write turns out to be rubbish, at least I'll have a shape to the days. And, she thought, with sudden confidence, if I work through the night, and sleep in snatches during the day, I shan't be so frightened of the sounds outside my door. I probably shan't even notice them.

Maise seemed to sink into a not-unpleasant drowse in the middle of the day and taking an afternoon nap turned out to be easy. As darkness fell Fael switched on all the lamps, built up the fire, and ate her supper off a tray. Afterwards she propelled the chair to the window-seat, and read for an hour, a glass of wine to hand, paper from the desk set out for preliminary notes.

She sent up a little paean of thanks for that collection, and then wondered, wryly, how many beleaguered females had cause to be grateful to Oscar Wilde's mamma for helping them to endure a solitary captivity. Cheers, Oscar, thought Fael, lifting her half-empty glass of wine, and then wheeling across to top it up, so that she could raise it again to his mother – what was her name? – Jane Francesca Wilde. Nice. Cheers, Jane Francesca.

The fire was dying and the room was growing cold and the premature night that fell on this part of Moher had long since shrouded the old house when he returned on the third night. Fael raised her head from her notes, listening, and felt her heart lurch with the remembered blend of panic and anticipation.

His light, quick footsteps came up the stairs, and there was the sound of the door being unlocked, and then he was there. And his presence fills up the whole room, thought Fael, looking at him. I wonder if he's driven the chattering ghosts away?

Although he had presumably driven through most of the night after the ferry journey, there was no suggestion of fatigue about him; he moved with the suppressed energy of a tightly-coiled spring, and Fael suddenly realised that fury was driving him. Against me? But when he strode into the room, she saw that he was carrying a half-crumpled playbill in one hand. He thrust it onto the desk in front of her, and when he spoke, she heard for the second time in their strange relationship the uncontrolled dissonance of his speech that indicated extreme anger.

'Read it.'

'What—'

'*Cauldron*. It's being brought over here—'

'Why? Is it a tour?'

'It can't be a tour,' said Christian. 'There hasn't been time to form a touring company and bring it to concert pitch. It's the original company – it must be. And they're bringing it to a fifth-rate slum theatre in one of the most run-down parts of the west coast.' Through the mask his eyes were narrowed into slits. But is he angry because of the slum theatre? thought Fael – because he believes the show will be devalued by appearing there? Oh hell, what wouldn't I give for the full use of my legs right this minute! He's so unbalanced and unco-ordinated at the moment that I could push him aside and be down the stairs and out into the night, yelling for help!

No point in dwelling on that. She said, 'Why would it tour so soon? You either try out in the provinces and come in to the West End when you're sure of your audiences, or if it's a West End hit you negotiate for tours afterwards. You don't run for a few days and then tour with the original cast. And it went like a bomb on the first night – it ought to have been set for a long run at the Harlequin— What have I said?'

'Nothing.' He turned away, and Fael thought: But I *have* said something, I've touched a raw nerve somewhere. Something to do with *Cauldron*'s first night, was it?

With the idea of probing further, she said, 'I didn't see the

278

notices, because you dragged me out of the country, but I bet they were raves.'

'It'll be the decision of some ledger-balancing finance clerk,' said Christian, but his voice was easier to understand, as if he was regaining control once more. Damn! thought Fael. Whatever I said to disconcert him, he's recovered his balance. She reached for the playbill, which was colourfully printed and illustrated, but gave only the information that a spellbinding musical, based on old Irish legends, would be opening at the Gallery Theatre in Ennismara in two weeks' time. Good wording at least, thought Fael; that ought to bring the audiences in. She looked in vain for a note of the company or the promoters. Anonymous. Like everything else about this wretched set-up. But hope was burgeoning, for if the company – the original company – really was here, it meant that people she knew, people who might help her, were close at hand. Is that why he's furious? she thought, and felt her heart bound upwards. Is he starting to feel unsafe? Maybe I'm nearer to freedom than I know.

Flynn had delivered his *Peter Pan* designs on his way to the ferry at Fishguard. He had bound them in two of the large, workmanlike folders he always used for presentations, and had included two balsa-wood and card scale models; one for Captain Hook's pirate ship, and one for the Lost Boys' island.

'You'll want me to take you through it all,' he had said to the rather startled director, who had not previously dealt with Flynn Deverill, but who had heard the stories. 'And we can do it now if you like, but I can only give you an hour because I'm catching a ferry, or say an hour and a half if I drive like a bat out of hell. Oh, and I'd need to know by the beginning of February whether you want me.'

'Well—'

'That's partly because of booking the warehouse I normally use in Blackfriars for the building work, but also because I'll be supervising the removal of the *Cauldron* sets to Ennismara.'

'Good God, they're never opening up the Gallery again, are they?'

'Providing they can stop up all the holes in the stage and mend the roof so the rain won't come in on the audience, they

279

are. Now, will I show you the device we could rig up so that the Lost Boys' island transforms into the pirate camp? No, that's not it, that's the nursery, and it's based on Arthur Rackham illustrations, by the way, and beautifully Edwardian. This one here's the island. See now, we'd bring down a gauze scrim here, and have pools of blue and green waterlight to fall here and here – providing you've got a good lighting man, that is – and I've given the trees a kind of faintly human aspect. If you turn to the next sketch you'll see it in enlargement. From a distance they'd all have gnarled faces within the trunks, that's an echo of the old druid religions and the tree spirits so each face is different. It gives a terrific atmosphere of menace, doesn't it? Children love horror these days, you'd maybe need to spike up Barrie's original text a bit to grab them, wouldn't you?'

'Well yes,' said the director, who was already involved in arguments about this with the purists, but who was not going to admit it to Flynn Deverill. 'You're rather expensive,' he added, a bit weakly. 'This fee you've put in—'

'Yes, I'll be the most expensive of all the submissions,' agreed Flynn at once. 'But I'll be the best you'll get. It depends if you're answerable to accountants or real theatre people.' He got up to leave. 'Oh, and if they're putting on *Dear Brutus* as part of the Festival, would you leave me out of the reckoning please, because it's a play I can't stand at any price.'

The *Peter Pan* designs would almost certainly be accepted. Flynn knew, without any vanity at all, that they were extremely good, and he knew that they were precisely what the Barrie Festival Committee wanted. But it amused him to play the prima donna. He spent the first half of the journey looking backwards, thinking about the designs and how he would enjoy being associated with the Festival, but as the Irish coast drew near, he began to think about the search for James Roscius's son. Because whether this creature's the professor's son or not, there's some kind of link, thought Flynn. As well start here as anywhere.

It ought to be relatively easy to search record offices and land registry files in Galway. Roscius had only mentioned his house near the Moher cliffs once or twice to Flynn, but there had been a note of unmistakeable wistfulness in his voice. A house that had been in his family for several generations, he had said. His great-grandfather had held on to it in the teeth of the Famine years and the tempestuous squabbles about Home Rule; his great-great-great-grandfather had held on to it through the Unionist quarrels a hundred years before that.

'And now it will go out of the family,' Roscius had said, sadly.

'You can't be absolutely sure of that,' Flynn had said.

'Oh yes I can.'

But for all his occasional abrupt spurts of confiding in Flynn, Roscius had never told Flynn precisely where the house was situated, and he had never mentioned the house's name. Assuming, thought Flynn cynically, that it did have a name, and it was not something like 5 Railway Cuttings. It was almost impossible to imagine the gentle donnish professor, with his paradoxical streak of theatrical brilliance, living in the Irish equivalent of Railway Cuttings, but people were constantly surprising.

Moher did not cover a hopelessly large area, but it was difficult to know quite where you stopped calling the area Moher and started calling it something else. And 'near to the Moher cliffs' was a very vague identification indeed. But then Roscius didn't want it identifying, thought Flynn, disembarking at Rosslare and setting off behind the wheel of his ramshackle car. He wanted it to remain unknown. And if that half-mad creature I saw at the Harlequin and the Greasepaint is truly his son, it isn't surprising.

One of the problems was going to be that the area surrounding the stormy Moher coast was full of little clusters of houses, and sprinkled with tiny, rather inbred, communities. Flynn, who knew the place only slightly, thought you might come upon the answer to a quest there within the first five minutes, or alternatively you might search for five years without finding a thing.

He was not expecting to derive any amusement from this wild search of the haystack for the pin. His own family had come from this part of Ireland, from Connemara farther north along the coast, but his mother had died shortly after his graduation and he could not remember his father who had died when Flynn was very young. There was no one left there to draw him back, and it struck him as rather sad that he should be returning under such conditions.

Beneath everything else was the insidious, nagging worry for Fael. I'm not in love with you, alannah, said Flynn, to Fael's image. I hardly know you. Let's say I'm suffering from an attack of chivalry, and let's say I'm doing this against my better judgement.

But he did know her, of course; he knew her through *Cauldron*, because if James Roscius's son had created the music for *Cauldron*, then Fael Miller had written the book and probably the lyrics. The more he considered this idea, the likelier it seemed. All the facts fit the case, thought Flynn, driving through the Irish countryside, enjoying the indefinable scent of Ireland that he always thought was made up of woodsmoke and peat fires and something else he had never managed to identify. All countries had their own scents, undetectable to their inhabitants; it was only when you visited them as a stranger you noticed it.

If Fael had written *Cauldron*, then she was more than worth saving from the creature Flynn had so nearly caught in the Harlequin. She was worth saving in any case, but it was remarkably distasteful to think of her in the hands of her father's murderer. I'm probably chasing a chimera, thought Flynn, scowling and driving impatiently towards Galway. I might even be playing a part in somebody else's fantasy, because I don't think that young man I encountered has a very good grip on reality.

As he neared Galway with its silvery river and curiously modern cathedral, he realised that for the first time he had used the expression 'young man'. Because I've three-quarters identified him? Because I knew his father so very well, and because I still have this affection and respect for James Roscius's memory? Oh hell, thought Flynn, changing lanes on the dual carriageway, I don't know anything any more. But I do know that I've somehow been dragged into this, and that if I don't find Fael I'll have to live with a feeling of loss for the rest of my life.

Chapter Twenty-Four

The intricate network that Christian had so carefully set up in London and that had served him so well there, served him again now.

The drifting, raggle-taggle world of the streets had its own brotherhood and its own information system, and the spider network could be extended so that its threads stretched very far indeed. Several of the itinerant musicians who entertained theatre crowds and tourists and tube travellers, had been delighted to accept cash from the mysterious gentleman who had ruled part of Soho for so long, because even with the Shadow apparently leaving London for a time, the authority still somehow held and no one wanted to offend him.

It was an easy enough task to keep an eye on the young man, Flynn Deverill, and even easier for three or four of them with Irish blood to mingle with the motley collection taking the ferry at Fishguard, and to travel unremarked to Rosslare. It was great altogether to be making this trip, and great to have the cash in your pocket, along with the fare back to England. But after the message was delivered to the Shadow they were going to try their luck in Galway City, and after that they might wander across to Dublin for a time. Hadn't you great opportunities in Dublin; there was the Abbey Theatre and there was the Royal Dublin Horse Show, never mind all the tourists with money to throw away. And if none of it worked as well as they were hoping – if the streets of Dublin were no more paved with gold than the streets of London had turned out to be – well, they would simply take the ferry back again. And if they could find the queer, remote place the Shadow had described to them and leave the information about Flynn Deverill that he wanted, there would be the plastic-wrapped pack of money waiting for them to collect. At the foot of a certain stone it would be, the Shadow had said, and one of their number, who was inclined more to whimsy than the rest, said wasn't it exactly like the gold at the end of the rainbow, and paid no attention when his fellows jeered and said, fool's gold, more like, and him the biggest fool of all to trust to it!

Even though Flynn Deverill was driving his own car and they were reliant on lifts and thumbing and their own two feet, they had managed to follow him and learn his plans, particularly since he had the way of talking to people in a careless fashion. Once on the ferry he had had a few drinks down in the bar, and they had tossed a coin for who was to go in and drink with him and fall into carefully casual conversation. As far as the busker who had won the toss could tell, Deverill had been wholly unsuspicious, not to say generous with his money. He bought several drinks, until the busker, who was secretly a bit guilty about his spying role, felt obliged to buy at least one back. After drinking two large whiskies at Flynn's expense, he made a quick calculation of the joint funds, and bought a round on his own account; not to have done so might have caused comment, and also it meant he got a third whiskey.

It was during the course of the third whiskey he found out what they wanted to know: Flynn was driving to Galway City, where he was going to book in at the Royal George.

As Christian locked the door on Fael and went quickly down the turret stair, the twin streams of hatred – the one against Flynn, the other against whoever had brought *Cauldron* to the tumbledown Gallery Theatre – were fusing angrily together in his mind. Two sets of enemies: *Cauldron's* organisers, and Flynn Deverill. *Cauldron* could probably be dealt with relatively easily – Rossani would show him the way, as he had done on those other occasions – but Flynn was a different matter entirely. Flynn would die slowly and terribly.

It was possible that it would be some time before Flynn began the search for Maise in earnest, but Christian did not think that was very likely. He had laid sufficient clues, and he thought Flynn would pick them up and walk unsuspectingly into his, Christian's, trap. And Flynn had too much impatience and too much energy not to travel out here at once, and he certainly had sufficient intelligence to have worked out Christian's identity by now.

Christian had employed three separate groups of people to watch Flynn, but he thought it would be the street musicians who would succeed. They were more nomadic than the rest; they would think nothing of uprooting themselves for a few weeks or a few months, and crossing to Ireland. Quite a few of them were Irish to start with, and the Irish had the restless gypsy strain from birth.

He waited until he had been back at Maise for four days, and then he waited until he caught the faint chimes of midnight from the little wayside church. Midnight, the hour that looked kindly on lovers and plotters and murderers. As he walked down the deserted cliff road and onto the narrow track that dipped below the road, a storm was blowing in from the Atlantic – he could feel it and he could smell it. The ocean was lashing itself angrily against the foot of the cliffs, far below, and the sea was black and menacing, the waves topped with little froths of white.

But the Self-Bored Stone reared up clearly in front of him, and Christian paused, staring up at it. Seen like this, against the backdrop of scudding storm clouds, the old tales came vividly to life, so that you wondered whether you might not have fallen into the seductive world of myth and legend and evil enchantments. When the moon was full, the silvery radiance poured through the aperture and laid a circle of cool light on the ground, but tonight the storm was blotting out the moon, and the stone's tip was in darkness. It made you believe that if you could but scale the stone's heights and peer through the round, smooth opening, you would find yourself looking down into worlds you had never dreamed existed. *And finding deliverance there?* said Rossani's evil voice in his mind.

Christian stayed where he was, his eyes going to the jagged cliff-edge, only a few yards away from where he stood. He thought that no one would know or care if he simply walked over that cliff tonight and was dashed to pieces on the rocks below, and with the thought, his mind rocked, he felt the wild madness seize him anew. To step into that tempestuous darkness, and to step beyond it, into oblivion and peace . . . To die . . . But supposing death was only the prince's hag-ridden sleep after all? Aye, there's the rub.

I believe I'm quite mad now, thought Christian, dispassionately. I believe I've crossed a Rubicon or forded a river somewhere, but whether it's the Jordan River or Charon's Styx or the measureless sacred Alph, or something else altogether I have no idea. But if I'm mad, then I ought not to care any longer and I ought not to be still hurting, and I do care – oh God, yes, I do, and I'm still hurting. Because Fael cheated me and because I ruined *Cauldron* . . . I can't bear to think about either of them. I don't think I'm entirely alone out here. I think the *leanan-sidhe* are very near to me tonight.

The people of Moher told how, when the wind whistled through the stone's smooth aperture, they could hear the *leanan-sidhe* calling to the shipwrecked sailors, luring them onto the murderous black rocks. People told stories of banshees, they said, the Celtic *bean si*, but in Moher they had their own banshees, and they were fearsome and cunning beyond belief. You heard stories of how they prowled this stretch of coast, all the way back to the days when people could not read or write; when Ireland had bards and story-tellers, and when they were regarded with as much respect as was these days given to the priests. Even Father Mack, when he had taken a drop of gin in Flaherty's Bar, agreed that the bards had been Ireland's aristocracy, preserving her history and keeping alive the legends. Sinead O'Sullivan, whose family had lived in Moher for longer than anyone could count, said her grandmother had told how the *leanan-sidhe* haunted this stretch of the coast, and her *great*-grandmother used sometimes to see them, washing the blood-stained clothes of those about to die, the scarlet webbed feet of them plain to see. Even today, said Sinead firmly, hadn't you to be blind and deaf not to occasionally hear the keening voices inside the wind?

Christian knew the stories, which the people of Moher loved to tell, and he knew that they did not really believe them. It was mostly only the Irish love of a good story, and it was partly the Moher people being jealous of their own snippets of folklore. He strode on down the narrow cliff path, the wind lifting his cloak so that it billowed out like huge, ragged, black wings. He bent to the stone's foot and slid his hand inside the crevice, his heart beating faster. Had the buskers done what he had asked them? Or had they simply taken the cash he had given them and vanished? He saw at once that the thick wad of banknotes wrapped in several thicknesses of plastic had gone and there was a moment of hideous doubt: have they cheated? Or has the cache perhaps been discovered by a tinker? But tinkers never came down here, and most people were too fearful of the stone's eerie legend. And then his hand closed around the thin envelope, also in its weatherproof plastic covering, and relief rushed in. He unfolded the single sheet of paper.

The writing was uneven and hurried, as if it had been written in extreme haste or in difficult circumstances. The deck of a ferry boat? Leaning against the trunk of a tree or a bar counter?

But it was perfectly legible, and Christian scanned it quickly. Flynn Deverill had reached Ireland two days earlier, said the note, carefully setting down times and dates. He was making for the west coast, driving his own car, and he would be staying in Galway City at the Royal George Hotel. There was even an addition saying that the car was a scarlet Volkswagen, and an apology that it had not been possible to get the number.

Christian tore the short, highly satisfactory note into dozens of tiny pieces and scattered them into the wind. It was working. Flynn was walking deeper and deeper into the trap. As he walked back to Maise, the knowledge was like a sexual charge, so strong that he actually felt a hardening between his thighs.

As he let himself into the house, he was smiling the secret, difficult smile, and once inside with the familiar scents of the old place closing about him, he paused, listening for sounds from the turret rooms. Nothing. Then Fael must be asleep. For a moment he struggled against a sudden longing to climb the narrow turret stair and to enter her room and lie in the bed with her. And then memory flared, lighting a different plane of awareness, and he saw again the revulsion in her eyes and the pity, and he remembered that she had cheated him over the child, and the desire turned to cold hatred.

He crossed the hall and went through to the stone-floored sculleries. At the far end was a low door, blackened with age, sealed with a huge iron ring-handle. Christian lit a candle and wedged it in a metal holder, pocketed the box of matches from the pantry, and bent down to turn the handle. As the door swung inwards, a noxious breath of dry, fetid air gusted out.

Inside the door steps wound steeply downwards, and there was a dank, oppressive atmosphere. The stairwell was narrow and the walls had a faint slimy look to them. Here and there lichen and pale fungal growths sprawled over the old brickwork.

As Christian went lower there was the suffocating feeling of the great old house overhead, and as the steps spiralled around to the right, he caught from somewhere below, the sound of water dripping against stone, followed by its own thin echo. Once or twice he thought that something flitted across his vision: something that was child-sized but not childlike, and something that was hunched and wizened, with a round hairless skull and long bony fingers . . .

He did not count the steps as he went down, but he knew there were eighty-one. Nine times nine, said his mind, with faint cynicism. The magical nine times nine of all the best fairy stories. At the foot, the steps gave onto a dank underground room with an earth floor, and black brick walls. The room was bare save for the gaping black abyss at the centre that was Maise's disused well, and that was surrounded by a narrow brick parapet. A faint mustiness drifted up out of the well and the parapet was stained and blackened, with several of the old bricks crumbling. Against the far wall was the well cover: an immense, saucer-shaped disc of clanging black iron, lipped and rimmed. In Christian's father's day the well had always been covered in case of unwary servants falling in, although no servant ever came down here except under protest and accompanied by at least two other people.

Once there had been some kind of investigation into the well, because it was thought that there was some danger of erosion by the sea at the foot, for the water had first turned brackish with salt, and then ceased to flow altogether. Christian could remember how it had taken two people to lift the cover and drag it free of the yawning hole. He could remember how the sound had reverberated through the entire house.

He stood at the foot of the steps, his eyes on the yawning

cavern: the ancient underground well that gave Maise its slightly macabre legend. The alleged opening to the subterranean water cave, where in some other time the *leanan-sidhe* had held court. After a moment he moved to its edge, seeing now that iron staves had been driven into the inside of the well-shaft, to form a makeshift but serviceable ladder. The staves were rusty, but they looked sound enough. So it would be possible to climb down inside the well, would it? Could I do it? thought Christian, caught between fascination and repulsion. If I had to, could I set foot on that rusting ladder, and go down and down into the darkness? And does it truly lead to the hinterlands of the *leanan-sidhe*, or is that only another of the jumbled myths about this part of Ireland?

Whether or not the ancient disused well was the doorway into the legendary, under-ocean worlds of the *leanan-sidhe*, it would provide the means for Flynn Deverill's death, when eventually Flynn reached Maise.

The warped smile twisted his lips, and he leaned forward over the well's mouth. For a moment there was not the tomblike stench and the impenetrable darkness, but something else, something that ruffled the air with its sweetness . . . A stillness came over him at once; he thought there was a flash of turquoise at the darkness's heart – the glint of iridescent wings, the sinuous bodies of eerie sea creatures with not the smallest drop of human blood in them . . .

Because this is what we really look like, human creature . . . If you came down to us, you would see what we really look like, and you would see how we are more beautiful than your human eyes can imagine and how we are more dazzling than your human soul can comprehend . . .

Christian stepped back, lifting the candle higher, and it was then he saw, in the ancient dust surrounding the well, tiny footprints, dozens upon dozens of them, light and swift and darting, as if the owners had traced circles inside circles inside circles . . . As if tiny creatures had come swarming up out of the well's depths while the humans slept, and had danced and cavorted to their own chill music . . .

Rats? said his mind. Or something else? Something that's remaining on the outer rim of consciousness, and something that's hungry for human souls, and that lusts after first-born children ... But Fael betrayed me! cried his mind again, and instantly came the response: but there are others. There are others you could use for the child and the bargaining.

But Fael was mine! cried Christian. I made her mine, body and soul and blood and bone, exactly as the *sidh* prince made Mab his own in *Cauldron*!

Mab.

The two things came together in his mind with such sharpness it was very nearly audible. The little wide-eyed redhead in the theatre, who had played Mab, not brilliantly, but very well, and who had certainly understood about being in thrall to inhuman creatures. Christian remembered Gilly from the Soho meetings, and he remembered the way she had always looked at him. And she would soon be here, the entire Harlequin company would soon be here. Mab, thought Christian, turning to climb back up the nine times nine steps to his own part of Maise, the smile lifting his incomplete mouth again.

Flynn had drawn a blank with his first line of enquiry, which had been to search the birth registrations for twenty-five to thirty years previously.

This did not mean that the son did not exist. If Roscius's wife had given birth to a creature so pitifully deformed, it was not impossible that they had concealed the child's existence, even to the extent of not registering it. Flynn thought the professor had been sufficiently well-off not to need to worry about welfare benefits and National Health or education; he had also been sufficiently unconventional, as Flynn himself was unconventional, not to have cared about the morality of what he had done. The boy would have been brought up in obscurity, and Roscius himself would have provided the education. Flynn grinned wryly, because if the professor really had done that, it meant his son was probably better educated than a great proportion of his generation.

He ate a thoughtful lunch in the Royal George, considering other methods. If he could not find the person, could he find the place? How did you set about finding a house whose name you did not know, in a place you were unsure of, and which might lie anywhere between the Connemara Mountains and the mouth of the Shannon, and which might as easily lie at the end of a wild-goose chase or the bottom of the rainbow, or the other side of Ireland altogether?

If you were looking for a house, didn't you usually start with a map?

Flynn left the Royal George's bar and went back out into the town.

Well no, said the assistant in the largest stationers that Galway boasted, no, you could not precisely buy Ordnance Survey maps of Ireland as you could for England – he knew exactly what the gentleman meant – but certainly there was an equivalent. Was it any particular part of Galway?

'That's the devil,' said Flynn. 'All I know is that the house I'm trying to find is somewhere near the Moher cliffs.'

This, it appeared, did not necessarily present a difficulty. There were some very good large-scale maps of the west coast, and there were several concentrating on that part. What scale would be needed? Most people had the one-inch-to-the-mile kind, which were ideal for touring, said the assistant; would they suit the purpose?

'They sound exactly what I want,' said Flynn.

After tumbling out and unfolding half a dozen different maps, during which time the helpful assistant several times became shrouded like Laocoon in the sea-serpent's embrace, Flynn bought three of the inch-to-the-mile maps, and carried them back to his room at the hotel. Probably this would be the wild-goose chase after all, but it was worth a try because properties on that coastline were so sparse that a great many of them had to be identified by their name. Flynn spread the map out on the floor, and frowned over it.

And there it was, as clear as a lighthouse beam in the darkness. Maise. *Maise*. The house that could only belong to one person, because that person had many years ago written a piece of music for a children's play at the Harlequin – a light, inconsequential piece of froth and frivolity that he had called Maise, which he told Flynn was a derivation of an old Gaelic word for happiness.

291

Surely only Professor James Roscius would have called his house Maise.

I believe I've got him! thought Flynn, and sat down to calculate the distance between Galway and the house called Maise which stood on the very westernmost tip of the cliff road.

Chapter Twenty-Five

The countryside surrounding Maise was the bleakest place that Flynn had ever encountered.

When he slowed the car down, looking for somewhere to break his journey and have a bite to eat, it was twilight; the heady, heavy gloaming that never fell over anywhere else in the world in quite the same way that it fell over Ireland, and that Flynn always thought of as weighed down with old enchantments and dreams.

But this was a short-lived twilight, and, as he parked the car, rain was already pattering outside the long, low building with the lighted windows and the neatly-lettered sign proclaiming it as Flaherty's Bar. There was the suspicion of white tipping the churning waves, and a flurry of rain blew across the road into Flynn's face. He shivered, locked the car, and went inside Flaherty's, ducking his head under the low doorway.

Whoever Flaherty was, he – or maybe she – had managed to bring the place comfortably up to date without entirely killing the atmosphere of the old building. Flynn was ensconced at a small, round, oak table near to one of the tiny, leaded windows, with chintz curtains in a strong, good-quality fabric. There were small, candle-shaped wall lights, but there were several clearly-functional oil lamps set about as well. 'We've the occasional power failure out here, you see,' remarked the barman. Any hint of whimsy or tweeness was put firmly in place by the blackened oak floors and the worn stone steps leading down to the tiny eating area, and the smoke-scarred hearth where a huge peat fire was burning. The storm was getting under way now, and the sound of the driving rain beating on the windows mingled with the warm flickering of the flames.

All of this greatly pleased Flynn, who had a designer's eye

for a setting. He drank a pint of strong draught Guinness with appreciation, and ate a substantial supper of home-made soup, soda bread spread thickly with butter, and the kind of huge juicy prawns you seldom got in England and which were served here with light, puffy potato pancakes. Afterwards he gravitated, apparently absent-mindedly, to the bar itself and asked for a second Guinness.

His fellow drinkers were inclined to be friendly. Flynn thought only a purist would have called them inquisitive, but it suited his mission very well to fall into conversation and to ask about the area generally. He bought several drinks and after a time, judging the mood carefully, said, 'I'm hoping one of you will be able to direct me on the last lap of my journey. I'm trying to find a house called Maise. I don't know its exact whereabouts. Would any of you know it?'

The stunned silence that fell on the roomful of people was akin to the kind of silence that descended in remote country pubs in films about werewolves and vampires, where the unsuspecting traveller seeks food and rest, and then trustfully asks if he can be directed to Castle Dracula. Flynn found himself particularly remembering the darkly-tinged Roman Polanski film, and the extraordinary Francis Ford Coppola epic. And the look of furtive fear that was now showing on every face was exactly the look that the extras in those films wore, just before they began to talk about wolfbane and wearing a string of garlic and a crucifix, and better still beat the hell out of here sir, because no one ever goes up to the castle, and if you do you'll never be seen again . . . Flynn took a deep breath and drank half of the Guinness in his glass at one go, because weren't there enough fantastical nightmares in this already without looking for the film-makers' versions?

Flaherty himself, a genial, rotund person who had been amicably dispensing drinks and conversation, and who had, not ten minutes previously, been recounting a highly spiced tale of somebody's daughter's exploits in Dublin, stopped dead, and, leaning over the bar, said, earnestly, 'Maise, did you say? That's not a place the likes of you would be wanting to visit,' which was so in keeping with Flynn's half-frivolous, half-serious analogies, that he stared at the man.

'Why the devil not?'

'Well, because it's a very weird place,' said Flaherty, now busily polishing the bar counter, and evading Flynn's eyes. 'A bad name it has, Maise.'

'They tell some nasty tales about it,' put in someone.

'What kind of tales? Is it haunted, or something?'

'It's not so much the house, as the owner,' said one of the men who Flynn thought had been identified as Seamus O'Sullivan, and who was memorable chiefly for the amount of drink he had put away.

Flynn's mind sprang to attention at once, but he only said, 'The owner? What's wrong with the owner? And who is the owner anyway?'

'No one knows his name,' said O'Sullivan. 'And he's not there so very often, thanks be to God.'

'He's there now,' put in an oldish man. Flynn saw for the first time that he was wearing a priest's collar, although this did not apparently stop him from enjoying what looked like a double gin. 'He's up there now, because we've all seen the lights burning.'

'Those of us who've ventured that far out,' observed Flaherty.

'Are you not a Galway man then?' enquired the priest, with what was plainly an attempt to turn the conversation.

'No,' said Flynn. 'I'm from London.' There was a stir of vague disappointment. 'But I was born in Connemara,' he said, and the disappointment perked up into approval. People looked pleased, and started to talk about Connemara, wasn't it the finest place ever, you'd never see the like of some of the sunsets over the mountains there. Somebody – Liam O'Sullivan, was this? – said the girls there were the best as well, and this was clearly a reference to some long-standing source of merriment because a shout of laughter went up. The atmosphere lightened by the minute and there was the feeling that an awkward, potentially dangerous corner might have been safely negotiated. Flaherty was heard to remark that it was blowing up for a wild old night outside, and would somebody please to throw a few more peat turves onto the fire. The smoky scent of the peat drifted pleasantly into the room, and it was observed that it was a great thing to see Flaherty had the oil lamps to hand, because likely the power would go before morning.

Flynn nudged his drink nearer to where the priest was sitting at the end of the bar. 'Did I hit a nerve just now?'

'Mentioning Maise? You did, of course. They're shockingly superstitious these people, but on the whole, you know, there's good reason.'

'Why? Will you have another drink, Father – I'm sorry, I don't know your name.'

'Michael MacKenna, but I'm Father Mack to everyone.'

'Flynn Deverill,' said Flynn, accepting the brief handshake. 'Gin, is it?'

'It is. My only vice.'

'I wish it was my only vice,' rejoined Flynn. 'Tell me about Maise.' Tell me about Maise's owner, said his mind. 'Why is there good reason for people to be superstitious about the place?'

'Well now, he's a very odd creature, the man who lives there,' said Father Mack. 'You could say that he's almost kept the old legends going in people's minds.'

'How? And how is he odd?'

'For a start he spends a great deal of time away from Maise altogether. You and I know that's not so very remarkable, especially in this country—'

'Absentee English landlords,' said Flynn, not altogether in jest.

'Oh, I don't think he's English,' said Father Mack at once. 'I think he's an Irishman, all right. Anglicised, of course,' he added, fairly.

'Like me.'

'You're not Anglicised in the very least, Mr Deverill,' said Father Mack.

Flynn grinned and said, 'Thank the Lord for that at any rate,' and raised his glass in a mocking salute.

'The thing is, you see, that when a house – a big house – is empty for any length of time, and when it's almost on the edge of a lonely clifftop; well then, you'd be almost certain of finding a few odd stories growing up around it,' said the priest, sipping his gin reflectively.

Flynn, choosing his words carefully, said, 'But does no one ever see the owner? Even if he doesn't mix with the local people, he's surely got to have some dealings with them? Doesn't he eat, or drink, or buy petrol or socks or firewood or—'

'We think he brings provisions with him,' said Father Mack. 'Food and so on. From Dublin or Galway, or even London, if that's where he spends so much of his time. Occasionally he sends down orders for fresh stuff, mostly to Flaherty there, or maybe O'Sullivan's – they've the franchise for milk and eggs hereabouts. There'll be a list of what's wanted and cash inside the envelope, almost the exact sum. He knows the price of things, your man.'

'But doesn't anyone see him when he delivers these arrogant requests?'

'They're put through the door at midnight as far as anyone can tell.' The priest glanced briefly over his shoulder, and appeared to draw nearer to the fire. 'You know, that's a tough old storm getting going out there, Mr Deverill. Have you really to go out again tonight? Flaherty has a couple of rooms he lets – nothing so very grand and not expensive, but clean enough, and a bite of breakfast included in the morning. It's no night to be driving along the cliff road, or anywhere else, for that matter.' It's no night to be driving out to Maise and its owner if that's where you're really going, said his tone.

'I might take Flaherty up on that,' said Flynn, glancing to the nearest window, where the rain was pattering relentlessly. 'Tell me more about Maise's owner. He's a creature of the night, seemingly.'

'Indeed he is, Mr Deverill, and whenever any of us catches sight of him it's always after dark,' said Father Mack.

'Really?'

'He prowls a certain stretch of the cliff road,' said the priest, glancing over his shoulder and lowering his voice. 'Wearing a black cloak the like you'd never see outside of a horror film. And,' he added, with the Irish genius for parenthesis, 'how he escapes notice in London – if that's where he lives – is a mystery. Even in London you'd think he'd stand out, and you've the oddest people there, so I hear.'

'We have,' said Flynn. 'But he does stand out there as well.

I rather suspect that he trades on his oddness, in fact.' He paused, and then said, half to himself, 'So he prowls the cliff road, does he?'

'He does, and always near to the place everyone believes is the source of the old legends,' said Father Mack. 'It's that that unnerves them so much. Do you know the belief of the Self-Bored Stone by any chance?'

'Tell me.'

'Well, it's a monolith, a good thirty or forty feet high, and it stands very near to Maise.' Father Mack took another drink of his gin. 'At the tip is a round aperture – probably a natural formation, of course, but I'd have to admit it's evocative enough on a moonlit night. The belief is that if you climb to the very top and look through the hole, you'll see through into other worlds. One version tells that you'd see spread out the chronicles of the *leanan-sidhe*, written in the ancient tongues of the lost tribes of Ireland. You'd be able to read the names of their victims.'

'Engraved in gold and soaked in blood? I've heard of the *sidh*,' said Flynn cautiously, wondering if he was about to see a wild version of *Cauldron* coming to life. 'But I don't think I've ever come across *leanan-sidhe*,' he said. 'It translates as – fairy mistress, doesn't it?'

'Near enough. You've retained a word or two of Gaelic, then.'

'You were the one who said I wasn't Anglicised. What are the *leanan-sidhe*? No, I'm not being polite,' said Flynn, anticipating Father Mack's look of enquiry. 'I'm never polite. I'm genuinely interested in what you're saying. You're very knowledgeable, by the way.'

'Oh, I've had plenty of time to learn about the folklore of this stretch of coast,' said Father Mack. 'And it makes for interesting study, you know. Around here, the *leanan-sidhe* are believed to be a kind of water spirit, and they're supposed to bestow genius rather maliciously on those who see them. One version of the legend swears blind that what they're really after is human children to steal down to their dark realm—'

'The changeling belief,' said Flynn, half to himself.

'Exactly.' Father Mack nodded briefly towards the lady sitting with the hard-drinking Seamus O'Sullivan. 'Sinead O'Sullivan there is supposed to have had a great-aunt who was suspected of being a changeling.'

'What happened to her?'

'The family burned her alive when she was a year old, in an attempt to drive out the black *sidhe* heart.'

'Jesus Christ.'

'Well, yes. He'd have been looking out for the poor murdered soul, of course,' said Father Mack, and Flynn spread his hands, accepting the veiled reproof and indicating apology.

'Forgive me, Father, for I have dwelled too long in the blasphemous cities of the English.'

'I don't know about blasphemy, you're certainly an irreverent one,' said the priest. 'Will I get you another drink?'

'Let me. By way of penance.' In fact Flynn was angry that he had so nearly antagonised this unexpected source of information. Serve you right for forgetting you're back in devout Catholic Ireland, said his mind. When the drinks came, he said, 'It's an interesting legend.'

'It is. But of course, it's no more than just a legend.'

'Of course not. Tell me, Father, would you know if there was ever a musician lived at Maise?'

Father Mack looked at Flynn very steadily, and then said, 'Now how in the world did you know about that, Mr Deverill?' and Flynn felt a surge of triumph. Got him!

When it came to it, nobody seemed very happy about him leaving the safe warmth of the bar and haring off to Maise. Wasn't it the worst night ever to be driving anywhere, they said, and no night at all to be driving out to Maise, for God's sake?

Flaherty contributed his mite to the persuasions, saying that the guest room could be made ready for Flynn in a trice, and appealed to his daughter for confirmation. His daughter, a buxom female, eyeing Flynn with a hopeful and appreciative eye, enthusiastically agreed that it would not take the shake of a flea's whisker to have fresh sheets on the bed, hot water in the ewer and a fire burning in the hearth. She added that Flynn would be made very welcome indeed. The picture conjured up by the description of the bedroom was so tempting that Flynn found himself arranging to just take a look around the locality and return within the hour.

'And you could leave your luggage here, Mr Deverill,' suggested Flaherty's daughter, hopefully.

'So I could.'

Liam O'Sullivan helped Flynn to carry his luggage in, observing that it was a wild old night and a man would be the better for staying indoors.

'It is indeed. A pity I can't do it,' said Flynn. He gave Flaherty a token cash deposit for the room, bought Liam a large whiskey, and glanced round the bar. 'And now isn't anyone going to provide me with a necklace of garlic cloves or a newly-minted silver crucifix for the journey? Or even offer to act as guide? Even if I pay in silver ducats rather than by a pound of carrion flesh? No? No takers?'

There were not, it appeared, any takers at all, although a murmur of laughter stirred the company in uneasy recognition of the black humour of the remark, and Father Mack looked as if he might be wondering would it be appropriate to pronounce a blessing, and if so, which one.

'Not even a sprig of wolfbane, or the fragment of an ancient rune to protect me?' demanded Flynn, donning his overcoat. 'Mother of God, you're a dismal lot. Well then, in the absence of any other form of help, spiritual or practical or demonic, I suppose somebody can at least give me directions.'

The directions were provided, albeit reluctantly. It was easy enough to actually get to Maise, said the inhabitants of the bar, leaving unspoken the suggestion that even though you might get there it was anybody's guess where you would finish up afterwards. But Flynn was to carry on down this road, watching for the potholes which would tip a man over the cliffs into the sea if he did not know they were there, and then to look for the narrow private road on the left. About three miles along, it was, and then there was the turning, and the Maise road, winding steeply up to the house.

At this point there was a pause, and the question as to why Flynn was going up to Maise in the first place hovered in the air. Liam O'Sullivan in fact started to say, 'Would you tell us—' and then caught Father Mack's reproving eye, and stopped.

Father Mack said, firmly, that there was no knowing what business a man might have of a night, and no telling where that business might take him and everyone agreed there was not, that was very true.

'Seriously though, Mr Deverill, won't you delay until morning?' said the priest, glancing at the rain-drenched windows.

'I'm afraid I can't,' said Flynn. 'But if I don't return within forty-eight hours you have my permission to call out the cavalry.' As he went out, turning up his coat collar against the driving rain, the lights in the bar flickered in ominous presage of a power cut.

From an artistic point of view the storm added atmosphere, of course, because it looked as if this was going to be the traditional journey along the long, dark, lonely road through the equally traditional raging storm. Flynn had already decided that he would have to approach Maise unseen and under cover of darkness, but he had not quite visualised such impenetrable blackness as this and he had certainly not visualised a cliff road with hairpin bends and a hundred-foot drop into the ocean on one side. He tried to see if there was any kind of crash barrier in case he skidded off the road and thought there was not.

The rattle-trap car was not suited to these conditions; before Flynn had gone fifty yards it was shipping water to an alarming degree. The rain was so violent that the windscreen wipers were virtually useless, and the headlights made only the thinnest of beams through the darkness. Flynn kept having to lean forward to wipe dripping condensation from the windows so that he could see where he was going, and even then, he ran onto the grass verge several times, grazing the nearside wing. He began to have terrifying visions of meeting another car head-on, but there was no sign of life at all and Flynn supposed no one with a grain of sense would be driving along this road on a night like this. He reminded himself that he had wanted to reconnoitre Maise unobserved.

If the rain had not slackened a little, and if he had not been peering through the murk for the turning, he would have missed it. But there was a small dip in the road and there it was, exactly as it had been described. Flynn pulled thankfully over, and as he engaged second gear for the slope, there was a sudden crunching jolt and a grating noise, and the car bounced as if it had been punched from underneath. The engine stalled and Flynn swore profusely and turned the ignition key. There was a sound like a loose tin can being rattled, and then the engine fired with an ominous grating sound from somewhere below. Exhaust dislodged by a rock? But you could drive without an exhaust, couldn't you? He would pull onto the grass verge – always supposing there was one – and he would walk the rest of the way to the house, take a good look round, and then drive himself back to Flaherty's using extreme care.

But as he let out the clutch again, the car careered wildly across the track, as if it was skidding on ice, and the steering wheel twisted uncontrollably out of his hands. Steering. The bloody steering's gone! thought Flynn, who knew virtually nothing about cars except that they usually refused to go when you most needed them. He got out, kicked each wheel in turn, tried the steering again, and finally faced the fact that the car was undrivable. Which meant he was stranded. And I wouldn't put it past that black-hearted villain to have planted a socking great boulder in the centre of his path to trap people, either! he thought, bending down to peer with difficulty under the car. Yes, it looked as if there was a damn great chunk of rock there, and a very integral-looking length of steel tube seemed to have torn away from the car's underside. This helped Flynn not at all. He got back in, switched off the lights to conserve the battery, and considered his situation.

It was the classic horror story opening, of course. The hero stuck in the middle of the blackest night Ireland ever spawned, in the middle of a raging storm, with little alternative other than to go up to the sinister house on the clifftop and ask for help.

I'm between the devil and the deep blue sea, thought Flynn, grimly, except that in this case the devil's almost certainly a maniacal killer, and the deep blue sea is a wild, storm-tossed ocean, probably inhabited by human-hungry succubi and homicidal siren maidens. And I wish, he thought, searching the glove-box for a torch, I really do wish that Father Mack hadn't related that bloody legend!

He found the torch and dragged an old waterproof out of the boot. The rain had lessened a bit, but the wind was moaning like a monster in its death throes, and it was bitterly cold. The sensible thing would be to walk back to the bar, trusting to get there before dawn broke and pneumonia took hold. It would probably take a good two hours and he would be soaked to the skin before he had gone ten yards. He looked back up the track. No lights showed anywhere, and Flynn wondered if the house really was up here. And surely only a fool or a reckless hero would walk up to the dark old house on the hill and request admittance. Especially when the hero knew that the arch-villain was inside. I'm not that reckless, thought Flynn.

But there might be other dwellings quite nearby where he could get help, and if he walked partway up the cliff path he would be able to look down on the countryside a bit and see if lights showed anywhere. As long as he kept clear of Maise itself—

No choice really, thought Flynn, setting off up the hill.

Walking up the cliff path was unspeakably eerie. The night was filled with the sounds of the storm: there were shrieking voices inside the wind and eldritch laughter within the sudden gusts of rain that still tore through the darkness.

There were no signs of human habitation anywhere, but Flynn walked doggedly on, shining the torch at intervals to see his way. The rain was definitely lessening and there was a cold, clean taste to the wind. If you were unduly fanciful – or if you had been so foolhardy as to listen to a load of superstitious rubbish from a romantically-minded priest in a bar – you might almost believe you were hearing the keening shrieks of inhuman creatures in the wind. It was very likely this that had started the legend of the *leanan-sidhe* in the first place. Flynn was just starting to feel pleased at having found an acceptable solution to at least one of the grisly sub-plots surrounding his arch-villain, when he became aware that someone was creeping along the road behind him.

It was a very bad moment indeed. He stopped at once, listening, trying to distinguish the sounds, trying to identify where they came from. Had it only been the product of an overstretched imagination? Yes, but if that creature is really holed up in some Gothic nightmare mansion up here, then he's going to be keeping a lookout for intruders. It's a bit of a coincidence, though, Flynn argued, if he just happened to be out checking the barricades at the exact minute you're sneaking up to the portcullis.

After a moment he set off again, straining every nerve-ending to listen. Yes, there was no doubt about it; someone was either behind him or over to his right, stealing furtively through the darkness. The thought of being suddenly attacked, and possibly struck down from behind without any warning was infuriating. Flynn cursed at not having brought some kind of weapon. But the torch was a large, heavy-based one, and it would deal a telling blow if necessary. The torch . . . If he can see me, let's even the score, thought Flynn, and he swung it around in all directions.

Nothing. Rain-slicked crags, the narrow, winding track, blades of grass caught and frozen in the beam of light. And then – oh God, yes, the house was there after all. Flynn stared up at it, for several seconds almost forgetting the creeping footsteps. The house rose up out of the swirling mists, black and forbidding, as much a part of the craggy cliffs as if it had simply grown there of its own accord. It was not quite large enough to seriously audition for the nightmare mansion of legend, but it would certainly never be cast as the woodcutter's cottage either. He swung the torch in the opposite direction, scanning the darkness.

Flynn shouted, 'If you're out there, show yourself, and let's fight this out!' and heard his words bounce off the rocks.

'Damn you, come out into the light! Or do you have to cower in the shadows all the time?' This time his words were snatched away by the wind and flung into the dark wastes beyond the cliff road. Nothing stirred and Flynn waited, his heart racing. He's out there, he thought, furiously. Damn it, I *know* he's out there!

And then rearing up from the darkness appeared the figure he had been waiting for. The pitiful, macabre being who had prowled the Harlequin, and who had held a portion of Soho's denizens in his power. *Cauldron*'s composer, if Flynn's guess was correct; Tod Miller's killer almost certainly; surely James Roscius's never-acknowledged son, hidden away out here for God-alone knew how many years, until his mind had warped and his soul had become helplessly embittered.

The dark cloak billowed out as he came forward, giving him the semblance of a monstrous black bat. Hands, curving into murderous claws, reached for Flynn's throat, and the very force of the onslaught knocked Flynn backwards onto the ground. Flynn swore and lashed out and felt again the frailty-over-steel of his assailant. As he struggled to lift his right hand, to bring the torch smashing down on the other's skull, Christian forced him back onto the ground, and taking Flynn's head between both hands, knocked it hard against the rocky path.

Flynn's world exploded in a cascade of spiralling stars and jagged lights, and the dark night spun away as he tumbled down into unconsciousness.

If Christian had left it another day he would not have met Flynn on the dark cliffside, and he would have had to create another opportunity. But he had not left it another day; he had acted immediately on the buskers' information, and no opportunity had needed creating.

He had telephoned to the Royal George Hotel in Galway that morning, using a call box on the main Galway road so that the call could not be traced, and asking if Mr Flynn Deverill was still staying there. He had sounded friendly and ordinary, and the hotel receptionist had said, Oh now what a pity, Mr Deverill had left only that morning.

'Damn, I was afraid I'd missed him. I wonder if he's on his way here – did he mention where he was going?'

The receptionist thought Mr Deverill had not precisely done that, but he had certainly asked which direction to take for Moher. 'And it's barely an hour since he set off.'

Christian said, lightly, 'Oh, then I know where he's going. I can reach him there. Thank you very much indeed.'

It had been an ordinary and normal telephone call; the kind that the receptionist would not think twice about, and would probably not even remember.

But it had told Christian what he wanted to know: Flynn was

coming out to Maise. He was walking straight into the trap. Christian waited until night fell; taking Fael's supper up to her, and then going quietly down to the old hut on the edge of Maise's land, that had been built by his father as a hide for the many bird-watchers who had once come out here.

The hide smelt of the night and of the old, damp timbers, but Christian barely noticed it. He half-closed his eyes and clenched his fists, because he must remain in control, he must not let the dark inner creature take over before he had Flynn in his power.

It was possible that Flynn would wait until morning and daylight, but Christian thought Flynn would come tonight. He dragged the large boulder across the mouth of Maise's private road, positioning it carefully. If Flynn was driving, there was a good chance that he would run straight into it in the dark and damage his car, forcing him to get out. Even if he spotted it, he would not be able to drive round it; he would have to get out and move it. That was what Christian wanted; he wanted Flynn alone and vulnerable in the dark.

He was aware that he was shivering violently, but he knew it was not from the cold. His mind was singing with hatred of Flynn, and the thought of rendering him senseless, of dragging him up to Maise and down to the subterranean room with the ancient disused well, was like a thrumming electrical current through his whole body.

Chapter Twenty-Six

The *Cauldron* company arrived in Ireland in untidy little clusters of threes and fours, variously by plane, ferry, road and train, depending on their personal inclinations and who was paying the travelling expenses. Most of them looked at the Gallery Theatre with dismay, and all of them regarded Julius Sherry with disbelief when he said it was nowhere near as bad as when he had first seen it. Wonders, said Sir Julius firmly, had been performed.

What had actually been performed was a compromise between Julius and Gerald Makepiece, resulting in some hasty, if rather makeshift, repairs. 'Cosmetic work,' the cheerful, erratic builders from Galway had called it, and said weren't they only papering over cracks, but in the end even Sir Julius had been forced to admit that the old place was looking a bit healthier. It was still a pity about the rampant rising damp and the Victorian flavour of the dressing rooms and backstage lavatories, and complete re-wiring would certainly have made everyone on the lighting deck feel a lot more comfortable, not to say safer, but at least the front of house area was freshly painted, and sections of new carpet had been laid. It was amazing what good carpeting did for a place. New washbasins had been fitted in the cloakrooms for the audience and the graffiti painted over, and the moss on the theatre's exterior had been removed by pressurised water jets. Gerald said hopefully that it quite spruced the whole area up, but Sir Julius was still annoyed with Gerald for opposing him, refused to be mollified, and said once a slum always a slum and the entire surroundings were a pustule on the face of the Irish countryside.

The compromise had meant that the work had partly been funded after a few persuasive telephone calls to people of authority and several expansive lunches for a few more people of generous inclination, and partly with the aid of a further investment by Gerald himself. Simkins of the bank had written a number of increasingly gloomy letters, advising Gerald strongly against throwing good money after bad, and prophesying ruination and bankruptcy, but Gerald, with a weak man's obstinacy, said he might as well be hanged for a sheep as for a lamb.

'Turkey,' said Sir Julius, sepulchrally.

'Pardon?'

'The correct theatrical expression for a flop is a turkey.'

'This isn't going to be a flop.'

But even with the repairs and the carpets and new paintwork, and even with the re-gilding of the once-famous stair in the main foyer, the prospect of staging *Cauldron* in such surroundings, and attracting enough audiences to balance the books, was formidable. Julius had arranged for a series of very carefully-worded press releases to appear before the opening, and there was to be an on-stage party after the first performance, to which local dignitaries were being invited. Simkins, getting wind of this in London, sent off another flurry of letters, warning that this would cost the earth because everyone knew that the Irish drank like fiends, and he hoped nobody would expect the wine merchants to be paid by the company.

Gilly, seeing the Gallery shortly after her arrival, thought it was the atmosphere as much as the theatre's actual condition. She thought you might renovate the place to within an inch of its life and the depressing aura would remain. It was as dismal as anything she had ever encountered, even in her worst days, even when she had been living in that dreadful squat near Mornington Crescent. Danilo thought the atmosphere was actually worse than the squat, which was where he and Gilly had met, although he admitted this might simply be because there was so much more of the Gallery than there had been of the Mornington Crescent house.

'And if we don't all fall through the stage it'll be by the grace of some saint or other,' said Danilo, surveying the place on the first afternoon.

'Is there a theatre saint?'

'I don't think so. There's always Jude.'

'Who's he?'

'Patron saint of lost causes,' said Danilo, gloomily.

'Oh. Well listen, will all this rot and mildew and whatnot make it any easier for us to keep a look-out for – you know, *him*?' It seemed absurdly melodramatic to use the Shadow's title; Gilly was annoyed to find that she flinched from it.

'I don't see why it should make any difference one way or another. How long do you suppose it will be before he finds out where we are?'

'Flynn thought he would come out here as soon as he knew,' said Gilly. 'It was in one or two of the papers in England. But it wasn't banner headlines; it was only a small paragraph and it laid more stress on the murders than anything else. He might easily have missed it; I nearly missed it myself.'

'Even so,' said Danilo, after a moment, 'I think I'm going to walk round the auditorium and the backstage area every night after rehearsals finish. And before every performance once the run starts.'

'What do we do if we find he's here? Prowling about?'

'I *think*,' said Danilo, after a moment, 'that first off we tell Julius Sherry and Stephen we've seen an intruder. We needn't tell them the whole story – at least, not yet. It sounds too far-fetched for words still. But at least the police could be tipped to keep a look-out. What do they call the police out here? Gardai, isn't it?'

'You're being very – very *rigorous* about it,' said Gilly, curiously.

Danilo paused, and then said softly, 'Yes, I am. I think this is *Cauldron*'s last chance, Gilly. If there's the least hint of sabotage here, I think it's finished.'

'Doomed.'

'Don't mock. I don't want anything to destroy this show.'

'I didn't know you cared so strongly,' said Gilly.

'Didn't you? Don't you care just as strongly?'

'Oh God yes. Oh yes, I do. I'm sorry, I was just being flippant.'

'Then let's try to find this bastard before he knackers the thing all over again.'

Chapter Twenty-Nine

Gilly had fought like a wildcat when the Shadow carried her out of his car and down the narrow track to the massive black stone. Her hands were still tied, but her feet were free and she had kicked and bit, and twice she heard his quick indrawn gasp of pain. Good! thought Gilly viciously. And if I get the chance I'll do it again! I'll yell for help and run like a bat escaping hell!

But then he tied her feet and twisted a gag over her mouth and she was helpless. He left her at the foot of the huge, menacing black stone and, over the sounds of the wind and the lashing ocean below the cliffs, she heard the car start up and growl away into the night.

It was somehow important not to look up at the great black stone. Gilly thought if she once did that she would start being frightened in a totally different way. And I've got quite enough fear to be going on with already! she thought. I've got a chance to get free, because if I can get these bloody bonds loosened even a bit I can be away! She dragged furiously at the ropes, swearing and sobbing, but the bonds around her wrists and her ankles were strong and the knots were secure. Gilly tore her skin in several places before she faced this. But what about trying to get back up the cliff path to the road? Could she drag herself along the ground? Worth a go. But she found that to move along in a half drag, half crawl was excruciatingly difficult; it would take what was left of the night to reach the main road. And the trouble is that I don't know if I've got the rest of the night, thought Gilly in anguish. I don't know how long he'll be gone. I don't know what else might be out here either— She glanced uneasily up at the stone again. No, I won't think that. I'll keep going because when he does come

'Yes, but look here,' said Gilly, who had been thinking about this. 'Look here, will he really do anything a second time? We're agreed that he removed Mia because she would have ruined the London production – doesn't that mean he wants it to have every chance? Isn't that logical?'

'Gilly, love, a madman isn't logical. Remember he's mad. Keep remembering it. He may have reasons that make sense to him but that wouldn't make any sense to anyone else. And what about Tod Miller?' demanded Danilo. 'Don't forget that he killed Tod Miller as well.'

'I'm not forgetting it,' said Gilly.

'Now,' said Danilo, 'unless we can bring anyone else in on this—'

'We can't do that.'

'No, we can't, can we? Then that means we'll have to split the patrolling between us.'

'What about if I do the after-rehearsal check, and you do the before-rehearsal one?'

'Other way round,' said Danilo at once. 'It'll be dark after rehearsals, or at least darkish. We'll work out a route when we've seen all over the place. And let's be very casual over it.'

'We could pretend to be looking for something or someone,' suggested Gilly. 'I'll call for you as I go, and you do the same. That ought to look pretty innocent.' She looked at Danilo. 'You think he's still dangerous, don't you?'

'I don't know. But Flynn thought he was. And Flynn's no fool. What I do know,' said Danilo, firmly, 'is that we aren't getting into any mad fights with this weirdo. At least, you aren't. Agreed?'

'All right. Yes, agreed,' said Gilly, rather white-faced. 'Has Flynn got here yet, by the way? Somebody said he'd probably have to come over to supervise the resetting.'

'I don't think he's here yet. If he is, no one's seen him. He's probably gone to ground with a female somewhere – you know what he's like.'

'Yes,' said Gilly, and felt depressed.

'Oh, he'll get here. He'll never let his precious sets be butchered by the ASMs.'

The company had been billeted in two or three small guest

houses and hotels around the area, but Gilly had been allotted a very plush double room in the Ennismara Castle Hotel which had at first gratified, and then unnerved her.

'You don't think it's just because you're playing the lead?' said one of the *sidh* girls, enviously. 'Star rating and all that. You might find that it's only that.'

Gilly thought that the rating she was being given was of a different category entirely, and the only thing to be found out was whether it was Julius Sherry or little Gerald Makepiece who was paying the Ennismara Castle's bill, and therefore expecting a half share of the bed. Maybe even entitled to it.

'A moral entitlement,' she said, worried.

'More like an immoral entitlement,' said the *sidh* scornfully. 'And will you?'

'Nothing to do with you.'

'Oh, so you will. Which one?'

'I don't know,' said Gilly, crossly. She thought, but did not say, that it was ridiculous in the extreme to pretend to squeamishness after the two years in Soho, but she had wanted to be finished with all that.

'It's worth thinking about,' said the *sidh* girl.

It was, of course. On the one hand Julius Sherry would be preferable on account of his prestige and the title, but on the other hand Gerald Makepiece was more timid and probably more easily managed. Also he was rather endearingly old-fashioned and he might even think it necessary to marry her once he had stopped being a sorrowful widower over that greedy vampire Mia Makepiece. Yes, it all needed thinking about very carefully.

'There's also the fact that Makepiece is richer than Sir Julius,' pointed out the *sidh*.

'That's being cynical.'

'No, it's being realistic. You'd be surprised the men that some girls sleep with, purely for cash.'

Oh, no I wouldn't, thought Gilly and went off to bed, intending to make a sensible mental list of the pros and cons of the two gentlemen concerned, and ending up dreaming about Flynn Deverill until breakfast-time, which was very irritating indeed.

The rest of the company were less lavishly housed than Gilly, and inclined to be disgruntled about it when they all fore-gathered for the first rehearsal, although the lodge-keeper said they had none of them known what it was like in the old days, when you had to put up with bedbugs and rusty bacon, to say nothing of cheating landladies permanently pickled in gin. He contrived to make it sound as if he had rubbed shoulders and shared discomforts with the likes of Jonathan Miller and Ron Moody and Julie Andrews, or even Gertrude Lawrence and Noël Coward, so that it was rather a pity when, at the first break, his stage wife told everyone that most of the discomforts had been endured under the dubious banner of a third-rate touring company, whose only claim to fame had been putting on things like *Getting Gertie's Garter*, and bad revivals of *Rose Marie* and *The Desert Song*.

It was next found that the *sidh*'s bawdy rape of the lodge-keeper in Act One had been drastically moderated, in what Stephen Sherry and Maurice Camperdown explained was diplomatic courtesy to the conventions of the country in which they were performing, but in what the lodge-keeper said was a downright sodding liberty, pardon for swearing.

'I'm afraid it's necessary if we're to be well received over here,' said Stephen. 'It's tactful.'

'It's not tactful to Tod Miller's work. Or,' said the lodge-keeper deliberately, 'to whoever wrote *Cauldron*.'

There was an abrupt silence. Gilly thought: So we aren't the only ones who are suspicious.

Stephen glanced round the dusty stage and, raising his voice slightly, said, 'Tod Miller presented *Cauldron* to my father and the trustees of the Harlequin Theatre. He presented it as his own original work – music, book, lyrics, everything. Since he's dead—'

' "And never called me mother"—' murmured an irreverent voice from one of the *Fianna* soldiers who had played in Victorian melodrama.

'Since he's dead,' said Stephen, 'we can't ask his permission to cut the scene. Since Fael is still missing, we can't ask hers, which we'd normally do, as next of kin.'

'Flynn Deverill's missing as well,' observed the stage manager.

'What, literally?'

'Well no, I don't suppose so. But he hasn't turned up to supervise the rebuilding of the sets.'

'We gave him the dates and so on, but he's so unpredictable it's anyone's guess whether he'll actually turn up,' said Stephen. 'There's no problem, is there?'

'Not really,' said the stage manager. 'We can manage the sets without him, although I'd prefer him to oversee.'

'You'll probably get them up a damn sight easier without him,' said Stephen. 'He's probably tucked up somewhere with a female,' he added, unwittingly echoing Danilo's earlier view.

'Oh, well, in that case—' said the stage manager glumly.

Stephen looked back at his cast. 'The rape scene,' he said. 'It's my responsibility to do whatever I think best for the show, and I think it's best that we cut it.' He looked at the lodge-keeper. 'I'm sorry about it, but we simply can't risk explicit sex on stage here, they don't approve of it.'

'It's the first *I've* ever heard of the Irish not approving of sex,' said the lodge-keeper huffily, not best pleased at losing three-quarters of a scene, never mind the titillating intimacy with the leading *sidh* girl.

'Not in *public*, Bransby.'

'Rot, they're at it like stoats all over the place,' said Bransby, and stumped off to the Green Room, whither he was followed by the *sidh* girl, who was cross at finding her best scene cut. The lodge-keeper's wife went along as well because you could not trust that saucy little hussy, and also if there were any tantrums to be thrown, the lodge-keeper's wife could throw them with the best.

The sorceress had discovered unmistakable signs of rats in the dressing rooms and was refusing to appear, and the quarrel between Gerald Makepiece and Julius Sherry had broken out again because each had discovered that Gilly had accepted an invitation from the other: lunch with Gerald and supper with Julius.

The first thing to penetrate Flynn's mind was the awareness that he was lying on a hard, cold floor, and that there was a skewering pain in his skull. He frowned, and fought his way up through the clogging unconsciousness, flinching when he opened his eyes. But it was not so very bright in here at all, in fact it was quite dark. It was only that his eyes were over-sensitive. After a moment he sat up, and at once sick dizziness swept over him. He remained very still and took several deep breaths, and the sickness receded slightly. Touch and go there for a minute, thought Flynn. But I don't think I'm going to throw up.

He had no idea where he was, but the swinging vertigo was lessening. Although I don't think I dare move too quickly or too much yet, he thought. At least I haven't got double vision, so I don't think I can be too seriously injured. He moved, wincing from the pain in his head, and made the discovery that he was tied up – his hands were bound behind his back, and a rope bound his ankles.

Memory was beginning to trickle back. He remembered Flaherty's Bar and the drive along the wild cliff road. There had been something wrong with the car – he had turned off the main road and run aground on a narrow track. Oh God yes, he had set off on foot – Yes, *of course*! Roscius's son, thought Flynn. I was trying to find him, only the bastard reared up out of nowhere and fell on me like a wild animal. He must have knocked me out – yes, I remember a sudden crack of pain and then spinning darkness. So presumably Roscius brought me here.

He thought he was in some kind of underground room. It was a largish room, low ceilinged, and with black brick walls and hard-packed earth on the floor. There was a stench of age and damp and as his head cleared a little, he made out worn steps on the opposite wall, winding upwards and away. And at the centre of the room was a yawning black abyss, roughly six feet across, with a brick parapet circling it. An old well. Flynn stared at it, and found it unspeakably sinister. A sour, tainted darkness seemed to waft upwards from the well's depths.

It was beginning to look as if Roscius had carried him up to the clifftop house and thrown him into the dungeons. There was an indefinable sense of suffocation as if the crouching old house he had seen earlier was directly over him, and Flynn was aware now of the faint, steady, drip-drip of water against stone somewhere beneath him. He looked uneasily at the well, and then away, forcing himself to remain seated upright, so that he could test the strength of his bonds. Oh God, yes, they're tight, he thought. If Roscius tied me up – and of course it must have been him – he did a very thorough job.

He was about to see whether he could drag himself across to the shadowy stair, and whether it might provide a means of escape, when he heard from above the sound of a door being unlocked, and the tortured creak of old hinges. A flickering light appeared on the stair, and with it, footsteps coming down. Someone's coming, thought Flynn, sweat breaking out between his shoulder blades. It's Roscius, of course – he's coming down here to deal with me. We're about to have our third encounter, and the way I'm feeling there's no contest as to who'll win this one.

The light grew stronger, and as the footsteps came down the last few stairs there was a moment when the shadows seemed to shiver and almost to flinch. And then he was there, framed in the stair opening, lit by the flickering flame of the candles inset in a branched holder. The young man Flynn had seen and fought below the Harlequin, and whom he had seen on the stormy hillside – how long ago had it been? A few hours ago? Longer? Hell, I'm losing track of time, thought Flynn, wildly. Mother of God, I feel dreadful, but I can't let him see it.

He said, 'Good evening to you. Have we no electricity down here, or is it only that you don't pay the bills?' It was not quite up to his usual form, but under the circumstances it was not bad.

Roscius set the candlestick on the floor unhurriedly, and straightened up. The soft voice Flynn remembered from the Soho basement said, 'You don't need to maintain the image down here, Flynn. There's no one to hear you.'

'Except yourself.'

'Except myself.' For the first time Flynn caught the faint Irish lilt.

'Are we to have a final confrontation?' he said, after a moment.

'No.' The single syllable was dismissive; it was very nearly bored. 'I'm simply getting rid of you.'

'The devil you are!'

'The devil I am,' said Roscius at once. 'Or so a great many people believe. But you knew that already.' He appeared to study Flynn. 'If you attempt any heroics,' he said, 'I shall shoot you in the stomach. And that's an agonising wound to suffer when there's no hope of medical attention.'

'I don't believe you'd do that,' said Flynn, and at once the other man reached into a pocket and levelled a black-mouthed revolver.

They looked at one another. 'Believe me, Flynn, I would,' said Christian. 'I'd enjoy it as well.'

'As a point of purely academic interest, why didn't you simply kill me while I was unconscious?' said Flynn. 'Wouldn't it have been easier?'

'I didn't want it to be easy. I want you aware,' said Roscius. 'I want you frightened.' He moved nearer, and Flynn tensed to ward off an attack, and felt the rope around his wrists bite into his flesh.

'I want you,' said the soft voice, 'to be sufficiently conscious so that you know what's being done to you, but not so conscious that you can put up a fight.'

'Be damned to that—'

'And we both know,' said Christian, 'that you're exactly in that state now.' He studied Flynn for a moment. 'To witness your terror, Flynn, will redress the balance a little.'

'What balance? Jesus God, you're mad—'

'Whether I'm mad or not doesn't matter. You can't fight me, you're far too weak.'

'Sod that, come over here and untie me, and we'll see if I can fight or not!' said Flynn, but he knew that Roscius was right. He could feel the man's thick gloating filling up the small room now, and he could feel the hatred. Why does he hate me so much? thought Flynn. Is it because I'm unflawed and he is flawed?

'A fight between us would mean brother fighting brother,' said Roscius very softly. 'And that might be against your principles, Flynn, always supposing you have any.'

He stopped and Flynn stared at him. After a moment, he said, 'What? What did you say? Did you say brother—?'

'I did. Didn't you know?'

Flynn said, 'Oh Jesus Christ Almighty, you bastard!'

'A lot of people have called you a bastard too,' said the soft voice. 'They're right to do so, of course, because it's what you are. You're James Roscius's bastard, Flynn. After I was born my father screwed a number of women in an effort to blot out the knowledge that he had sired a monster.'

'You,' said Flynn.

'Me. But you were the result of one of those screwings. That's all you are, Flynn. A nothing.' He paused, and Flynn said, half to himself, 'We're half brothers. But why didn't I know? Why didn't I guess?'

Before he could say any more, before he could start to assimilate this astounding information, Roscius was standing over him, the gun levelled. 'And now,' he said, 'I'm going to tip you into the old well and leave you there to die.' He studied Flynn for a moment. 'It's an immensely old structure, that well,' he said. 'And until about a hundred years ago it was still in use. But then it was found that fissures were letting in sea-water, and so my great-grandfather – your great-grandfather as well, if it comes to that – had it closed and sealed.' He paused, and Flynn saw that he was briefly enrapt in the strange legend. If ever there was a moment to take him off-balance and overpower him, this was surely it. He dragged uselessly at the ropes again.

'No one has ever found out how deep the shaft is,' said Roscius. 'But there's a legend that it winds down and down beneath the ocean, and that eventually it comes out in the underworld lair of the *leanan-sidhe*. You know about the *leanan-sidhe*, do you? Yes, of course you do. You depicted a version of them for *Cauldron*. But the *leanan-sidhe* of Moher and Maise are far grislier than your winged iridescent creatures, Flynn. Perhaps you'll find that out for yourself.'

Flynn said, 'You know, you'll never get away with this.'

'No? Let's see, shall we?' said Christian Roscius, and with a swift unexpected movement, he tore away the face-mask and advanced on Flynn.

The minute Roscius's hands closed over his arms Flynn fought him, dragging frantically at the ropes and swearing furiously.

But he was still infuriatingly weak from the blow to his head, and his captor had the iron strength Flynn remembered from their earlier encounter.

Roscius seized him from behind, circling his arms just beneath Flynn's shoulders, and dragging him across the floor. The dizziness was sweeping in again, and as Roscius pulled him towards the gaping void at the centre of the room, Flynn was aware of slipping helplessly into a half-faint that tilted his consciousness and distorted his vision, and that was worse than a complete blackout would have been. Through it, he was aware of the dry, tomblike breath of the ancient well and then of being dragged inexorably nearer the edge.

Roscius half-lifted him and gave him a sudden violent push, so that Flynn landed half across the parapet, his head hanging down into the yawning hole. There was an appalling moment when he thought he heard the well actually breathe out, and its foul stench surrounded him. Nausea seized him afresh, and he thought: Oh God, don't let me be sick in front of him! He gritted his teeth and after a moment the sickness receded. But I'm in no condition to fight him, he thought. He's doing something to the rope now – is he tying it more tightly? No, he's looping a second rope round my waist. Why?

But there was no time to wonder why, because Roscius was pulling Flynn over, so that he was lying on his back, still half over the parapet. The dreadful mad face was only inches away, and Flynn stared up at it, seeing it in all its horrifying deformity; seeing how the candle-light cast a reddish glow over it, and how the eyes – expressive and surprisingly beautiful eyes fringed with long lashes – reflected little pinpoints of light.

'As you see,' said the voice, in uncanny echo of Flynn's thoughts, 'I have unmasked, because I want my face to be the last thing you will see.' The words sounded ragged, as if he was slightly out of breath, and Flynn was unable to decide if this was simply due to exertion, or if Roscius was deriving a warped arousal from what he was doing.

He was still struggling, and although consciousness was slipping away again, he was aware that he was being pushed into the appalling abyss. He thought frantically: But I can't! I can't die like this!

Roscius gave him a final, vicious push, and Flynn went down into the ancient blackness.

He was jerked to an abrupt halt after a fall of only a couple of dozen feet, and the suddenness of this snatched his breath away, and jarred his whole body. For a moment there was only a confusion of pain and fear, but gradually he began to sort out and identify his feelings. He was not, in fact, injured, and he had not, in fact, fallen all the way to the shaft's foot.

I'm on the end of a rope, he thought, torn between relief and creeping horror. That bastard tied a rope round my waist – yes, I can feel it cutting in. Did he loop it around something at the top? He must have done, because I'm against one side of the well. I think I banged against the sides several times as I fell. He explored cautiously with his bound hands. The brick lining of the well felt clammy and rough and altogether repulsive. Even the smallest move caused him to sway slightly. He sent up a prayer that the rope around his waist would hold.

But now what? thought Flynn, wildly. He's not going to leave me here like this, surely? He managed to look upwards, to where he could make out the blurry circle of light that was the well's mouth. Against the dimness he could see the head and shoulders of his assailant. He's watching me, thought Flynn. He's watching to see what I do, although I'm not at all sure I can do anything. But if I could get my hands free I might stand a better chance. If I could somehow cut through the rope— Oh God, could I possibly use the iron rungs? They're meant for a makeshift ladder, I suppose, but most of them are rusty enough to be pretty abrasive.

The iron rungs formed a very makeshift ladder indeed; they were a series of horseshoe-shaped iron staves driven into the wall at intervals. But Flynn thought he might manage to swing himself across and use the staves to saw through the ropes. He would probably tear his wrists to ribbons in the process, and he would probably contract blood poisoning as well. But anything was better than hanging here like a spider on the end of a web.

If the well shaft had been wider he would not have done it. But it was barely six feet across and it was easier than he expected to brace his feet against the wall, and manoeuvre into position with his hands against the iron ladder. He began to rub the ropes against the jutting staves, wincing as the rusting iron scraped his flesh, but going doggedly on. Because if I can free my hands I think I can free my feet, he thought. And then I'll be out of this gruesome place and I'll strangle bloody Roscius with my bare hands!

He had no idea how long it took before the rope strands parted, but he thought it was not very long. There was a moment of delighted hope when he managed to pull his hands free and bring them around in front of him again. He rubbed his grazed wrists, and then braced his back against the wall again, so that he could go through the same process with the rope around his ankles. This took longer, and several times he over-calculated and sent himself spinning dizzyingly in the centre of the well, but in the end he managed it.

So far so good, thought Flynn. What I've got to do now is climb up to the top, and if I can do that, I'll beat the shit out of that warped, evil creature, even if he's got fifty guns!

He grasped the iron staves and began to climb, testing each rung before he put his weight on it, seeing how they were placed at carefully-spaced intervals so that they supported feet and gave a handhold at the same time. But it was a slow, difficult process. The sides were completely vertical, and the pull on Flynn's thigh muscles and on his shoulders was agony. Several times the rungs dislodged and went skittering down into the black depths below, and each time this happened Flynn clung on to the other staves, his heart hammering. But I'm still in one piece, he thought. And I'm nearly there.

He was within four feet of the top when he heard a sound that chilled his blood and froze his marrow. Above his head, something huge and clanging was being dragged across the floor of the underground room. It was a monstrous, an enormous sound, and it was the kind of teeth-wincing sound that made Flynn think of huge nails being scraped across immense iron surfaces. The well cover! he thought, in horror. Oh God, Roscius is dragging the well cover into place!

But even as he frantically grasped the next set of iron staves, the light from above was shutting off, and he heard the mad laughter of his gaoler.

320

There was a final massive clanging, that reverberated through and through the well shaft, and the black iron cover came down over the well's mouth. Flynn heard, very faintly, the scraping of a locking mechanism, and then blackness, thick and stifling and absolutely impenetrable, closed down.

Chapter Twenty-Seven

Julius Sherry donned his well-cut dark blue suit, and thought that for a man of his age he was looking remarkably trim. A good tailor did wonders for the more portly figure, of course, but really, he did not look his age.

He had found a very nice, discreet little restaurant just outside Galway, and he had arranged with the manager to have a table for two intimately tucked out of sight.

He knotted his tie carefully, and studied again the playbills that Mr Flanagan of the County Arts Association had had distributed. They were vivid and surprisingly well-designed, and Flanagan's minions had been thorough; the playbills and small posters were being displayed in most of the shops in Galway City, and in all of the hotels. There had also been talk of some kind of door-to-door mail-drop, although Flanagan had said they would have to pick the areas carefully, because folk in the Gallery's immediate neighbourhood would not know a good musical if it got up and hit them on the nose, unless it might be one of the raucous pop groups they all listened to at top volume. But a good mail-drop in the more up-market parts always stirred up interest, said Flanagan, and with the curious Irish talent for mixing city-wise ingenuity with downright parochialism, added that what you did, you arranged for the dairies to take the leaflets onto the milk floats, so that people got the information with their morning milk.

'Oh, I see,' said Sir Julius, rather blankly.

'And if you give the dairies a free advertisement for yoghurt and eggs on the back page, they'll do it for about half of nothing,' said Flanagan enthusiastically, and Julius remembered that the County Arts Association was to some extent accountable to the *Dail*.

As Gilly got ready, she supposed a bit glumly that she would have to go through with it. Looked at sensibly it would be no worse than the nights on the game in Soho, and looked at practically it would very probably be a great deal better; Julius Sherry was clean and reasonably intelligent, and it would doubtless all take place in a comfortable hotel bedroom – presumably this one.

A polite refusal could be given, but Gilly guessed it would not be very far-sighted. She wanted very much to continue in *Cauldron*, and she wanted above everything to go on playing Mab. She did not know, not absolutely, that doing so depended on going to bed with Julius Sherry, but it was not something she dared ignore.

She listened with only partly-feigned interest to Sir Julius's anecdotes throughout dinner, and laughed in the right places because even though he was not an actor, he had a theatre man's instinct for a good punchline. As the evening progressed, he became sufficiently confident to grope her under the table, and his complexion, never exactly pale to start with, grew increasingly sanguine. This was slightly worrying, because it would be awkward if he succumbed to a coronary at the table, although not as awkward as if he succumbed to one when they were in bed together.

And when he patted her hand and suggested in a thickened voice that it seemed a pity to end the evening so early, what did she think? – Gilly said, 'A very great pity indeed.' And greatly daring, added, 'Julius,' which was the first time she had omitted his title, and which ought to signal the green light.

And now he would say the waiter could call them a taxi, and then he would give the address of her hotel, and there would be sly looks from the night reception staff who would all gossip, and people in the company would get to hear about it, and those inquisitive *sidh* dancers would tell one another that now they knew how she had landed the leading part, and they had suspected all the time that she was nothing but a hooker. Damn and blast! thought Gilly, crossly, and resolutely squashed the horrid little voice that said: But if it was Flynn Deverill you wouldn't give a tuppenny toss what any of them thought! Castles in the air again, Gilly. Julius is calling for the bill. I'll pretend to go to the loo while he settles it, that's supposed to be tactful. And when I come out, he'll have the taxi and everything arranged.

In fact Julius Sherry was in a bit of a quandary, having reluctantly come to the conclusion that the Ennismara Castle, regarded as a love-nest, was not on. It was one matter to do that kind of thing in London where everybody was anonymous and hotel staff did not give a damn what you did or how many people you did it with, so long as you paid the bill afterwards. But out here it was different. He remembered that Stephen was bowd-lerising the Act One rape scene, and he remembered that this was Catholic Ireland and he found himself visualising, with extreme horror, a number of embarrassing scenarios, starting with a flat refusal by the hotel manager to allow him into Gilly's room (which would be a whopping irony when he was footing the bill); progressing to the manager and assorted minions bursting into the room with the pass-key while he was actually on the job (knowing the Irish sense of timing he would just have reached the short strokes!), and ending with a truly unthinkable situation in which he was ordered from the hotel, in the kind of humiliating *deshabille* you only saw in blue movies (of which he had only a very limited experience, but everyone knew what went on in them).

But here was Gilly being extremely on-coming, and here was Julius himself in a very gratifying state of arousal under the table, and something would have to be thought of. He did think of something, he thought of it after the pudding and before the coffee, which he refused on account of it sometimes causing wind in the bowels.

He would take Gilly to the theatre. They would go in through the small stage door, and they would tiptoe through the darkened auditorium together, which would be intimate and sufficiently tinged with the forbidden to be titillating. And they would cement their little relationship in the Gallery's Green Room. There was a satin-covered chaise longue in there – shabby but not distasteful – and the lights could be turned off, so that the shabbiness would look rather romantic.

'I hope,' said Gilly, when he explained all this to her, 'that there isn't a night watchman.'

There was not a night watchman, and there did not appear to be anyone in a watchman's guise.

But there was something inside the theatre, and it was something that was watching and listening – and *gloating*, thought Gilly, as Julius pushed open the stage door. She was suddenly aware of a rather unpleasant little chill. I'm being very trusting over this, she thought, glancing at her companion. I'm going in to precisely the kind of situation that Danilo wanted me to avoid. Alone, into the deserted theatre. . . But I'm not alone, I'm with Sir Julius, thought Gilly, and then a scary little voice inside her head, said: Supposing that's what Mia Makepiece thought?

Julius closed the stage door and slid the bolt across – 'Because we don't want any tramps or tinkers sneaking in after us, do we, my dear?'

'No,' said Gilly, who was still thinking about Mia Makepiece, poor stupid Mia, killed in the Harlequin, and from the sound of it, lured there by a fake message from an admirer. The police had not actually said this was what had happened, but you did not have to be Einstein to work it out. And nobody knew who the admirer had been. It might have been the Shadow, forging somebody's name on a note or imitating somebody's voice on the phone, which was what Flynn Deverill believed. But it might not have been. It could just as easily have been anyone in the company who had arranged that secret rendezvous.

And now here was Gilly herself going into a dark theatre for a secret rendezvous. She felt a spiral of panic uncoil, because was it conceivable that Flynn had been wrong, and that it had been Julius Sherry who had lured Mia into the Harlequin and killed her? And then killed Tod Miller as well?

She glanced at Sir Julius as they went through the dark, old theatre. It was a preposterous idea. Julius Sherry was not a schizo killer; he was very well-known in theatre circles. He did not act, but he financed things and helped produce them: Gilly thought the word 'magnate' described him. He backed shows and joined forces with like-dowered people to put on new plays. You saw fluorescent-lit boards over theatres saying that this was, 'A Sherry and Somebody Production'. Sometimes he lent his name to workshop ventures for drama students, or to the twinning of British shows in the States. He was the senior trustee for the historic old Harlequin Theatre and everybody knew about him. Everybody knew about his illustrious background as well – the cousin who had been knighted for services to the theatre, the great-aunt who had been one of Wolfit's favourite leading ladies, the great-grandfather who had been instrumental in reviving the Harlequin's flagging fortunes in the eighteen-nineties, and who had perked up the fortunes of several ladies of the chorus at the same time. All of which Gilly had learned during the last few weeks; none of which was proof against Sir Julius being a schizo killer.

Whoever had built the Gallery had not planned a Green Room as such, but there was a sprawling, untidily asymmetric area that abutted several sections of the backstage area: a kind of natural lobby which had developed over the years into its present usage. You could reach it by means of a narrow corridor just beyond the stage door which had the dressing rooms opening off, or you could go through the auditorium and the swing pass-doors on the prompt side; you could get to it from the carpenters' workshop at the very back of the theatre as well.

Sir Julius led Gilly along the narrow dressing-room corridor, which was the obvious approach, but which Gilly did not much like, because it was a one-way-street arrangement: once you started along it you could very easily be trapped, especially if you happened to be with an aspiring schizo killer who would bar your way out, and who might have cunningly locked the Green Room door at the other end.

But when Julius said, 'All right, Gilly?' Gilly at once said, 'Oh yes, perfectly all right. Just that it's a bit – well, spooky in here, isn't it?' She thought he might add, 'You won't feel spooky once I get going, my dear,' but he did not. Over dinner he had said they would have a very cosy little time, and he had leaned across the table and huffed wine-breath into her face. She had thought that he only needed to put on a maroon velvet smoking jacket and refer to his very interesting etchings, or offer some more Madeira, m'dear, to be his randy old great-grandfather reborn, entertaining Gaiety Girls.

The sight of the Green Room, with its tattered furniture and ramshackle shabbiness, was unexpectedly comforting. Gilly found it rather endearing when Julius fussed anxiously over the arrangement of the lights, and even dusted off the tatty sofa. In a minute he would say, 'And now, my dear,' and they would be off.

Sir Julius seated himself on the chaise longue, patted the cover invitingly, and said, 'And now, my dear,' and Gilly with a mental shrug, went forward.

It was no better and no worse than she had expected. He got a bit out of breath and he needed a bit of coaxing – this was a potentially awkward development, because if he was too stubbornly flaccid to be of any use he would be embarrassed and angry, but if Gilly displayed too many tricks of the trade it might make him wonder about her background. Still, this was the twentieth century, for goodness' sake: he would hardly expect her to be totally ignorant.

Between fumblings and strokings, Sir Julius's chancy manhood revived quite promisingly. To help him along, Gilly got up from the sofa, and, standing in front of him, stripped off, leaving on her stockings, suspender belt, and high-heeled shoes. This generally helped most men along, and it helped Sir Julius along very strongly indeed. He pulled her back onto the chaise longue and lumbered on top of her, and Gilly tried not to mind that the sofa had hideously uncomfortable walnut arms that dug into you in the most unexpected places. Over his shoulder she could see the door leading to the narrow corridor; they had left it partly open, and Gilly caught herself imagining that at any minute she would see the Shadow himself, standing in the doorway watching them.

Julius seemed to have judged his alcoholic intake fairly well, so that he did not struggle sweatily for half an hour before managing to climax. He moved off her as soon as he had regained his breath, which Gilly thought considerate, and pulled his clothes together, muttering something about a quick visit to the loo. Troublesome prostate, poor old sod, thought Gilly, not without sympathy, and smiled at him as he went out, using the swing-door exit that led down to the auditorium. She heard his footsteps going towards the men's cloakroom near the stalls.

I could do a great deal worse, thought Gilly, leaning back. He's very courteous, even when he's screwing, and that's worth a lot; people wouldn't believe the selfish ways of some men. What a calculating bitch I'm sounding. But she was not really; she was simply fighting not to return to the days of having no money – of not being able to pay bills, and of barely having enough to buy food. Those hideous weeks when there was often nothing in the pantry except maybe flour and a cheap tub of margarine, so that the only thing to do was make a kind of scone dough, which was pretty tasteless but at least stopped you feeling hungry. I'd do anything to avoid going back to that, thought Gilly, staring up at the Green Room's peeling ceiling. It's all very well to be high-minded and high-principled when you've never been really broke, and to say you'd rather scrub floors for a living – I'd have scrubbed floors gladly, if somebody would have employed me to do it, or I'd have— *There's somebody outside.*

She sat up, pulling her clothes around her. Had she imagined it? No, there it was again, a furtive darting movement in the shadowy corridor almost as if the shadows had reared up and tiptoed forward to peer through the chink in the door. Gilly caught the sound of extremely stealthy footsteps, and instantly began to scramble into her clothes, keeping her eyes on the partly-open door. There was no need to panic quite so comprehensively, of course; Julius would be back at any minute, and if anything appeared from the passage – the Shadow? Julius Sherry armed with a dripping axe? oh come *on*! – she could be through the other door, and out into the auditorium or into the carpenters' workshop.

And then Gilly heard, very faintly, the sound of a door opening and closing in the auditorium. Julius! she thought, thankfully. Or is it? And is he the one I've got to be wary of after all? No, I don't think he could have got round to the dressing-room corridor so soon – he'd have had to go out into the street and along to the stage door. She listened for Julius's footsteps, which were distinctive as are most people's footsteps. At any minute she would hear him coming back and she would call out and tell him what had happened, and they would take a look together and find nothing, and they might even be able to laugh over it.

328

think what to do or whether she could find her way out in the dark, a soft voice just behind her said, 'I really shouldn't bother to run, Gilly. You won't escape me, my dear.'

There was a terrible sense of inevitability at feeling his arms go around her and at being pressed against him in this abrupt intimacy.

So this is what it feels like to be in his arms, thought Gilly, dazed and helpless. Strength and authority and sizzling power. I didn't know it would be like this. I couldn't possibly fight against this, nobody could. He's mad, of course, but he's still a triple murderer, and he's probably going to murder me next. I think I might be a bit mad as well, because I'm not struggling, and I don't even know if I'm frightened.

The Shadow was carrying her out of the theatre, going easily and almost negligently as if she weighed next to nothing. As they went out of the auditorium, Gilly managed to twist round to see the stage. The Shadow had left it in darkness, but she could just make out the figure suspended at the centre, swinging gently to and fro. There was a terrible submissiveness about it. I think he's dead, thought Gilly. I don't think he could live – I don't think anyone could live with half his feet torn away like that. There'd be shock and loss of blood. When this is all over, I think I'm going to be very upset about Julius.

The Shadow was carrying her out through the stage door and if there was ever a minute to fight this was surely it.

'Don't fight me, Gilly,' he said, and Gilly shivered at the eerie way he had picked up her thoughts. 'Don't fight me and don't try to run away. If you do, I shall certainly catch you and overpower you.'

'Where – are we going?'

Incredibly she felt a stir of amusement from him. He really is mad, she thought, but it's a madness that's all mixed up with the night and the darkness and it's part of his own magnetism. 'We're going to the Cliffs of Moher,' he said. 'And once we're there, you're going to be a sacrifice, Gilly. Out there on the clifftops, in the dark storm. At exactly midnight, my dear.' *My dear* ... The words held a slurred, sexual note, and Gilly repressed a shudder.

They had reached a car now, and he opened the back door and threw her onto the seat, reaching in to twist her arms behind her back and securing them with twine. Gilly struggled into a sitting position, but he was already in the driving seat, and there was a click as he operated some kind of electronic door switches. She said, 'I don't understand what this is about—'

'Don't you? You really shouldn't have let Julius do that to you tonight, Gilly,' said the Shadow, and Gilly thought: So he *was* there! He was watching us!

But she managed to say, 'Why shouldn't I? What's it got to do with you?'

'You were Mab,' said the Shadow. 'And Mab understood about being in thrall to the beings of the old legends. You were to be the one who would give the *leanan-sidhe* a first-born,' he said. 'We were going to make the child, Gilly, you and I, out there at the foot of the ancient Stone. And it would have been pledged to the *leanan-sidhe*, who haunt those cliffs and scour the land for human children, and they would have taken it – I *know* they would have taken it, because I would have forced them—' He broke off suddenly, his breathing harsh and ragged. 'They stole my birthright, those creatures,' he said. 'And because of it I became a thing of darkness.' He glanced at her in the driving mirror, and she caught sight of the masked face, the eyes shining coldly through it. 'You know about the darkness, don't you, Gilly?' he said, softly. 'Well, we're going to meet it tonight. You're going to be given up to it.'

And then, almost to himself, 'And it may be sufficient for them to return my humanity.'

Chapter Twenty-Eight

The darkness that had closed down when Roscius's son dragged the well cover into place was more complete than anything Flynn had ever imagined possible. It was a thick solid blackness, and there was not even the knowledge that in a few minutes his eyes would adjust to night-vision. To have night-vision it was necessary to have a small amount of light ingress, and in here there was none.

He had climbed up to the mouth of the well at once, of course, feeling for the iron staves driven into the sides, stretching a hand cautiously up to feel for the underside of the cover. His searching hand found the other end of the rope that was tied round his waist. Roscius had secured it to the remains of what felt like an ancient hinge on the underside of the well lid. It felt rusty and so frail that Flynn realised with cold horror that it could give way under his suspended weight at any second. He tried not to think about this for the moment.

He had known, even before he tried to push the cover off, that it would be hopeless, of course; he had heard, with dreadful clarity, the sound of some kind of locking mechanism being used, but he still made the attempt, first managing to loop the rope around the top rung of the iron ladder which would at least reduce the slack if he fell, and which would go some way to saving him if the rusting lid-hinge gave way. He managed to knot it reasonably firmly, holding on to the rung with his left hand and using his right hand and his teeth to make the knot. So far so good. Now for the lid.

He steadied himself with his left hand this time, and placed his right hand, palm uppermost, against the underside of the lid. It felt horrid against his skin – as if lying across the ancient well for centuries had caused it to soak up the black, fetid air.

335

Flynn set his teeth and threw all his weight behind the effort. Twice he lost his hold on the iron rung and dropped sharply downwards, but each time the knots around the ladder held.

But after several attempts, which left him gasping for air and covered in sweat, he knew it was an impossible task. The well cover was immovable: Roscius had locked it in place and he intended Flynn to die down here. Flynn found the footholds again, and curled his hands around two of the staves, and forced himself to concentrate on his appalling situation, and on how he was going to escape.

There was a brief spark of hope when he remembered the people in Flaherty's Bar, and the priest – Father Mack – who had known of his destination, but this spark died almost at once. It was not very likely that they would send out the cavalry for a brief, chance-met acquaintance, and even if they did – even if the house was searched from cellar to attic and this part was scrutinised – all anyone would see would be a disused well shaft, the cover properly in place. There would be no reason to suspect that there was a prisoner hidden anywhere.

I'm clutching at straws, thought Flynn, his hands still curled around the iron staves. I'm absolutely alone. I'm more alone than I ever imagined possible. If I can't get out of here I'm going to die, and God knows how long it will take. I don't think I can hold on to these iron rungs for much longer. And when I can't, I suppose I'll just swing helplessly from the rope. It might take days to die. I'll probably become purblind from the dark and deaf from the silence, and I'll probably go mad with thirst— It's supposed to be a very nasty thing indeed to die from thirst. But that's what it's going to be, thought Flynn. Despair, the agony of the soul, closed about him, and he thought: I'm shut in an ancient well shaft, beneath a deserted old house by a mad creature with half a face, and no one knows I'm here.

He had no idea how long he stayed like that, half clinging to the iron rungs, half swinging from the rope. He thought he might partly have lost his grip on consciousness again for a time – he certainly thought he might have lost his grip on sanity at some point as well. But at length he began to think more clearly again. I can't go up, he thought. The lid's locked in place, and if Roscius unlocks it, I'll hear. And if I stay here

I'll go slowly mad. But supposing I could go down?

His heart at once began to beat faster with a mixture of panic and hope. What had Roscius said? There's a legend that the well winds down and down beneath the ocean, and eventually comes out in the underworld lair of the *leanan-sidhe*. I don't believe in the *leanan-sidhe*, thought Flynn, grimly. At least, we'll say I don't for the purpose of this exercise. But I can very easily believe in ancient wells that go down into sea tunnels. And anything's better than staying here, waiting to die.

Undoing the knot in the rope around his waist was more difficult than he'd expected. And I've got to remember that once this rope's undone, I'm wholly reliant on the iron rungs, thought Flynn, trying not to panic at the prospect.

He had expected to feel overwhelming fear when the knot finally loosened, but instead he felt a fresh surge of hope. It's another step towards escape, he thought. At least, I'll say it is. Here I go, then. Down into the depths. I'm not liking this at all, but I'm damned if I'll admit it!

The well got nastier the lower he went. It grew steadily colder as well, and the bad air seemed to get worse. It's like crawling down into the maw of a monster, thought Flynn. No, I won't think that, I'll think I'm going down to freedom. I wish I could see a bit better.

He thought it was not quite so silent now; once or twice there was the sound he had heard earlier, that was so uncannily like a massive, invisible creature breathing out. He caught the dripping of water more clearly as well and hoped very strenuously that this did not mean he was simply climbing down to a reservoir filled with stagnant water.

He had to feel for the iron rungs as he went, and to test each one before he dared put his weight on it. Several rungs were missing and he had to slither lower, his hands taking his entire weight; several times the rungs broke away from the brickwork as soon as he found them. When this happened Flynn froze at once, clinging to the remaining staves, listening to the sound of the fall. What will I do if I hear them splash into water? he thought in horror. But there was no splash, only a faint thud as the iron staves reached the bottom. Flynn tried not to think that it sounded a very long way down. He tried not to hear the curious breathing-out sounds as well, although he had the uneasy impression that they were louder. I'm getting closer to whatever's making the sounds, he thought. The air's getting worse, as well. He had no idea if this was because he was inside a sealed vault and using up oxygen, or if it was from some other reason entirely. He wished he had not lit on the expression 'sealed vault' and he wished he had not thought about using up oxygen.

His leg muscles were coping fairly well with the descent, but his arms and shoulders were aching abominably. He was just wondering how much longer he could go on, when, without any warning at all, the iron rungs stopped. Flynn, holding on by his hands, explored the wall immediately below him, using his feet. Nothing. Then either there was such a short drop to the bottom that the rungs were no longer necessary, or—

Or a whole series of rungs had rusted and fallen out of their own accord.

I'll have to jump and trust to luck, thought Flynn, appalled. There's nothing else for it. He took several deep breaths, which tasted dreadful and made his head swim all over again, and he was astonished to find himself sending up a prayer. But, Mother of God, if I land safely on terra firma, I'll return to the bosom of the Church immediately! I'll go to Mass every Sunday, and I'll even—

It was now or never. He let go of the rungs, and for the space of six heartbeats slithered painfully against the brick wall. And then incredibly and wonderfully he was on firm hard ground, slightly jarred by the short fall, but in one piece. I've done it! thought Flynn, hardly believing it. I've reached the bottom and I'm more or less unhurt, and I've even done it before I could swear away any more of my immortal soul. This unexpected spurt of irony cheered him up more than he would have believed possible. I mustn't get carried away, he thought. I'm a bit nearer to freedom than I was an hour ago, but I daren't get carried away.

The shirt he had donned a hundred years ago that morning was sticking to his shoulder-blades with sweat, but his head felt noticeably clearer. Because there was an ingress of air from somewhere? He had lost all sense of time, but he thought it could not be more than a couple of hours since Roscius's son had imprisoned him. I'll beat you yet, you evil sod! he thought.

But a sneaky little voice whispered that this might be as far as he was going to get, because if there really was a way out of here, Roscius would surely have known of it. Flynn could almost imagine that tortuous mind enjoying contriving a prison that allowed for escape, and then lying in wait for the hapless prisoner who believed himself free.

It was then that he realised that not only were the sounds of dripping water and strange exhalations much nearer, for the first time he could make out, very faintly, the outlines of the bricks. Light was coming in from somewhere.

The light was not good, but it was a million times better than the solid blackness had been. It was a dull, smeary light, rather horridly reminiscent of poison oozing from a wound, and it seemed to be coming from Flynn's left. He waited for his vision to adjust, trying to take stock of his surroundings before moving again. Above him was the well shaft, and at his feet was what seemed to be a solid mass of rock. Ahead of him, in the direction of the sluggish light, he could just make out the shadowy outline of a tunnel.

Flynn forced himself to stay calm. It was possible that the tunnel led absolutely nowhere and it was still possible that Roscius was tricking him, but it was a chance that had to be taken. He set off warily.

The tunnel was narrow and the floor was perilously uneven, but it was possible to walk upright and there was sufficient light to guide his way. It wound steeply downwards, and as Flynn went deeper he had the sensation that he was crossing a dark threshold and descending to a forbidden and very sinister realm. And I don't believe I'm entirely alone here, either, he thought. Is Roscius following me? Or waiting for me somewhere up ahead? I wouldn't put it past him. With every step he expected the shadows to part and to see the dreadful, incomplete face appear, but nothing moved and the only sound was the strange breathing, growing perceptibly louder.

The tunnel twisted and turned sharply so that for most of the time it was impossible to see more than a few yards ahead.

Flynn kept imagining creatures gathering just beyond each turn of the tunnel, their heads bobbing together, whispering and plotting ... *Clucking and gobbling, and mopping and mowing ... ?* Don't be absurd! he said to himself angrily.

But the feeling that he was entering some diabolic and devil-haunted nether-world persisted. There was something goblin-like about this place, there was the impression of small, bony bodies dodging out of his line of vision, and of peering, inward-slanting red eyes. Was he really going into the lair of the *leanan-sidhe* after all? And supposing they were not the sensuous, sensual creatures that Fael Miller had created and that Flynn had brought to life, but something very different indeed? But that's ridiculous! he thought. That's absurd.

He stood still for a moment, thinking he could hear other sounds now: dry little rustlings that might have been fleshless fingers rubbing gleefully together, or whisking, boneless tails poking out beneath trailing velvet gowns ... There was the smell and the feel and the imprint of bloodied legends waking, and of centuries-old elvish courts being convened, almost as if—

Almost as if the pitiful, mad creature who lived in the clifftop house had called to something immeasurably ancient and incalculably evil. And as if that something, once summoned, had stayed.

Flynn shook off the clustering thoughts, and went on again. The light was perceptibly stronger and the breathing-out sounds were all around him, but he had gone a fair way through the tunnel before it suddenly dawned on him what the sounds were.

It's the ocean! he thought, half relieved, half fearful of a different danger altogether. The well tunnel goes down beneath the ocean – Roscius said it did – and that's what I'm hearing. I'm probably under the ocean now, or at least I'm very near to it. I don't know that I much like the idea of being several fathoms beneath the Atlantic, he thought, sending an uneasy glance at the tunnel roof and seeing that it gleamed faintly in the uncertain light. I hope that's just phosphorescence, thought Flynn. I hope it isn't the ocean oozing through.

And now he could see that the dull light was in fact water-light that rippled and played on the rock walls. There were carvings in the rock as well: pictures of strange sea-beasts with horned heads or round, seal-like heads and sinuous bodies, with tiny wizened-faced creatures crouching at their feet. The *leanan-sidhe* with their servants? Or the *leanan-sidhe* themselves, in their stages of metamorphosis into humanish shape?

I'm not at all sure I'm really seeing this, thought Flynn, staring in repulsion at the carvings. And where did I get the word 'humanish' from? It's got a distinctly unpleasant sound to it, that word. I'm not at all sure I didn't die inside that revolting well, or that I haven't toppled over into real madness. Because I think I'm crossing over into *Cauldron*'s world, and although it isn't quite the world I designed in London, there're some alarming similarities.

I'm very likely approaching my own particular hell or at the very least purgatory, he thought. I'm very likely going towards hell's fire-drenched caverns, and I'll be torn to pieces by the red-eyed demons who hold gobbling malevolent court there . . . Or at best, I'll find that I'm flung into the iron-hued dungeons where pieces of time are frozen inside the molten furnaces . . .

And those are quite interesting images, he thought with sudden wry humour. If I ever get out of here, I'll use them for a stage-set some time.

Fael had been so immersed in the legend of the Self-Bored Stone, and in the strange bargains that had been struck at its base, that she had not noticed the hours slipping away. She had left the lights burning through the day because of the winter darkness that enclosed Maise, and day had slid down to twilight and then to full night almost without her noticing.

Once, somewhere in the middle of the evening, she thought there was the sound of something massive and heavy being slammed below her in the house – a door? – and she lifted her head to listen. But there were no more sounds, and Fael plunged back into the ancient myth-worlds which were peopled with heroes and giants and princesses, and laced with heady, heavy enchantments. There were upwards of half a dozen plots here, and any of them would make a terrific follow-up to *Cauldron*. And this time I'm spinning the magic all by myself, thought Fael, in sudden delight.

She was vaguely aware of the old house settling into silence all about her, but she was absorbed in the unravelling strands of myth and in any case she had started to know the house's sounds now; she was in fact beginning to find the little night creakings and rustlings familiar and rather friendly.

It was only when she heard the turret door being unlocked, and turned to see her captor in the doorway, that she realised it was almost midnight. He had discarded the wide-brimmed hat he so often wore, and droplets of moisture clung to his dark hair. His eyes behind the mask shone, and there was a crackle of energy from him, as if his whole body was alive with electricity. Fael felt a hammer of panic begin to beat against her mind. Something's happening. Something's changed.

He crossed the room and caught her wrists in one of his hands, and she felt the remembered magnetism again and was suddenly and angrily aware that it would not take much, it would barely take the crooking of a finger to lure her to bed. If he beckons, I'll go, thought Fael, staring up at him in mingled horror and stirring fascination. If he really set the magic spinning again, I believe I would. Does he know it, I wonder? But it isn't bed he's got in mind tonight: it's something far darker and far more sinister. Oh God, is this the reckoning – the real reckoning?

He lifted her in his arms then, and Fael at once struggled and said, 'What are you doing? Put me down, damn you! What is all this?'

'It's another phase of your captivity, Fael,' he said, carrying her down the steps. 'Probably it's the last phase.'

'Well, whatever it is, you needn't think you'll have it all your own way!' said Fael, and was pleased to hear quite a respectable note of defiance in her tone. 'Don't think I won't fight you, because I will!' she added, for good measure, and as he carried her down the narrow turret stair she twisted around in his arms as much as possible, and glared at the covered face. 'Listen, if you don't tell me where we're going and what you're going to do, I'll claw your eyes out. I really will, you know.'

'Without eyes I can still shoot you, my dear.'

There was a very nasty echo of *all the better to murder you, my dear*, about his tone. Fael heard it and flinched.

342

'You've still got the gun,' she said, after a moment.

'I have. And it's interesting to contemplate where a bullet could go, isn't it?' He paused on the curve of the stair, the narrow eyes studying her. Fael felt a breath of cold air, and saw the curtains on the half-landing stir slightly. She repressed a shiver. 'Straight into the spine, perhaps,' he said. 'A bullet in the top of the spine might be the best place – below the brain but above all the nerve centres. Yes, I believe I could be fairly accurate about that. And you'd suffer irreversible paralysis this time, Fael. But there'd be complete mental awareness. You'd be dependent on other people for absolutely everything. How would that feel? You came close to it after the car crash, didn't you, but the damage was repairable. How would you cope if it wasn't?'

He paused, and then said, very coldly and very deliberately, 'And you'd be alone this time, Fael. Tod's dead, you know. Or didn't you know?'

Fael said, 'Oh get on with whatever you're going to do and stop being so bloody melodramatic!' But she thought: Yes, of course Tod's dead, and of course I guessed it. Only I can't think about that now – because I daren't think of anything other than what's happening now.

They reached the ground floor and *Scathach* threw open the door and stepped out into the night. The wind snatched at Fael's hair and took her breath away.

He moved with the swift, cold efficiency she remembered, depositing her in the back of the car, and tying her wrists behind her back. Fael said, 'You don't use much variation, do you? We've done all this once already,' and as he drove off, struggled fruitlessly to loosen the ropes.

She thought they drove only a very short distance – perhaps a quarter of a mile – before stopping, but it was very dark and the wind was driving little flurries of icy rain against the car's windows. Fael shivered and glanced at the dashboard clock. Just coming up to midnight.

He parked on a narrow grass verge on the roadside and lifted her out. The rain had stopped, but the wind was driving the clouds across the night sky and there was a full moon, a pale globe that rode high in the sky, and cast a cold radiance that

Fael found unspeakably sinister. She looked about her, trying to identify landmarks, trying to see if there were any nearby houses with occupants who might hear or see what was happening, or hear if she yelled for help. Nothing. He picks his spots, she thought wryly.

It was not until *Scathach* carried her down a roughish track that wound down from the road and she saw the black outline of the Self-Bored Stone that she understood where they were. He knows this path very well, thought Fael, and he's approaching the stone with familiarity. But behind the familiarity was something else. Respect? Something even stronger? Submission? It was absurd to think of the word in connection with him, but Fael did think it.

And there's something else out here with us, she thought suddenly, feeling the fear rev up again. It's something I can't quite see but it's something that shrieks inside the wind and that screeches with laughter. He was holding her firmly, but she managed to twist her head to look back. The path was sparsely covered with scrubby patches of grass, and the wind was whipping miniature dust-storms across it. Ridiculous to think that dozens of little footprints were appearing on the wind-tossed ground, as if invisible creatures danced along in *Scathach*'s wake. Absurd in the extreme to imagine figures half-forming in the darkness and to think they were forming a circle around *Scathach*. The *leanan-sidhe* with their chill, seductive music . . . ? I'm hearing things and I'm definitely seeing things, thought Fael.

But as they approached the huge silhouette of the stone, she thought the shapes came a little more clearly into focus. As if they're shedding their outer skins, thought Fael, in sudden panic. I daresay I'm going mad, but I can hear their music! cried her mind. And I *can* see them, I truly can! They're linking hands and prancing in a wild devils' dance, and although they wear gloves of human skin, under it their fingers are fleshless and horny-nailed . . . *All the better to dig out your heart, my lady, and all the better to steal your new-born babe, my lady* . . .

Is that why he's brought me here? thought Fael. Because of the night we spent together, because there might be a child? But it's the most outside chance in the world – he must know that. And it won't be a first-born – he knows that as well.

Even so, a different, more primeval fear started to uncoil, and for the first time she thought of the tiny speck, that might or might not exist inside her, as a living thing: a child with dark eyes and hair and with feelings and emotions – perhaps with a slightly other-world perception and an intuitive ability to spin marvellous music and twist it around people's emotions . . . *His* son. But I don't want it! cried Fael silently. I don't want to feel like this! Oh God, I'm not believing any of this at all! I must be in a nightmare or somebody's drug-induced hallucination!

But I can see shapes forming in the darkness, and I can make out huge, ragged wings that they sometimes fold around them like cloaks, but that sometimes beat frighteningly on the night when they're hunting the humans . . . Their faces are hidden, but if they weren't they'd be gnarled and sly: cats' faces and rats' faces with evil wizened features— The *leanan-sidhe*, the water-demons who can bestow genius but who steal human children. And it's a fearsome, grisly process watching them form – he told me that and I didn't believe him, but tonight I do.

Scathach stopped in the lee of the stone, and only then did Fael see that lying at its foot, gagged and bound, was a girl with dishevelled red hair and frightened eyes and vaguely familiar features.

Mab. Mab from *Cauldron* who was caught in thrall by the soulless *sidh* prince and who fought against yielding to him lest she become his, body and soul and blood and bone.

back I might be far enough away to hide.

But she had only covered a few feet when car headlights sliced through the darkness and swung off the road. The Shadow returning? With a feeling of despair she recognised the car. Damn and bloody blast. There was the sound of the doors opening and closing, and then he was coming back down the cliff path. Gilly could see that he was still wearing the black silk mask, but he was hatless and for the first time she saw that he had thick, glossy dark hair. In his arms he carried a girl with wide-apart eyes and short hair so pale it looked silver when the moon came out. He set her down, near to Gilly but not so near that either of them could reach the other. Fael Miller, thought Gilly, incredulously. And he's bringing her down here. Is this some kind of sacrifice, then? He's tied her hands as well, thought Gilly. I don't think either of us can get free. If I could cut through these wretched ropes I might make a run for it. And leave Fael? No, of course not. But I could make a fight for it at least. She began to surreptitiously feel around on the ground under her hands for a sharp stone that might saw through the rope.

With his eerie way of echoing a thought, the Shadow said, 'You are both going to be a libation to the creatures of the *leanan-sidhe*. Fael has cheated me, and so have you,' he looked down at Gilly, 'and so you will both die tonight.'

Fael looked across at Gilly. 'I don't know how well you know him, but he's quite mad,' she said, and Gilly looked at her gratefully, because however helpless they both might be, it was heartening to have Fael with her.

'He thinks,' went on Fael, still in the same half-dispassionate, half-contemptuous tone, 'that he's entered into some kind of bond with creatures who don't exist. He thinks that if he gives them a first-born child they'll – make him whole,' she said. 'I failed him, and so, it appears, did you.'

Christian said, 'The *leanan-sidhe* do exist. They are my people—' He was standing near to the edge of the cliff, and he turned to look out to the black wastes of the Atlantic; his hands were outstretched, the palms uppermost, in the age-old gesture that was both supplication and pledge.

'They exist, and they enjoy full-grown humans just as much

as they enjoy new-born babies,' said Christian, and both girls heard, with helpless terror, the slurred madness in his voice. Fael thought: He really has crossed the line now, and I can't see anything that either of us can do to stop him. But we've got to think of *something*! He's bound Mab hand and foot and he's gagged her – no, her name isn't Mab but she's Mab to me. She's Mab tonight, because she's half-caught in his spell already. He's tied my hands as well, but not my feet. He doesn't need to tie them though, she thought, bitterly. I could walk a little way; I could probably get to the base of that malevolent stone without too much difficulty. But by the time I'd managed it he'd be onto me.

'You shouldn't have cheated me of that pawn, Fael,' said Christian, turning back. 'You should have given me a first-born child – it was what I wanted you for.'

What I wanted you for . . . Fael beat down a sudden wrench of pain, and said, sharply, 'What about *Cauldron*? Have you forgotten that? You wanted me for *Cauldron* as well.'

'*Cauldron* was yours,' he said, at once. 'I wanted you for the child; you wanted me for *Cauldron*. *Quid pro quo.*'

For a moment neither of them spoke, and then, 'My God,' said Fael, softly. 'Is that really all it was?'

'That's all it was, Fael. I made a bargain with the *leanan-sidhe* and tonight I'm making assurance doubly sure.'

Fael stared at him, because with the almost unconscious quotation – and it's *Macbeth* and how appropriate – the final piece of the jigsaw that she had been seeking fell into place. I know who you are, she thought. Oh God, I really do know, and I see now what I should have seen before. The pieces whirled around in her mind, and then fell neatly into place, each one in its appointed slot to make up the picture.

The secret house in Ireland . . . The familiarity with James Roscius's methods . . . The haunting sense of having met *Scathach* before in another place or another time or another world . . .

And now the remembered quotation from *Macbeth*, the quotation that the professor himself had so often used. 'Let's make assurance doubly sure, Fael,' he used to say. 'Let's make doubly sure you pass the next music exam. Let's make assurance doubly sure that we're doing justice to Mozart, to Scott Joplin, to Aaron Copland . . .'

She heard her voice saying, 'I know who you are.'

There was a moment when everything – wind, storm, the lashing waves of the ocean – seemed to pause and to freeze into absolute silence. Hell and the devil, thought Fael, now I've done it.

After several lifetimes, he said, 'Do you indeed?'

'You're James Roscius's son,' said Fael. 'It's the only answer that fits all the facts.' She paused, and then said, 'That's who you are, isn't it?'

Again the silence. Then he said, very softly, 'It is. And isn't it a pity you realised it, Fael.'

'He had a son,' said Fael, still staring at him. 'I never knew that. I thought I knew him quite well, but there were parts of his life that he kept closed from the world. We all respected it, even though we speculated a bit. I don't think anyone knew he had a son.'

'No one knew. He made sure of it. He kept me,' said Christian, savagely, 'hidden from the world.' He studied her, the moonlight shining on the mask, so that his eyes glittered coldly. 'And now, of course, you really will have to die,' he said. 'You do see that, don't you? And it'll have to be Rossani's way. Now that you know who I am you'll have to die like all the others died – Leila and Mia Makepiece and your father—'

Because there's a primitive belief that safety is inter-dependent with identity, my dear . . . Because the dwarf's power will be broken if once his name is discovered, my dear . . .

'It's unavoidable, Fael,' said Christian, staring at her but not making any move yet. Gilly, listening closely, still trying to see a chance of escape for them both, was unable to tell if it was hatred that held him in its grip, or passion. Does he hate her violently or does he love her just as violently? Or is it both? Does he hate her because he loves her? This is all too deep for me, thought Gilly, uncomfortably. The night's all filled up with complex emotions and too-fierce feelings – it's seething and boiling with them – and I don't understand them. I don't want to understand them. I wish I was a thousand miles away, thought Gilly, still frantically feeling around for a sharp stone that might make some impression on her bonds.

'I'll give you to the *leanan-sidhe*,' said Christian, still speaking in the same soft tone. He glanced towards the black, jagged cliffs where spumy spray rose up from the foot. 'I'm sorry about it, but it will have to be done.' He came towards her, and Gilly caught a snatch of Rossani's music, hummed very faintly. Her skin began to crawl with terror.

Rossani's a-prowl and he's looking for fools;
He'll grind down your bones and he'll shred up your soul.

Grind down your bones, thought Gilly, in horror. He's sticking to the grisly song. Or is it Rossani who's doing that? But he *is* Rossani. And that's what's going to happen on those rocks below the cliff. We'll be ground to pulp.

Fael was staring at the masked figure in fury, and when she spoke, Gilly thought: Oh good for you, Fael! You're still fighting him!

'You're an evil, twisted bastard!' shouted Fael, and the wind snatched her words and tore them into harsh ragged splinters.

'I'm no bastard, Fael,' said the Shadow, and incredibly there was faint amusement in his tone.

'Well, you won't do it,' said Fael, defiantly. 'I don't believe you'll really do it.'

'That's because you keep losing sight of one important fact, my dear.' He reached up to his face, his movements slow and deliberate, and peeled off the face mask, flinging it away from him. 'You keep forgetting that I'm the villain,' said Christian, and bent to pick her up again.

The light in the sea tunnel seemed to have grown as strong as it was going to grow. Flynn thought this might be because he was nearing its source, and he was torn between burgeoning hope that the tunnel was about to open out into freedom, and dread that he was about to come smack up against a dead-end. He had lost all sense of time and his wristwatch appeared to have stopped. He supposed this had happened when Roscius over-powered him on the hillside and cursed all over again.

But looked at logically it did not matter if he had been

imprisoned for half an hour or a couple of days. On balance he thought he had been in the underground room and the well shaft for no longer than three or perhaps four hours, and he thought he had been in the sea tunnel for about twenty minutes. He had left Flaherty's Bar just after eight p.m. so that if his estimation was right, it was coming up to midnight. None of which made any difference to his situation if a dead-end was ahead.

He had arrived at this conclusion when, without the least warning, he was confronted with what appeared to be a solid wall of rock. Well, so I was right, thought Flynn, staring at it in bitter anger. It's the dead-end I was fearing, may the devil rot its black Protestant soul!

He stepped back and studied it. But I can still hear the sea, he thought, suddenly. In fact I can hear it more strongly than ever. That might be because it's on the other side of that rock, of course. But the light's still trickling in – it's a bit fuzzy, but it's coming in from somewhere. And then he saw that the rock wall was in fact a jutting spur, and that behind it was a narrow opening.

There was probably nothing more useful than a water-filled cavern on the other side of the rock, and by this time it seemed to Flynn perfectly possible that he was trapped down here for ever, and doomed to wander the tunnels for the rest of his life. I'll probably end up as a leading character in the folklore of this bloody place, he thought, and people in Flaherty's Bar will whisper fearfully about me, and tell tourists how, on moonless nights when the wind's in the right quarter, they can hear me moaning beneath the sea-bed, trying to find the way back up to the world again ... Or maybe I died back there in the well shaft, and this is purgatory, and never mind that it's nothing like the priests told, because I'll be stuck here until I've expiated every sin I've ever committed. Well, if that's the case, I'm due to be down here for a devil of a long time!

Still, here I go, he thought. Will I get through or not? God, it's a tight squeeze. Probably designed specifically for penitents in the last stages of starvation, or those inhuman things carved into the rock back there. Only I don't think I'll think about those carvings until I'm free. If I ever am free. No, it's all right, I'm going to get through. Praise every saint in heaven.

Beyond the rock spur the tunnel widened and there in front of him was an expanse of night sky, with, beneath it, the dark wastes of the ocean. And it might be the Atlantic, thought Flynn, in immense relief, and it might be cold and bleak and stormy, but at the moment it's as fine a sight as ever Homer's wine-dark sea was.

The stinging night wind whipped in and out of the cavern, and Flynn gasped as it struck his face like a blow, and then breathed in enormous lungfuls. The wind tasted cold and clean and salty, and nothing had ever felt as good anywhere in the entire world ever. His eyes prickled from the cold, and he was suddenly filled with huge affection for the entire world. I'm free, he thought, leaning against the side of the cave, tasting the salty wind on his cheeks. I'm out of that hell-spawned place, and I'm unhurt except for a few stretches of skin that Roscius's ropes tore away. What now, I wonder? And where exactly am I? The tunnel was behind him, and directly ahead was a broad shelf of rock. And beneath the shelf—

Flynn inched cautiously to the edge and looked down. At once his stomach lurched with panic and his mind tilted with vertigo, and he retreated to the shelter of the cave. The cave opened out on the side of the black cliffs he had seen when he drove to Maise earlier on. He was partway down the cliff-face, and immediately outside the cave was a sheer, hundred-foot drop. At the bottom the black, angry waters of the Atlantic pounded unceasingly against the craggy Moher rocks, throwing up great clouds of spray. Flynn was drenched within minutes, and he moved farther back into the cave and sat down to consider. To climb down the cliff was impossible and unthinkable: it was too far and he would almost certainly fall and be dashed to pieces on the rocks below. But how far was it to the clifftop? He went out again and looked upwards, waiting for the scudding clouds to race across the face of the moon and give him a little more light. Surely it was no more than twenty feet to the top? The thought of climbing up was terrifying, but Flynn could not see anything else to do. Down into the well and now up the side of the cliff, he thought. It's not a nightmare I've fallen into or a black fantasy, it's a bloody nursery rhyme!

In the event, it was easier than he had dared hope. The cliff was not as sheer as it looked; Flynn thought it might have been eroded or even worn back by the constant onslaught of the wind and the sea-storms. But it had not been worn smooth; there were footholds and handholds, and there were even clusters of toughly-rooted plants. Flynn climbed determinedly up, not looking down, trying not to think about the hundred-foot drop below him, certainly trying not to think what would happen if he missed his footing.

The wind tore at his hair as he climbed, and several times he thought he caught the sounds of strange cries inside the wind, and of keening creatures who beat enormous wings on the night and mocked him.

You'll never escape . . . You'll never get free . . .

Oh, won't I! thought Flynn, grimly. I'll get to the top of this damned cliff, and I'll go after that accursed Roscius. The top of the cliff was within arms' reach now, and he grasped at the tiny stunted plants sprouting out of the rock, and hauled himself thankfully up. Made it! He lay on the cold ground, recovering his breath, staring up at the night sky, giving thanks to whatever powers might be appropriate that he had escaped.

After a moment he sat up and looked about him. He thought he was some way off the main highroad, partway down a half-slope that broke the terrain between the road and the start of the cliffs proper. He thought Maise was somewhere over to his right, but he had lost all sense of direction and it was too dark to be sure of anything. I don't want to go back to Maise, he thought, but if I could see the turning to the private road I'd at least know where I was. Wouldn't you have expected Roscius to provide a bit of light for wayfarers trying to reach his nightmare mansion, the miser? thought Flynn. Some villain, who won't light the path for his victims!

He stood up, brushed himself down, and set off up the grassy slope. Once on the main highroad, I might get to a phone, or even flag down a car. Oh sure, he said to himself sarcastically. And what cars do you suppose will be driving out here at midnight on a wild night like this? He spared an angry thought for his own car, presumably within a few minutes' walk, but the steering snapped and useless.

It was then that he saw headlights coming down the road

towards him. Someone was abroad in the storm after all. And I suspect, thought Flynn, narrowing his eyes, and keeping well back in case the headlights picked him out, I rather suspect that that car's coming from the direction of Maise.

The car was about two hundred yards away when it slowed down, and then turned off the road. The headlights swung around, illuminating the grass verge and the start of the cliff. Flynn made out the rearing, monolithic stone he had noticed earlier on, and then the headlights were switched off.

Roscius, thought Flynn. Or is it? Mightn't it be a couple out for a bit of illicit screwing on the back seat? No, it's Roscius, I'm sure of it. No one else would be abroad in this storm, and no matter how sexed-up you were, you'd never park on the edge of a cliff.

Keeping to the shadows, he set off towards the car.

No one in Flaherty's Bar had taken Flynn Deverill's remark about sending in the cavalry after forty-eight hours precisely seriously; you could tell he had been making a joke, and in any case, wasn't it precisely the kind of thing they would have said themselves, setting off for such a sinister old place?

No one was really worried when Flynn did not return, although Flaherty's daughter was disappointed, the shameless creature. She said crossly it was nothing to do with being shameless; it was only the waste of work. Hadn't there been the large front bedroom all made ready, and lavender-scented sheets on the bed, never mind a fire lit in the grate and fresh towels and hot water put out.

But what with all the to-ing and fro-ing of the evening, and what with a grand, spirited argument starting up in the public bar and everyone joining in and one or two tempers getting frayed, nobody thought any more about Flynn for some time. It was only when Flaherty was calling for them to get off to their homes – Did they think he wanted to fall foul of the gardai? – and when he and his daughter were surveying the pile of dirty glasses and saying wasn't it beyond belief how much washing up piled up of a night, that they realised Flynn had not come back. Seamus and Sinead O'Sullivan had stayed to give a bit of a hand with the clearing up, which they often did, and Liam had stayed as well on account of being enamoured of Flaherty's daughter, which was an arrangement that would suit all parties, and was therefore being enthusiastically encouraged. Father Mack was still there as well, half dozing by the fire, which could be forgiven on account of him having said early Mass in two parishes that morning.

And so what with one thing and what with another, it was nearly midnight when Flaherty finally finished, and then Father Mack woke up and they all had a tot of whiskey to keep out the cold for the homeward walk. Seamus was just saying wasn't it a wonderful thing that the power had held up, what with the storm and all, and the O'Sullivans were getting ready to go, when the lights flickered and went out.

They were all used to power cuts – although it was admittedly startling to get one so bang on cue as you might put it – but it was only now, in the flurry of finding candles and hurricane lamps, and looking out a good torch to lend the O'Sullivans for the walk home, that Flaherty's daughter tripped over one of Flynn's suitcases and they realised he had not returned from Maise.

And it was now midnight.

They sat round the fire talking it over, and the lamps burned low and the fire burned low as well, and the storm lashed against the windows. Liam, who was apt to be fanciful, said wasn't this the way their ancestors used to sit: huddled round a peat fire by lamplight, fearful of a number of enemies – the press-gangs or the English, or the demons out at the house that they had known as *mera*. And now it was himself up at Maise they were discussing, said Liam, and they were all just as fearful.

Flaherty went round with the whiskey again, and Father Mack said hadn't they in common humanity to make sure Mr Deverill was all right, and Seamus said that was all very well only it was Maise they were discussing. Liam said for Christ's sake hadn't they better do something instead of sitting here on their bottoms, and Father Mack reproved him for blaspheming.

Flaherty's daughter held by the opinion that Mr Deverill had intended to return, and then Flaherty remembered the sum of money Flynn had left by way of deposit for the room, which had been generous and wholly unnecessary. You did not do things like that and then vanish. And if the vanishing was intended, you did not do it without taking your luggage.

Flaherty's daughter and Sinead were all for the men going off up to Maise there and then, which, as the men pointed out, was all very well for them: they would be safe and snug here while the rest of them were entering the lion's den.

'Or the demons' lair,' put in Liam, and was told to hush.

'There're no demons inside Maise,' said Flaherty's daughter. 'I've been up there a dozen times, and never spied sight nor sound nor whisker of a demon, or anything else. Sinead's been there with me.'

'We'll go along by ourselves if you're scared,' said Sinead. 'We'll take the four-wheel drive – Seamus is in no fit state to drive anyway – and we'll just take a look to see if your man's there or if there's been an accident on the road along the way. Has anyone thought of that?'

Nobody had thought of that until now, but Sinead's words decided the matter, because none of the men was going to be bested by a woman, and that woman Sinead O'Sullivan. After more arguing, it was decided that they would take Liam's truck, with Liam driving, and Seamus and Flaherty in the rear, leaving Father Mack to travel in the passenger seat with the dignity befitting a man of God.

'Pray for us,' said Father Mack as they set off.

'Did he mean that literally, do you suppose?' demanded Sinead.

'He did.'

Chapter Thirty

Look in the chronicles . . .

The Taming of the Shrew, William Shakespeare

Fael was as unable to close her mind against the appalling face, as she was unable to shut out the mad agony that streamed from Christian's mind into hers.

As he lifted her in his arms, the wild night and the shrieking wind that held the voices of strange inhuman beings blurred and began to spin in a dizzying maelstrom. This is it, she thought. I'm going to die – we're both going to die – and it's going to happen *now*. I'm about to be thrown onto the rocks in a warped sacrifice to creatures out of an ancient legend, and if I'm not smashed to bloodied splinters on the rocks, I'll drown in the freezing Atlantic Ocean. And no one will ever know what happened to me, and I'll never know what it feels like to walk normally again!

As he carried her towards the cliff edge the clouds moved across the pale moon, as completely as if a black curtain had been pulled down. I'm going to die in this darkness, thought Fael, struggling in vain against the iron grip that held her. This is unbearable. But it won't happen – it can't. Something will stop him! He won't kill me, not when it comes to it – I don't believe I meant nothing to him. With the thought, came the memory of the strange, dark passion that had blazed between them, and to Fael's astonishment she heard her voice say softly, 'So I was just to give you a child, was I? Come on, admit that's not true.' She felt him pause, and as he did so, the moon began to slide out from behind the clouds. Light, pale and uncertain, began to sprinkle the Self-Bored Stone.

'Admit it,' said Fael, meeting the beautiful eyes in the appalling face unflinchingly.

'I admit to nothing.' But he did not move.

'Tell me your name. Your first name. You owe it to me. And where's the harm any longer?'

For a moment she thought he would refuse, and that he would simply walk to the cliff edge and throw her over. But then he said, 'Christian.'

'Christian. Yes, of course,' said Fael. 'The soldier of light, the force against the principalities of darkness. She called you that deliberately, didn't she? Your mother, I mean? As a safeguard.'

'*No.*' It came out violently, as if it was forced from him. Fael heard the blurred undisciplined note and knew that control was slipping from him. Is that good or bad? Will it make it easier to keep him talking or not? Oh God, what's the point of keeping him talking? I've probably got about three minutes before I die!

But she said, 'Christian – you aren't really going to kill me, are you?'

The moonlight was growing stronger, silvering the stone, and Fael shivered and remembered its legend: other worlds. You would see other worlds through the Stone's tip. And one legend tells that you could read the ancient chronicles listing the names of creatures bound by the *sidh*'s dark enchantments. . . . And if you name the dwarf you break his power . . .

Behind them, a soft voice said, 'Christian Roscius,' and Fael felt him whip around. Standing no more than three yards away was Flynn Deverill.

As Flynn moved forward, the moon came fully out from the bank of cloud and shone directly through the Self-Bored Stone onto Christian.

It was an extraordinary moment. The moonlight rayed through the Stone's opening and showered Christian as if it were a cold, pale cloak, showing every dreadful detail of his uncovered face.

He and Flynn held one another's eyes as if they had been clamped together, and to Fael, still in Christian's arms, and to Gilly, still trying to escape her rope-bonds, it seemed as if neither man would ever speak. They're fighting, thought Fael, suddenly. They're each trying to impose their will on the other. And then with a sense of unreality, she heard Christian say, on a note of loathing: 'Flynn Deverill,' and thought: He's spoken first. And by doing that he's yielded something, he's somehow given way mentally to Flynn. Do they both know that? Yes, of course they do.

Flynn had felt Christian's sudden submission, and he had felt the other man's smouldering hatred as if it was an open furnace. But almost all his concentration was on reaching him and freeing Fael, and he was aware now that Christian was holding Fael to him as if he could not bear to let her go. He either hates her or loves her, thought Flynn. But whichever it is, it's too strong for him, it's burning him up. She's reached something in him that nobody else ever has: something that he's never let anyone else get close to, and he doesn't know how to deal with it. Oh Christ, the poor sod, thought Flynn, torn between helpless compassion and raging fury.

But if I don't do something fast he'll simply walk to the edge of the cliff and throw her over, and then come back for Gilly, he thought. And I can't let Fael die – I can't let either of them die! On the crest of this thought, he shouted, 'Come over here and fight me, Christian! Let Fael go and we'll fight it out between us!'

'The final encounter?' said Christian, mockingly, but Flynn heard the uncertain note in his voice. It's now or never, he thought. If ever I'm to go for him, I'll have to do it now. The cliff edge is nearer than I like, but it can't be helped. He tensed his muscles, and then three things happened all at the same time.

Flynn sprang forward, knocking Fael out of Christian's arms, and sending Christian falling towards the cliff edge.

Car headlights sliced through the darkness, mingling with the cold, eerie moonlight.

And there was the sudden sound of huge wings beating triumphantly on the air, and there was the vivid unmistakable impression of darting elongated bodies, swooping out of the sky.

Christian had been half-stunned by the fall, and he had lain for a moment on the ground, trying to regain his senses. He knew he was suddenly and dreadfully vulnerable. Flynn Deverill, he thought. And the two girls – he's freeing them, I can see him. And someone else is coming – there are car headlights on the road. I've got to get away, he thought frantically. I can't stay here – I can't be seen, not now they know who I am—

And then between one heartbeat and the next he caught the silvery ruffle of something on the air and his senses leapt and something deep within his body responded.

The *leanan-sidhe* . . . They're here, he thought with sudden surprised joy, and so deep and so sweet was his own response that he forgot all the other dangers, he forgot that he was lying on the cold ground and that the mask had been discarded. They're coming out of the heart of the storm, he thought, half kneeling and staring up at the night skies. They're coming from out of the eye of the tempest because that's where they live, in all the old stories it's where they live, and it's where they draw their power.

He stood up, no longer aware of Flynn and the girls, neither seeing nor hearing the screech of Liam O'Sullivan's battered truck as it parked untidily. He was moving in a trance towards the cliff edge, staring out across the wild, white-topped waves of the ocean. Had he heard it in truth, or had it been the wild imaginings of a disordered mind? Voices in the wind, nothing more, said the logical part of him, but—

But it's more than that, said the mystical side, the poetical side that Fael Miller had uncovered and that she had drawn dangerously close to.

And then from out of the scudding darkness and the driving wind and rain it came again and this time Christian knew there was no mistake. Silvery mocking voices, and threading in and out of the voices, music so beautiful and so seductive that you would sell your soul if it would go on and you would barter your sanity if only it would never stop . . . But have I any sanity left to barter with? he demanded. Oh God, what have I left that I can offer them?

They were coming closer, they were riding towards him through the darkness, breasting the wind and the storm. He was shivering in the biting cold, but he was no longer aware of it. He threw his whole mind outwards to them. Take my mortal soul! he cried silently, flinging out his arms. Take my mortal dreams! Only give me back my birthright! Return what you took and let me be whole! Let me be as other people!

There was a moment of the most profound silence he had ever known. It seemed as if the wind paused to draw breath, and as if the ocean froze in its ceaseless beating on the rocks. Christian felt something rise up exultantly from the darkness and come towards him.

And then they were there. Twisting, twining creatures, exactly as he had visualised them, exactly as the old stories described them. They had discarded their goblin carapace in which they prowled and hunted the world of the humans, and they were forming in all their dazzling, myth-drenched beauty. Slender, nearly-formless bodies, round sleek heads, worn smooth by centuries of living in the soft, silken under-water realms. Christian caught his breath, and behind him heard Fael gasp. But there was no room in his mind even for Fael now.

The *leanan-sidhe* were drawing him forward, their hands all around him, stroking, caressing. He could feel their tapering, fingerless hands closing around his head, stroking his poor shameful face, cradling it in their boneless arms. Their silvery laughter filled the night, and sweet perfumed breath blew gently into his face. Christian, straining to see them, cried, 'Will you give me back what you stole?'

Are you bartering with us, human ... ?

It was not quite like human speech, Christian was not even sure if he heard them in human words, but there was an understanding, an exchange. He drew in a deep shuddering breath. 'Yes! Yes, I am bartering with you!'

But for bartering, something must be given in return ...

'What?' cried Christian. 'Tell me what you want!'

What have you to give us, human ... ?

'The child! There may be a child!' He half-turned, trying to see Fael through the darkness. 'It will be yours!' he cried. 'I give it freely and willingly to you as soon as it is born!'

But it would not be a first-born ...

Not a first-born, because she shared that with someone else ... 'Must it be that?' he said, almost humbly.

Always . . .

'Then there is nothing I can give you.'

You can give us your soul, human . . . You can give us yourself . . . Do it now, human . . . Come with us now and be ours for all of time . . .

Body and soul and blood and bone . . .

And once you have let us love you, human, you will never want human women again, for we are more loving and more passionate than ever you can dream . . . But you must surrender willingly, you must not resist . . .

'All right!' cried Christian, flinging back his head and holding wide his arms in a gesture of obeisance.

At once the night was rent with shrieking, malicious laughter that ran eerily in and out of the wailing, driving wind. Blue-green iridescence split the darkness and Christian felt the mood of the night change; he felt it no longer wistful and elusive, but wild and as rapacious as a pack of wolverines. Cold silken arms wound around him, like thin spring water, soft and sensuous beyond bearing. He could see the *leanan-sidhe* more clearly now – voluptuous beings with beckoning arms, and bodies that burned against the darkness like blue-green flames in a peat fire on a frost-ridden night.

They swarmed over him, screeching their eldritch delight into the night, twining about his legs and sliding between his thighs. He knew now he was truly mad, because none of this could be happening, these creatures had no reality outside of legend, and their sensuous whisperings did not exist outside of the keening wind. But his body would surely not respond to a legend with such violent arousal, and if the stinging wind was still lashing the darkness, he could no longer feel it. There was only the cool, velvet caresses against his skin, and the silvery voices in his ear.

We will have it all, human, we will take blood and marrow and juices, and we shall empty your loins, over and over, and you will be ours for ever . . .

He moaned softly, feeling the smoky incomplete hands stroking him to helpless longing, his body toppling towards a scalding climax. Pain was clawing through his body and the tempestuous night was blurring and dissolving all about him.

As the beckoning arms drew him forward, the purest ecstasy he had ever known, white-hot in its intensity and so violent it was painful, began to explode through his body.

As he walked towards the cliff, he was smiling and holding out his arms. There was a final eldritch shriek that might have been the wind but that might have been something else, and the tormented creature who had believed himself a changeling, who had fought with the strange, dark persona awoken by Tod Miller's eerie, beautiful musical, and who had cast a mysterious, compelling mesmerism over almost every person who encountered him, walked deliberately over the cliff edge, to the raging seas beneath.

There was a final cry that might have been triumphant voices, or that might have been an agonised death scream, or that might only have been the wind.

The moon slid behind a bank of cloud and darkness fell about the Self-Bored Stone.

Chapter Thirty-One

The power was still off in Flaherty's Bar, but Flaherty had banked up the fire with thick slabs of peat, and Seamus O'Sullivan had set the oil lamps around the long, low-ceilinged room. Sinead and Flaherty's daughter had brewed a huge pot of coffee over the kitchen range. Gilly had tried to help but was told to sit down and recover after her ordeal. Did she think they all wanted her passing out on them?

Seated in the deep inglenook that smelled pleasantly of peat and woodsmoke, Gilly and Fael had finally managed to stop shivering. Thick warm rugs had been looked out and wrapped around them and Liam O'Sullivan had gone back to the farmhouse and routed out a couple of thick sweaters for Flynn.

'I'm warming up a bit, are you?' said Fael, leaning back, her hands cupped gratefully around the strong fragrant coffee which was liberally laced with whiskey.

'Yes, but I think it'll take days to feel properly warm again.'

'Weeks,' said Fael. She thought it was remarkable how well she and Gilly seemed to know one another, and how well they both seemed to know Flynn and the people in this bar. Or was that only the slightly unreal closeness that came from having traversed a danger together? I'm free, she thought. The spell's wound up and the rough magic's abjured ... Buried fathoms deeper than ever did plummet sound ... And he's dead. He's lying out there at the foot of the cliff and if he isn't drowned, he's certainly battered to shreds on the rocks ... and he was my father's murderer, and I shouldn't be feeling like this about him ... She took a deep breath, and across the table met Flynn Deverill's eyes and was insensibly cheered.

Father Mack was saying something about it being a sad and solemn night for them all, and Fael thought: Yes, of course he'd

364

see it like that. She heard herself saying, 'Did you know who he was? I mean that he – that Christian – was the professor's son?' The name came out awkwardly as if her mind had flinched from it.

'Well, we didn't know for sure,' said Father Mack, who had the kind of calm, warm Irish voice that managed to be reassuring and gossipy at the same time.

'And of course, we never knew his name,' put in Sinead O'Sullivan.

'But there was always the possibility of some kind of connection. Living in the house and all.'

'Coming and going between here and Dublin and England,' put in the elder of the two O'Sullivan men. Seamus, thought Fael.

'We all knew the professor,' said Flaherty, who had fetched out a bottle of Irish whiskey from under the bar. Gilly noticed that Flynn Deverill had accepted a very large measure indeed.

'I'm keeping up the image,' said Flynn, meeting her eyes and grinning in a friendly fashion.

'So I see.'

'We knew the professor quite well,' said Seamus O'Sullivan. 'He was a great man altogether. We knew his lady as well. That's his wife, you understand.' This was to Flynn.

'Of course.'

'He found one or two consolations,' said Liam. 'Aside from his wife. You'd have to admit that he had one or two consolations, that professor.'

'So it seems,' said Flynn. 'Did you know my mother was one of the consolations?'

'Ah. Was she now? Yes, you have a look of the professor yourself,' said Father Mack, consideringly.

'Ah now, there's no shame in the odd consolation,' said Seamus to Flynn. 'Even though your man there would preach about sin and adultery and God knows what else.'

'I would,' said Father Mack, to whom this last remark was more or less directed. 'But I'd have to say it's not for any of us to judge.'

'I'm not judging,' said Flynn.

It was then that Seamus O'Sullivan looked across at Fael and said, 'You're very like your mother, aren't you?' and Sinead said comfortably, 'The spitting image, isn't she?'

Fael stared at them both. 'What did you say?'

'Your mother. You have her looks. The eyes and the hair.'

There was an abrupt silence.

Aine was here, thought Fael. She was at Maise and I never knew. But of course she was here – she had to have been, argued her mind. *He* knew her. *Scathach* – Christian. He said so at our first meeting . . . *Our first strange and fatal interview* . . . And where else would he have seen her, but at Maise?

'She came to stay at Maise a few times,' said Seamus, and, as if in answer to this, Fael saw Father Mack nodding in agreement and caught Flynn's sudden sharp attention. Her thoughts veered on to a totally different path. Dear God, she thought, what's going to be brought out now?

'It would be around twenty years ago,' said Flaherty. 'Wouldn't it? Or was it less than that?'

'It was certainly no more than twenty,' confirmed Sinead. 'Because I remember that she'd the little one at home who she wouldn't leave for long – that'd be you, of course, my dear,' she said to Fael, who stared at her and tried to take hold of several different whirling thoughts.

'She – didn't come to Maise before then?'

'If she did,' said Seamus, 'it was the best-kept secret of the century, and secrets aren't kept so very well out here, you know.' He laughed and everyone joined in.

'Did she come to – visit Professor Roscius?' Fael was grateful to Flynn for asking this.

'She did,' said Seamus. 'I remember it very well, because it had all to do with the writing of a grand musical show. It was called—'

'The *Dwarf Spinner*,' said Fael and Flynn together.

The fire was burning up brightly in the large front bedroom with the patchwork-quilted bed and the flames washed the white walls with a rosy glow. Ten minutes earlier Flaherty's daughter had beamingly brought up a huge copper ewer of hot water, and the firelight reflected fathoms down in the polished surface.

'Will you be all right in here?' said Flynn, seating himself on the small window seat and surveying the room.

'Yes, of course.' Fael looked round the room with pleasure. 'Thanks for bringing me. Stairs are still a bit of a problem. They're putting Gilly next door. She's still a bit shaken over what happened to Sir Julius.'

'Not surprising,' said Flynn.

'I've taken the room you were going to have,' said Fael. 'Haven't I?'

'Yes, but it's all right. I'll be downstairs,' said Flynn. 'Trying to get some well-deserved rest on Flaherty's under-stuffed sofa.'

'Drinking with Father Mack and Flaherty for what's left of the night,' observed Fael.

'That as well.'

He studied her, apparently waiting for her to speak, and after a moment, Fael said, 'So my father never wrote *Dwarf Spinner* after all.'

'That's not the surprise of the decade,' said Flynn. 'Does it matter to you?'

'I don't think it does,' said Fael, who had been thinking about this, along with the fact of Tod's death. 'It'd be nice if my mother could have had the recognition,' she said, 'and it'd be nice if she could have it now, but— No, I don't think it does matter, not really.' She eyed him thoughtfully, and then said, 'She wrote it with your father. I mean – James Roscius.'

'So it seems.'

'And after she died Tod let everyone think it was his own.'

Flynn said, 'Just as he let everyone think that *Cauldron* was his own.' They looked at one another. 'I am right, aren't I?' said Flynn, at last. 'You did write it, didn't you?'

'Some of it.'

'With Christian Roscius.'

'Yes. He wrote the music.'

'It's a wonderful story,' said Flynn, and fairness forced him to add, 'and it's wonderful music.'

'Oh yes.'

'And,' went on Flynn, thoughtfully, 'it's almost history repeating itself, isn't it? Your mother and the professor with the *Dwarf Spinner*. You and the professor's son with *Cauldron*.'

'Yes. I wonder why Roscius never denounced my father all those years ago.'

'It would have created publicity,' said Flynn at once. 'And publicity was the one thing he had to avoid.'

'Because of Christian,' said Fael.

'Yes. The professor was already starting to surround him with that extraordinary secrecy by then.'

He still hasn't managed to refer to Professor Roscius as his father, thought Fael. But she said, 'It all fits, doesn't it?' And then, after a moment, 'Did you know that you were Roscius's son?'

'Not until Christian told me just before he left me to die in that accursed well. But the pieces slot into place,' said Flynn. He leaned back against the curtained window. 'Did you care for him, Fael?'

'The professor?' But Fael knew he had not meant the professor.

'Christian.'

Fael took a moment to reply. Then she said, carefully, 'I don't think anyone could have known him and not been – affected by him. I don't think anyone who knew him could ever quite forget him, either.' Forget *Scathach*, she thought. Forget the mad, helpless agony that streamed from his mind into mine and the eerie shared passion . . . God, no, I'd never forget that.

I might not be allowed to forget, either, she thought suddenly. Because for all your inherited intuition, Flynn Deverill – and I'll acknowledge that to be formidable – there's something else, something you don't know, and something I don't even know myself yet . . .

The child. The child that he intended for the bargain. *The child you cheated me of, Fael . . . You shouldn't have cheated me*, he had said. The tiny speck of life that probably did not exist, but that, if it did exist, might be made up of fire and darkness and torment, but also of light and music . . . The changeling's son, born of the wild night tempests and flurrying rain, and the shrieking storms that hold the voices of inhuman creatures from Ireland's ancient past . . . Was that what Christian had seen in those crowded, confused minutes before he flung himself over the cliff? Had he finally seen the *leanan-*

sidhe? I didn't see them, thought Fael; at least – I don't think I did. I don't think Flynn or Gilly did either, although I can't be sure. But I think Christian saw them, and I think that was why he held out his arms in that last, pitiful, pleading gesture. I can't bear to think about it, not yet, probably not ever. But I don't want there to be a child, thought Fael. And then – or do I?

But none of this could be said now, and none of it might need to be said ever. Fael was grateful when Flynn's voice broke into her thoughts.

'Do you know,' he said, 'for a moment, I thought we were going to find the circle completed a bit—'

'A bit too neatly? Yes.'

'You thought your mother and – Professor Roscius might have been lovers?'

'Yes.'

'So did I.'

They looked at one another. 'We were nearly half brother and sister,' said Fael.

'We were.' His eyes began to dance, and Fael thought: He's enjoying this. Whether it's a reaction to what we've both just been through, or whether it's something else entirely, I've absolutely no idea. I don't know how reliable his mood is, either. He ought to be exhausted and flaking out on Flaherty's under-stuffed sofa, but he's not. *I* ought to be exhausted and flaking out on this brass-railed bed with the beautiful quilt, but I'm not either, she thought. And then, with a kind of incredulous delight – I'm enjoying this as much as he is.

'So, now,' said Flynn, with an edge to his tone that Fael had never heard before, 'I'd better be getting to my lonely couch.'

'So you had,' agreed Fael. 'I dare say the Irish whiskey's already poured out and waiting for you.'

'Father Mack has a generous hand with the whiskey.'

'I noticed.'

'Then,' said Flynn, 'I'll say goodnight.' He came over to the bed, and bent over to brush her lips with his. Fael at once felt as if an electrical circuit had been completed. Sparks against the darkness, she thought dizzily. Skyrockets and comets. The brief kiss exploded into something very much deeper and very much

369

more intimate. If he keeps kissing me like this I could well be lost, thought Fael.

Flynn drew away at last, but he stayed where he was, half sitting on the bed. He said, 'You understand that was meant only as a brief goodnight-and-sleep-well kiss.'

'It got a bit beyond that, didn't it?' Fael was sitting up on the bed, her hair tumbled and her eyes brilliant. She said, 'It's probably reaction to – to everything that's happened. I don't suppose either of us is in a very – normal state of mind at the moment.'

'Speak for yourself,' said Flynn at once. 'I never felt more normal.'

'No, but we shouldn't lose sight of the circumstances.'

'Oh, I'm not losing sight of them, my darling girl. Come here to me again.'

Some immeasurable time later, Fael said, 'Listen, normally I wouldn't dream of— Certainly not on such a very short acquaintance—'

Flynn said, his mouth muffled against her hair, 'But don't you think we've known each other from the beginning of the world and a bit before that as well?'

Fael leaned against him, and thought: He's got the Irish trick of suddenly injecting a caress into his voice. Christian would have had it as well, if he hadn't— She drew away and looked at him. 'That's quite a good line. I bet it's been useful to you a number of times.'

'It is a good line, isn't it?' agreed Flynn. They looked at one another, and then for the first time Flynn smiled properly. Fael felt her heart turn over.

She said, 'Won't Father Mack's whiskey be waiting for you?'

'It will,' said Flynn, and bent over her again.

Gilly, helping Flaherty's daughter and Sinead to wash up, found that she was timing how long Flynn had been upstairs. It was after three a.m. now, and it was more than an hour since he had carried Fael up to the bedroom . . .

Mad to be counting the hours like this. Mad to be so aware of the two of them up there in that warm, safe, firelit bedroom. Insane in the extreme to be feeling anything other than immense gratitude at being safe and at having been rescued, and at knowing this frightening, bizarre episode was finally safely over.

Oh damn, thought Gilly. Of course they'll be together. They'll probably stay together as well. She's absolutely right for him. Suitable. Not like me. She's from the same background, more or less – no squats in Mornington Crescent there, and no shameful Soho street-walking episodes either! – and if she really wrote *Cauldron* she'll certainly match him for talent. She'll never bore him and he'll never bore her, and she'll keep him in check, although not too much so. They'll probably become quite a famous theatrical family, thought Gilly. They'll start a dynasty, and in about twenty-five years' time there'll be articles in glossy Sunday newspaper supplements about their dazzling children all starting to make a name on their own account. He'll stay sharp and good-looking and she'll never fall out of love with him, and he'll always adore her, and she'll be beautiful at ninety because she's got those indestructible kind of looks, and she deserves it anyway, because she's lovely all the way through. And he'll certainly be dynamite in bed . . . Oh *damn*.

I don't mind at all, she thought, very firmly. I really don't. There's a lot of good things in my life already – *Cauldron* can probably return to London, which will be terrific – well, as long as they let me stay in it, it will. And Soho's definitely behind me, and all kinds of exciting things are probably ahead. Danilo. Yes, there's Danilo, thought Gilly, and suddenly and astonishingly found herself wanting very much to talk all this over with Danilo.

All the same, she thought, I won't go up to the room next to Fael and Flynn just yet. I don't think I could quite manage to lie in that nice little bed they've so kindly made up for me, and know that only a couple of feet away—

I'll just sit here by the fire for a little while longer.

'Flynn?'

'My lady?'

'That's the dawn chorus starting outside. Imagine listening to it like this.'

'Imagine,' said Flynn, pulling her against him again.

'You hadn't noticed the dawn?'

'I hadn't noticed it. But,' said Flynn, softly, 'by dawnlight and by firelight and by the light of the noon-day sun, and by yonder bless'd moon, lady, and for years and years until we're both surrounded by dozens of children and scores of grand-children, and multitudes of great-grandchildren—'

'How extravagant,' said Fael. 'That almost sounds like a proposal.'

'So it does. This almost feels like an acceptance.'

'I believe you're right,' said Fael.

It was generally agreed amongst the *Cauldron* company as they prepared for the re-opening at the Harlequin, that they might never have been away. The Irish episode might almost have been a dream, said several people, and then remembered Sir Julius Sherry's extremely unpleasant death and instantly looked solemn. A bad business, that had been. But still, life went on, and there had been talk of some kind of award within the theatrical profession to commemorate him – someone suggested calling it the Sherry Cup which was either nauseatingly whimsical or unexpectedly adroit – and there was a rumour that *Cauldron* might be the first recipient which would be exciting, even though the cynics were all saying, Oh dear, not *another* meaningless trophy.

And here they all were again, with a good run ahead, and the promise of a new show after that. Someone had even said something about a permanent company being formed under the aegis of Fael Miller – soon to be Fael Deverill – with the present players forming the nucleus, although it was not yet known how likely this was.

And so life went on and it looked as if *Cauldron* would go on as well, which was God's mercy when you thought about the level of unemployment within the profession. Gilly had secretly taken singing lessons from Danilo's music teacher in case anyone might look askance at her understudy role, but nobody had done so and it had seemed to be taken for granted that she would continue. She and Danilo had been on a half-working, half-recuperative holiday to Siena, where they had stayed with Danilo's cousins. They had eaten huge amounts of pasta and delicious Italian bread, and drunk inordinate quantities of wine.

They had gone for long walks and talked a lot, and they had begun to discover some quite surprising and rather intriguing things about one another. It had been noticed that their Mab and Aillen mac Midha scenes were beginning to take on an unmistakably sexual slant, which Stephen Sherry thought very good indeed. He told Danilo he would not be surprised if Gilly did not become quite well thought-of and successful, and Danilo told Gilly.

The cauldron-sorceress had given the *Fianna* captain his marching orders, and bets were already being taken in the *sidh* dressing room on who would replace him. Several quite sensible, quite likely nominations were put forward, until one of the dancers observed caustically that it was an impossible task, because he happened to know *rather* particularly that the only qualification the sorceress required for a lover was the ability to keep it up all night.

'*Really?*'

'Really,' said the dancer, managing to look smug.

The lodge-keeper had rethought his approach to his scenes with the *sidh*, giving them a bawdy tweak which was worrying Simkins of the bank considerably. It was worrying the lodge-keeper's wife as well, although for different reasons, but she was keeping a stern eye on the *sidh* girl who figured so prominently in the scenes in question.

'Don't worry, dear, I wouldn't touch him with a bargepole,' said the *sidh*, disdainfully. 'I've got bigger fish to fry.'

'Who?' demanded half a dozen voices in the *sidh* dressing room.

'*Wouldn't* you like to know!'

'Pass me the calculator somebody. Who'll offer even money on the identity of the fish . . .'

'No time now – there's Beginners being called.'

'And there's the overture starting up.'

'Come on everybody, we're off!'

Gerald Makepiece and Simkins of the bank had a drink together in the theatre bar before the curtain went up. Both of them were feeling very charitably disposed to the world in general. Both had something to look forward to.

Gerald was going to a nightclub with the little *sidh* girl who had so astonishingly and so promptly accepted his diffident invitation. Really, it seemed as if he might be more of a success with these dear young creatures than he would have dared imagine a year earlier. A pretty little thing, the *sidh* girl. A very polished little dancer as well. She had told him all manner of extremely interesting things about the *Cauldron* company: Gerald would never have believed it to be such a hotbed of intrigue. They would talk some more tonight, partly because it would postpone the bed-thing and also because Gerald loved intrigue, in fact he preferred it to the bed-thing if possible, which he found a bit chancy these days. Also, it aggravated his indigestion.

But he was going to talk to Fael and Flynn about the possibility of a really good part for the *sidh* girl in the new show which Fael was writing and Flynn was designing, and which was apparently going to be called *Stone*. Simkins had scoffed at this title, and said people would instantly dub it *Stoned* and the critics would all write that it sank without trace. It would not sink without trace at all; Gerald had read some of the book and listened to some of the music, and it was beautiful and disturbing and macabre. The music was a kind of mosaic of Christian Roscius's notes, found in the music room of Maise, and very early stuff written by Professor James Roscius. It was going to be Gerald's pleasure to back *Stone* – along with Simkins's bank, of course; it was odd how that desiccated little man had taken to the raffish world of the theatre.

Simkins of the bank, finishing his whisky, was glad to see that Makepiece seemed to have cut down on his drinking, because the poor little man had gone on quite a binge when his terrible Mia had been killed. Of course, he was a pushover for these greedy young actresses – he was after one of the *sidh* dancers at the moment. Simkins was very glad to think he himself had more discernment. It was one thing to invite the lively and very talented young lady playing the cauldron-sorceress to a *tête-à-tête* supper, and it was another to get tangled up with rapacious harpies. Gerald was actually taking the *sidh* girl to what sounded like a very seedy nightclub after tonight's performance; he was apparently looking forward to it enormously and had bought a silk shirt especially for the occasion. Simkins was glad to know himself much more prudent, and to think that his own supper with the sorceress was to be a very discreet affair making sensible use of the bank's service flat near St Katherine's Docks. All very circumspect, although they might discuss the idea of the sorceress playing a stronger role in the new musical, which she was perfectly capable of doing. Simkins did not see why he should not make one or two minor stipulations, particularly when you remembered how much the bank were investing in the new project, along with Makepiece, of course. He studied Makepiece over the rim of his glass, and thought it was strange how such a dried-up little herring of a creature had become at home in the colourful world of the theatre.

'Overture and Beginners,' said Gerald suddenly, his head cocked in the direction of the auditorium. 'Time to get to our seats if we aren't to miss the opening.'

'Oh, we don't want to miss that,' said Simkins, and the two rather dried-up, slightly desiccated, and somewhat gullible gentlemen drained their glasses and went happily into the darkened theatre to make sure of not missing anything.

As Fael took her seat at Flynn's side, she felt the soaring anticipation of the audience, and as the orchestra, under Maurice Camperdown's direction, struck up *Cauldron*'s overture, beneath her own anticipation was a lingering sadness.

This is yours, Christian, she thought, for the moment unnoticing of Flynn's presence. This is yours as much as it's mine. You spun it for me out of nothing, and you wove the magic and set the spell working. And if I cheated you, Christian, at least I put your memory to this: 'Lyrics by Fael Miller; music by Christian Roscius'. We've named you at last, Christian, she thought. There wasn't, after all, anything else to name for you. No child . . . I'm not sorry. Or am I? No, it's better like this.

As the lights dimmed a shiver of pleasure went through the house, and the first notes of the opening music began to drift through the theatre. There was a moment when Fael could almost see it: coruscating strands of brilliance, laced with silver and gold and so fragilely beautiful that you knew that if you touched it, it would shatter under your hands.

And then the orchestra gathered itself together and the music written by the lonely, tormented creature, who had fought to stay behind his own enigmatic legend to the end, poured out and wove all over again its golden, shining spell.